RYAN G. PLUT

The Belfair Pinch

First edition

ISBN: 979-8-9888043-2-1

This book was professionally typeset on Reedsy.
Find out more at reedsy.com

PINCH, verb (British English, informal)

1) To steal (a thing).

2) To arrest someone.

— the Oxford English Dictionary

Contents

Foreword

May you enjoy this tale as much as I enjoyed writing it.

Acknowledgement

I'd like to thank my friends (and often proofreaders) who read early draft manuscripts and made valuable suggestions. In order: The Revd Mark Rudall for corrections to the religious details; John Hope; Wayne Breidford for his valuable insights into continuity and details about weapons; Mark Plut; Dave and Jan Bell. Thanks also to the Veterans Museum in Chehalis, Washington, for details on certain weapons that appear in the story. If I have forgotten to include any person, my sincerest apologies.

Cover artwork by the author. Portions of the ship depicted on the cover courtesy of Nordisk Film Kompanie a/s, Denmark. Sibenik buildings in background © Xbrchx | Dreamstime.com.

1

April 1941, Sibenik, Kingdom of Yugoslavia

Vlasnik Golubić was happy, yet also nervous. Happy, because his *konoba* was raucous with loud patrons having a good time. Nervous, for he had just been called to meet a man outside, the man with the scar on his face, whose name he did not know, and did not wish to know. A man he had met only twice before, and fervently wished never to meet again after this.

As he made his way to the side door, his agitated state wasn't noticed by the inebriated Swede who stopped him to ask the way to the toilet. He pointed down the hallway beside the kitchen and excused himself, then stepped out into the alley.

It was narrow, as most alleys here were. One might stretch both arms out and nearly touch the walls of adjacent buildings, if not for the group of some twenty men that now filled it. Beyond the end of this alley was a ship, the ship of the party-goers inside. It was many storeys tall and now blocked the rays of the setting sun, throwing the alley into shadow. In times of peace, it was said Šibenik had the best sunsets in all Yugoslavia—but today was not a time of peace.

He had expected the man with the scar would be alone as before, and was dismayed to see he was not. Even more so because the men here were in uniform, and were heavily armed. With a shudder, he saw their weapons were not the normal Russian-supplied type, but of German issue. Their uniforms showed no insignia. The man he feared now stepped forwards. Most unusually he had no beard, revealing an ugly scar extending from the outer corner of his left eye down to his jawline. It had not healed well.

"Good evening, Golubić," the man said, soothingly. "Business is good, I hope?"

"Ye-ye-yes, Herr Oberst," Golubić stammered.

"You will not address me as such," he barked, his soothing tones evaporating. "We are not German. We are the Royal Yugoslav Army."

"Yes, yes, of course you are. I mean nothing else!" Golubić agreed, bowing to show respect, his hands clasped before him to prevent their trembling.

"You remember our agreement?"

"Bring the Swedish captain out this side door. Make some excuse why he cannot use the front entrance, then bring him out here."

"Very good."

"And my daughter, Herr O– " he caught himself in time, " – pukovnik?" The Oberst snapped his fingers above his shoulder, and a soldier stepped out of the group to thrust a girl forward roughly while retaining a grip on her arm. Her wrists were tied behind her and a gag bound her mouth. She whimpered. Golubić embraced her and stroked her hair.

"How touching. She will be released to you unharmed when we have the captain. Go."

"Please sir, may I take my daughter with me now?" Golubić pleaded.

"No—I have changed my mind: do not bring out *only* the captain. Now you must bring out *all* the Swedes. All of them! Have you anything more to say?"

"No, no, I understand completely." His daughter was ripped from his arms. The Oberst turned away, then back around with a finger raised, as he thought of something else.

"Oh, one more thing, Golubić: is there some place nearby you know of, a place having a blank wall with no windows, in a courtyard, perhaps?"

Golubić trembled. "There is a square beside a small church, that way, two streets in and turn to the right." He scurried back into the building, and into his kitchen. Burying his head in his hands, he took deep breaths and tried to remain calm. When he felt sufficiently composed, he went in search of the Swedish captain in the crowd. The man held a Berlitz phrasebook for tourists and was struggling to speak Serbo-Croatian words to him, not least because his voice was slurred by too much *rakija*.

"*Hvala ti …*" the Swede shouted over the din of the lively accordion, "*na divnoj … oproštajnoj …*"

"*Kapetan* Söderberg, please just use your English, it will go much easier." The publican patted him on the shoulder.

"We want to thank you for the wonderful going-away party. It's been just grand!"

"It's been wonderful having all of you here these weeks," he responded with distraction, his demeanour one of joviality. Only a person of keen perception could see it was false. " … but, have you heard the news? Yugoslavia has surrendered. It happened yesterday!"

"Yes, I heard," he slurred, then hiccuped and continued, "we're getting out tomorrow after we refuel, just in time."

"Lucky you. But I must warn you, lorries of Italian soldiers from Zadar have been seen entering the town," he lied, "I think it best if you return to your ship now but, you should use my side door into the alley, yes?"

"Yes, yes, good idea!" He turned and, clapping his hands, shouted for attention to make this announcement. The accordionist stopped playing. The Swedes downed their drinks. They all stood and formed an orderly queue as they wove unsteadily past the proprietor on the way to the door. A few stopped to shake his hand and exclaim, "Lovely party Vlasnik. Thank you." As the last of them exited, there was the sound of many tramping boots heard through the open doorway, then loud cries of "*Hände hoch!*"

Just then, the Swede returning from the toilet appeared in the hallway, at the very moment a soldier stepped in through the alley doorway. Golubić stopped the Swede with a hand on his chest and pushed, sending him staggering backwards down the hallway. Snatching an apron from its hook he flung it at him.

"How many times must I tell you to wear your apron in the kitchen!" he shouted in annoyance, then in a whisper hissed, "Put that on and stay in the kitchen." The soldier thrust the publican's daughter into the room, where she tripped and tumbled to the floor. Her father helped her get to her feet, and clung to her, her gag still in place as she sobbed. The soldier took another step into the room to confirm it was indeed empty, then slammed the door as he left. The sour-faced accordionist had paused to watch this drama play out, then continued securing his instrument in its case. Minutes later Vlasnik Golubić hustled the lone Swede out the front entrance door.

"Go, run for your ship," he urged, "and don't come back!"

2

Cairo, Kingdom of Egypt

The Egyptian date seller loitered on the pavement in a street just off the square, and across the way from the old Semiramis Hotel. This was now British General Headquarters (Middle East). His ass stood patiently at the end of its rein, its woven baskets of dates suspended on both sides.

The day was getting increasingly hot as the sun beat down. The passers-by wore garb of many types. There were the Arabs like himself, wearing a white robe, a *ghutrah* and *agal* upon their heads, and there were businessmen in westernised pin-striped suits, a red *fez* upon their heads, on their way to an early lunch. Only a very few women, and these wore a black robe and a shawl over their heads, which also covered most of their face. Always, a male child or two scampered alongside them. They only occasionally stopped to buy a paper sack of dates, which was just as well because selling dates was not his primary reason for being here. In an hour all these passers-by would be indoors to escape the heat, as everyone here did between the hours of one and six – everyone, that is, except the damnable British.

The date seller was looking forward to seeing his wife Fatima and their children for a lunch of tea and *eish baladi*, delicious *kofta*, and for dessert, honeyed *Feteer meshaltet.* Then he will enjoy a cold bottle of Sakara beer which Fatima buys for him, clandestinely of course. They eat well, all made possible by the Egyptian Pounds he gets from his handler, Herr Gelbherz. Not for him to subsist on a few measly *piastres* like his neighbours. Idly, he wondered if the notes given him are authentic.

He popped another date into his mouth and bit down, then slowly stopped chewing, for a vehicle had rounded the corner. Boxy and camouflaged rose-pink and olive green in colour, he could see it was British because it lacked a windscreen, had twin machine guns mounted ahead of the passenger seat, and there were two jerrycans strapped to its bonnet. It squeaked to a halt at the foot of the stairs to the building entrance.

It was time to go to work. The date seller tucked the date into his cheek for the moment. He tethered the ass to a nearby cast-iron bollard, then reached up his sleeve to retrieve the Leica camera that hung by its strap from his arm, and began to snap pictures. One of two door sentries, who wore a kilt just like the other, now shouldered his rifle and started down the steps. All four men piled out of the Jeep and stretched, then dusted themselves down. They also wore the *ghutrah* and *agal.* They collected kit bags, a duffel bag, and various weapons from the car.

"See you chaps at Shepheards for gin and tonics," the bearded driver said to his companions. One of the other three said, "Righto," and waved a weary reply as they started up the stairs. The sentry arrived at the vehicle. "Good afternoon, sergeant," the driver greeted the sentry.

"Lieutenant. That date-selling ass is back," the sentry replied. He didn't salute the man, as that would identify him as an officer.

"I see him, and his donkey too."

"He has a camera up his sleeve."

"You don't say. What a surprise. Which sleeve?"

"The left."

"I'll fix him. He won't come back here when I'm through with him! Help me unload these jerrycans of petrol." Together they unstrapped and took down the full jerrycans, setting them on the pavement. The lieutenant settled himself into the driver's seat and reached up to pull back on the charging handle of the nearest Vickers 'K' machine gun.

"Give me your tie, sergeant," he said, unbuttoning the right-hand pocket of his tunic.

"My tie?"

"Yes, quickly now!" The sergeant laid his Lee-Enfield on the bonnet and worked at the knot. He handed the tie over and retrieved his rifle. The lieutenant started the Jeep and engaged first gear. In a Jeep, one always started off in second gear unless you were towing anything, but the Lieutenant had in mind a clever plan.

He let out the clutch and made a very slow U-turn. When the Jeep was approaching the date seller, the engine howling, he pumped the accelerator rapidly to make the Jeep buck in apparent distress and then, without touching the clutch pedal, stamped on the brake pedal. The engine stalled and died. He slipped the gear lever into second and got out. Lifting the bonnet, he rested it against the upraised barrels of the twin Vickers. He looked the engine over and touched a few wires, his back to the Arab on the kerb a few yards away. Leaving the bonnet raised, he exclaimed, "Damn!" then went around to the left side of the vehicle to climb in behind the steering wheel. He picked up the tie and draped it around his neck, then sat forward to peer through a drilled hole left in the bonnet. He waited.

The Arab stepped off the kerb and crept forwards, believing himself to be hidden from view, and continued snapping pictures. He leaned in for a close-up of the engine. What a coup! Herr Gelbherz was going to be pleased with all this information.

The lieutenant pressed the starter button, then stepped on the brake.

The Jeep jerked a yard forwards and the bonnet collapsed. The Arab was thrown to the ground, his robe trapped under the wheel. Bystanders rushed to help. The lieutenant triggered the Vickers overhead, the sound of gunfire echoing off the face of the surrounding buildings. The ass bucked and brayed, scattering dates everywhere, and the bystanders fled. The lieutenant leapt out and grabbed the Arab by the robe at his throat.

"Are you armed?" he demanded, holding his knife before the man's face.

"No!" the Arab wailed, the whites of his eyes wide with terror, hands held palm out in denial.

"Let's have a 'shufti', then." He reached up the man's sleeve and yanked the camera upwards, bringing his arm with it. "Sure you are, here's an arm right here." He stuck his knife in the arm and lifted, cutting the camera strap. The man screamed. He spit pieces of chewed date in the lieutenant's face.

"One day, *in sha'a Allah*, you British shall be driven from Egypt!" he snarled. The sergeant came pelting across the street, kilt flapping, his rifle held out at "port arms". The lieutenant dropped the camera into his tunic pocket, letting its bloody strap dangle. While the robe's white sleeve rapidly turned crimson, he used the other sleeve to clean his blade. When he'd finished fashioning a tourniquet on the arm using the sergeant's tie, he stood and wiped the flecks of sticky date from his face.

"Sergeant, take him in for—oh, bloody hell, look!" The sergeant whirled to see an Arab making off with the jerrycans. He raised his rifle and took aim. The lieutenant knocked it upwards, and the shot went high.

"Don't *shoot* him sergeant. He can't get far carrying two full jerrycans now can he? Go after him!" At the sound of the shot, the Arab dropped the jerrycans and ran away with his hands raised overhead, soon disappearing around the corner of the building. All this gunfire had attracted attention, and army personnel erupted from the headquarters entrance to see the commotion. The sergeant trotted across the street to retrieve the jerrycans, passing another sergeant who was crossing the other way. Staff Sergeant Ellice had a pencil moustache, his hair parted in the middle and slicked down with brilliantine, his mouth readily twisting into a smirk. His fellow soldiers were uniformly regarded by him with a contemptuous mien, and superior officers with a disdainful tolerance. When he reached the Jeep, he saluted in a somewhat idle manner.

"Don't salute me, you idiot!" the lieutenant said, irritated.

"Just as you say, *sir*," Ellice said pleasantly, the word "sir" managing to sound a bit disparaging. "General Stone has ordered me to tell you that you're to pick up a Roy Mallinson from an aeroplane before it departs, and go now. He's one of those fellows off the *Dominion Empress*. You'll find him waiting to board a Dakota at RAF Fayid."

"RAF Fayid? The Great Bitter Lake? You must be joking, that's 70 miles away!"

"Then you'd better hurry, hadn't you," the staff sergeant said, with a smirk. "General Stone said, and I quote: 'Auchinleck wants him. This is of the highest importance. Tell him not to return without him'."

"Then, sergeant, *you* have charge of this spy. Take him in for interrogation. He's to be detained and not released before I return. Here's his camera. Keep it safe as evidence—mind the blood." The sentry brought the jerrycans and set them down, then returned to his post. Ellice helped the lieutenant fasten the bonnet and strap the jerrycans down. The Jeep was started and reversed off the Arab's robe, then Ellice escorted the spy across the street, prodding him along. As the lieutenant drove away heading east, street urchins materialized from nowhere, scrambling to scoop up as many dates as their shirts could hold. But it wasn't until he was within actual sight of RAF Fayid, that it occurred to him: perhaps General Stone had ordered Sergeant Ellice to do this task?

Captain Reginald Wallace, with his licensed officers and nurses, queued to climb the short ladder into the 'Dakota' aeroplane that sat baking in the mid-afternoon sun. Nearby sat three Spitfires that were to be their escort. They found their bench seats and sat in the stifling heat with their backs to the aeroplane's fuselage. Except for his three deck officers and his second engineer they all, including him, wore second-hand civilian clothing that had been provided them. When the SS *Dominion Empress* had been torpedoed four nights ago on the third of January, those not on active duty had been forced into the lifeboats wearing nothing but their pyjamas. It was dark inside, but toward the cockpit he could see the pilot, co-pilot, and navigator standing deep in conversation, illuminated by the sun shining through the astrodome above. In between there were five stretcher cases of injured men being evacuated, a nurse tending to them, and a one-star general and his wife. She held a trembling little Yorkshire terrier on her lap. No doubt the presence of this general was the reason for the extra Spit. Reggie tucked his legs aside as Nurse Doris went forward to see if any help was needed with the stretcher cases. When they were all seated the radio officer came through with a clipboard to sign them in. After the man had checked him in, Reggie asked, "This is an American DC-3, isn't it?"

"No sir, it's a C-53. You're fair observant, as she's within a gnat's whisker to them."

When the radioman stepped to the next person, the captain sat back and shut his eyes. He tried to relax for what seemed the first time in 'donkey's years'. He concentrated and focused, and was able to bring up images of England in January: foggy, damp, green England! He'd not been home in two and a half years. He'll get six weeks of R&R

– rest and relaxation – before being assigned to command another ship, if one was available. First stop will be to visit his mum and dad in Goudhurst, having a pint in the Olde Starre and Crowne pub, catching up with the gossip as they gaze over the High Weald of Kent. Perhaps he'll tramp over to Flimwell for another pint and a visit with George and Helen, and why not? They might even combine their petrol rations, pick up Laura, and drive north to Whitstable in George's ancient Hillman Wizard saloon for a bit of a winter's holiday. No, not Laura; he'd proposed marriage and she'd replied she preferred they remain friends. Dorothea, then, a better choice—not really marriageable, but a bit of fun all the same.

He briefly wondered how Nurse Becky McKenzie and Captain Roy Mallinson were enjoying their new life together, retired in sunny Australia. He smiled with the delicious memory of her, how he'd thought she might've fancied him, but in this he was mistaken: she only had eyes for Roy. His reverie was interrupted by the roar of an engine and a squeal of brakes from without. A bearded man entered the Dakota and made his way to the front, between the stretcher cases, to speak with the pilot, who shook his head and pointed aft. The man walked aft, looking over the occupant of each seat. He wore Italian boots and German gloves, a Arabian *ghutrah* and *agal,* and motorcyclist's goggles which now perched on his forehead. His face was dusty all over, except for where the goggles had been. There was no indication of any rank on him, with the sole exception of a golden badge of a scorpion and the letters LRDG on the man's collar.

"Which of you is Roy Mallinson?" he asked of the seated passengers. No one answered. "Roy Mallinson?" the man repeated. Reggie spoke up.

"He's in Australia, private."

"It's lieutenant! When did he leave?"

"He was never here. I'm Reginald Wallace, his replacement."

"Oh? Is he dead?"

"No, but I believe he's definitely in heaven."

"What do ya mean by that?" the lieutenant replied, irritated. He had a rather poor opinion of having to pick up these new recruits, and then waste his valuable time and efforts to train them, only for them to get killed on their first mission in the desert.

"Never mind." Reggie had briefly thought to mention the beautiful Becky McKenzie, but decided against it.

"Are all of you from the *Dominion Empress*?" the lieutenant asked, looking over the group.

"Yes, we are," Reggie replied, as the rest of the group nodded agreement.

"Well, that's correct. You're to come with me, now."

"We're on our way back to Britain."

"Look, Mr Wallace, I'm under direct orders from General Claude Auchinleck, to bring a Roy Mallinson back to Cairo. I was ordered not to return without him. You've just told me you're his replacement so, you're it! Follow me."

"I'm sorry, but I can't."

"I don't care. Now, we can do this the hard way, if you'd like, but either way you're coming with me." The Lieutenant smacked one gloved fist into the opposite palm. Reggie thought for a moment. He was sure this had to do with some paperwork needing straightening out, about the sinking of the *Dominion Empress*.

"Oh, all right then." *I guess we can always board a later flight*, he thought. He stood and all his officers and nurses stood too. They began to gather up what little belongings they had.

"No, just you. No one else," the lieutenant insisted. Reggie ducked his head out the loading door to see a rather dusty, small and squarish, oddly-camouflaged vehicle. One that couldn't possibly hold more than a few persons. He looked at the others, and made up his mind.

"All right, I'll come. Just ... give me a minute will you?" The man crossed his arms and leaned against the fuselage, to listen while he waited. Reggie turned to his crew. "I'm sure it's just some paperwork that needs straightening out. I'll get a later flight." He thought, *Why this can't be done when I reach Britain is beyond me.*

"Good luck in your retirement, Engineer MacCallan." He shook Hamish's hand.

"Aye, Good luck to ye, laddie."

"Carpenter Nowiczski, it's been a pleasure having you on my crew." They shook as well. He stepped over to his second engineer and three deck officers.

"Sinclair. Taffy. O'Malley. Fred. Good luck with your next assignments. I'm sure you'll all do well. I only wish I had time to provide a letter to whoever is—tell you what, I'll write those letters and forward them to the Ministry of War Transport. You can pick them up there." As he shook each hand, they thanked him, wished him well, and sat.

"Best of luck to you in California, Miss Kee." He hugged the nurse, careful to not disturb the gauze encircling her head.

"Thank you sir, but I'm going to Portland, Oregon, with Gene," she replied, and bit her lip. It seemed to him she was about to cry. He turned to Gene and put out his hand.

"You take good care of her, do you hear me, Eugene?" The thin young man, his sandy hair always neatly parted, seemed to him to be about to cry, too.

"Yessir, you bet I will!" They shook hands. Gene sat, then a moment later leapt to his feet and shouted, "Three cheers! Hip-hip!" and they all responded three times, "Hooray!" Reggie reached out and playfully mussed Gene's hair before shoving him down into his seat.

"I'm ready now. Let's go."

"No luggage?"

"Just what I'm wearing, and this logbook." They climbed down the aeroplane's ladder, walked to the vehicle, and got in. He set the book on the floor. The seat was somewhat hard and uncomfortable. Reggie twisted to look it over from where he sat. He was puzzled because he noticed it was left-hand drive, similar to a car from The States. It seemed rather bare-bones to him, with a minimum of gauges and switches. What seemed most strange to him were the three gear-change levers.

"What is it?" Reggie asked.

"The paperwork says it's an 'MB four-by-four', but everyone calls it a Jeep."

"A sheep?"

"No, it's spelled Jay-ee-ee-pee; – Jeep. It's American."

"What's that mean?"

"No one seems to know." One after the other, the three Spits started their engines. Suddenly, a shout came from the Dakota. He turned to see Nowiczski standing in the doorway, and Nurse Doris coming down the boarding ladder clutching her skirt and holding out something in her hand.

"Wait, wait!" she shouted.

"It's our nurse," he explained, for the lieutenant's benefit. She scampered from the Dakota to the Jeep. When she arrived she threw herself into his lap and wrapped an arm around his neck to keep from falling out.

"Ow, ow, ow, that tarmac is *hot*," she exclaimed, fanning the air with her feet. Doris liked going barefoot whenever the opportunity arose. She presented him with Nowiczski's silver flask. "Piotr wants you to have this," she announced, then in his ear whispered, "He says he doesn't need it since his distillery went down with the ship." He waved his thanks to the carpenter, who stood on the bottom step of the ladder, then put the flask on the floor. "You know, Reggie," she continued, "I have something to confess to you!"

"Confess? Now, what could our Doris possibly have to confess to?" he said, teasing her.

"Well, you remember that time on Christmas Island, when we all picnicked on that beach?"

"Yes, vividly." He smiled.

"And Nurse Kee went 'starkers' to go swimming, and walk the beach with Eugene?"

"Who could possibly forget that?" he said.

"Well, ... I really did want to frolic naked on that beach. I almost did go naked – I really would have too! ... that is, if Ruth hadn't stopped me." She spoke as if the lieutenant wasn't sitting right there. He was, and his mouth was hanging open.

"I know. We all saw Ruth restrain you. You're a very special woman, you know, and don't let anyone tell you any different." Doris wasn't what you might call a classic beauty by any stretch. She had a round head, her teeth were crooked, and her nose too big. Even so, she did exude an enormous amount of sex appeal. But she wasn't one of those women who was aware of it, or used it to manipulate men. It was just her being her.

"Now, I have some news, something I didn't want the others to hear quite yet, but I'll tell you now because you're leaving."

"What is it?"

"Piotr and I are *engaged*, ... and I'm soon to be *Mrs* Doris Nowiczski, and, ... and I'm *pregnant*!"

"That's a lot of news. Congratulations to you and Piotr!"

"Thank you. I'm going to miss you, Captain Wallace." She gave him a quick smooch, and not on his cheek.

"Doris, believe me, I'll never forget you." Turning to the lieutenant, he said, "Excuse me," then picked her up and carried her to the Dakota where he deposited her into Piotr Nowiczski's waiting arms. As he walked back to the Jeep, the ground crew tossed the ladder inside and the door was secured. One at a time the Dakota's engines sounded *chew-chew-chew-chew* and roared to life. The lieutenant started the Jeep and began to drive off.

"Just a moment lieutenant—I'd like to watch them leave if I may."

"Sure." He faced the jeep towards the runway and turned off the motor, and they sat for a minute as the Dakota ran up each engine. The ground crew called out "chocks away!" and ran. They watched as it taxied to the end of the runway. The lieutenant decided he wanted some clarification on just who this new recruit was, and how he was meant to fit into the Special Operations Executive.

"You're a captain?" *Meaning, I've just discovered you outrank me.*

"Yes, lieutenant, I am."

"You have a nurse?"

"Yes, two actually."

"Why two?"

"Well, that nurse with the gauze on her head is also our translator."

"You called that old Scot 'engineer' – what is he, your explosives expert?"

"Why, yes, he is," he answered, surprised the man knew.

"And that Yank kid with the twelve-bore. What's his speciality?"

"He's my wireless operator."

"And who's that chap Carpenter?"

"His name isn't 'Carpenter', he *is* a carpenter – that's his job."

"Why do you need a bleeding carpenter?!" the lieutenant demanded.

"Why shouldn't I have a carpenter?" Reggie replied, annoyed. The Dakota roared down the runway to lift off. The three Spits all went together right after, and they all winged away to the west-south-west. The lieutenant seemed to him to be in a sulky mood.

"Is there something the matter, lieutenant?"

"Look, just this morning when I'd come it from the desert, I never even had a chance to clean myself up, and then I'm ordered to pick *you* up. You're the reason I had to spend my entire day driving, and miss my usual gin and tonic at Shepheards."

"Oh. Sorry." He picked up the flask and offered it to him. "Here, have some of what we call 'panther piss'." The lieutenant put it to his mouth and took a healthy slug and then coughed, spraying his mouthful across the Jeep's bonnet. He pounded his chest with a fist.

"What *is* this?" he gasped, eyes watering.

"Potato Vodka. 150 Sikes proof, I believe. Did Nowiczski not add any juice this time?" The lieutenant handed the flask back, and Reg took a cautious sip. "Mmmm, rather nice. No juice, but he did add a bit of honey this time."

"Best I not have any—I want to get there alive." He wiped his chin with his *ghutrah*. Reggie capped his flask and pocketed it.

"Lieutenant, are you aware you've got dried blood on your tunic front?" He pointed at the stain.

"I knifed a spy this morning," he boasted. "Makes a nice change of pace from blowing up aerodromes and supply dumps."

"We blew up a submarine two months ago. Killed seventy Japanese and took seven prisoners," Reggie announced.

The lieutenant scowled. He handed him a pair of goggles, started the Jeep, and they drove to Cairo in silence.

3

"SOE" Comes Calling

Reggie sat quietly in a hard chair in an anteroom of BGH(ME) – British General Headquarters (Middle East) – waiting to be shown in. He'd arrived the day before in early evening and everyone had already departed the building, but he'd been issued a hotel room. He didn't know for how long. He didn't feel himself this morning, as he hadn't had the time to shave, or the razor, and so had quite a bit of stubble. He hadn't shaved since before the sinking. He drummed his fingers lightly on the ship's logbook in his lap.

The clerk at the desk, a rather fit brunette in the tunic and knee-length skirt of the Auxiliary Territorial Service, clacked away at a typewriter. Her hair was done up in a roll at the nape of her neck, as was usual for these ATS clerks. Beyond her was a mahogany door with a frosted glass panel, and on it was printed the name "Lieut.-Gen. Robert Stone". A staff sergeant sporting a pencil moustache sat perched on the corner of her desk and chatted her up. His demeanour was somewhat smarmy. From snatches of his monologue Reggie gathered he thought of himself as God's Gift To Women. The clerk stopped typing.

"Sergeant Ellice, *please*, I'm trying to get some work done here," she pleaded, "Can you *please* just leave me alone?" The man stood and straightened his tie, then left with only the barest glance in Reggie's direction. The typewriter's clacking resumed. While waiting to be seen he sat back, rested his head against the wall and shut his eyes, tired. If he was to give testimony, or an accounting of events during the sinking, perhaps he should marshal his thoughts. He went over again in his mind what details he could remember. The anteroom's outer door burst in suddenly and a man of about Reggie's age strode through the room and into the office. He had a bristly moustache but otherwise was clean-shaven.

"Sir, you can't go in —" the clerk shouted, but was cut off by the slamming of the door. Indistinct muffled voices came from within. She turned back to her typewriter and apparently saw an error on the page. "Fuck!" she blurted, her fists clenched. She ripped the paper from the machine, balled it up and binned it in disgust. Spotting Reggie where he sat quietly, she turned as red as a beetroot. "I'm so sorry, Mr Wallace," she said, flustered, "I forgot you were here."

"That's all right. I've heard worse, Miss ...?"

"Featherstone."

"Well, Miss Featherstone," he said wearily, "it seems I'm here to give an accounting, for the record, of the sinking of my first command. I've been trying over the past few days to remember all the details, and I want to get it all down on paper before I forget anything. May I have a sheet of paper and a pencil, and a clipboard if you have one, please?"

"I'm really not busy at the moment. I could type it for you?" she suggested.

"Can you type it while I dictate?"

"Can I? Just watch me!" She said, enthusiastically. She turned into the roller a carbon flimsy between two fresh sheets of paper. "What's the name of your ship?" she asked.

"The SS *Dominion Empress*, Ellerman Shipping Lines, home-ported

London," he replied. She checked the wall calendar and wall clock and typed those too. Sitting up straight, fingers poised over the keys and eyes bright, she smiled and gave him a nod to begin. Reggie sat back, composed himself, and shut his eyes. His exposition should be neutral, without embellishment. He cleared his throat and began to speak, slowly. The typewriter began clacking.

"The SS *Dominion Empress* proceeded westbound out of Alexandria, Egypt for Valletta, Malta, with a deck cargo of aeroplanes for that island, and taking a regulation zig-zag course. Navigation lights were off. It was the third of January 1942. My First Mate Dafyd ap Morgan had command.

"I was in my bunk when Morgan called me to report we'd been briefly illuminated by a powerful searchlight off the starboard beam. As I reached the bridge I saw the time to be 2302 hours. The first torpedo struck without warning in line with the bridge. Heavily laden as we were with a cargo of lead and rubber, she still lifted in the water. Her back was broken. I knew this because the wooden bulkhead of the chart room flexed and splintered, and the door came off its hinges.

"I ordered my wireless operator to send a mayday at once. The second of two torpedoes struck aft, in hold number four, which hold carried sheet rubber. When I saw flames from the hatch and black smoke coming from the ventilators, I knew then she was done: a rubber fire cannot be put out.

I rang for full astern – this to prevent the lifeboats overturning. I pulled on the whistle cord, seven short and one long, then announced on the tannoy, 'Muster stations, abandon ship' three times, and repeated this down the engine room voicepipe. *Let's see, what happened next? Oh, yes, I remember.*

"The lights went out. Eugene appeared on the bridge to tell me the power was out and his mayday was cut short. I remember seeing he was carrying his pump twelve-bore. I ordered Eugene, Morgan, and my helmsman to the boats. When the ship was nearly at a stop I rang the telegraph 'finished with engine', picked up the ship's logbook, and followed them.

"As best as I can recall, the time then was 2308 hours. I can find no fault with any of my officers. There was no panic, even among my passengers. When I reached the deck, four of our six lifeboats had been occupied and were being lowered, or already in the water. Two were not needed.

"An Italian motor torpedo boat rapidly approached and raked the ship with machine gun fire. Here I must commend the actions of Eugene Graham, for without question he undoubtedly saved our lives: he shot out its searchlight. The Italian left the area to the Northwest. We pulled away some little distance and I made a head count. Two civilians – both of them American – were missing: Nurse Susan Kee and Wireless Operator Eugene Graham."

"Half a moment." Miss Featherstone interrupted, "I need to start another page." He paused as this was done. "Go ahead, sir."

"I then ordered three boats to pull away, this to avoid the suction when she went. I returned to the ship, and called for volunteers to accompany me because I intended to re-board for a search. As my boat arrived at the midship bulwark gate, the ship's main deck was then level with the water's surface. As the ship was now settling rapidly, we were all aware she could go without warning. Mr Graham appeared, carrying Miss Kee who was unconscious and bleeding from a head wound, and stepped into my boat with her.

"We pulled away and the ship foundered on an even keel less than a minute later. The time was 2314 hours. We arrived at Marsaxlokk harbour, Malta, at mid-morning on fifth of January. The ship's company were flown out to Alexandria, Egypt, where my unlicensed crew were assigned to other ships, after being afforded the usual period of rest and relaxation.

"Attached hereto please find a list of ship's personnel and the logbook. This affidavit given this day and month, *et cetera*, – signed *et cetera*." Reggie sat motionless for a moment, eyes shut, wondering if he'd left anything out. The typewriter stopped its clacking. He opened his eyes and sat up. Miss Featherstone pulled the sheets out and put it with the others.

"I'd no idea what you blokes went through. Now I do." She plucked a handkerchief from her handbag and blotted her eyes. "I didn't know the spelling of the names you mentioned so I left spaces. You'll need to write them in. Then I'll type up a clean copy for you, and you may pick it up tomorrow."

"That'll be fine, Miss Featherstone, I'll do that. Thank you." The office door opened and the man emerged. He turned and shouted back into the room. His voice had a plummy upper-crust accent to it, and he had a rather pompous manner and a slow way of speaking.

"This mission should be mine. After all, I speak the language," he said. There came a reply from within.

"Don't you worry, Fitz, you'll get your chance soon enough."

"I'll speak of this to Winston!"

"You do that, Lance-corporal Maclean."

"It's *Sir* Fitzroy Maclean, if you don't mind," he huffed.

"Tell me, have you ever navigated a four-hundred-foot ship before?" asked the unseen voice.

"No, but, aren't there people? People I can delegate to —"

"They're called 'crew'."

"Yes, crew."

"May I remind you, David has you still in training! Have you completed the *required* six parachute jumps?"

"Er, ... no."

"Have you *started* them yet?"

"No."

"Fitz, just you keep in mind that in this theatre General Auchinleck is in charge, and he's already made the decision. Dismissed!" Fitz shut the inner door and left the anteroom in a huff. Miss Featherstone watched him leave with a frown, then turned to Reggie, and smiled.

"You may go in now." Reggie knocked on the door, then entered, to see a three-star general seated behind a desk, and just picking up a folder.

"What was that all about?" Reggie asked, jerking a thumb over his shoulder.

"Fitzroy Maclean. He was a Tory politician, and erstwhile diplomat."

"No kidding," Reggie said, with a roll of his eyes.

"What can I do for you?"

"I was told to report to you, sir."

"Oh, then you must be Roy Mallinson! Excellent, excellent. We've been expecting you." He stood and leaned over his desk to offer his hand. They shook.

"Sorry to disappoint, but Captain Mallinson was never 'in country'. I'm Reginald Wallace, his replacement," he replied.

"But, you *are* a Merchant Navy captain, am I correct?"

"Yes sir. ... er, I should mention, a 'brevet' captain, pending my arrival in London."

"Excellent! Just go down the hall, five doors on the left, and see Major Stirling. He'll interview you." He sat down and picked up the folder again. Reggie shut the door, was given the typed sheets, asked Miss Featherstone to have supper with him that evening, and left.

He counted the doors as he walked, until he came to an unmarked door with a brown sign jutting out above it that in white letters mysteriously proclaimed 'SOE'. *SOE? What does that mean?* The door had a window and he could see a man seated at a desk. He knocked and entered. Here, there was no anteroom nor any clerk, and the major seated at the desk looked up in surprise.

"May I help you?"

"I was told to report to you, sir."

"Roy Mallinson is it, then? Good of you to come. Major David Stirling." He stood, and Reggie was surprised at his height, a tall 6 feet 6 inches with an athletic physique and heavy eyebrows that met. They shook hands.

"Captain Mallinson is retired. I'm Captain Reginald Wallace, his replacement. May I ask, what does S-O-E mean, major?"

"Well, this is a borrowed office. I'm actually head of SAS but we do often work together. Have a seat, captain." They sat. *Didn't answer my question.*

"I'm told you'll be interviewing me. Is this about the sinking of the *Dominion Empress*?"

"Och, aye, heard about that. A week past was it? I'd heard all of you survived with not a single injury. Well done." His accent was Scottish. *Still didn't answer my question.* Reggie sat back and crossed his legs. It seemed his giving evidence was going to take some time.

"Well, sir, we had one injury, a concussion. I was on my way to England yesterday with my crew, and was prevented from leaving so, if we can wrap up my testimony today, I'd appreciate being able to continue my journey. England awaits, you know."

"Please, you can call me David." He cleared his throat. "Yes, ... well, ... this has nothing to do with the *Dominion Empress*." He opened a folder on the desk, and perused it for a moment. "You served under captain Mallinson, correct?" he began.

"I was his first mate, yes."

"And in your time with him, you fought a Japanese submarine in a running gun battle in the Java Sea at night and survived?"

"Yes."

"And you fought off a Japanese bomber?"

"It was an observation seaplane that bombed us. 'Fought off' is a bit strong, ... we 'evaded' it."

"And you sank a Japanese submarine in the Indian Ocean with an improvised bomb, and took seven prisoners? Including the submarine's commander?"

"Yes, we did. David, is this line of questioning going somewhere? Because if I'm not here to give testimony about the sinking of the *Dominion Empress*, I'd really prefer to continue my trip to England as soon as possible."

"We, that is to say, the Special Operations Executive *not* the SAS, want to offer you the command of a ship."

"A ship!" he repeated, surprised, sitting up and leaning forwards.

"Yes. We'd like you to take command of the HLV *Belfair*." David opened a drawer and brought out a bottle of Dewars White Label and two tumblerglasses. He held one up and raised an eyebrow. Reggie nodded.

"Uh, ... you said 'H.L.V.'? What's that mean? His Majesty's something-or-other?" The major poured out a heavy dram and handed it across.

"Heavy Lift Vessel. It's a sister ship to the HLV *Belpareil* and HLV *Beljeanne*. She's 414 feet long by 68 feet wide and draws 33 feet when loaded. 10,446 dead weight tons, all up. She's twin screw, has a cruising speed of nine knots and is capable of eleven knots. Built 1926, and equipped with three cranes, each able to lift 100 tons. Interested?"

"Hundred ton cranes? Great Scott!—but, just a moment, you've not explained who or what this Special Operations Executive is." Reggie sat back, took a sip of his dram and waited. The major hesitated, and then spoke with care, his fingers steepled before him.

"The SOE doesn't exist, officially. We're responsible for conducting espionage and clandestine raids into enemy territory, and coordinating with the resistance movements of foreign governments. It was formed at Mr Churchill's personal request. Winston refers to us as his 'Ministry of Ungentlemanly Warfare'." David took a drink and smirked. "You saw the vehicle that brought you here?"

"Yes, a Jeep. I was impressed. I gather it's American. During the drive here it seemed it could handle anything." He took another sip.

"I can confirm that, personally." He winked. Reggie consulted his wristwatch.

"Major Stirling, I'm very interested in your offer to take command of this ship. So, the day is young. Shall we requisition one of these Jeeps and go have a 'shufti' at the H.L.V. *Belfair*?" The major shifted uncomfortably in his seat and said nothing. "Oh, is it not in Alexandria?"

"Actually, it isn't, but there is a similar ship, the *Belray*, here in Port Said, although it's less than half the displacement. We could view that if you wish."

"I'd rather have a look at the *actual* ship, if you don't mind." Reggie responded.

"Ah, ... yes, well ..." the major left his reply hanging.

"Oh, I see. You're trying to tell me it's too far away to conveniently drive there?"

"You could say that." The major reddened, embarrassed. "It's in Yugoslavia." Reggie's eyes narrowed.

"You mean, *occupied* Yugoslavia?"

"True," said David in confirmation. "On eighteenth April last year the country surrendered unconditionally, and Mussolini and Hitler officially recognized the formation of the Independent State of Croatia. That country is now a German puppet state, yet Italian-governed, but they're so incompetent the Germans have re-assumed command of the Serbian part of it because of this. The *Belfair* lies in the Italian-governed portion.

"There are so many political factions it seems things have degenerated into a state of civil war. There are factions of fascist *Ustaše* led by the ultra-nationalist dictator Ante Pavelić, and the royalist Chetniks led by Brigade General Mihailović, and then a shadowy group known as 'partisans', but who knows who is leading *them* – all we know at the present time is they're Communists. But, at the same time they're all either fighting each other, or collaborating with each other, or the Nazis or the Italians."

"Sounds confusing."

"You don't know the half of it. There are also the mercenary troops of Hungarians or Roumanians, or maybe Bulgarians or Albanians, we've really no idea how many factions are involved. But really, all you need do, is go in and bring the ship out. In essence you'll just be a delivery captain."

"Delivery Captain? Don't you think one of those factions might want to lodge a slight objection to that?" he asked, with heavy sarcasm. His sarcasm was ignored.

"Here, let me explain: we've recently learned the ship is owned by Belships A/S, a Norwegian company. When the Germans invaded France in 1940 the founder of that company, a man by the name of Christen Smith, saw what was coming. He had twenty-six ships in African ports and these had already been seized by the Vichy French. He knew he had to act quickly in order to stay in business, so he sold the *Belfair* to a Swedish 'holding company' on a clandestine 'handshake deal' for a nominal sum, with an agreement to get it back the same way at the end of this war. The Nazis know nothing of this.

"For all intents and purposes, it's now Swedish flagged and has a Swedish crew. Sweden has declared neutrality. Diplomatically speaking, the Nazis can't touch it, although we have our suspicions they're itching to get their hands on it. It's currently laying empty in the port of Šibenik, and it's been sitting there since April of 1941. We think the Nazis had a hand in this somehow. We believe they may have sent in an agent to prevent its departure, but have no actual proof of this."

"You make it sound all so simple," Reggie sneered. "You're asking me to pinch a ship from an occupied country. I'm no agent. I've never killed anybody. I've never fired a gun in anger in my entire life. I've even attended grouse shoots in Scotland and missed every shot. I think you'll be better served sending someone who knows what they're about."

"The agents we have know nothing about ships this large. We need a qualified Merchant Navy captain to take charge. You're available now and, speaking frankly, your credentials are far beyond anything we could have hoped for. We need you to bring it out 'under diplomatic immunity' to Alexandria, when your part of the mission will be done, and others will take it over from there."

"Šibenik, Yugoslavia to Alexandria, Egypt, in an empty neutral ship. Why?"

"On the face of it, it's to be taken back to Sweden but, as it passes England by, we plan to seize it. We've already obtained the Swedish Government's tacit agreement to do this. Naturally they'll issue protestations and condemnations of this supposed act of piracy, and these will be trumpeted in the world-wide press. We then intend to re-flag it as Norwegian, a member of the Allies, and turn the ship over to be managed by 'Nortraship', the Norwegian Shipping and Trade Mission."

"So, we get another ship to add to the allied fleet. So what? What's so important about this ship in particular?"

"Sorry, but that sort of information is strictly on a 'need to know' basis, you see," the major informed him.

"If I'm to risk my life going into an occupied country, I'll need to know the reason why before I make any sort of decision." He downed his drink and stood up. He began to button his suit coat. The major looked alarmed.

"All right, all right, *please*, sit! You're not to repeat this to anybody, agreed? Strictly 'Hush-Hush'!"

"Agreed," Reggie said, and sat. David stood and went to the door. He locked it and shut the Venetian blinds for privacy, then returned to his desk. He refreshed their drinks. The major settled back into his chair, and began speaking quietly and deliberately.

"There's to be an invasion of French North Africa, planned for November, only ten months away. It's been tentatively assigned the code name Operation Torch. Naturally, we expect the Vichy French to oppose us. Talks are in the works to have the French resistance stage a coup just prior to the landings, but who knows how those will pan out. We could be facing a major battle.

"Monty tells us that General Patton says he is America's 'best tank man', or so he tells everyone. Patton's been tapped to command 250 Sherman tanks to be landed on the coast of Morocco. It seems he's never commanded a tank brigade in a major battle, you see, and is rather keen to get stuck in.

"Now, a third of these tanks will be unloaded from the USS *Lakehurst* at Safi, Morocco. But the *Belfair* alone has the capacity to carry the other two-thirds, and with those three massive cranes they could be unloaded quickly, six all at once, directly into the port facilities at Casablanca. Don't you see what this means? With speed like that, think of the lives saved!"

Reggie could see the benefits. The ship was Swedish-owned and neutral, even protected diplomatically, so the risk was minimal: the world press would be reporting on it, and the eyes of the world would be following his progress. The Nazis couldn't make a move against a neutral ship under the gaze of the entire world. Well before the time of this 'Operation Torch' he'd be well distanced from any international repercussions. It was indeed tempting.

"I'm still an employee of the Ellerman Shipping Line. I'll need to speak—"

"Yes, certainly. You'll still be their employee and pull your normal pay while seconded to our organization but, we'll provide you a salary as well. Consider it 'hazard pay' – don't let Ellerman Shipping know of this, as officially we don't exist. You can tell them you've temporarily joined the Port of Alexandria's staff in a managerial role, just to 'gain experience' as it were. We'll draw up paperwork to make it look official." Reggie thought for a moment: *I could be in and out in a matter of weeks, certainly no more than a month, tops.*

He made up his mind. "I'll do it!"

"Thank you, Captain Wallace. You've no idea how relieved we all are you've accepted." They clinked glasses and drank. Reggie then had a thought, something hanging in the back of his mind over the past few minutes.

"You mentioned the ship is unable to leave Šibenik. Is this because of diplomatic disagreements between Yugoslavia and Sweden?"

"No. It seems the captain went missing. The Swedes then were allowed to send in another naval captain, a Captain Jules Söderberg, to bring it out."

"Oh? Why didn't he?"

"He was murdered. It's the reason they turned to us."

4

Preparations

He awoke early Saturday morning, the sun streaming in, the top of Millicent Featherstone's head buried in his armpit. Supper and dancing at the Turf Club had ended here in his hotel room. The cocktails had been splendid, the supper exquisite. As he'd spun her about the dance floor, Milly had complimented him on his abilities. They'd fit very well together last night. As he dressed he watched her sitting on the edge of the tub in her panties, shaving her legs. When she finished she offered the razor to him, but he had to decline.

"Major Stirling told me not to shave; I'm to grow a beard." Milly slumped on the edge of the bed, her forearms dangling between her legs.

"Oh, God, they're sending you to the Balkans, aren't they?" She pouted, and threw herself on her back, a forearm over her eyes. "Why is it every ..." she complained, leaving the rest unsaid. "Do me a favour: if you run into 'Marko' give him a swift kick in the 'ghoulies' from me."

"Why?" he asked, laughing, "What did he ever do to you?"

"We had three dates, and he stood me up for two of them." She sat up.

"I think I won't. You'll get much more satisfaction out of doing it yourself, when you see him next."

"You mean 'if' I see him again," Milly replied, standing and reaching for her brassiere. "Men who go there have a tendency to disappear. I need to go to work."

"I'll walk you there," he offered, but thought to himself, *That sounds ominous.*

"Nice bit of stubble there." Major Stirling greeted him when he entered. "Having a beard in Yugoslavia is regarded as *de rigueur.* Every man sports one. Those without a beard are regarded with suspicion. We want you to look as much like a local as possible. Once you reach the ship you can shave."

"I've been meaning to say something about that. After a sinking it's usual to be given six weeks R&R. Will I be —"

"Sure, six weeks will give you a good start on your beard. In the meantime you can brush up on your Serbo-Croatian."

"Not that I know any now."

"I was being facetious. It's an extremely difficult language. We think you'll be best served if you only learn a few key words and phrases that may help you bluff your way out of a difficult situation. You should talk as little as possible. Just leave the talking to your contact. He's fluent in it." The Major brought out a number of items from his desk and grouped them on the desktop. They got stuck into it straight away. He pushed a tiny bible at him, a raised golden cross embossed on its morocco-leather cover.

"This is a phrasebook you'll do well to study, disguised as a bible. We'll arrange for a tutor to coach you on certain days about pronunciation." Reggie opened it to find onionskin pages filled with tiny type. David then pushed a short stack of paper money at him.

"This is the money they use in Yugoslavia. It's called 'dinar' and we'll provide quite a lot of it, more than you'll need, to bribe your way out of any spot of trouble. Corruption seems to be a way of life up that way. Familiarize yourself with the various denominations. You'll carry this in waxed envelopes sewn into your clothing, for the drop." Reggie glanced at it, then pocketed it.

"Also sewn into your clothing will be a new set of papers saying you're Swedish. We'll take your photograph and gin those up later. Apropos clothing, you'll be given clothing befitting the country so you'll blend in while you travel to the ship. We're working on assembling those for you now."

"You said, 'for the drop'? I won't be parachuted in, will I? I don't think I can do that."

"No, we'll drop you by submarine. You'll need to walk in the dark approximately five miles overland through dense scrub, the last half mile through town."

"Do I get a compass? A map? How do I know the route?"

"You'll be met on a specific beach by your 'in-country' contact, Bill Hudson, an agent we planted there in September '41 for another operation, Operation Bullseye. He'll guide you there. His *nom de guerre* — sorry, *nom de guerre* is French for 'War Name' —"

"I know what it means, sir," Reggie interrupted.

"Oh. ... Well, ... anyway, as I was saying: when you're in-country you're *never* to refer to *any* of our agents by their *actual* names. Never call your contact 'Bill' or 'Hudson' within earshot of any other person. You're to call him only 'Marko', got it?" Despite himself, Reggie laughed. The major regarded him with a bewildered expression. "What's so funny?"

"Nothing, nothing. Carry on."

"Marko will have a wireless transmitting set with him. When you reach the ship, Marko is to send the coded message 'The goose has landed'."

"You're joking."

"Not at all."

"No, that's just too stupid." The major bridled at this and frowned.

"What do you suggest?" he asked, peevishly.

"Well, I'm from Goudhurst in Kent, … how about, … 'The Hedgehog Has Burrowed'?"

"Have it your way." The major said, with a shrug. "Now, we come to this: if your words or your bribes fail, this will be your last resort." He unwrapped a folded cloth to reveal a pistol laying next to its magazine. "This is a Walther P38 and is an early model – notice the walnut grips. It's 9mm Parabellum." Reggie picked it up and hefted it. It was short. The German eagle was stamped on one side, and there were various other numbers on it.

"Walther P38? So, it's German?"

"The Czech resistance took it from a dead *Gestapo* officer. Standard issue in the *Wehrmacht* except the barrel's been shortened." Reggie noticed the snub barrel had been machined for threads, and so there was no front sight.

"Does it come with a silencer?"

"No. If you find you do need to use this, you'll likely be standing within feet of your assailant so I shouldn't worry about missing."

"Splendid," he replied, without enthusiasm. "As I said, I've never fired a gun in my entire life – that is, only long guns, never a pistol."

"Now's your chance to learn, eh? Take it with you now. Familiarize yourself with it, until you feel comfortable handling it. You'll be taken into the desert and we'll coach you. There's no ammunition in it: we won't give you that until later." The major took the magazine and cloth back and placed them in the drawer. "Now just go down the hall to the door marked sixteen, and they'll snap a photo for your new Swedish identity papers. They're expecting you. Well, that wraps it up for today. Enjoy your rest and relaxation." Reggie pocketed the pistol and the phrasebook. After the photo session Reggie surprised Milly in General Stone's anteroom.

"Have I got news for you! Want to have lunch?" She accepted at once.

They were in the restaurant of Shepheards Hotel, chosen for its view of the Nile. Lunch had been excellent and they now sat back, each with a cocktail. Milly was still in uniform since they had come here directly she had ended her work day at noon, this being a Saturday. He'd already told her his contact was going to be Marko, and they'd had a good laugh at that, but he still refused to kick him where she demanded.

"So, I've been given five more weeks for rest and relaxation," he announced.

"That's wonderful! What do you intend to do with it?"

"I must spend some time studying and practising but, outside of those hours, I guess I can do whatever I want. What say you to hiring a pair of camels this afternoon and touring the Sphinx and pyramids?" Reggie was dismayed at seeing her reaction to this question. She set her drink down and squirmed in her seat, avoiding his gaze.

"Reggie, I ... I have to use the powder room." She rose and fled the room.

He sat looking at a lateen-rigged felucca slowly gliding upstream, wondering what had upset her. *Oh. She must be married and I've just put my foot in it. No, wait, that's not it; she's a 'miss'. Then what could be the problem? She must not be as attracted to me as I am to her.* The felucca was now out of sight. He polished off his drink. *What could be keeping her? Oh, her handbag's gone. I've been stood up.*

"Sorry about that." She sat. "What were you saying? Something about pyramids, was it?"

"Yes. Scrub the camels. We can do horses instead."

"Well, I prefer ..."

"Milly, are you married?" he interrupted. Again with the squirming. She sighed.

"No, I'm not married." She sipped her drink.

"But, you're not interested in me. You put on a good show last night, I must say."

"It was ... not a show. God! Far from it." She took a sip of her drink. "It's not you. I suspect you're looking for the right woman, the one you can marry."

"Yes, I am. I'm twenty-nine and 'not getting any younger', to quote that old chestnut." *After all, mum was twenty-nine when I was born*, he thought.

"It's true I'm holding myself off from marriage. I have a career to think of." She lowered her voice. "You're not in the Royal Navy or RAF or Army, so maybe you don't know what women in the services go through out here."

"Go through? Can you explain?"

"We want to do our bit for the war effort. I work a nine hour day, sometimes longer, we all do. At least three times a day, sometimes more, I'll have a boob squeezed, my bum pinched, my knee or sometimes my thigh fondled. All ranks too. Some blokes dive straight in for a kiss. It's humiliating." She glanced about to see if she'd be overheard by nearby tables, then continued *sotto voce*, "At least once a fortnight some feckin arse will try to touch my fanny!"

"Your actual *fanny*?" he said, gobsmacked.

"One staff sergeant did manage to touch it, and I bit his shoulder so hard I drew blood."

"Astounding. Have you tried lodging a complaint with your ATS superiors?"

"There's no use in that. I've tried. They seem to think we're here as a kind of a 'safety valve' for the men to blow off steam." Reggie then related his experience, as she sipped her drink.

"As first mate last year on a voyage from Batavia, Java, to Perth, Australia, my merchant navy ship, the *Dominion Empress*, carried nine civilian Commonwealth nurses, and I'm dead certain everybody aboard treated them with the utmost respect the entire time. I know I did."

"Perhaps I should join the merchant navy." She tossed off the remainder of her drink.

"I'll have to admit, not all our ships are like that. It probably had more to do with the way my captain, Roy Mallinson, looked after us. Another drink?"

"No, thank you. Shall we go see those pyramids now?"

"Oh, – I got the distinct impression you're not interested in me."

"I'm not interested in *marriage* at this stage of my life. That's not to say I'm not interested in *sex*. I knew you to be a real gentleman the moment we met, not at all like any of the others here. I most definitely am interested in sex, and specifically with you, and only with you. Blimey! You've no idea how long it's been!"

"Hmmm." He scratched the stubble on his chin. "Even looking as unkempt as this?"

"Yes, Reggie, a woman can see through all the surface bits to the real man inside. Are you game?"

"Where do you live?"

"I share a studio flat with three others. Kind of crowded."

"You've seen my hotel room. How about moving in with me until I go? Sex or not – always your call – it will be a pleasure having you for company, Milly." He held up a hand as if swearing an oath, which in a way he kind of was.

"Done, Reggie. But one condition!"

"Which is?"

"We keep this known only to ourselves. I've my reputation to consider."

"Agreed. Now, let's go get those horses, shall we?"

"Camels!!!"

The remainder of the afternoon was spent viewing the pyramids and Sphinx by camel.

The next weeks were spent in training. His language tutor was patient and only occasionally irritated. He found the same word as a noun might be a completely different spelling as a verb. He was started out on single words:

"*Zdravo* – Hello."

"*Doviđenja* – good-bye."

"*Molim* – please." In coming days they graduated to short phrases he might need:

"*Imate li ikakvu?* – Have you any?"

"*Koliko je to?* – How much is that?"

"*Ne pucati.* – Don't shoot."

"*Predati se* – I surrender."

He despaired at how difficult the words were to pronounce. He was of the opinion there were not enough vowels in some words. Consonants were grouped in ways never seen in English and, blimey, those accent marks!

"*Doviđenja.*"

"No, it's *doviđenja.*"

"That's what I said!"

"Now say it properly: *doviđenja.*" And so it went, over and over again.

In the desert his weapons instructor was equally patient. They taught him how to disable an attacker by bending fingers or limbs in directions they were never meant to go. He was shown the proper grip to hold the Fairbairn-Sykes fighting knife for an upwards or a downwards thrust, and how to keep the knife in the scabbard when it was mounted inverted, with a bit of an elastic loop over the pommel. He was shown how to reload the magazine properly. A dozen empty tins were set up at the base of a high dune. At twenty-five paces, only one was hit. This could not be repeated. At six paces, all were hit. It was the same a week later, and the week after that. "Oh, well, good enough. Let's go back," the instructor said.

In the beginning, Milly and Reggie's negotiated agreement had been in earnest, but gradually they both began to anticipate with growing eagerness the approach of each day's teatime. But it was each new weekend where things really came alive. There were many new destinations to experience with Milly. They browsed the bazaars, sampled sweet desserts from hawkers in the streets, shopped in the *souk*, bathed at Alexandria's popular Sidi Beshr Beach on the Mediterranean, but never in the Nile (crocodiles, you know). One Saturday they boarded the Thomas Cook side-wheel paddle steamer *Arabia* to stay at the railway hotel near the border of Anglo-Egyptian Sudan, in Wadi Halfa on the bank of the Nile. Walking through the gardens they selected a bench under the Medemia date palms with a view of the hotel fountains. Reggie cradled his head in Milly's lap as she quizzed him. She leafed through the tiny Serbo-Croatian/English dictionary, selecting Croat words at random, and he had to come up with the English equivalent.

"*Soba*," she announced.

"That's easy: 'room'."

"*Janje!*"

"Yan-yay? Don't know that one."

"It means lamb. *Meso!*"

"Meat."

"Very good. Now, what is '*Čaj*'?"

"Easy. That's tea – they pronounce it 'chai'."

"*Zdjela.*"

"Bowl."

"Yes, but it can also mean 'plate', or any container. *Diktat.*"

"Diktat means 'dictation' in German, so I'll guess it also means 'dictation' in Croatian."

"Very good, Reggie!" And in this way he made progress.

Returning on the Sunday, they missed boarding the downriver steamer PS *Sudan*, so had to take the train. Along the way there was a delay of some sort that concerned the ancient locomotive, but they eventually arrived at Cairo near midnight.

Frequently on many nights they might make love—no, that's not the word for what they did—for with a keen willingness they fucked. At times tender and dreamy, at other times zealous, but always the mood was just right. Never did they quarrel, nor even exchange a cross word. Despite all their stated intentions and assertions at the beginning, were they falling for each other? That couldn't be, could it?

5

A Warning Given

In the middle of his fourth week of R&R, just before lunchtime, – it was the fourth of February – he was called to an emergency meeting with Major Stirling. When he arrived in the SOE office he was met by a waiting corporal and rushed down the hallway to another room. The major, not smiling, seemed to him to be in something of a rush. He thanked the corporal and dismissed him with the order, "Get Mr Sayeed!"

"Don't sit. Stand here please." He was brought to a position in front of a table. There was no preamble nor pleasantries. "Strip off, please." He saw an array of clothing laid out on a table. There was a full length mirror in the corner. Next to this was a battered second-hand suitcase.

"What is it? What's going on, major?"

"Clothing first. We'll talk after." As his clothing came off it was piled in a chair. "Pants, too." When he stood naked he was handed pieces of clothing and, as the major explained them, he put them on. "This is what Yugoslavian men wear underneath and, here is your singlet – put these on. They wear this type of sock." There was a knock and a short balding man entered, a tailor's tape measure dangling around his neck and a fabric marking chalk in his hand. He was Egyptian, the

41

same man who had taken his measurements two weeks before. He said nothing but stood off to one side to observe.

"Put on these trousers, and here's your belt – it's Bulgarian leather." He then was handed a rough long-sleeved shirt of stiff cream-coloured cotton.

"This is your shirt. It's Osnaburg cotton because wearing Egyptian cotton will look suspicious. Now, here's your waistcoat." He put them on. "Sorry there's no jumper. The only wool jumpers available are British service issue and inappropriate for our needs, but we do have this." The Egyptian then held up a jacket that had toggles and loops instead of buttons, and some minimal embroidery about the stand-up collar. It was not of wool, but rather a green-dyed leather, and there were brown corduroy sleeves, and corduroy panels sewn into its front and back. He shrugged into that. He patted it and could feel a stiffness in the front, low down, and looked up quizzically.

"That's your money and Swedish identity papers. They're sewn into inside pockets with a stitch or two of thread. Should you need to produce them quickly the thread will just break." Major David Stirling then looked the captain directly in his eyes and issued him a stern warning: "Captain Wallace, mind you're not to lose, nor discard, *any* of this clothing under *any* circumstances, do you understand?"

"Yes sir, I do."

"Very good. Remember that! Now, these boots are Italian military issue. Rather popular where you're going. Everyone wears them. Don't tuck your trousers into these, as you don't want to be mistaken for anybody military." He could see they were indeed finely made of a brown leather, and laced all the way up to above the ankle, providing good support.

"And now for your trench coat. This is waterproof." He was helped into this. The major turned to the tailor. "What do you think, Mr Sayeed?" The Egyptian held his tailors chalk in his teeth, and stepped up to pull at various bits, and tugged on his lapels, and smoothed his hands over the shoulders. He nodded and pocketed his chalk. The major then handed Reggie some fine black leather gloves. He would later learn these were of German manufacture.

"And now, for the *pièce de résistance*, your hat." This was a black lambswool affair, something like an Astrakhan, or as the Canadians referred to them, a "wedge Busby". The ridged peak did not run fore-and-aft but instead from side to side. It sat square upon his head and was tilted slightly to the rear. He turned and regarded himself in the mirror. His beard was not yet long enough, but he did indeed look Yugoslavian.

"What do you think, Reggie? Satisfactory? Everything fit?"

"Yes, I think I look rather authentic. Mr Sayeed did a bang-on job."

"Thank you very much, Mr Sayeed, you may go." Mr Sayeed bowed and left. He hadn't said a word. "Here's your pistol and spare ammunition." He handed over a dagger in an odd-looking sheath. "This is a Fairbairn-Sykes knife which is standard commando issue, you may find it handy. It may be mounted in any of various positions, and you can experiment with that later. Get dressed in your civilian clothing now, and what you're wearing goes into this suitcase. Do you have anything in your room that's valuable, anything you don't care to part with?"

"Why, yes, I've half a dozen shirts. There's a flask of vodka that was a gift, and this wristwatch." The major took Reggie's wrist to look closely at the watch.

"That'll pass. What kind of flask is it?"

"It's Polish silver."

"That'll pass too. Leave the shirts. Don't forget your toothbrush and tooth powder. Pyjamas too."

"I don't wear pyjamas. My toothbrush?"

"Yes. We've a submarine waiting for you in the port of Alexandria.

There's a driver waiting to take you there now. You're to meet your contact on Monday the ninth of February at eighteen-hundred hours local time, on a beach just north of Brodarica, Croatia. Awfully sorry about the short notice, old chap, but it's the war you know, it waits for no man—oh, and Captain Wallace?"

"Sir?"

"We're in something of a desperate rush just now, but I reckon we can allow you a quick word with whoever that 'bint' is you've been shagging."

Major David Stirling never saw his fist coming.

6

The Croatian Drop

It was half-three when the Jeep skidded to a stop in a cloud of dust. This Jeep was new, so new it had a windscreen, was dark green, and "USA" was still stencilled in white on the side of the bonnet and bumper. Staff Sergeant Ellice set the handbrake and waited.

"Thank you for taking the time to drive me out, sergeant."

"Not a problem, sir, happy to oblige," he said, blandly. Milly sat stoically in the passenger seat, her eyes on the submarine in front of them, yet not seeing it. At the sergeant's suggestion, General Stone had agreed to let her off duty at noon so she could accompany Reggie, who sat on his suitcase in the rear of the Jeep behind Milly. He jumped to the ground and retrieved his suitcase, setting it on the bonnet to open it. He removed an armload of his wrinkled shirts.

"I'm sorry I must go so early. This is not what I'd intended." He piled the shirts in her lap. "I want you to have these to keep. Sorry, they're dirty, you'll likely need to wash them." Expressionless, she accepted them. "Thank you for seeing me off. I'll see you in two weeks." He bent to kiss her. She didn't turn her head to meet him, so he kissed her cheek. She still hadn't looked at him. *Oh, I'm an idiot – It's a long drive back to Cairo. Part of that trip will be in desert and in the desert anything*

*may happen, and who's to know? – if the Special Operations Executive
expects me to act like some sort of an agent, I might as well start now.*

"Staff Sergeant Ellice, you're General Stone's 'dogsbody', correct?"
He asked, using an old Royal Navy term.

"I'm his aide-de-camp, yes." the man countered with a sneer.

"And Miss Featherstone here is the General's personal clerk, isn't
that right?"

"You already know that ... *sir*," he said, unctuously. Standing in
such a way as to make sure the sergeant had an unobstructed view of
him, he dug the Walther out of the suitcase, pulled the magazine out,
examined and replaced it. He transferred the pistol to his left hand and
rested his left arm on the back of Milly's seat, so the sergeant could
see the weapon up close all the more easily.

"How's the shoulder, sergeant, all healed up?" he asked casually.

"Yes sir, it —" Ellice shut his mouth and glared at Milly. Reggie's
left forearm was touching the back of Milly's right shoulder, and he
could feel how she trembled.

"I'll say good-bye, then." Reaching across Milly, Reggie put out his
right hand. They shook hands, and as they released Reggie grabbed
the man's thumb and bent it back towards the elbow and twisted that
arm to the rear. Ellice grimaced in pain.

"On the drive out," Reggie hissed, "do you think I didn't see you
watching her tits bounce as you made sure to hit every washboard and
pothole in the road? I've heard stories, sergeant, awful stories." He
increased the pressure. With fire in his eyes, he shouted, "You are not
to touch her! No squeezing, no pinching nor fondling of anything,"
– his voice dropped an octave – "and no raping! Is that clear?" The
sergeant grunted, eyes squinted with pain.

"Answer me! Is that clear?"

"Ye-yes sir." The sergeant stammered. The slightest smile began
to play on Milly's lips.

"Sergeant, 'chancers' of your sort make me ill. You are to treat her like the lady she is – and this order applies to every woman you meet from now on, because when I return, if I hear anything different—" He raised the pistol so the sergeant was looking down the barrel, "I will find a clandestine way to murder you." The sergeant swallowed hard. He released the man, and turned to put the gun in his luggage, snapping the case shut.

"Don't bother complaining to your superiors, because this never happened. That's right, isn't it, Milly?" He placed his left hand on her shoulder, to find she no longer trembled. She gazed up into his face.

"Yes," she nodded, "we drove in silence. Not a word was said." The sergeant cradled his elbow and rocked in his seat.

"See you in two weeks," he repeated, and kissed Milly again, properly this time. He started across the gangplank to the submarine. A bearded man above in the conning tower waved to him. When he reached the deck of the boat he saluted the White Ensign. Looking back at the Jeep, he saw her raise the lap-full of his shirts to bury her face in them. It occurred to him then, that perhaps she had no intention of laundering them. The gangplank was withdrawn to the shore with a mobile crane. He made his way around the three-inch deck gun to the base of the tower. Hooking the suitcase handle onto a grappling hook dangling there, it was hauled up ahead of him as he climbed the rungs. When he reached the top, the man there helped him over the coaming, and introduced himself.

"Lieutenant-Commander David Wanklyn. Welcome aboard *Upholder*."

"Captain Reginald Wallace, sir. Happy to be aboard." They shook hands.

"Let's get you below. We're late as it is." Reggie turned to look, but the Jeep had gone.

They assigned him a cabin he shared with a junior officer. The

Upholder motored to the west-northwest on a heading of 300 degrees true. In daytime it ran submerged on batteries and at night on the surface so the diesels could charge them. He was told the voyage might be 1,100 nautical miles or more. At certain times "Wanks", as his men called him, kept him updated as to their position, telling him when they had cleared the island of Crete, or that they were now entering the Adriatic Sea. He spent his time practising his Croatian pronunciation, or field stripping the pistol. One day he wrote out the letters of recommendation for each of his *Dominion Empress* officers. He gave these to Wanks and asked him to send them to the Ministry of War Transport. The trip itself was uneventful, except for when he was told they had "torped a freighter" but, unfortunately, he had slept through that event.

In late afternoon on ninth February, Reggie dressed in his Yugoslavian clothing and sat nervously waiting to be called. When the crewman knocked, he found it was a great relief to finally be going. All his civilian clothing and suitcase was left in the room. He was shown the way to the control room. Reggie stood in the cramped compartment with leading seaman Mr Turner holding a deflated yellow life raft, the small two-chamber kind used by bomber tail-gunners when forced to bail out over water. Commander Wanklyn was there peering into the periscope, and turned to him.

"We meant to drop you after dark, but we've only just received a decrypted alert an 'Eye-tie' ship is scheduled to depart Brindisi and we must go sink it. We're dropping you off early. Sorry."

"What time is it?"

"1648 hours local." Wanks said.

"What time is sunset?"

"1717 hours."

"Won't I be seen?"

"Let's hope not, eh? Want a look at Brodarica?" he asked, and stepped aside. Reggie put his face to the rubber cups of the eyepiece and gripped the handles as he had observed the commander to do. Towards shore there were lights. This was the village of Brodarica. There were lights on the left as well, and in between was darkness. As he watched, there were three short flashes of a torch.

"I just saw three flashes from the shoreline," Reggie said.

"That would be your contact's signal. The man must be early. So much the better, eh?" Reggie stepped aside, and the commander had a look. "Down periscope," Wanklyn barked. "Surface slow."

"Surface slow, Aye." There was the unique sound of ballast tanks being blown.

"Take this torch. Clip it to your trench coat epaulette. When you see his signal, answer it with two short of your own." Mr Turner handed him the torch, then draped the raft over his shoulder and climbed the ladder up the conning tower. Reggie followed after, getting splattered with saltwater. The Commander followed. When he emerged it wasn't yet dark, but getting there. The clouds to the west had a rosy salmon yellow colour on their undersides. He reckoned the temperature to be hovering about the freezing mark. There was a slight breeze, its direction variable; his breath danced before his face before dissipating. Mr Turner was already halfway to the deck. The captain and commander both looked to the east at the dark portion of shore. Reggie flashed twice, and was answered by three short.

"How far do you reckon, sir?" he whispered.

"About half a kilometre," Commander Wanklyn whispered, "and not having a coastal chart of the area, this is as close as we dare."

"One quarter of a nautical mile. Easy peasy."

"The tide is ebbing now. We wanted to drop you at the slack but, as I said, we're early."

"Hmm ... what's the tidal range here?"

"The tables say about a metre. Do you want us to stay surfaced until you get there?”

"I don't think there's any need. You don't want to be seen. Good luck getting that ship."

"Cheers. Go now, and good luck." They shook hands and exchanged salutes. He followed Mr Turner down the ladder. The seaman put a foot inside the raft and yanked first on one toggle, then another, and the tiny craft inflated with a noise much too loud. He held it at the beginning of the slope of the hull, and spoke quietly.

"Get in and sit. I'll lower you. When you're in the water haul this line in. There's a paddle tied to the end of it. Kneel in the centre with your knees apart, and stroke on alternate sides."

"Thank you, Mr Turner." He reached into his pocket and offered the flask of vodka to him. "I only just realised I won't be needing this where I'm going. You might as well have it. Enjoy!"

"Awfully kind of you, sir. Good luck."

He slid down the hull seated in the tiny craft. In the water he reeled the painter in and coiled it to stow it. The single-ended paddle was an aluminium affair with a tubular shaft. He started away, stroking as instructed. Behind him *Upholder* reversed away and then soundlessly submerged.

The coil of line was getting tangled in his feet and he found this irritating, so he untied it from the paddle and raft, and jettisoned it overboard. He occasionally paused to flash the light, and was answered every time. The breeze was no longer variable, but came from his left and was strengthening. What is more, the air temperature had dropped precipitously. He reckoned he had only some 300 yards to go. As he switched the paddle from side to side he was dribbling water inside the raft. His knees were getting wet and the water was cold. This raft was hardly longer than it was wide and its directional stability was awful. As he stroked on the right, it rotated left, and as he stroked on the left it rotated right. He appeared to be making little headway.

Then he had an inspiration: he wouldn't spin so much if the thrust of the paddle was down the centreline of the raft. He'd use a sculling motion, and to do that he'd need to reach the stern. Still kneeling, he scooted around to face the raft's right side and hung the paddle over the stern, holding it against the tube with his right hand. With the very first figure-eight stroke: success, it worked! Now he was making progress toward shore, and not a moment too soon, for the wind had picked up dramatically and it began to snow. The coast here ran generally from northwest to southeast, but this wind came from the north, pushing him south. He redoubled his efforts. The effort expended in sculling was making him overheat and sweat. He paused to unbutton the trench coat, and pushed the bulk of it behind him.

Just when he thought he might be in the wind-shadow of the land, he heard a *pop* and a hiss of escaping air. He felt behind him and found his knife scabbard had punctured the tube. He tried stopping up the hole by putting his gloved finger in it but to no avail, it was too large. The raft deflated quickly and he toppled backwards. The cold shock took his breath away. He spit out a mouthful of seawater. Grappling frantically for the other buoyant chamber of the raft he succeeded in catching it. His hat floated before him and he snatched it, then stuffed it into his coat pocket. Hanging both arms over the tube he tried kicking toward shore but with boots on nothing happened. He tried dog-paddling, but against the wind and current it was no use. He couldn't believe how cold it was. How much time did he have before he was unable to grip this tube? Fifteen minutes, maybe twenty at the most? Maybe.

"Help me! Help!" he screamed. The wind was howling now, and the snow now blew horizontally, his words carried away. He pulled his open trench coat up until its belt was under his arms, and tried buckling himself to the tube with it. He couldn't work the buckle wearing his leather gloves, so he removed them and stuffed them into the other coat pocket. He buckled the belt around the tube, and this supported him. But with the belt on the centre of the tube, its ends protruded upwards in a vee-shape, and this made a perfect sail which was caught by the wind. He was being blown south in the same direction as the ebbing current. Screaming again, he realized he couldn't be heard over the wind, so conserved his energy. My God it was bloody freezing!

He fumbled for the switch on the torch and couldn't feel his fingers, or his nose or ears either. When he succeeded in getting it to flash he saw the other light was still there – sometimes ahead or behind, and often disappearing, but always reappearing. The light was following him, and then it wasn't. South of him, in the direction he was being carried, a chain of small islands appeared across his path. Paddling and kicking as hard as he could he made no headway, and was swept between and past them. The effort exhausted him and he panted, the vapour of his breath torn away.

He caught a brief glimpse of the distant light before it was obscured by a peninsula. Now he knew he was off a deep bay, because the travelling light had disappeared. The ferocious wind took the tops off the waves and flung the spray in his face, stinging it. His body hung straight down, a useless weight. With a tremendous effort he lifted one leaden leg and succeeded in getting a boot onto the deflated tube that hung below. He locked his knee and stood on it, and this relieved the strain on his arms. He was terrified this remaining inflated chamber might burst. With all this waterlogged clothing he'd sink like a stone without it. Unbidden, a vision entered his mind of a smiling Milly holding out her arms to him. Would he ever see her again?

The sun had set. He was far from the mainland and hadn't seen the light in awhile. There was a light in the sky and he craned his neck to look upwards. In the dusk a lone four-engined bomber passed overhead heading south just beneath the cloud cover, yet high enough to still be illuminated by the rays of the setting sun. It was rapidly losing altitude and one engine was burning brightly. He watched until it ditched in the sea. *The Germans don't fly four-engined bombers that I know of—that's a British Halifax. Poor sods.*

Minutes later he was carried helplessly between a tiny island and the mainland. He attempted to flash the torch again but his fingers wouldn't work. With his teeth he succeeded in switching it on. He left it on. The very minute it came on, it was answered by three flashes from shore and then that man left his light on as well. Now he was travelling parallel to a dark wooded shore, and there were clusters of lighted houses at intervals, darkness separating each one. The light now kept pace with him, and this gave him hope. The spray still lashed his face, he just couldn't feel it any more. His teeth chattered. As before, he was carried between another tiny island on his right and a dark peninsula of trees to his left. But the current here swept him behind this land mass and, mercifully, this blocked the howling wind and stinging spray.

Before him was an island, in actuality another peninsula, because it was connected to the mainland by a low neck of sand. A village entirely covered its rounded hill, a light here and there giving it shape. Through the driven snowflakes he could see at its summit a monumental dark church and bell tower limned against the slate-grey sky. He drifted hopefully towards this sand beach, but at the last second the current turned and carried him parallel to the shore. He floated past the end of a medieval wall that came right down into the water. Now a shoreline of boulders and massive slabs of stone was only yards away. Fearing he might be carried past this village – so close! – he left one arm over the tube and stroked with the other arm and then, his foot touched bottom! Panting with the exertion he waded painfully up a monolithic slab of rock and collapsed, sobbing with relief.

How long he lay there he didn't know. Rolling onto his back, with pained stiff fingers he clawed at the belt buckle, but couldn't free it.

With his knife he stabbed at the tube and it deflated. Working the raft from side to side he pulled it from underneath the belt. The fierce wind snatched it away, and it disappeared into the sky on an updraught. The wind. He had to get out of this deadly wind. It was snowing heavily and wind-driven flakes stuck to his bare head. He brushed them off and felt ice crystals crusted in his hair. *My hat. I've lost my hat. Why am I not wearing gloves? Have I lost them as well?*

Standing was difficult. Walking even more so. Staggering up the slope of bare rock he encountered a pathway skirting the shoreline here, below dark houses set cheek-by-jowl. He was still exposed here, and was shivering violently. The air was very much more colder than even the water had been. A sign here read "Plaža Rosi." *Is this the name of the town?* he wondered, *am I still in Croatia?*

Picking a direction at random he turned left. His knee joints only bent with searing pain. Everything he wore was saturated with water and weighed a ton. His boots were filled but he didn't dare take them off, for fear of never getting them on again. Each leg felt like a tree stump. In thirty yards a narrow steep stairway appeared, zig-zagging upwards between houses, and this he took with painfully slow progress. The wind at his back buffeted him with powerful gusts and many times threatened to knock him down, if not for the assistance of a massive iron chain stapled to the walls of the limestone houses. At the top, this stairway ended at a relatively wide alley. Uphill to his right he could dimly see the square top of the church bell tower. Downhill to his left some fifty yards away was some sort of Croatian pub – a *konoba* – its sign lit and looking inviting. Shaking uncontrollably, teeth chattering, his mind was made up: *I don't have the energy to go uphill any more. Anything is better than out here.*

He shuffled downhill. When he reached the pub, he had to flatten himself against a wall, for just beyond the next building was a square. The far side of this square was a medieval wall, and guarding the archway through it were two armed Italian soldiers under a street lamp. They were checking the papers of a peasant who stood with a donkey, on its back a towering faggot of sticks. A howitzer stood to each side of the archway and covered the landward approaches to the village. This was a peninsula, so that gate was the only way in or out. Wherever this place was, it was occupied by Italians, and he was trapped here by that wall.

The carved and painted sign over the door read *Tri Labud* and showed three white swans swimming within a gilded pretzel. He paused to feel for his pistol, to make sure it was still there, and was startled to find his sodden hat. He squeezed the water from it as best he could and put it on. He pulled his torch from the epaulette and dropped it in the pocket. Taking a shivering breath, he steeled himself for whatever he might encounter, and opened the door.

The room felt very warm, at least compared to outside. It was large with a low ceiling of heavy dark wooden beams and pillars, and filled with men at round tables. Men who looked like farmers or fishermen. As the door banged shut behind him they all, to a man, turned to look at him and then went back to their games of dice or dominoes. He looked about. There was a rock fireplace with a cheery fire at the far side of the room, but every seat there was occupied. The only remaining open seat was a hard pew-like affair against the wall near the door, a tiny square table positioned in front of it. He sat. The table was sticky. He dripped water, forming a puddle at his feet. Then he noticed with dread that nearly everyone here was armed; some men had a fowling piece, or a squirrel gun, leaning against the table by his side.

A barmaid squeezed between chair-backs and approached, to wipe his table. Her golden blonde plaited hair encircled the top of her head like a crown. She had an embroidered blouse, and a dress somewhat like a *dirndl* but with a short red and black vest, quite fancy. He racked his brain for the word "tea" and could only remember the word for "coffee" in Serbo-Croatian is "kava." She stood, hand on hip, impatiently waiting for his order. He had to try. There's always a first time for everything.

"Zdravo," he said, putting on his best smile.

"Zdravo," she said, bored.

"Molim, kava."

"Nema kava." The barmaid replied. The word for tea suddenly popped into his mind.

"Molim, čaj."

"Nema čaj," The woman responded, in irritation, "Samo pivo, rakija, sljivovica." *She's telling me: No tea. Only beer, spirits, and plum brandy.*

"Molim, pivo." She left. A man seated at another table nearest to him set his litre glass down and turned to regard him for a moment, then went back to his game. A moment later he turned again to look, then stood and swaggered over to him. Snatching Reggie's hat off his head, he dashed it in his lap and pointed at the wall while saying something in irritation. Reggie saw a row of hats hanging on pegs, and only then realized every man here was bare-headed. He ducked his head, gave a smile, and put his hat beside him on the bench. The man wiped the water from his hand on his trousers and returned to his game. The barmaid brought his beer, slapped a menu down, then went back to the bar. Holding the glass between his palms, he took big draughts of the beer and, even though it was cold, it was refreshing. He began to feel human again. *Perhaps I can pull this off, after all.*

His fingers were pruned and it was painful to bend his swollen knuckles, so he flipped the menu open on the table and was dismayed to see there were no pictures. He could not translate, nor even guess, at what any of this meant. He brought out the phrasebook and tried to open it, but couldn't separate the thin pages. They disintegrated under his thumb; the pages had been reduced to a watery pulp. Putting it back in his pocket he missed, and it fell in the puddle at his feet. He abandoned it. She came again and stood, hand on hip. He needed to buy time to think. Gulping the last swallow, he traced his finger down the page, pretending to read it, as he pushed the glass over to her.

"Molim, pivo." She took the glass and left. *I need something inside me that'll warm me up quick. Soup! How do you say soup in Croatian? Not a clue.* He thought back to his public school language classes. He was rubbish at Latin, but excelled at German, and this stood him in good stead when his father had taken him to the Continent when he was but a thirteen-year-old lad, to show him where he had fought in the Great War. He'd had a wonderful soup while there. A soup that was said to be common to all of eastern Europe. He tried to remember what they'd called it. She came again and set the beer before him. He took a long draught and set the glass down. *That's it! I remember now!*

He smiled up at her. "Gulaschsuppe, bitte." Chairs scraped on flagstones as the men at the nearby tables stood. Bolts were withdrawn and pushed home, and he was staring down the barrels of more than half a dozen rifles. The barmaid scarpered. *Bloody hell, I said that in German—Idiot!*

7

A Rather Pleasant Death

A man, a very big man dressed all in black, pushed through the throng to confront him. He was easily well over six feet tall and broad-shouldered, with a beefy build. The men murmured "Stjepan" as he approached. Reggie could see a nasty scar running from the outer corner of his left eye to his jawline. He could recognise a "Heidelberg scar" when he saw one. He tried not to show how panic-stricken he was.

"Zdravo." Reggie said, forcing a smile. The big man downed his beer and set the glass down. He gathered Reggie's trench coat lapels in one ham-like fist and, lifting him out of his pew, slammed him against the wall and held him there. The farmers put up their rifles. The man went through Reggie's pockets. He showed to the crowd his black leather gloves, and the spare ammunition box, and his knife and torch, and his wristwatch, and as each item was discovered he held it up to view and made the announcement "*Njemački.*" – German – saying this whether they were or not. When he found the Walther pistol he held it up and said "*Gestapo.*" All the men nodded knowingly. He then wrapped an arm about Reggie's neck, nearly cutting off his windpipe, and made a speech in Croatian to the room. Reggie was like a rag-doll in this man's grip. Most raised their hands – a vote must have taken place. The man "Stjepan" left all Reggie's things on the table, and dragged him by his neck through the room into the kitchen, through a door and down a flight of stairs to a cellar. The cellar was very cold. Stjepan dragged him past a row of beer barrels, a butcher's block, a table, and through an open barred door like in a gaol at the far end of the room, then threw him down under a window. He kicked Reggie and stood over him.

"You're making a mistake. I'm not Gestapo." Reggie rasped, in English. Stjepan uttered a string of Serbo-Croatian at him. Reggie tried again, this time in German, the only other language he knew. "You are making a mistake. I am not a German," he repeated. Stjepan replied in German as well.

"Shut your mouth. I know you're not German! You are English. Did you parachute here?" Stjepan demanded. Reggie thought of the bomber that had ditched.

"I crashed."

"Are you a pilot?"

"No."

"For you, the war is over!" Stjepan sneered.

Reggie knew exactly what this meant. He'd seen short films in the cinema, often produced by London's Ealing Studios, explaining to British subjects what a downed airman could expect from his enemy captor. In every case the actor playing the part of the Nazi would say this very line. He'd now be arrested and bundled off to an *Oflag* or a *Stalag* of fellow airmen, to sit out the remainder of this war in hopeless boredom, or until an exchange of prisoners could be arranged. It might be years until he saw Milly or his parents again. He frowned. *What a miserable way for my mission to end.*

"Still, you may have some interesting information," Stjepan said, scratching his scar as he thought aloud. "Tomorrow I will torture you until you give up your secrets. You will be unable to keep them."

"That's against the Geneva Convention," he protested. Stjepan only laughed.

"You are in the new Independent State of Croatia; we are not a signatory to this Geneva Convention you mention. You are not dressed as an airman. You must be a spy. The penalty for espionage is death. After interrogation we will take you to the Plaža Rosi beach and you will be executed there. We will dump your corpse in the sea." He kicked Reggie again and laughed. "Pray to God. Tomorrow you will be dead." Stjepan locked the door behind him, hung the ring of keys on its peg, and stomped up the stairs. The electric bulb on the ceiling snapped off and he was left in darkness.

Reggie stood and rubbed his side where the boot had landed. Cautiously he took a deep breath. It didn't feel like any rib was broken. Stjepan had spoken German fluently, as if he was a native-born German. Much better than Reggie's school German. The light snapped on again. Another man, this one wearing an apron, came down and deposited Reggie's things on the table. He hung up a chef's honing steel on a hook.

"I'm an Englishman. British airman. Help me!" he pleaded to the man, in English. The man, not understanding, ignored him. But this man happened to be standing within arms reach, so Reggie lunged at him through the bars and nearly succeeded in grabbing a handful of clothing. Startled, the man pulled away, afraid. He hurriedly picked up a ladle and pot, and fled up the stairs, forgetting to turn off the light as he went.

Reggie looked about his prison. It was not an actual prison, but a cellar pantry; on every limestone wall were wooden shelves filled with tinned goods, bottles, and boxes. Sacks of corn-meal sat on the table. He watched a rat scurry from around one sack and along the wall, and shuddered. He wouldn't be sleeping tonight, or he'd wake up minus an ear. He went to the barred door and shook it, but it was locked tight. There was no handle, just a large keyhole. The large medieval skeleton keys hung out of reach a dozen feet away.

He could see his breath. The temperature here was below freezing. The room was unheated and he found the reason why: the window was not a window at all, just a rectangular opening to the outside with four solid iron bars an inch thick and spaced a foot apart. Snow sifted in and collected on the floor. He took a few tins off the shelf and stood on them.

Over the bars there were remnants of chicken wire mesh that no longer kept out the rats. He tore this away. Holding onto the bars, he hoisting himself up on tiptoe to put his head out. It was a snow-covered alley. Letting himself down, the bar second from the left rotated in his hand. He shook it. It was slightly loose. The bar was held in sockets in the limestone blocks at top and bottom. When was this place built? 1330? 1540? Whichever century it had been, the surface hadn't been sloped to drain outside, and over time water had collected on the sill, freezing and thawing, to leave the limestone weathered and weak.

Looking about for a tool, he reached through the bars of the door and took down the chef's honing steel. He jammed the point of it in beside the loose bar and pried and chipped away at it, until he'd broken out enough limestone he could shake the bar back and forth a couple inches. When prying and chipping no longer removed any material, he tried the point of the honing steel in the keyhole to pick it, but it had no effect. He rehung it.

The wooden floor overhead creaked as the cook walked back and forth in his kitchen. All this time he could hear laughter from above, and sometimes a concertina played. But eventually the sound of voices died down, and he heard the frequent slamming of doors. The cook came down the stair and hung his apron. Once again he pleaded with the man in English but was ignored. The cook went up, the light snapped off, and a few minutes later there was the slam of a door and then silence. Watching out the hole, he saw the cook trudge away down the alley. It was still snowing.

He needed to sit and suss this out. He took tins off the shelves and stacked them to form a seat, so he wouldn't be forced to sit on the wet and cold stone floor. There on the lowest shelf at the back was a tin. It was the largest tin there. He dragged this out and hefted it. Holding this up to the dim light reflected off the snow outside, he saw the label read *GULAŠ* and had a picture of a cow standing in a green pasture. The label read 3,000 grams – nearly 7 pounds!

Building up the platform of tins with even more tins, he stood on it. Gripping a firm bar with one hand, and balancing this heavy tin on his opposite palm, he reared back, intending to slam it against the loose bar with all his might. Just before he attempted this feat, a bicyclist rode by outside, and he caught himself in the nick of time. He watched and waited but the alley stayed empty.

Now he reared back and let fly, again and again. On the sixth try the bar clanged out into the alley and the tin followed after, tumbling down the slope and out of sight in the dark. He put his head out, but his body was much too bulky. Shedding his wet clothing, he pushed the trench coat, then the jacket, and finally the waistcoat outside into the snow and tried again, and succeeded in worming his way out. It was still snowing heavily, but between these close-set buildings the fierce wind was lessened. He struggled into his wet and cold clothing again. He had no hat, nor gloves. When they discovered him gone, surely they would search. Where to go now? Who in this godforsaken town would risk sheltering him? To them he was an enemy alien. *Godforsaken? The church! Hadn't the church historically offered sanctuary to those in need?*

He struggled uphill in the gale, the snowflakes sticking to him, and growing ever colder. A hundred-fifty yards later, shivering violently, he found the churchyard. A square stone plaque embedded in a nearby wall was carved with the words *Crkva Sveti Juraj* – Church of St George. He was so cold. He'd never in his life been as cold as this, ever.

The church was surrounded by a large graveyard, and as he left the relative protection of the houses behind and plodded into this open area the violent gale bowled him over. He could only make headway by crawling on hands and knees from one headstone to another but, no matter, he was nearly there! Safety was at hand! Reaching the wall of the building, he could stand while leaning against it as the wind shrieked, breaking around it like a sea around a rock. An oval cartouche of the Virgin Mary above the door looked down on him. The double doors of the church, six wooden panels with crosses in their centres, had no knocker. He pounded on it and waited. There was no answer. He shuffled around the building to try a second door. The windows showed no lights. When he reached the front door again, he kicked it and screamed over the wind but again, no one came.

He huddled for shelter behind an above-ground marble sarcophagus. He should probably keep moving, but he didn't know to where. It was odd, though, very odd: he wasn't shivering any more. He stood and started down a street, the wind buffeting his back. He was confused – had he been down this street before, or not? Every joint ached. There were ice crystals in his hair. He couldn't feel his face or any of his extremities. He was surely going to lose fingers or toes to frostbite, or gangrene. That is, if he lived at all. As he stumbled along he wondered at how he had come to be here. *Why was I doing all this? All to get command of a bleeding ship. A ship that wasn't even British. From a foreign country that wasn't even an ally. If I get back, I'm resigning my commission, handing in my resignation. I'll move to New-bloody-Zealand, or to some place warm, and as far away from ships as possible. Kenya, maybe. I'm so tired. I'll just sit in this doorway for a moment. Only a moment. So tired.*

He sat on a raised threshold before a recessed door, then sagged to the left and rested his head against the stone jamb of the doorway. He shut his eyes. He lay there, and let the snow cover him. Cover him like a blanket. A nice warm blanket. *So tired. Mustn't close my eyes. Keep them open. Open. Keep them ....*

His mouth fell open and he drooled, and the drool froze in his beard.

Good old Captain Mallinson. As his first mate I learned so much from him. He must be so happy with Becky in warm Australia. Wish I were in warm Australia now. And the others before him; stern Captain Harris, kindly Captain Bowen, and that old Greek, Captain Neroutsos. I learned so much from them, too, as I rose up through the ranks.

The Goudhurst railway station platform wet from the recent rains where mum, in tears, stood with dad to see me off to join the Merchant Navy as a newly qualified Third Mate. Waving to them from the train window as it left the station. The Royal Navy 'quack' rejecting me for some medical reason I can't even remember.

Dorothea. What a kick. She scooped me up after Laura had refused my proposal. Dorothea knew – we both knew – she had caught me on the rebound, but neither one of us cared, the sex was that good.

After graduation from the academy dad took me to Scotland for a grouse shoot. Utter rubbish at it, but so wonderful to be in the company of dad's old army mates. The broad Scots dialect of the gillies so hard to decipher. I was allowed to taste whisky for the first time ever, and liked it.

Whilst still in public school I bought and restored (against my parent's wishes) my first motorcycle, a Triumph "Model H" made surplus after the Great War. Hadn't known at the time, this model had a weakness in the front fork spring, prone to break on rough ground. That didn't go well, as I crashed while at speed, breaking my leg in the bargain.

How I hated school. Hazed and bullied. Always my lungs so weak. So continually out of breath I really couldn't participate in footie or cricket in any meaningful way. That was all right, because my mind was more attuned to mechanical things anyway.

Earlier still, 1926, at age thirteen I'd never been away from Britain before, but dad took me to Europe to show me where his Great War battles had been fought. We toured where the Battle of Albert was fought in 1918, and the battlefields of Passchendaele and the Somme. We continued on to see Germany. I loved Germany! Everything I saw so fascinating. So foreign a place to me, foods so different from what I knew. Begged dad for money to see the German *Kino* – the cinema. At thirteen I'm old enough to go places on my own now, even in this foreign country, aren't I?

On my way to the cinema, a trio of drunken German sailors stumble out of a cabaret. One is sick in the gutter and passes out. His friends carry him away, but the sailor's hat is left behind! Scooping up this prize I put it on. A tall lad for my age, I pause to admire my reflection in a window. A swarm of florid-faced burghers mistake me for an actual sailor, sweeping me along with them as they hurry into the cabaret. A man with beery breath laughs in my face, slaps me on my back, hands me a litre of beer.

This adult world is strange to me. Instinctively, I know it's wrong for me to be here, but I don't leave, taking a seat in the front row, right up against the stage. I drink some of the beer and it makes me feel woozy. The Weimar Republic is at its peak and Germany is awash in decadence, especially in its stage theatre world. There's an emcee with a cane, in top hat and tails, a raucous jazz orchestra off to the side. Even after all these years I can still hear the accented English of the compère: "Ladies und chentlemen, mein damen und herren, vee hope you vill find zee amusement mit our Ode to Springtime."

The curtain opens. It's a pantomime play about springtime, and seems to start innocently enough with six dancing women dressed as bluebells. Their knee-length skirts are blue, their legs, even the slippers, powdered with a golden glitter. Each has a fat green "stem" atop their head for a hat. The stage lights dim. Offstage, photographer's flashbulbs pop in imitation of lightning. A thunder machine rumbles. Arms interlocked in a chorus line, the flowers dance to the left and right and back again, blown about the stage in a "springtime storm." A bright light appears offstage – it is the sun, and it drives the storm clouds away. The lights brighten – the storm has passed.

A man dressed as a bumblebee appears, his papier-mâché body rotund, fuzzy, yellow-and-black. He wears a Tyrolean hat and lederhosen. The "bee" chases the flowers about the stage, leering and mugging at the audience, and the jolly burghers guffaw at these antics. In their efforts to avoid the bee, the flowers dance very close to the front of the stage, jiggling and shaking as if in a breeze. The bluebells may be wearing blue skirts but are otherwise topless, their upper bodies only painted blue to match the petalled skirt. Never before had I seen bare breasts.

One by one, the bee catches each flower in its turn, and then that woman's skirt "blooms open" – each is naked beneath the skirt and her golden legs wave from the centre of the dress "petals" in imitation of golden stamens. Soon all the flowers have "bloomed", their "stamens" wave and kick so close above. A line of blooming bluebells dancing overhead, and they are beautiful.

Whilst the trombones and saxophones jokingly blow off-key notes, the bee produces an enormous papier-mâché penis and pantomimes sex with the flowers. The burghers howl with glee, slapping me on my back, but I don't mind: for the first time I see an anatomy so different from my own, and am fascinated. At thirteen years of age and newly pubescent, I know the first stirrings of what I later learn is called lust.

I did not tell father what I did, but from that day forwards I'm smitten with girls.

Reggie had a vague understanding as each memory had arisen from his subconscious it was from an earlier and earlier time. Was this what was meant when they said, "his life flashed before his eyes"? Nothing was flashing here; it was all rather slow ... and somewhat dreamlike ... and actually quite pleasant ....

8

Into the Bear's Den

He lay on his left side. The snow is a blanket to him. It's keeping him warm, yet he knows instinctively he is still cold. He opened his eyes and in front of his face is the limestone. He moved his head and felt the hard limestone grit against his forehead. He pushed aside the blanket of snow and touched the limestone. It was real enough, but the snow was warm and dry. Snow shouldn't be warm. How strange.

He shivered. Why did he shiver now? He hadn't been shivering when he curled up in this doorway, but now he did. With every shiver a thousand-million needles pricked his skin over his entire body. They lanced into his nerves like fire. He was in agony as he shivered. The pain was excruciating and he whimpered.

There was a rustling sound and a vertical bar of flickering orange firelight appeared on the limestone above his head. Had someone opened this door behind him? Painfully he lifted his arm and felt for the door at his back but it wasn't there. The firelight vanished. Someone lifted his arm, and then from behind him a warmth suffused him from head to heel. He slept.

He awoke. He lay on his right side now. Before him was a body, and he was pressed to it. This body was very warm, yet he was still cold, and shivered. What he'd thought earlier to be a layer of snow, he found to be a downy white eiderdown many inches thick. This was a bed and only then did he realize he was naked. Above him in the limestone wall a tiny window, hinged at the bottom and open, admitted daylight so he could see the bed enclosed by dark polished wood, and dark velvety curtains. The curtains parted and the bar of flickering firelight appeared once more. Someone lifted the duvet from his feet and cold air rushed in, and he recoiled from it. Then a wonderful heat warmed the soles of his feet and the duvet was replaced. He raised his head to see a young girl with strawberry blonde plaited hair encircling the top of her head. She carried a brick on a towel. Expressionless, she paused to look at him, then shut the curtains. He slept.

Again he awakened, still on his right side. Now he no longer shivered. Before him lay a woman facing away from him, and she is nude. She is pressing her full length against him, warming him with her own body heat. How wonderful she should do this, and for him, a stranger! He is grateful beyond measure to her, for saving his life as he lay dying. Memories came flooding back to him: he was being dragged by his feet, sliding along on his trench coat and could see stars above. The back of his head bumped the cobblestones.

She stirs. She rolls to face him, her eyes still closed. For long minutes he gazes at her face and is struck by her astonishing beauty: her natural wide and dark eyebrows angled upwards then tapering downward at the end, her raven hair, her long lashes, her high cheekbones in an oval face, the chin strong yet not pointed, her complexion smooth as new cream, her lips, her eyes—her eyes! She's awake! Long moments pass as they gaze silently at one another. He could see something extraordinary in those tawny brown eyes: tiny flecks of gold that glint as she looks over his face. Her lips part. She is about to speak. What will the voice of this strikingly beautiful woman sound like?

"Your breath, it stinks."

"Sorry. Who— ?"

"Shh." She placed a finger at his lips.

"Sorry. How— ?"

"Do not speak," she said, a command.

"Sorry."

"You are English." She made it a statement of fact.

"How do you know?"

"You have said five words, and three of them were 'sorry' – now, face the other way. Go to sleep!" Determinedly, she shut her eyes, an indication to him he should do the same. He rolled to face away from her. Her arm snaked around him and pulled his body to hers. He's bewildered to think that, even when drunk, he'd never in his life woken next to a nameless woman. Soon they are both asleep. While they sleep, the solemn girl with the strawberry blonde plaits returned, to replace the heated brick wrapped in a towel at his feet.

He rolled over and snuggled into the duvet, hugging his feather pillow.

"How do you feel?" He opened his eyes to find her standing by the high bed, intent on buttoning the fly of khaki jodhpur breeches. The tiny window admitted daylight.

"I don't know yet. Thank you for saving my life." He hiked himself up on his elbows. Unmistakably she was only now beginning to dress, because she was nude from the waist up, and barefoot.

"Is nothing. You will lie still." She pushed him back down on the bed. "I will check you for frostbite." She pinched his cheeks and nose and chin, asking "Do you feel this? And here, this? This you feel?" She pinched on his ears and nose, and felt his throat and shoulders, and his chest with both hands.

"Yes," he answered to each question. He looked her over as she worked on him somewhat roughly. Her black hair was parted down the centre. He made the mistake of looking up at her beautiful face, – the wonderfully shaped eyebrows, those gorgeous eyes, her lips, the high Slavic cheeks! – and instantly became aroused. *Good thing I'm covered by this duvet*, he thought. With the skill of an expert phrenologist, her fingers worked over every inch of his skull, testing it with her sharp nails. Her breasts swayed scant inches above his face, tantalizingly close. When her probing fingernails reached the back of his head, he sucked in his breath and winced.

"That hurts," he told her.

"Yes, it would," she replied, flatly. Turning her head over a shoulder she barked an order in Croatian. The girl with the strawberry blonde plaits appeared at once, holding open a field-grey tunic for the woman to put on, then left again. The girl wore a frilly embroidered blouse with short puffy sleeves and a boy's knee breeches. She was barefoot.

He recognised the tunic as an Assault Artillery Jacket, – what the Germans called a *Sturm artillerie geschutz jacke* – of heavy *feldgrau* wool. It had epaulettes and an officers stand-and-fall collar, but all indication of rank had been cut away. He watched as she pulled the left side across the right, forming a stiff double layer, and fastened its many buttons. The girl returned with a wide leather belt for the woman and left. She buckled this around her waist, over the tunic. She wore no brassiere, and the thick front of this men's uniform flattened her breasts. *That must hurt*, he thought. She didn't seem to be bothered.

The girl returned with a seamstress's pincushion, which she held up for the woman with both hands. The woman gathered the edge of the duvet in both hands and threw it back, exposing him. Startled, he curled into a fetal position in an attempt to hide his arousal.

"Lie still! Hands at your sides! Relax! She has seen you before," she commanded. Gripping his arms and legs she forcibly put them where she wanted.

"Seen me before? What is she, twelve years old?" Reggie redoubled his efforts at visualising a doctor's office, thinking of the time he tried to join the Royal Navy, before failing a physical examination. His efforts were for naught.

"Eleven. Who do you think helped me drag you here? Take your clothes off? Lift you in this bed? You are too heavy for one person."

"Oh." *That's reasonable I suppose.* The woman pinched or squeezed each leg and arm. She selected a pin and pricked the tip of each toe, and around the perimeter of each heel, and each time he flinched in pain. She repeated this procedure with each finger, thumb and palm in turn, and got the same reaction. During this entire routine, the young girl and the woman chattered on continuously. He shut his eyes as he listened to the flow of their foreign conversation and relaxed, eventually succeeding in getting his erection to go limp.

He opened his eyes. The girl, curious as ever, carried on talking while she looked him over. He scowled at her. She ignored him. Satisfied with the results of her tests, the woman stuck the pin in the pincushion and the girl left with it, returning with a towel. They helped him stand. He wrapped the towel around himself. They parted the curtain to enter the main room. Hobbling, bent like an old man, they held his arms as he was escorted across to the water closet. Inside, he paused at the wash-basin and was startled to see himself in a mirror; his lips purple and chapped, his eyes puffy and bloodshot, his forehead, nose and cheeks pocked with tiny red cuts from the wind-blown ice crystals. He scraped his fingers through hair stiff as wheat-straw stubble. When he emerged, the woman was busy setting up a gate-leg table in the centre of the room, and it was then the aroma registered in his nostrils: goulash! *Beef* goulash. It smelled delicious!

"We have our baths. You have salt all over. You are next," she said. At a word from her, the girl beckoned him through an archway into the kitchen. A grey-haired grandmother stood there, her back to him, stirring a pot on a square cast-iron wood-stove. A large copper washtub of water waited in the centre of the room, a ladder-back chair next to it. He stepped into the water. It was cold. With a word, the girl held her hand out. He supposed she wanted his towel. *I'm not going to take my towel off in front of an eleven-year-old*, he thought.

He shook his head and pointed to the other room. She took hold of the towel and gave a tug. He only gripped it tighter. Her lips compressed in annoyance, she sat on the chair and folded her arms to wait him out. It seemed they'd reached an impasse. In a minute the girl's face brightened, and she spoke to the grandmother, who handed her a bar of brown soap. She in turn helpfully offered the soap to him. He put his hand out, but she pulled it out of reach. He snatched for it but missed. With a quickness that belied the older woman's age, his towel was whipped off from behind. He squatted and manoeuvred to sit, grimacing at the coldness of the water. The grandmother handed the towel to the girl and went back to tending her pot.

The girl gave him the soap, then stood and used the folded towel to grasp a long vertical pipe at the side of the stove, one which was hot, apparently. She swivelled this pipe outwards and down to be horizontal and it just reached the washtub, resting on its rim. This pipe ended in a valve. The towel was neatly folded and left on the chair. Now she opened the valve gradually, and a cloud of steam vapour shot out until a spirt of water erupted. She shut it off, then held out both hands towards the valve handle, palms up. He took her meaning to be: there it is! Use it! *Oh, I get it now: she was refusing to leave because it was her 'duty' to demonstrate the system for me so I wouldn't scald myself. This village mustn't have pressurized water. They must have a gravity water tank, likely in the attic, and this wood-stove heats the water here. Primitive but workable.*

He gave the girl a 'thumbs up'. Her nose wrinkled up, she impertinently put her tongue out at him, then flounced into the other room. He put hot water in the washtub, and then lathered up with the scratchy brown soap. With amusement he looked after her, smiled and thought,

Clever child. In ten or twelve years, whoever marries her is going to have his hands full!

When he was done rinsing, he towelled himself dry and went back to the alcove bed, where his clothes were laid out for him. All of it, except for his leather and corduroy jacket, had been washed and was now dry. He stood in the space between the bed and curtain and dressed in all his clothing except the jacket, trench coat, and boots. When he emerged the woman had a question for him.

"You are hungry, yes?" He agreed. "We will sit." The gate-leg table was set with four bowls of goulash, steaming and fragrant, over soft chunks of boiled potato redolent of paprika and slices of red peppers, and garnished with sliced hard-boiled eggs. There was a shredded pickled cabbage salad. The girl was already seated. The grandmother came to the table holding a bottle of red wine, and sat. Everyone, including the girl, had their glass filled.

He could see the entire cottage from where he sat. This room was the largest, yet also crowded with comfortable overstuffed furniture. Framed sepia-tone photographs lined the mantelpiece and walls, and there was a crucifix. Everywhere on every surface was a crocheted doily, lace tatting, a knick-knack, or porcelain figurine. There was a fire in a fireplace. To the left of this an adult's bicycle with a luggage rack over the rear tyre leaned against a wall near the front door. To the right of the fireplace was the door to the water closet, and he now realized he hadn't seen any shower or tub in it. In addition to the alcove bed in this room, he could see a bed through another doorway. On the far side of the kitchen was a boot room at the back door, where the copper washtub now hung by its handle from a hook on the wall.

"I am not catholic. You wish to say prayer?" the woman asked.

"Before I answer that, I need to know something: ... who *are* you?"

"You are permitted to call me Pavlina."

"What is your family name?"

"That is my family name."

"Is this your family?"

"My friends. This is the safe house. They know not English."

"What are their names?"

"I will not tell you. If you are caught and tortured, you will not know that."

"That's … actually dead clever."

"What religion are you, if I may ask?"

"My parents didn't raise me in any religion. I guess you could describe me as an atheist."

"An atheist Jew! Haw-haw!" she guffawed at his jest, "You are being funny, yes?—but, do not mention those things in my country, if you want to remain alive. I am serious!" It puzzled him about being called a Jew, but he decided it was best to say nothing, passing it off as a harmless mistake.

"Please, I insist your friends say grace," he said, by way of invitation. The grandmother spoke to the girl, and she spoke the Serbo-Croatian words, hands clasped in prayer. As they ate, Pavlina told him how they usually did not eat this well, but the girl had found a dented three-kilogram tin of beef goulash in an alley gutter. When they had finished eating, Pavlina refilled their glasses with the last of the wine. The girl carried the tableware to the kitchen to wash up. The grandmother sat in her rocker near the fire, and was soon drowsing. He used the fire irons to rearrange the ember-red logs, and the flames leaped up anew. Pavlina moved to a horsehair upholstered armchair, and Reggie to a sofa matching this, placed opposite the grandmother's rocker but facing the fireplace. They spoke in low tones, trying not to disturb the older woman.

"Where did you learn your English?" he inquired.

"I work in London as the servant to the child of the family, for one year and the half."

"Only half a year? Why did you leave?"

"The usual reason—the husband's hands."

"Oh."

"I speak five languages; Croatian, Russian, some French, and a little Greek. The English I teach myself!" she said, proudly.

"I speak only English, and my German is limited to what I learnt in school. I read Latin in school, but found I had no aptitude for it." The clock on the mantel chimed half-five in the afternoon, and this attracted his attention. "How long have we been asleep?" he asked.

"Is Wednesday."

"Oh, that's just splendid! I was supposed to meet my contact forty-eight hours ago. How am I supposed to find him now?" he complained. She laughed, and regarded him with eyebrows raised.

"I am your contact."

"You! You're Marko?"

"No, I am Pavlina. This I tell you before."

"But, I was told to meet Marko."

"Marko can be ... not relied on. Do not depend on him. He hopes to make united the partisans and the Chetniks but is hopeless. The rules he makes are his own." She pointed to the bicycle. "I was exhausted. I pedal from my home, to Brodarica, and then Primošten, and over all the town looking for you, eighty kilometres all in one day, chasing you from where you come. All in the Bura." They paused to sip their wine as he thought of the questions he wanted answered.

"Primošten. Is that where you live?"

"No. We are in village of Primošten, here."

"How did you know I was in this village, and not some other place farther down the coast?"

"Coast is turning east now. The next land you touch will be Italy, in a few weeks," she said, with a shrug. His mind boggled at how narrowly he had escaped certain death.

"But, you knew I was here. How is that?"

"Is because I see boat without you."

"You saw my raft?"

"Yes, that. I see 'raft' hanging—is in tree. You are lucky raft is yellow."

"The Bura. Is that the name of the province we are in?"

"No. The Bura is the name of the wind. It can be like ..." she paused, searching for the right word, "... the *ciklon*, but not turning. Is straight wind, yes?"

"Like a cyclone? I can testify to that!"

"How are you here with no weapons? Not even hat or gloves? This I think strange."

"I had a hat once, and gloves, and a gun and knife. They were all taken from me." He told her the tale of The Three Swans pub, his mistaken identity, imprisonment, and subsequent escape. She shook her head sadly at the tale. "I need to contact my headquarters. They'll be desperate to hear from me. Will you bring out your wireless transmitting set, please?"

"I have no radio," she stated, blandly. The girl came from the kitchen with a pencil and paper to sit at the table, and began to draw.

"Oh." *Things just go from bad to worse here*, he thought. "Pavlina, in all this time you haven't once asked me my name."

"Is because I know your name. You are 'Shlomo'."

"Shlomo! How do you reckon that?"

"Is name inside your coat." Reggie crossed the room and returned with his jacket. Inside its collar in green thread was stitched the name Shlomo. He laid it aside.

"This jacket is part of my disguise. It was taken from an Italian prisoner of war." Pavlina grimaced at this.

"That Italian must have taken this coat from a Jew, – a Jew who is now dead." She paused for a moment, her face thoughtful and then, with a sidelong glance at him, pointedly asked, "You are not a Jew?"

"I am not. I'm a captain in the British merchant navy. My name is Captain Wallace. Reginald Wallace. I'd be pleased if you would call me Reggie."

"Réži," she said, and laughed delightedly. "Has the nice sound. I like it! Is sound of growling—is sound how like the bear make." She held up her hands, fingers crooked like bear claws, her eyes flaring to show the whites. Her nails were sharp points. "Réži," she repeated. The girl looked up from her paper and nodded at this, then continued drawing. In English, Reggie's name was pronounced "Redd-jee," but the way Pavlina pronounced it, it sounded as if there was a quality of a soft "purr" to it: "Rezz-shee." From now on, and for as long as they knew each other, she would say his name in this same manner, and each time she did he was thrilled right down to his toes.

"I tell you now Yugoslavia politics. This I do to keep you safe. You do not wish to be killed, yes?"

"No, I mean yes, not killed. Sure, please continue."

"Here you must know who you *will* and *will not* trust. Do not trust the *Ustaše*, they are fascists like Nazis, and collaborate with them often. Do not trust the regular Croatian Army – these we call the *Domobranstvo*. Both are worse than Nazis.

"The Chetniks are Royalists, and the sworn enemies of partisans. They only wish to return the king to the throne. Two months ago, over two thousand Muslims were killed in village of Foča by them. This they say is act of vengeance against *Ustaše*.

"Chetnik leader is General Dragoljub 'Draža' Mihailović and the English and the Americans support him. Partisans do not understand why is this, for Mihailovich does nearly nothing. Is better to support Josip Broz: he plan soon to make the DFY, the Democratic Federative Yugoslavia.

"Unless Bosnians, Serbs, and Montenegrins are together with us partisans, do not trust them! That is the sure way to be killed. In this country you do not know how religious a person is become. If you say to them you are the atheist, to them that is maybe the blasphemy: they will be happy to kill you."

"I'll keep that in mind," he replied, alarmed. "But, why doesn't this General ... 'Mee-high-low-vitch' do anything?"

"German forces hang or shoot everyone, including women, the children and old people, up to one hundred hostages for every one German killed, and fifty shot for every wounded German – because of this, the Chetniks have stopped killing Germans. The *Ustaše* and *Domobranstvo* also kill everywhere without any reason, and enjoy this. The *Ustaše* let the churches fill with people, and then burn them down."

"How horrible!" he said, appalled. *Did Major Stirling know about any of this, when he asked me to take on this mission?*

"Now the partisans! I am partisan," she said with pride, tapping a finger on her chest. "Josip Broz is leader. Yes, *personally* he is communist, but is different communism, not like that of Stalin. You can trust partisans. Do not discuss politics or military matters with us. Do not call us Communists – is not true!"

"So, if the leader of the partisans is a communist, you're a communist too, then?"

"More a socialist I am thinking. We have all peoples in our ranks. Communists make only five per cent of us, but the Serbian Chetniks and *Ustaše* and Germans say partisans are hundred per cent Communist. Do not believe this. Is false! Is propaganda! One day we partisans will make a free Yugoslavia, where all peoples will live together in peace and prosperity!"

Her earlier impudent behaviour toward him forgotten, the girl brought her drawing to Reggie to show him, and said "Réži." It was a bear walking to the left on all fours, and the word balloon above its head read "Réži." Across the top of the page was a range of snow-capped mountains. Smiling, he gave her a nod of encouragement. She took her drawing back to the table to draw some more. Reggie took another sip of wine, and looked in the girl's direction.

"Where is the girl's father?"

"Executed." He looked at the grandmother napping in the rocker.

"Where is the grandfather?"

"Executed."

"And you are not the girl's mother—also dead?"

"Executed" she said, sadly. They sat in silence for a bit, sipping their wine, the only sounds the snoring of the grandmother, the ticking of the mantle clock, and the scratching of the girl's pencil. Reggie was feeling relaxed, and also rather domesticated and at home in this strange country. They gazed at the fire for a time, and while she was mesmerized by the leaping flames, he studied her profile. She wore no cosmetics whatsoever, not even lipstick, nor even any jewellery. She did nothing special with her hair, only letting it hang straight, although it did curl inward slightly at the end and was neatly trimmed at chin length. Her eyebrows were not plucked, but left in a natural state. Her unadorned beauty greatly attracted him, and he was aware it wasn't only because she had saved his life. He gazed at the fire, spellbound, and knew there was something else to these feelings, working at him deep down inside. The mantle clock chimed six. Pavlina stirred and patted his arm to get his attention, then pointed to the girl.

"For two nights," she murmured, "we are sleeping in her bed, and she sleeps in bed with *Baba*." She sipped her wine.

"Perhaps we should go out now, before it gets too late, to find a hotel for me?" At this, Pavlina chuckled softly.

"You make the joke, yes? There is no hotel in Primošten. You will sleep with me." Reggie thrilled at hearing her make such a statement, and so boldly, too! His mind ran wild with anticipation of events later tonight, but he kept his expression under control, revealing nothing outwardly of his desire for her. The girl came again, a hand pressing her drawing to her chest, and smiled shyly at him. She plumped down on the sofa to his right. His arm encircled her shoulders, and she showed him her drawing. It was the same large bear as before, but now below it there were two smaller bears. He guessed they might be cubs, so this bear had to be a female. On the left side of the page she had drawn another larger bear standing on its hind legs and facing the viewer. This bear startled him and he coughed, for she had depicted it much like the Cerne Abbas Giant, but with rather more detail. And then he tumbled to what had happened.

"Pavlina, did you *use me*," he demanded, "use me as a ... as a teaching tool?!" Pavlina put her hand out palm up, and waggled her fingers for the drawing, so Reggie passed it over to her. She grinned and then explained herself.

"She has friend at school, his name Jaakob, and she asks why you are looking so different from him. These questions I must answer with the truth." At mention of this name the girl smiled and hugged herself. Pavlina then spoke to the girl, and was answered. She then held up the drawing to him. "This is a bear family. You are the standing bear. I am the other bear. She will allow me to keep her drawing." Carefully she folded the drawing to save it. The girl returned to the table to start another drawing.

That night Pavlina brought a lighted candle in a holder to the small table between the head of the bed and the velvet privacy curtain. They undressed quietly in this space while facing away from each other. Turning down the bedclothes she got in first, laying on her back. With her legs together and hands clasped, she shut her eyes and composed herself for sleep. He knelt beside her, already aroused and quite eager, then kissed the side of her neck.

"Réži, please, you will not to do this thing!" she said, squirming away from him, both hands protectively shielding herself between the legs, her body tense.

Have I misconstrued what she meant? he thought. He didn't want to do anything that might distress her, so lay at her side facing her, a hand resting motionless on her belly, all the while keeping his posture non-threatening. After a minute or so of laying quietly together, he felt her tension melt away as she relaxed. Her hand came up and she interlaced her fingers with his, and he had to assume she did this as a way to keep control of his hand.

"When was the last time you slept with a man?" he asked, his tone hopeful.

"You have the short memory."

"It's a euphemism. What I mean is, when was the last time you made love?"

"Before when I become *vojnik* – a soldier – in 1937. I am partisan *vojnik* now and if I 'get with child,' Josip Broz will have you executed to preserve the safety of his partisan troops."

Reggie was astounded at this, but had to remark, "That's a rather good deterrent!"

"I know not this word."

"Never mind. Where is Josip Broz now?"

"Now? He is maybe in Foča, three-hundred-fifty kilometres by road to the east."

"You mean to say Josip Broz will send a soldier all that distance, just to execute me?"

"No, he will not, because he has already a soldier here for that. Goodnight."

"Goodnight." He rolled over and blew out the candle.

9

Escape!

They breakfasted on the freshest of eggs, and delicious little peppery sausages she called *ćevapčići*. There was dense rye bread with butter, and also tea. It was unmistakable to him they were serving out the best they had. The breakfast things were then cleared away. Reggie laid his jacket on the table and snapped the threads of the inside pockets. He brought out his counterfeit Swedish passport and removed its waterproof envelope. The grandmother and granddaughter came to see it, curious. He ripped open the other waterproof envelope and spread the Yugoslavian dinar notes out on the table to dry, as they were slightly damp. The girl clapped her hands and hopped in delight, smiling broadly. The grandmother gasped, a hand pressing her forehead, and sat heavily. Pavlina came to see what was the matter.

"Is much money," she declared, "Is much more than year of living. Where do you get this?"

"I was given this to use in your country. I want you and your friends to have half of it, because I'm grateful."

"Oh Reggie, you are kind, but this is being the old notes; today in Croatia we use the new 'Kuna' notes."

"So, all this dinar is useless?" he asked, exasperated at how British

Intelligence could have bollixed up their preparations so badly.

"I am afraid is so," she said, sadly. She spoke with the grandmother. "Perhaps all is not bad. *Baba* will take to bank where is friendly man. She will say her husband died, and she finds these old notes hidden under mattress. She will ask for exchange to Croatian kuna. We will see." The notes were gathered up when dry, and the grandmother was sent off on her errand.

* * *

"Featherstone! Get me yesterday's casualty figures," General Stone barked, as he rushed through the anteroom to his inner office, " ... and the list of the week's out-of-commission tanks and lorries. I've a meeting with Claude in a minute."

"Yes sir," she said, and jumped to the task. She entered his office to find him standing at his desk before an open briefcase, just adjusting his peaked cap. "Here they are, sir." He placed them in the case, snapped it shut, and rushed to the anteroom door with it, but then hesitated.

"Miss Featherstone, before I forget—David tells me we were expecting a coded message from Marko two nights ago at the latest, telling us Captain Wallace had reached the ship. It never came. We've no idea why." Milly bit her lip, and her eyes glistened.

"If he's truly dea—" she choked, and swallowed.

"Now, now, it's only possible at this stage to say he's missing. You're fond of him, aren't you? Chin up, old girl! Why not take the rest of the day to recuperate? We can get by without you for a day."

"Thank you sir, ... if he's truly missing, could it remain private, just between us?"

"Yes, certainly. And Stirling."

"Stirling too, – I'd prefer it if no one else knew," she said.

"Off you go then, and we'll see you all fresh in the morning." The general ushered her through the anteroom door and, as they parted to go their separate ways, unthinkingly he gave her backside a pat.

* * *

Pavlina pulled on her knee-high black leather boots, then stood.

"We go now," she declared, and hugged the girl.

"Shouldn't we wait for the grandmother to return?"

"She will be at bank a time. We will get your things at the *konoba*." They stepped out into the alley. There were no clouds. The sun was out and the winter sky was a brilliant blue. The temperature was in the forties – compared to a few days before, it was positively balmy. The snow had melted, but the limestone pavement was still wet in the shadows.

"Is that wise? What if Stjepan is there?"

"Stjepan is not a problem. I can handle Stjepan." Reggie had his doubts about that, but had to trust her. It was her country, after all. They walked through narrow alleys in a confusing path, and at every corner she first paused and peered around it, because she still wore her partisan uniform. "Primošten is occupied by Italians," she explained as they walked, "but they keep to themselves, and we keep to ourselves. They are out during the day, but do not come into the alleys at night, because we will shoot them. These Italians, they really do not want to be here. They are more afraid of us than we are of them," she said, with a mischievous grin. He pointed out for her the cellar opening with its missing iron bar. They turned the corner to stand before the *konoba* door. Reggie hesitated.

"I don't think I should go in. Are you *sure* you can handle Stjepan?"

She laughed. "Stjepan is *dječak prijatelj* since June. *Dječak prijatelj* is man-who-is-friend-of-woman."

"A boyfriend?"

"Yes, that."

"I'll wait for you out here," he said. She entered the *konoba*. As the door shut behind her, he saw a paper tacked to it, something he hadn't seen before during the night. In two lines of bold letters it read NIENTE ITALIANI! NEMA TALIJANA! He didn't need to speak either language to guess this meant "No Italians!" He found a narrow gap between the houses on the other side of the alley and loitered there to await her return.

He was a little unnerved to hear shouted Italian. Something was going on in the village square beyond the mouth of this alley. He peered out cautiously to see a Bersaglieri officer, identifiable by the cockade of black feathers on the side of his helmet, strutting in front of a platoon of armed Italian soldiers, shouting and gesticulating. He could see only a sliver of the square, not the full extent of the entire company without exposing himself to view, and anyway, he didn't want to. They appeared to be going through some kind of drilling manoeuvres, as in unison they moved their rifles into various positions with each command.

Glancing about his section of alley, on the wall of the *konoba* across from him was a glass-fronted display case, the kind that usually contained village meeting notices. He stepped over to it to see what was there, even though he couldn't read any of it. The pictures alone told him enough. There was the usual church notice, identifiable by a crucifix. Next, there was a sketch of a kitten, and also a sun-faded photograph of a terrier. It was a good guess these might be lost. A very good drawing of a pair of hands holding knitting needles and a ball of yarn told him this village had some version of a Women's Institute. Another notice showed a drawing of a boat and a tray of various types of fish, the prices listed in *kuna* and *banica* per kilogramme. He spied a poster tacked there, a swastika in each of its corners. It was in German, in the angular *Fraktur*-style lettering the Nazis often used, and he read it: *Mörder! 28 Tote!* – Murderer! 28 Killed! The poster showed a head-and-shoulders photograph, taken from the front, of a heavily bearded man with black hair and a trim moustache. His name – a single name that was obviously his *nom de guerre* – was "Buga" and the reward for his capture had recently been increased to 500,000 reichmarks, but only if taken alive! *That's a lot of money. They must really want this fellow.*

He turned to go back to his gap to wait but stopped, bemused. He gazed at the poster again. He was sure he'd seen this fellow somewhere before, but that was impossible. Putting his hand up to it he covered the beard. It was Pavlina, of this he was certain. Her black hair was slicked straight back with pomade, and she was wearing a tie, white shirt, and a man's suit coat, but it was most definitely her! He tried opening the display case but it was padlocked. The hinge pins couldn't be easily pulled without tools, so he reached for his knife but the scabbard was empty. Briefly it crossed his mind to smash the glass with his elbow, but before he could do this, he became aware the shouting had stopped. There came the sound of hundreds of tramping boots. The first of several platoons of soldiers, flanked by an officer, was approaching this alley! The closest path of escape was into the *konoba* so he rushed to the door and inside. He found the place empty. Many might be out in the fields, or fishing. Pavlina stood there alone. Before he could open his mouth, she spoke.

"I tell him you are English airman, and Josip Broz orders me to take you out of country. He brings your things. He thought you were German. He apologises for the misunderstanding." Stjepan appeared, carrying all his things. When he saw Reggie, he grimaced. He dumped the items on a table, none too gently. Reggie stood back and waited while they finished their conversation, and busied himself stowing articles away in his pockets. The battery in the torch had died. As Reggie pocketed the gun, he decided there was no harm in putting on a forced attempt to be cordial.

In German he said, "Guten Morgen. Wie geht es dir? Gut, hoffe ich?" Stjepan didn't respond.

"Reggie, Stjepan speaks only Serbo-Croatian. He knows not German."

Reggie tried a second phrase: "Das Wetter ist heute gut, viel besser als vor ein paar Tagen, ja?" Stjepan had no reaction, not a muscle twitched. Stjepan turned to Pavlina with a confused look, and shook his head.

"I tell you before: Stjepan speaks not German!" Pavlina admonished him.

"Sorry." *This man is a top-notch actor. She doesn't know Stjepan's secret. Pavlina doesn't speak German. Stjepan doesn't speak English. I'm in a very unique position here: I know both.*

"Is the good breakfast, but I will use the toilet now," she said. The facility was across the room and down a side hallway. When she was out of sight they heard a door click shut. Reggie took this opportunity to speak to Stjepan, in German.

"Pavlina is beautiful, and so loving, too," he casually commented. "I plan to ask her to marry me just as soon as I can find the proper engagement ring – but don't let her know this: I want it to be a surprise." Stjepan grabbed Reggie's collar with both fists.

"You have slept with her?" Stjepan demanded, also in German.

"Yes, have you?" Reggie replied, twisting away from his grip but not succeeding in breaking it.

"Yes. She is a very talented lover," Stjepan declared. *Pavlina would never permit that. Stjepan just lied to me*, he thought. They stood awhile, not speaking, just locked in a silent struggle while Reggie tried to extricate himself.

"You know, I think I'll ask her now," he said, again in German, "and she'll surely want you to stand up as my best usher, because you're such a good friend to her." They both heard a door click shut. Stjepan let him go. Reggie picked up the last item, his knife, and didn't put it back in its scabbard, but continued holding it, the point resting on the table. Gripping the handle for a upwards thrust, in English he muttered low, "I'll plunge this into your throat." Stjepan had no reaction. *Good. He really doesn't know English.*

Pavlina now approached them. He sheathed his knife and turned to her as soon as she arrived. Stjepan shut his mouth and glowered, unable to make any reply in front of her.

"Pavlina," in dulcet tones of English Reggie said to her, "in a moment I'm going to kneel. What I want you to do, is to take my hand and help me to stand up." He dropped to one knee. Stjepan looked down at him.

"What is happening?" she asked, also in English. Stjepan looked over at her.

"I saw a wanted poster of a man. It's you, isn't it?" Reggie replied sweetly, and took her hand in both of his own.

"Oh, that. Yes!" Pavlina said, nodding, and laughed with delight. "It was all Stjepan's idea to present me as the bearded man. No one will ever look for the woman, only look for the man who does not exist!"

"You are in great danger," he said, keeping his voice honeyed. "We have to go, and go now." She helped him to his feet. He took her arm in his, patting her hand. Stjepan looked from one to the other, then seized her upper arm in a vice-like grip and yelled something Serbo-Croatian in her face. Pavlina winced in pain and recoiled from him. Stjepan realized he had hurt her and let go of her arm. In shrill tones Pavlina yelled right back in his face and pushed him away.

"Let's go." Reggie said, tugging on her arm, and she nodded while glaring at Stjepan. He hustled her out the front door before Stjepan could say anything more. Once outside, after a few paces he stopped her.

"Why did Stjepan yell at you?"

"He asked if we had sleep together."

"And what did you say?"

"That we did, because is true: we sleep."

"How would he know to ask a question like that?"

"You must have told him," she accused. She slapped his face, and raised her hand to slap him again. Reggie seized her wrist. His next question was the most important one.

"*How* could I tell him? Stjepan doesn't know English. I don't know Croatian. We both know German. Stjepan speaks flawless German, because he must be native-born in the Fatherland. A moment ago he told me you and he had slept together, and you are a very talented lover."

"No! We did not! Is impossible!"

"*We* know that. Don't you see? He's a Nazi – he's *using you* to get to Josip Broz." A look of sudden understanding dawned on Pavlina's face.

"That makes sense. Always he ask to meet Josip in person, but always I make the excuse." The door to the *konoba* burst open and Stjepan emerged at a run, only to skid to a halt abruptly when he saw them. He scratched the back of his head while looking up and down the street. He then directed a casual remark at Pavlina in Serbo-Croatian. Pavlina shook her head and shrugged her shoulders, palms up. Stjepan stepped back inside, and the door shut.

"What was that?"

"He asked if we had seen his janitor."

"We need to go back to the safe house now! Can you find a confusing route so we won't be followed? We'll need to run," he urged. She didn't hesitate.

"This way!" As they rounded a corner and were out of sight, somewhere behind them they heard a door slam. They put on a bit more speed, running while holding hands. Bursting into the house she locked the door, he pulled the curtains, and they collapsed in the chairs panting from their efforts. The grandmother and girl looked at them in surprise. It was nearly noon, and there were pita sandwiches on plates laid out on the table for lunch. Reggie turned to Pavlina.

"You're in great danger! I have to get you out of this village, now!" With fresh eyes, Pavlina saw a man whose only concern was for her own safety.

"Is both of us in danger! *We* must go now," she replied. Hurriedly he collected the stack of Croatian kuna notes from the table, handing it to her.

"Split this in half," he demanded. She counted it out quickly. "Do you know a way off this peninsula, where we can avoid going through the village gate?"

"Yes. Follow me! *Doviđenja, doviđenja!*" They said their good-byes. "*Doviđenja!*" He handed half the money to the grandmother, and hugged her and the girl, as did Pavlina. The grandmother quickly wrapped two of the sandwiches in a sheet of newsprint for them. He put on his Astrakhan. She donned her Russian *pilotka* forage cap, on its front the emblem of the partisans: an enamelled badge of a red five-pointed star without a yellow hammer and sickle. Pavlina wheeled her bicycle through the kitchen and boot room, out the back door and into the garden. Chickens scattered at their approach. They passed a cast-iron hand pump near the high wood fence. At the garden gate they cautiously peeked out. The alley was deserted. The church bell began to toll—it was noon.

"Pavlina," he whispered, "I saw Italians marching through the village!"

"This I know. They go to the church first for the long sermon, then around the village edge, then to the harbour, then the barracks. Is the same every day." In narrow alleys and through gaps between houses, they made their way to the peninsula's southern harbour. The tide was out. By dropping down the face of the quay onto a narrow bit of shingle, they were able to creep unseen around the end of the medieval wall separating the village from the mainland. Once beyond the wall she paused.

"Give to me your coat. I must cover my uniform. There might be *Ustaše* or *Domobranstvo* on our way." She buttoned the trench coat up to her neck, took off her *pilotka* cap and put it in the pocket.

It was sixteen miles to Šibenik. They went by little-used back roads, and paths overland through high brush and often olive or fruit orchards, but always avoiding the main roads. They skirted the upland village of Primošten Burnji. The only difficult part was getting over the 800 foot high ridge beyond it. While on the back roads, at her behest he went ahead, and she followed two-hundred yards behind pushing her bicycle, "For safety because of the price on my head, so we cannot be caught together." Only once did a car approach, and he kept his head lowered and didn't look at it – just another farmer trudging home from his plot of land. Glancing back, he saw she did the same. It didn't stop.

In mid-afternoon they stopped to rest, deep in a copse of trees, and munched on the cheese and *ćevapčići* pita bread sandwiches the grandmother had prepared. As they ate, she told him the source of her *nom de guerre*: in the seventh century when Croatian tribes migrated from the Pannonian Plain westward towards the Adriatic Sea, there was one tribe ruled by a family of five brothers; *Klukas, Lobel, Kosjenc, Muhlo* and *Hrvat,* and their sister *Tuga.* The other sister had a reputation as a strong and fierce warrior who led her own army to victories over the peoples already inhabiting the coast.

"I name myself after this warrior: her name was *Buga*." He told her about having seen the wanted poster. She laughed and said, "The Nazis set the reward and pay for printing and distribution. Our cost is nothing. Is clever, yes?"

"No, because Stjepan knows who you really are. Whether he can eventually get to Josip Broz to assassinate him or not, his backup plan has always been to turn you in for the reward. Either way he wins." Pavlina scowled at this and said nothing. Reggie then changed the subject. "So, you've killed twenty-eight men?" She bit her lip as she silently ticked off the fingers of both hands.

"No, Stjepan only invents this number. *Twenty-six* fascists I kill, now." She was silent a moment, her face masked in thought as she chewed. She swallowed, then continued as if delivering a lecture, "The Russian forces have women fighters in their ranks. Women there are valued as soldiers, as snipers, as pilots, and here in Yugoslavia is the same! Is well known the Germans think of us women soldiers as not equal to them, and call us by a word in their language '*flintenweiber*' and this insulting word is meaning 'rifle broad'. Germans are under orders that when we are captured, they must execute us on the spot without trial. Is known women fighters are raped many times before execution." She shrugged, as if resigned to the thought such treatment was only to be expected, and took another bite of her sandwich. After swallowing her mouthful, she declared, "Is luck I find my talent as the best assassin!".

Reggie nodded, reminding himself she had used, "*when* we are captured" not "*if* we are captured". He had the sudden realization that, in the short time he'd known her, she'd never displayed any weapon.

"So, how do you kill them? You carry no weapon, not even a knife." She only smiled coyly and didn't answer.

They dusted down and continued on their journey. They passed signs pointing down crossroads that led to other villages: Grebastica,

Zaboric, Jadrtovac, and Brodarica. They tramped into Šibenik following a railway line through an industrial neighbourhood just at twilight. When that ended before a string of shut waterfront warehouses, they walked north on a road tracing the shoreline of the bay, the sign reading *Obala hrvatske mornarice*. They began to see darkened lampposts and commercial buildings, now locked tight. As they rounded the corner of a decrepit four-storey waterfront hotel, its shutters hanging broken, suddenly there it was before them: the ship he'd come so far to reach.

They were looking at the side of the ship that faced the bay, from its aft port quarter. On the fantail stern of the ship, in white letters on a blue hull, he read BELFAIR and beneath that in smaller letters its home port, STOCKHOLM. Reggie could tell it was unladen by how much of the ship's red bottom paint showed above water. Most striking was a large Swedish flag painted on the hull. After this old hotel the waterfront met a substantial stone mole jutting out into the bay, and perpendicular to the shoreline. The far side of the mole was longer than the near side, and crossed the stern of the ship. Then the quay continued north, and this was the seawall to which the ship was moored. As they cleared the stern of the ship, Reggie seized her arm and froze. He drew her back out of sight.

"What is wrong? Here is your ship."

"Look, there at the gangplank to the ship," he whispered, "See the red-and-white striped sentry box? That's not normal." As they watched, a guard with a rifle stepped out and checked his wristwatch. His uniform was grey. He wore a 'coal-scuttle' helmet. The German then slung his rifle on his shoulder and resumed his guard duty, pacing first towards the stern. "Let's go around, to get a better view of the situation," he said. They retreated around the corner the same way they'd arrived. Taking a roundabout way through the back alleys of the city they found themselves at the mouth of an alley that opened out onto the quay. It had a hip-high black iron bollard that kept any car from driving in. To their left was a *konoba* rather unimaginatively called *Sidro* – "The Anchor" – and lively accordion music poured forth from this. Here they were nearly straight across from the sentry box and gangplank. They remained back in the shadows so they couldn't be seen.

This gangplank was a long planked affair adorned with frets for grip, rising at a shallow twenty degree slope up to the ship. Here it was attached to the ship at the side of the bridge, where there was an open gate. A swivelling platform here allowed the ramp to point in any direction, but now it was oriented at an angle to the ship's side, pivoted towards the stern. It had handrails on both sides. This gangplank was suspended from a shipboard crane, and its end hung above the quay at waist level.

A wide promenade lay between the face of the buildings and the ship – at a guess he supposed this to be more than twenty yards wide, including the road – and a lamp-post illuminated the intervening space. The guard now stood smoking in front of his sentry box. Another guard, this one Swedish, stood on the ship next to a belt-fed heavy machine-gun mounted on the bulwark near the bridge. It was obvious his job was "to repel boarders", if any. The sentry box was placed between the end of this gangplank and the ship's side, to keep it out of this Swede's arc of fire.

"Is a German guard," she said, stating the obvious. "What will you do?"

"I guess there's only one thing for it: I'll have to brazen my way in. Let me have my trench coat, please."

"Brazen? What means this?"

"You'll see." She shed his coat and helped him into it. He turned and took both her hands in his. "Thank you for saving my life, Buga Pavlina. We'll not see each other again," he said, allowing himself the pleasure of using her full name. Her grip tightened.

"This I know, Reggie Wallace."

"I've enjoyed our time together." *I'm going to miss her.*

"I also." Taking hold of her shoulders, he kissed both her cheeks, in the continental fashion. She hugged him then, a bit wistfully.

"Good-bye, Pavlina," he said in her ear. "You'll be all right, getting back to your home?"

"Good-bye, Reggie, do not worry about me," she replied. He turned to face the ship and straightened his clothing, fastening buttons, adjusting his trench coat belt and making sure his collar was straight. He smoothed his hair down and replaced his hat. He left his German-issue gloves in the pocket, but brought out her *pilotka* cap. She pocketed it. He took his Swedish passport out and opened it. They'd given him the Swedish name "Leif Magnuson." Holding his passport open to the photo in his left hand, he took a deep breath and strode forth. Pavlina watched him go from the shadows. He marched out briskly, arms swinging, and when he was halfway there he looked up at the Swedish guard and waved heartily, as if they were acquainted, and the man returned his wave. The German guard set his cigarette on the windowsill of the sentry box and warily levelled his rifle with its bayonet at this approaching stranger. The Swedish guard leaned over the rail for a better look at him. He strode up and displayed his passport.

The German reached in the door to bring out a clipboard, a pencil on a string dangling from it. He compared the passport to the clipboard, and shook his head. Putting the clipboard away, he stood in front of the gangplank holding his rifle at port arms. It was quite obvious what his meaning was: you shall not pass. Reggie tucked the passport in a pocket, did a military about-face, and marched back to the alley. When he was sufficiently within the shadows of the alley, he sagged against a wall for support, and wiped a hand over his face.

"What happened?" Pavlina asked, gripping his arm.

"There's a list," he replied, shakily. "I wasn't on it."

"I cannot leave now. My orders are to get you on that ship. Have you your kuna notes?" she asked.

"Yes, in my coat pocket," he said, patting the trench coat.

"Give to me the coat! You will follow me." As he followed her, he felt a strange gratitude to the guard for allowing him more time with Pavlina, and wondered if she perhaps felt the same about him. Thinking of Milly he felt guilty, but assuaged his guilt with the knowledge Milly wasn't seeking marriage. They retraced their steps to another, wider, alley behind the buildings fronting the promenade. They ranged back and forth here, skirting the outdoor tables filled with patrons of the bistros and cafes, searching for what, he didn't know, until she pointed up to a sign on a building that read *Gostionica Palme, 24 sobe*, and below this hung a second sign reading *Sobe raspoloživ*.

"Is saying 'Palm Tree Inn, 24 rooms. Rooms available'," she translated for him. "We get the room. I do all the talking. Busy yourself looking and say nothing. Our name is now— "

"Magnuson," he interrupted. "Get a flat overlooking the ship, as high as possible."

"No. I must have my bicycle with me at all times. Is very important."

"First floor it is, then," he replied. She pulled at a knob vigorously, and somewhere inside a bell jangled. In a minute a plump matron in a floral apron and slippers unlocked the door. A *Gauloises caporal* dangled from her lips, an eye squinting against the smoke. Her thinning auburn hair was in curlers. Pavlina launched into rapid Croatian. They were admitted and the door with its glass panel was locked behind them. The building's interior was open from the ground floor all the way up to a skylight. The floor was tiled in a lovely mosaic pattern, and a heavy and ornate baroque table graced its centre, holding only a large vase of dried flowers. A half-dozen bicycles lined one wall. A ginger cat appeared at their feet. Reggie bent to stroke it and was ignored. A pleasant looking young woman in a long coat and holding a purse smiled and nodded at them as she locked a glass door that read in gold leaf, *Frizerski Salon.*

There was no lift. Led up a curved stairwell to the first floor, carrying the bicycle, they saw a balcony with a railing went all the way around each floor, the numbered flats opening off of this. Stopping before a door with a brass numeral "8" above a small nail, Pavlina propped the bicycle on its wheel-stand. The matron unlocked the deadbolt with a modern key, then unlocked the door itself with an ancient skeleton key. When the door was open, she stopped Pavlina from entering by grabbing her hand and pointing at it. Pavlina strenuously argued with the woman. Reggie thought, *She's noticed we're not married—I'll need to fix this.*

He hugged Pavlina, whispering in her ear "Play along," then swept her up in his arms and carried her, all the while she hugged his neck and waved her feet, smiling, across the threshold where he set her down. Pavlina and the matron resumed talking. Reggie wandered about. He tested the bed, opened cupboards and drawers, turned on the taps in the kitchen and bath, and generally kept out of their way. The high-ceiling flat was stifling hot. He noticed the steam heat radiator had no handle. There was a sink, and on the counter an electric kettle and electric cooker, a wire toasting rack on it. Pots and pans and dishes were in the cupboards, and cutlery and tea towels in the drawers. Soon the matron accepted a handful of kuna, handed over the ring of keys and left them alone. He wheeled her bicycle inside. When the door shut, Pavlina collapsed on the bed giggling like a schoolgirl. Reggie had never heard her giggle before.

"What did you tell her?"

"We are newly-wed on the honeymoon, jewellery is hard to find these days. What you did convinced her!"

"My word, this flat is hot." It was, and there was no way to regulate it, as there was no handle. *When was this place built? Pre-Great War? 1900? 1870?*

"We must open windows—she tell me, if we shut off, rooms above will suffer. The washerwoman from the alley laundry will visit every week on Tuesday and Thursday. The price is reasonable, she tell me. I pay for one month. She will take nothing less."

"Pavlina, that's all right. Well done!" He went to the windows and opened them both, each into their recess, and shut their protective doors over them. He pushed the green-painted louvered shutters outward. Leaning as far out as he dared and looking left he could see the mouth of an alley, and just beyond this was The Anchor pub. He was here for the ship, however, and this flat afforded an unobstructed view of it.

The ship had large Swedish flags painted on top of all three of the hatchcovers, and on both sides of the ship near bow and stern. Between or beside these blue and yellow flags he saw the painted words SWEDEN and NEUTRAL all in white, and in German, Italian, and English. He reckoned the crew had done this so the ship wouldn't be accidentally bombed, by either side. The hull was a very dark blue, almost black, the superstructure the usual white. What was most prominent were the three giant buff-coloured cranes. He knew this ship to be empty but, curiously, the booms of these cranes were left swung out on both sides. He wondered why. Their normal position should be set inboard.

Down the centre of the promenade there was a line of palm trees alternating with lamp-posts. The lamps bathed the promenade and quay in a cheery glow. These palms were not the tall "Royal Palms" he'd seen in Singapore last year, but instead were short and had thick trunks, and these had a rough diamond-patterned surface. The fronds at the tops of each formed a dense clump. It was after sunset and he could see couples strolling under the lamps, some of the women pushing prams with infants. It looked most inviting and picturesque. He called Pavlina to the window to see the view, but she didn't answer.

He went to her, and she was indeed sound asleep on top of the duvet. They hadn't eaten supper and there was no food in the flat. He shook her awake and they went to the alley to find a restaurant. When they returned, he prompted her to disrobe while he turned down the duvet and fluffed the pillows. He shut the door behind him as he entered the bathroom. Lining the bathtub with a heavy woollen blanket, he curled up with his pillow and pulled the blanket over. Minutes later there was a knock.

"Reggie, are you well?" said Pavlina through the door.

"Yes. Do you need to use the toilet?"

"No." After a few seconds, the door opened and the light snapped on. She stepped to the side of the tub and looked down at him, hands on her hips. She was starkers. He smiled at being presented this enjoyable sight of her, and from such an unusual point of view. Wagging a finger, she chastised him.

"Reggie, is normal to put water in tub, also not use blanket as towel!"

"I'll sleep here."

"Do not be idiot. Come to bed now – I trust you." He undressed and hung his clothes in the armoire, then joined her.

"Sleep tight," he said.

"The bugs, do not make them do the biting," she recited.

"Don't let the bed-bugs bite," he corrected.

"Yes, that." That night, as on every night, they heard accordion or fiddle music from The Anchor. But sometimes there were heard single gunshots in the city, and distant explosions. Often, they heard bombers passing overhead, above the cloud cover, and wondered — ours, or theirs?

Buga Pavlina and Reggie Wallace held each other, and hoped Šibenik's turn would never come.

10

Interlude

"Good morning, Buga!" Pavlina awakened and sat up, to yawn and stretch luxuriously. Reggie set a tray holding a teapot and cups on saucers at the foot of the bed. "Sorry there's no cream, nor any sugar."

"What is this? She asked, perplexed.

"It's tea. I found it in the cupboard. I hope it's still good. Haven't tasted it yet." He fluffed her pillows, propping them up behind her.

"But, why you make tea?" He balanced the tray atop her thighs, then slipped into bed beside her.

"Why? You must have tea in this country, or is that not your tradition?" He poured out a cup each.

"Yes, tea, but why *you* make tea? *You!* Slavic men do not do this for women."

"That's strange. They should. Drink up!" He had a sip, and frowned. "We'll need to buy some fresh somewhere."

"Is not bad." They sat and enjoyed the tea. "Thank you, Reggie," she said, giving his shoulder a squeeze. She then slowly brushed her hand downwards, across his chest as far as his navel before withdrawing it. He thrilled at the touch of her fingertips. He wondered, *is she deliberately teasing me now?*

"Reggie, how old are you?" she asked casually, and sipped her tea, as if she didn't care if he answered or not.

"Twenty-nine. How old are you?" he responded, not expecting an answer.

"I am thirty-three. I know you think maybe I am old, yes?" she asserted.

"No. No. I don't think that at all," he said. Their tea finished, he began to dress while she went to stand in the centre of the room and began to do stretching exercises, twisting this way and that. She then laid a towel on the floor for her ritual morning exercises.

"These I do every morning if I have time," she explained, "I do not want to make my clothing with perspire, so this I do without."

"Perspiration."

"Yes, that—perspiration. You will not mind?"

"You exercise however you like," he agreed. He clothed himself while he enjoyed watching her as she counted out twenty star jumps. Tucking her feet under the end of the bed, she did thirty sit-ups. When she finished she wiped herself down with the towel, then put on her panties. She seemed to his eyes to be somewhat dispirited as she sat on the edge of the bed.

"Are you not going to dress?" he asked, when she didn't continue.

"I do not think to be away from home for more than one night. I cannot walk around in partisan uniform here in daylight. Is very dangerous," she fretted.

"Tell you what: I'll get you some new clothes."

"I cannot leave this Inn," she declared. "How you will buy for me?"

"Let's suss this out."

"What is meaning this word 'suss'?"

"Suss out? It means to solve a problem."

"Reggie, thank you for suss out Stjepan. I believe Stjepan to be honourable Croat. I was confused by love." Reggie sat by her side, an arm about her waist to console her, and said nothing. She laid her head on his shoulder and sighed.

"I've got it!" he exclaimed, and stood up. He emptied the pockets of his trench coat and had her put it on, buttoning it up to her neck. He put a handful of kuna notes in its pocket. He put his pistol in his trouser pocket, and stood by the door. "Come here. You are to go knock on the other tenant's doors. Ask for a woman: what is a rare Croatian name?"

"Vesna?"

"You're to ask for 'Vesna' until any woman answers. If a man answers, ask for his wife. If there's no woman, make an excuse and move on. You are to tell them this: you are a newly-wed bride on your honeymoon and lost your suitcase on the train, then ask if she has any clothes you can buy. I'll stand here and keep watch so you're safe, all right?"

"Yes. Thank you, Reggie." She started along the balcony and knocked on the first door. He stood in their doorway and watched. A heavyset man answered. The next door was a very tiny, frail woman, who shook her head. The next woman had nothing to sell. The next a tall elderly man. Each time she made an excuse and moved on. On the sixth try, the ploy worked, and she went in. She emerged fifteen minutes later with an armload of clothing, and Reggie waved his thanks to the tenant. Inside the flat Pavlina spread her haul on the bed and shed the trench coat.

"Look what is here!" she exulted. There were two dresses, three skirts with pockets, five blouses, a cardigan, two shawls, and a pair of flats: these were purple leather with a little leather bow for decoration. She snatched something up from the pile and hurried to the bathroom, emerging a minute later in a lacy black lingerie top. With a hand she adjusted each boob in its cup and then, hands on hips, strutted the room modelling for him. Where before she had always flattened them under a stiff man's jacket, now they stood out beautifully shaped and contoured.

"You look more feminine than ever," Reggie said, drawing near to straighten a shoulder strap that had turned. "Why do you wear a man's jacket, one that fastens so tight? Doesn't it hurt you?"

"Yes, is not comfortable. I wear it to make men respect me, so the orders I give will be followed." She put on her clothes, selecting a blue woollen skirt, and the warmest blouse there, and a knitted tan shawl. Now they were able to go out to see Šibenik, like any ordinary local couple. She would not — could not — wear her boots and cobbled together partisan uniform here. It was best to go incognita.

Breakfast was at a bistro in an alley. It was tea, and a very small pita bread filled with *ćevapčići* sausages, scrambled egg, red peppers, and feta cheese. It even had a rare slice of onion! Back in wartime London, one couldn't find onions for love nor money. When they returned to the flat, Reggie drew a bowl of water from the kitchen tap and sat at the table. He field-stripped his pistol and emptied the magazine, rinsing the salt crystals out of every crevice. He patted it dry with a tea-towel and spread the parts on the floor under the steam heat radiator for a few minutes to finish drying.

Reggie was well aware he was here for the ship, and he was on an important mission, but after the previous day's debacle he felt he – both of them – needed a break to recover, to formulate a plan. They spent this first day strolling the city to familiarize themselves with its layout and landmarks. It was discovered that, generally, streets that ran north to south were predominately wider pedestrian alleys, and streets that ran east to west were usually narrow stairways, but not always. Reggie learned the Croat word for 'stairs' was *stube* because this word was engraved on the building corners at the top and bottom of stairs. There were many shops in public squares, and these were connected by these alleys. Tiny shops lined these alleys, too. Often an alley wasn't straight, but might zig-zag at random. Walking downhill anywhere always brought you back to the harbour front, and this was where the main road was, along the quay. At the mole, where the stern of the ship was positioned, the main road turned inland and ascended the slope, going east. Other than churches, there wasn't a building anywhere taller than four storeys. They found the public square where the weekly farmer's market was to be held tomorrow, a Saturday. They strolled past the largest cathedral they'd ever seen here. Facing it across the square was the city hall. No one needed to tell them it was the city hall, as it was quite obvious: there were long red vertical banners with prominent swastikas, hanging above armed German soldiers flanking an entrance. An armed German soldier patrolled the square with an Alsatian dog on a lead. Today a courier's BMW motorcycle with sidecar was parked nearby, but within the hour had gone.

High up on the slope behind the city hall they came upon another church. On the north side of this was a beautiful and peaceful rock grotto, dripping with water and filled with ferns and mosses. A statue of the Virgin Mary gazed down on them from within it. And there were moggies everywhere. Many, many moggies, and they lolled on the limestone in the warmth of the midday sun. Everywhere they saw a slogan daubed on walls or buildings, the partisan motto *Smrt fašizmu, sloboda narodu!* This she translated for him: "Death to fascism, freedom to the people!"

Fuel for civilians was always in short supply, so there were few cars, but Italian military vessels did visit this port to refuel, and there was no shortage of military vehicles passing through. There were food shortages of course. Red meat was unobtainable, but when it did appear it was usually horse meat. Deliveries were made by push barrow or horse-cart. The one thing that seemed to be plentiful was the seafood. The fishermen always brought in the catch, and they fished every night under lantern light. For the most part the Germans and Italians left them alone.

Supper that evening was at a restaurant off a well hidden alley. Pavlina ordered for them both, and when the plates were served Reggie was dismayed to see it heaped with suckered tentacles, for this was grilled *hobotnica* – octopus. Not a thing you might see in London, if at all. On the side there was a most delicious dip of pureed eggplant and red pepper. Occasionally armed German or Italian soldiers might choose to eat in a restaurant, and when they did it was always three or four together, never one alone. The owner would always seat them away from the other patrons.

After supper, Reggie and Pavlina joined the couples and families promenading along the quay before sunset. He was relaxed. It seemed to him there wasn't even a war going on, almost. He stood gazing at the ship, not even concerned about how he might gain entry, just enjoying the chill evening air, when Pavlina rushed up to him all aflutter. A young couple stood not five yards away, and it was to this pair she pulled him. She introduced them but he forgot their names immediately, as was easy to do with these often unpronounceable Serbo-Croatian names. They appeared to be very much in love.

"They are getting married in that church, on Saturday. Tomorrow." She pointed.

"That's nice," he said in English, putting out his hand to the fellow, "Please convey my congratulations to them." He turned to the young lady and shook her hand as well. They appeared to be younger than him, perhaps twenty-three or twenty-five.

"But Reggie," she hugged his arm, bouncing on the balls of her feet, mad with joy, "they have invited us!" The young man beamed at him and nodded.

"But Pavlina, we don't know these people."

"Is no matter. We will accept, yes?" She seemed about to burst. The couple smiled, waiting. It seemed he had no choice in the matter.

"Yes, of course we'll go," he said, nodding. The young man bowed, and the couple strolled away. Pavlina was positively swooning with delight. How she was going to sleep tonight he hadn't the faintest. They returned to their flat as the sun set. Pavlina drew a bath and entered the tub. Reggie swung open the windows and shutters, and sat on the deep windowsill. The room light was off. His back was to one side of the opening and his feet against the other. He wasn't cold sitting here, as the high heat from the flat kept him warm. Soon the sun had disappeared and the lamp-posts switched on. He sat and watched the promenaders on the quay. He could see both guards too, and there was activity on the ship's deck. The crew was just finishing touching up the colours of the Swedish flags. He saw the end of the gangplank now hung at about head height. *Had the Swedes raised it for some reason? No, I forgot about the tides!* "About a metre" *Commander Wanklyn had said. Then it must be high tide now. This means the gangplank will never be on the ground, making it not at all easy to get aboard.*

Pavlina was drying herself, a towel over her head, and he turned his head to watch. He had never before known a woman for whom nudity mattered so little—well, with the exception of Nurse Susan Kee who last year had skipped naked into the surf whilst we all picnicked at that beach on Christmas Island. Wasn't she a stunner! Even Milly had always waited until the lights were off before removing her knickers. With Milly he knew it to be "that English thing about privacy," but on the other hand, Pavlina could easily stand before him absolutely starkers, and be completely unconcerned about it. Was Pavlina just being Slavic? He didn't know. Mind you, he wasn't complaining.

A sound began from outside and this attracted their attention. It seemed to be coming from the ship. Pavlina came to the window, the towel now about her torso. It was a tannoy announcement from the ship, but in Croatian.

"What are they saying?" he asked.

"Ugh, that is badly said. Is dreadful. Something about shooting?" Then it was repeated in German, and finally in English.

"Attention! Attention! Please do not shoot out our lights. They identify us as a neutral ship. Your city is also protected by our lights." As the announcements ended, a powerful flood lamp at the end of each boom blazed on, to illuminate all the flags and words painted on the ship.

The wedding was to be at noon. Pavlina togged-up in her best ensemble, a brown corduroy skirt paired with a floral and cream-coloured silk blouse, its neckline elastic. Naturally it was without a brassiere as it was an off-the-shoulder affair. This was not tucked in, but paired with her leather belt over it at her waist. Reggie was thrilled at the sight of her, looking as she did, quite fetching. He had to wear his 'farmer's disguise' again, only leaving off the jacket and trench coat this time. This revealed his waistcoat over his Osnaburg cotton shirt. Good enough.

After breakfast they browsed the Saturday market, buying enough fruit, vegetables, bread made from ersatz flour, and tinned food to last a week, for they had no icebox. This food lasted two weeks for they often ate in the local bistros. Major Stirling had been correct: this money was vastly more than he needed. He bought a few nice second-hand shirts with some trousers, and a pair of used shoes in his size. Also a used suitcase to hold her clothes. On the way back to the flat, they followed the sound of singing to find a traditional Dalmatian *klapa* choir practising in a courtyard, and paused to listen to the four men singing in beautiful *a cappella* harmonies.

At noon he sat in a church, and listened to the spoken Serbo-Croatian without understanding any of it. Pavlina sat leaning forwards, attentive to every nuance of the ceremony. Afterwards they followed the guests to a nearby hall, where they nibbled on rather plain *canapés*; little squares of ersatz rye bread that was half tree flour – that is, "sawdust" – topped with cheese, with an olive or bit of seafood. There was a cake, but they didn't partake, preferring to stand back and leave it to the families. Men, both young and old, stood to make speeches to the assembly. Someone handed him a glass of a rather good Croatian wine for the toasts. Pavlina was laughing delightedly as she flitted from group to group, and seemed to be engaged in sparkling conversation with just about everyone here. He was chuffed to bits she was having such a wonderful time. He was thinking she was just as, ... no, *even more* beautiful than last Tuesday night, when first he saw her gorgeous tawny hazel eyes.

Then the chairs were cleared away from the centre of the room, and the dancing began. A circle was formed, much like the Greeks do, as people held hands. The music and the dance started together with whistling and yipping, and there were two accordions, a Croat fiddle, and rapid drumming. Reggie had never in his life seen such rapid movements as this dance. It was astonishing, really. Pavlina leaned towards him to shout over the music.

"Is dance called '*svadbeno kolo*' – *kolo* is meaning 'wheel' – this I dance at my own wedding." Reggie hadn't known she was married, as she wore no ring, and had never mentioned having a husband. Pavlina wanted to dance and stood up to join, tugging on his hand, but Reggie resisted, knowing he couldn't manage it, and had to decline. He watched from where he sat, observing carefully to trace what was happening: both men and women moved to the left a few steps, then to the right even more steps, so the circle gradually rotated in one direction. The men wore their shoes, but most women chose to dance barefoot. Each person's movements were identical with the next: a leg crossing first ahead and then behind the other, but at the same time pivoting on a heel as a foot was set down. Yet each step somehow included a sort of hop, and this made the women's breasts whip up and down. It was incredibly complicated, and all of it happened in a fast blur, yet none lost their place. When the dance ended all of a sudden, Pavlina returned to his side to sit with him, breathing hard. Reggie waited until she'd caught her breath.

"Do you have children?" prompted her.

"Yes, one," she replied. "He was not-born."

"Stillborn."

"Yes, that." She fanned herself with the wedding announcement.

"I'm so sorry. Where is your husband now – in the military?"

"Dead," she replied, her voice flat and inexpressive. She didn't offer any more information than this, so he didn't press, but privately was relieved.

"I'm sorry," he responded, "Do you think you might remarry?" He quailed inside, sensing instinctively it was the wrong subject to raise, but once the words had left his mouth, it couldn't be unsaid. She said nothing, and looked away from him, seeming to find something on the far side of the room suddenly rather interesting.

Shortly after two o'clock they wished the newly-weds all good fortune, and left. Since they had met, when the two of them walked anywhere, it was always side by side, but slightly apart. Now Pavlina took his arm as they strolled, and from then on this is how they always walked. It had been a mere five days since they had first met, but he felt like he'd known her forever. He hoped she felt the same about him, but she was so hard to read, he really couldn't tell.

At ten minutes to three in the afternoon they were strolling along the waterfront, just another couple amongst many, when the people around them began walking toward the alleyways. Soon the prome-nade was deserted, and a young man they didn't know dashed out and guided them into an alley. They waited here with a group of locals, but unsure as to why. Precisely at three o'clock a grey *Kübelwagen* approached from the north, a *Wehrmacht* officer in the passenger seat wearing a peaked cap, and three soldiers in 'coal-scuttle' *Stahlhelm* helmets. This *Kübelwagen* was a small open four-door car of high ground clearance, and it carried a spare tire on its slanted bonnet. It motored south to stop before the sentry box. A soldier climbed out and stiff-arm saluted the officer, the other soldier climbed in, and it motored away to the north. During this exchange the soldiers had their *Maschinenpistoles* levelled warily at the face of the buildings opposite as a precaution. One held a *panzerfaust*. The people now emerged to reoccupy their promenade. Pavlina questioned the locals and relayed to Reggie that this guard, and others elsewhere, were replaced every 6 hours around the clock. The Germans were so precise, people here learned to scatter at three and nine o'clock every day, just like a clockwork.

In the early evening Reggie donned his leather and corduroy jacket, and they went next door to The Anchor *konoba* to quench their thirst for a beer. When they sat, the Croatian publican bustled by, stopped to look him over, but then barked something at him. Reggie listened as Pavlina translated.

"He says only a foreigner wears such ridiculous clothing. He wants to know if you're Swedish. He sounds angry. I think Swedes may not be welcome here."

Reggie thought for a beat. *I need to say something that will put the man off from any further interest in us, let him know talking to me is not worth his effort.* He leaned over and, cupping a hand to her ear, whispered, "Tell him I speak only Welsh — and order a litre of beer for me, and something for yourself." She relayed this information to the man, who seemed satisfied with the answer. The man turned on his heel and left, to bring the drinks shortly. He seemed to be in a better mood. Pavlina had ordered a *Višnjovik*, and Reggie had a sip. She explained this sour cherry wine was a favourite of her leader, Josip Broz, and she liked it, too. Pavlina raised her glass and, clinking it against his own, exclaimed, "*U vaše zdravlje!*", and they drank.

With a sense of relief he saw that, unlike in Primošten, none of the other patrons here were armed, and this was certainly because this city was being administered by the Germans. They drank, and listened to the music. It was familiar to them, for they were easily able to hear it from their flat. An enjoyable day all around, but it wasn't over yet: that night Pavlina whipped up a delicious supper from the provisions and spices they'd obtained that morning, and he discovered she was a most excellent cook. He insisted he act as her '*chef tournant*' and this became his habitual task when they weren't going out. In time he became very adept indeed at slicing and dicing.

In bed that night he lay staring into the darkness, and thought about events at the wedding, and that wonderful supper, then shut his eyes and drifted off to sleep with visions of her. Her drying off after her bath – vigorously dancing at that wedding – laughing merrily – her eyes sparkling ....

Both knew he must get aboard ship, but not how to do it. Both knew also that when he did, they must part. But Reggie was also aware "Operation Torch" was slated for November, and that event was a long time in the future. Over the next weeks, they settled in and behaved like locals. Merchants and townsfolk began to recognise this new couple, for they were always seen together. They fell into a daily routine and Reggie and Pavlina became very comfortable with their new situation. He felt very much at ease here in the beautiful town of Šibenik. He was unsure about her, but he wondered if he'd be feeling this way if she were not by his side.

One day, when they were out and about in the town, Pavlina spied a particular store front and steered him inside. It was a chemist's shop, and Reggie learned a new word, for the sign above the door read *Ljekarništvo*. On the wall inside there was a very large exquisitely carved figure of Jesus on a cross. It was easily more than a yard tall and beautifully gilded and varnished, the wound in his side painted a bright vermilion, the cloth about his waist painted white, the crown of thorns green with black points, the halo gold-leafed and shining.

Pavlina picked up a wire basket and they browsed among the items displayed on the shelves. Reggie selected a toothbrush, tooth powder, and also a Gillette safety razor, shaving mug and shaving soap for use when he was finally able to get aboard ship. Then he found a nice black leather bag with a zip closure to hold it all. She selected a bottle of boot-black and a straight razor, then beckoned him over to a shelf, where she stood somewhat embarrassed. Glancing about, she saw they were the only customers here. He saw an advert placard on the shelf with an illustration showing what appeared to be a nursing sister wearing a wimple, her finger raised as if giving instructions. The text was in German and his eye picked out the words *zur menstruationskontrolle*. Pavlina plucked a slip of paper from a cup placed there and held it out to him.

"You buy for me, yes?" Pavlina asked, her voice hopeful.

"Yes, certainly," he said, with an encouraging nod, and took the slip from her. "How many do you want?"

"Oh, er, three?" she said, relieved. She went outside to wait for him. Reggie placed the basket on the counter and when the pharmacist came to assist him, he gave the slip to the man and said "*Tri.*" The pharmacist returned with three blue paper cartons, on each label the brand name of "Camelia" and a black-and-white illustration of a pretty woman wearing a string of pearls and a bright red camellia flower. The pharmacist pulled the lever of the cash register and it displayed the total. Reggie counted out enough kuna and laid it on the counter. He coughed into his fist, then attempted to use his newly acquired language skills.

"*Imate li ikakvu* prophylactic?" he inquired, enunciating the words slowly and distinctly. The man regarded him with eyebrows raised, then laid a Serbo-Croatian/English dictionary on the counter, and returned to his task of grinding at a mortar and pestle. Reggie looked up the word "prophylactic" but it wasn't there. The word "condom" was missing too. Frustrated now, he painstakingly looked up a string of words to assemble a coherent sentence, then called the man back to the counter. The pharmacist smiled tolerantly as Reggie asked his question.

"*Imate li ikakvu lijek koji spriječiti trudnoću?*" hoping it was coming out as intended: "Do you have any medicine that prevents pregnancy?" With Reggie's pronunciation of the final words, the man became extremely angry, waving his arms and shouting. Reggie paid the man, collected his change, and left hurriedly.

"What takes long?" Pavlina asked, "language difficulties?" He gave her the paper bag and explained what he had attempted. "Oh, Reggie, we are not in London, we are in hundred per cent catholic country. Did you not see the large cross on the wall?" She hugged him, and kissed his cheek. "But thank you for thinking of me," she whispered huskily in his ear.

Often a lorry filled with Italian – or occasionally German – soldiers might drive though on the main road on its way to somewhere else, but the Italians had learnt early on in their occupation that one didn't go into the back alleys, especially at night. These back alleys were the source of the gunshots heard at night. The resistance was hard at work.

He paid the monthly tariff on the flat to the matron on Sunday, the first of March. He'd have been quite content for things to carry on as they had, were it not for an incident in the first week of March: quite late one night, after midnight, they were awakened by an extremely loud gunshot echoing from the alley behind their block of flats. Not unheard of, though always coming from much farther away.

Before sunset the next day they'd eaten supper in a restaurant visited only once before, just off the narrow *Ulica fra Nikole Ružića* near the *stube.* It was seafood again, but a whitefish in a piquant tomato sauce this time, young dandelion greens with thinly sliced peppers for a salad on the side, a dollop of sour cream standing in for salad cream. Reggie liked octopus fried with garlic, just not every day. The beer was good.

Entering their block of flats from its door on the alley, they went up to their flat, and he hung his jacket on a chair back. Their bellies full, they collapsed on the bed to rest, and digest. Suddenly, a single gunshot was heard from the promenade. He peeked through the louvres of the closed shutter to see open lorries below and *Wehrmacht* soldiers holding at gunpoint a group of civilians, their hands in the air. A body lay sprawled on the pavement. When he told Pavlina, she frantically searched the room to find paper and a pencil. Reggie seized his pistol. He glanced over her shoulder as she scribbled, but it was in Croatian. There was the sound of breaking glass on the ground floor, from inside their building! She opened the door and poked the paper on the nail in the centre of their door, then turned the knob to throw the deadbolt.

He sat on the floor opposite the door with his back against the wall under the window and braced both forearms on his knees, aiming for the door. Boots thumped the stair, and then they heard pounding on doors, and indistinct German, and the screams of terrified women. She snatched up his jacket from the chair, rushing over to hang it on the doorknob. She stood at the hinge side holding their largest kitchen knife, but he waved her away, out of his field of fire. She retreated to the bathroom. Each pounding was coming closer. The tramping footfalls stopped outside their door. If the door opened he was prepared to empty his magazine. The doorknob rattled. He held his breath, waiting for the door to be kicked in. *They may kill us both but I'll take as many of them with me as I can before that happens!*

The footfalls faded away and there was silence. When he heard the lorries start their engines he looked though the louvres of the shutter. They drove away filled with standing civilians. An old woman in a black shawl fell to her knees over the body below, rocking to and fro and keening sorrowfully. He turned to find Pavlina standing there and they hugged and, surprisingly, she gave him a quick kiss. She had put on her *pilotka* cap. *Of course! If she had to die fighting, she would want them to know they were up against a partisan.*

"What was it you wrote?" he asked. She handed him his jacket, then cautiously opened the door to retrieve the note. She read it to him.

"Otto darling – The Italians have hired me to translate for them. Sorry I missed you! Come back tomorrow. Kisses! – Hildegard." Both of these were the most Germanic of names.

"Why did you hang my coat on the doorknob?" he asked.

"They can see you though the keyhole," she answered. *Yes, anyone could have seen me,* he thought, *even if the skeleton key had been left in the keyhole to block the view, that would have been a tip-off that the room was occupied. What an intelligent woman.*

Outside their room the other doors stood open and a few hung askew, splintered and off their hinges. Holding his pistol at the ready before them, they crept down the stair. In the foyer a broom lay there, and smoke rose from a cigarette on the floor. The glass from the locked door crunched under their feet. The murmur of voices made him look up. The heads of other tenants peered down at them from the upper floors. He pocketed his pistol. The door to the hairdresser's stood ajar and he glanced into the salon.

"Matron? It's Mr Magnuson!" he called out, hopefully. The cupboard door under the stair creaked open and she crawled forth. They helped her stand. The matron's ginger cat appeared, looking about doubtfully. Reggie picked up the matron's cigarette and handed it to her. She took a shaky drag, then began to sob. Pavlina and Reggie stepped through the shattered glass front door onto the promenade, over to where the old woman knelt. A young woman and a boy stood nearby, in tears, but dried their eyes when they saw this partisan *vojnik*, one who now began issuing orders. Together they each took hold of a limb and followed the old woman to a nearby house. After they departed, Pavlina told Reggie the man's name was Rados, and he was father of the boy and husband of the woman, and she had promised the family that, as a partisan, she would avenge his death at some time in the future. As they made their way back to their flat, a distant sound was heard: *brrrt – brrrrrt – brt*—bursts of machine-gun fire. It continued for some time. These were followed by the crack of pistol shots.

In bed that night, before switching off the lamp, his arm about her and her head on his chest, they discussed what they could do to get him aboard the ship, bringing up ideas at random.

"I don't mind telling you, what happened this afternoon terrified me," he said.

"You are a strange man, to admit such a thing," she replied, "but I like you are saying always what you think."

"I've *got* to get aboard that ship! — I could wait until the guard has paced to the stern, then make a dash for the gangplank from the alley. It's only what? Twenty yards?"

"But the ramp is so high up, and he has the rifle. If he sees or hears you, he will just shoot."

"Why not just walk up and shoot the guard?" he proposed. "He let me walk up to him once. Surely he'll recognise me."

"What if guard is different man?" she worried aloud. "Also, he could see your hands before. Now you will have your hand in a pocket on your pistol. He will just shoot you first."

"What if I shoot him first, but from the alley?"

"That is a long distance for a pistol. If you miss, there will be the gun battle."

"You're right, and I'm not that good a shot," he had to admit. "Could we find a member of the local resistance cell, someone with a rifle, to shoot him for us?"

"Šibenik is outside my area. I do not know the contacts here, and is dangerous to ask people I do not know such questions."

"Perhaps I could march up to him as before, my passport in my hand, and hold the pistol clamped under my left arm. Then, as I approach close to him, I pull it out and shoot him point blank?"

"I will not let you do that," she replied, vehemently. "He will be wary as you approach. Also, to shoot a German is dangerous. They will round up hostages and execute them. Hundreds will die! You have seen this." They switched off the bedside table lamp and snuggled down under the bedcovers.

She's right, he thought, *and it's possible she could be among those rounded up.* "What if the guard is Italian?" he ruminated.

"The Italians do not execute like the Germans do. This is what I hear."

"Well, we can get a message to the ship by attaching it to a weight and throwing it aboard," he said.

"How will that help?"

"It'll let them know I'm here, and who I am, and that they can expect me sometime."

"Good idea. We will do that tomorrow. Goodnight."

"Goodnight."

Pavlina stood in the centre of the room to do her usual stretching and her ritual morning exercises, beginning by touching her toes. He began to dress as she counted out twenty star jumps. These were followed by thirty sit-ups, and for these she invited him to pin her feet down. When she finished she lay breathing hard. With her hands still behind her head, she didn't look at him but up at the ceiling. He sat at her feet and looked her over frankly, first at her breasts as they rose and fell with each breath, and then at her taut belly coated with a sheen of sweat. She let her knees fall apart, and he could easily see the perspiration glistening on her curly black hair. *Is she ... flirting with me?*

"You seem to be quite fit," he remarked, casually. Her eyes met his then, and a sly smile spread on her face.

"Thank you. Help me up?" she suggested. He stood and took her hands, pulling her to her feet. She used her towel to sop up the perspiration from beneath each underarm and breast, and then wiped down her torso and limbs, and finishing up by squatting slightly, to blot between her legs. When she turned away, she looked over her shoulder at him with an impish grin, then flung the wadded towel in his face, where he caught it. Shaking out the towel by its corner, he let it drape and twirled it round and round. Her eyes widened; she knew what was coming. As he flicked it at her, she scampered towards the bathroom with a cry of "eek!" and the towel gave a resounding *crack!* as it just missed her backside. She slammed the bathroom door after her. He inhaled her heady fragrance from the towel and this excited him. *Oh, she's definitely flirting, no doubt about it!*

He heard the toilet flush and as the door opened she cautiously peeked out. He dropped the towel in the clothes hamper. She emerged and dressed, then they went out to breakfast. Afterwards they visited an ironmonger where Reggie bought an inexpensive used spanner and some wire. Back at the flat he sat to compose a note. He spoke the words aloud as he wrote them down.

"Hello. I am your new captain sent secretly by your government to bring your ship out to safety. Keep your gangplank on the ground. I will attempt to board soon (in civilian clothes). I am not Swedish. Do not shoot when you see me coming. – L.M."

"L.M.?" she asked.

"Leif Magnuson. If this note doesn't make it aboard, I don't want whoever finds it to trace it back to me."

"But, why not tell them you are English?"

"Same reason. They'll find out soon enough." He wrapped the note around the spanner and wired it in place. They went for a walk, and decided to stroll along the quay facing the store fronts as if window-shopping. It was instantly plain he couldn't approach the ship anywhere without being seen by the guard, except at the stern, when the guard had paced to the bow. Once again taking the back streets through the city they strolled arm-in-arm out the mole and spent some time admiring the view of the bay, just in case they were being watched. They then retraced their steps, and when he was within yards of the stern he stopped and looked all about. No one was within sight. The guard was far away at the bow. Unladen as the *Belfair* was, the deck looked to be about thirty feet up. He took the spanner from his pocket and, rearing back, let fly as hard as he could. The spanner sailed up, up, only to carom off the underside of the fantail with a clang, ricocheting outward to land on the mole. He scooped it up and tried again, heaving with all his might, and this time it sailed over the rail and clattered onto the deck. They turned and strolled back the way they had come.

At the block of flats he climbed the stair to the roof, four storeys up. It was over 100 yards to the ship's stern from this vantage point, but he could see a bit of white on the deck. The following day it was gone, and the gangplank end now rested on the quay.

11

La Petite Mort

A week passed while they examined the ship from every angle they could, all without arousing suspicion. Every day at 9am, 3pm, and 9pm they observed the changing of the guard, but it never deviated from what they'd seen before. The guard was German, always German. Wasn't this section of Croatian coast supposedly under the control of Italy? They thought of tossing another weighted note, telling the Swedes to drop a hawser off the fantail so Reggie could climb aboard, but it had been eighteen years since he had done hand-over-hand during gymkhana, and even then he had been rubbish at it. It was not something he felt he could still do at his age. Leaving a rope ladder to the mole would look much too suspicious, as well, and would tip off the guard.

They hired a fisherman's dinghy and rowed past the port side of the ship looking for access ports that could be left open, but there were none. The lowest freeing port was sixteen feet above the water. There were no portholes low down. Pavlina "camped it up" in the stern, hands behind her head and ankles crossed, as if Reggie might be rowing her along on the River Cam. The only thing missing was a parasol and a picnic basket. Serious as his mission was, it was good to have a bit of fun.

A man walking along the deck above them glanced down at them then continued on his way. Reggie shipped his oars then cupped his hands to his mouth to shout, "L! M!" The man leaned over the side, and Reggie repeated this while pointing to himself. The man disappeared. He returned with an armload of rope ladder, the kind with wooden rungs often used to board the pilots. He balanced the ladder roll on the rail, preparing to let it unroll down the side of the ship. The sound of engines alerted them and they turned their heads to look. A *Motoscafo Armato Silurante* – motor torpedo boat of the Italian *Regia Marina* – had entered the Bay of Šibenik from Saint Anthony's channel, which connects this bay to the Adriatic sea. Throughout the day, two or three of these vessels might arrive to refuel and depart. They spotted his dinghy and altered course towards him. The Swede crouched out of sight behind the bulwark with his ladder when he saw the MTB approach. Reggie rowed towards the end of the mole, trying his best to appear as just another Yugoslav fisherman. *Brilliant. Neither one of us speaks Italian. What will happen if they demand to know why we're near the ship, and we cannot answer?*

The Italian idled past them only yards away at dead slow, its exhaust burbling, and the crew lined the foredeck to look them over. There was a click and a crackle of static from the boat's tannoy. An Italian deckhand frantically waved an arm at the bridge, and put a finger to his lips for silence. The tannoy clicked off. The MTB crew's attention was riveted on Pavlina: she lounged relaxed in the stern sheets, her bare legs hanging over the side. With her hands clasped behind her head, her eyes were shut and she lay open-mouthed, fast asleep. The MTB idled away to refuel. When the sound of its engines had faded to nothing, she sat up.

"Did you have a good nap?" he asked.

"I do not sleep, I only decoy them," she replied.

"You've been married only once?"

"Yes."

"How is it you know so much about how men will behave?"

"Is a gift," she said, and winked.

After they returned the dinghy, the fisherman refused to let them hire it again.

Spring was on its way. Buds had appeared on the trees, and the crocuses had bloomed. The temperatures in the night routinely dropped to the mid forties now, but only very rarely into the upper thirties. It rained less often now, too. A week ago a brief light spring snow had melted the moment it touched the ground.

Reggie relaxed on the bed with her dictionary to study it, and occasionally looked up to study her. She sat on a kitchen chair industriously blacking her boots to a brilliant shine. Absorbed in her task, she didn't notice him watching her. He was growing very content always being with her, and smiled.

One night in the middle of the third week of March near nine o'clock they met as usual, each sitting on their respective windowsills, to watch the changing of the guard. The sun had set at seven o'clock. The flood lamps at the end of the ship's booms were aimed back at the ship and illuminated the flags as usual. The lamp-posts along the promenade gave off their cheery glow. Soon the strolling couples melted into the alleyways. Again, as on every night, the *Kübelwagen* approached from the north to stop before the sentry box. A soldier climbed out and saluted the officer, the officer touching his cap with a swagger stick. The other soldier climbed in, and it motored away to the north. The helmeted soldier stood outside his sentry box and watched the car until it was out of sight. When he was certain it was indeed gone, not to return, he stepped into the sentry box for a moment and emerged bareheaded, then scrubbed his fingers briskly through his curly hair. Taking a *bustina* side cap from his epaulette he settled it on his head, tilting it rakishly to the side. Pavlina sat up, suddenly observant.

"Reggie," she called in a whisper, so her voice didn't carry, "the soldier, see his hat? Is not German." Reggie sat up. The man wore a grey-green uniform, a colour similar to the Germans, but his hat was definitely not German.

"So?"

"So he is Italian. I can get you on the ship now!"

"How do you figure? Nothing has changed except his nationality," he whispered.

"I have idea. Take all your things, we are leaving this room now. Make sure your pistol is loaded." Reggie busied himself gathering his clothes from the armoire, and things from the dresser, and laid them all out on the bed. He filled his shaving kit bag with his toiletries and his knife. He shrugged on his jacket and inserted each toggle through its loop. He put on his Astrakhan. When he went to get his trench coat it wasn't there. He turned to see Pavlina wearing his coat, as she snapped shut the latches on her suitcase. He could see she had left it belted behind her in the Norfolk style.

"Pavlina, I'll need my coat."

"No, you will not. Is mine now."

Hmm, that's true, I won't need it on the ship. "Keep it. Wear it in good health," he said, and smiled. Now he made a circuit of the flat checking for any forgotten items, closing the shutters and latching the windows. When he turned back around she was gone and the door stood open, and her suitcase was resting on the landing. She was already below in the foyer with her bicycle, and looked up.

"Hurry!" she whispered fiercely.

"Coming!" he said. He locked the door, picked up her suitcase, and chased after her. They went out the door at the rear, as the entrance door was boarded over because of its broken glass. She led him to the mouth of the alley where there was an iron bollard. Here she propped the bicycle on its stand back in the shadows, but facing back up the alley for a quick getaway, and he strapped her suitcase onto its luggage rack. Fiddle music came from The Anchor. This *konoba* had an entrance door in front opening out onto the promenade along the quay. Behind them it also had a side door that opened onto the alley in which they were standing. There was an obsolete third doorway, filthy and long disused, near the mouth of this alley and it was to this old door she guided him. The door itself was recessed nearly a yard into the limestone and there was an eight inch step for a threshold.

"Step up," she whispered. He dropped his kit bag in the corner, stepped up and shrank back into the shadow. Pavlina stepped up and stood facing him.

"How will I look?" she asked, holding open the coat to reveal she was wearing nothing but knee-high boots and panties. She wasn't even wearing that brassiere. On this chilly night there were tiny goose bumps on her bare skin, and the cold night air made her nipples stand erect. Reggie was speechless. This was a time to be truthful. He found his tongue.

"Pavlina, you look fucking gorgeous!"

"Good. That is my intent!"

"What are you going to do? Kill him with kindness?"

"You will see. If my plan fails, is *you* who will do the killing. Have you ever killed a man?"

"No."

"You maybe learn ... I think soon." Leaving the trench coat open, she hugged him and through his clothing he could feel every delicious curve of her body. He buried his nose in her hair for the wonderful scent of it. "Reggie," she breathed in his ear, "in case I die—we kiss now, yes?" They kissed, and for the first time quite passionately, and for a long time. Then they held each other a minute longer.

She stepped away. As she buttoned the coat she instructed him, "You stand here and not be seen. Stay in the shadow. I go now. You watch for me. Here you will see everything." She retreated up the alley, the way they'd entered it, and disappeared around the corner heading north. Reggie stood in shadow with his shoulder against the door jamb, where he could see the ship and the promenade to the north of it. Halfway between the mouth of this alley and the ship was a lamp-post, only one of many down the centre of the promenade. These lamp-posts were spaced some twenty-five yards apart. Interspersed between each of these grew a hardy palm tree, or rarely two together. The guard paced idly in front of the sentry box, his rifle slung on his shoulder. There were few people out at this time of night, but still, no one spoke to this guard; no one ever spoke to these guards.

It had been eight weeks since his instructor back in Egypt had taught him about safe weapon handling, but he well remembered the lesson to always carry it with the chamber empty. It had no holster. The danger here was, if the safety happened to be off, and the external hammer caught on his clothing as he put it in his pocket, he might accidentally shoot himself in the leg, or worse. Better to be safe than sorry! While he waited, he took the pistol from his pocket. Racking the slide to chamber the first round, he ever so slowly let the hammer down, then just as carefully slipped it back into his trouser pocket.

Ten minutes passed. He'd heard a gunshot, but it was from far away and couldn't possibly be related to Pavlina. Nonetheless, it was worrying. Then he caught sight of her: she was leaning against a lamp-post, the third lamp north of here, and facing the bay. The guard hadn't seen her.

Reggie jumped, startled, as he heard the fiddle get momentarily louder and the entrance door to the *konoba* slam. Two men, very drunk, staggered past the mouth of his alley going north. They wore oilskins, fisherman's rubber wellies, and hats similar to a trilby with the brim upturned all around. When they spied her, they stopped to talk but soon lurched away. This attracted the interest of the guard. Pavlina watched them go, then left the lamp-post and very casually strolled south, to stop and lean her back against the next lamp-post.

The guard stopped his pacing and lit a cigarette. As he smoked, he faced her with apparent interest but she never looked his way. From his hiding place Reggie saw a hunched old woman with a sack of groceries come into view, shuffling north. When she passed Pavlina, the woman turned and spat on the ground at her feet. Pavlina laughed at her, and made a rude gesture. They had words. Pavlina left the lamp-post and again strolled south. The old woman watched her go, spat again, then shuffled away to the north.

How intelligent, Reggie thought, *she's 'playing the prostitute' to put the guard at his ease until she can get close enough to do the deed. How very cunning of her.*

Now Pavlina was leaning her back on the lamp-post between Reggie and the ship, facing south and still ignoring the guard. The Italian guard finished his cigarette and lit another. He said something, and Pavlina appeared to notice him for the first time. He said it again. Pavlina unbuttoned the trench coat, pushed off the lamp-post, and turned towards the man. She opened the coat wide for a few seconds, then shut it, resuming her position against the lamp-post. The casual interest of the guard was instantly transmuted. He tossed away the cigarette he'd lit moments before and looked both north and south. He took the rifle off his shoulder and worked the bolt to chamber a round. Holding it in one hand, he strode towards Pavlina, still looking about to make sure he wasn't seen. When he arrived she held her hand up in a "stop" gesture, palm facing out and then, turning her hand palm up, she rubbed her fingertips together. No common language was necessary for this "oldest profession." The guard dug into his pockets and brought out money, which he gave to her. She counted it, nodded, then pocketed the money. The Swedish guard on the ship had taken an interest and leaned his arms on the rail to watch. Again, she held her hand up in a "stop" gesture. Pointing overhead at the lamp, which threw a bright pool of light around its pole, she turned and pointed directly at his dark alley. She took hold of the man's hand and led him to the alley. Reggie could see now she was smiling broadly for the Italian's benefit. *What an actress!*

He shrank back against the door and put his hand in his trouser pocket. As slowly as he could manage it, he eased the pistol out of his pocket and brushed off the safety with his thumb, then held the gun flat against his leg. Reggie fought to slow his breathing. He hoped the music from the *konoba* would mask the sound of his breathing, and held his left hand cupped over his mouth to help disperse the vapour of his breath so the Italian wouldn't see it.

When they reached the mouth of the alley, the Italian held his rifle pointed at her and reached out to squeeze the pockets of the trench coat, which she had left unbuttoned and hanging open. She extended each leg one at a time, and he ran his hand over her boots, feeling for hidden knives. He was young, appearing to be not more than the age of twenty, if that. She held her hands upraised for this search, on her face an expression of boredom as if she routinely submitted to such actions every day. When the Italian had found nothing suspicious about her, she pointed to the alley's far wall. The man got the point straight away, and this is where he leaned his rifle. *He found no weapons! How is she going to kill him? With his own rifle? That's impossible! Has she left it up to me?*

Pavlina perched her bum on top of the bollard, then leaned back to let the trench coat fall open, exposing her body completely to view. The pair of them were now little more than a yard away from him. The Italian licked his lips and looked her over. She thrust her upper body forward and rocked from side to side to make her breasts sway invitingly. She cupped a hand under each boob, lifted, then released to let them bounce. She tilted her head back and, with eyes half-lidded in seeming desire, parted her lips and licked them. The man bit his lower lip and whimpered with eagerness. Stepping back, he glanced both north and south along the quay again whilst fumbling to unbuckle his belt, then opened his trousers and quickly pushed them down to his knees. Now she spread her feet further apart, and clearly this was done to allow the man to enter her all the more easily. She leaned back, putting both hands on the bollard behind her for more support. The man's hands were now on her panties, about to take them down. Alarmed, Reggie thought: *No! Surely she doesn't intend to bribe the man with sex just to get me on that ship! I can't let that happen, not to her! Nothing was worth that price.*

His mind was made up: he would take one step out, press his pistol against the man's head, and pull the trigger. In his mind he could see every movement he would need to make, as if he'd already made it. *This* was the moment! He would do this *now*! As he stepped down off the threshold, her hands came up and pressed the bicycle pump under the man's chin. There was a soft sound – *Phut* – and the man's cap flew off. He slithered to the pavement in a heap. He emitted a gurgling exhalation, and lay still. His eyes and mouth were wide open and he stared vacantly at the sky. Pavlina's behaviour changed in an instant. Dropping the pump into her pocket, she squatted beside the body. Seizing a handful of his genitals she yanked skyward with a viciousness that, had he been alive, would have made him scream.

"Give me your knife! I will geld this fascist swine," she exploded. A pool of blood, black in the dim light of the distant lamp, began to spread from his head. Reggie froze, rooted to the spot. *How had she killed him with a bicycle pump?* She looked up at him, her eyes aflame with anger, "Knife! Now!" she said, fiercely. Reggie set his pistol's safety and carefully pocketed it. He reached for the knife on his left hip, but it wasn't there. *Oh, yes, I put it in my shaving bag.*

"Pavlina, don't. It's wrong to desecrate a corpse!"

"He deserve it!"

"Why do it at all? He's dead!"

"I do for terror. Is sending the message, and the bloody fascist beasts will think again before invading my country!"

"But don't you see?" he pleaded, "If you do, they'll look for you. If we just place his rifle under his chin, they'll think he's a suicide, and no one will look for you."

She thought for only a moment. "Good idea. Do it!" She let the man go, wiping the urine from her hand on the inside of his trousers. They straightened the body's legs, pulled the trousers up and buckled the belt. Reggie retrieved the Carcano rifle and laid it atop the body, the muzzle under the man's chin, and inserted the thumb into the trigger guard. They stood a few seconds more as they regarded the corpse, until she said quietly, "Rados is avenged!" Suddenly, with a look of shock she gripped Reggie's arm and shook it.

"The bullet in his gun is not fired! They will know!" she whispered.

"We can only hope they won't notice—I really must go now!" he replied, urgently. At the darkened far end of the alley a rectangle of light briefly appeared on the wall and a door slammed. A man stepped into the alley from the side door of the *konoba* and began to walk unsteadily towards them in the dark. He stumbled into her bicycle, and it tipped against the wall. He set it upright again and stood looking at it stupidly. While he was distracted Reggie and Pavlina stepped up into the shadowed doorway.

"Give me that gun of yours," he whispered to her.

"Is no more bullets. Use your knife," she whispered in reply.

"I can't. It's packed away in my bag."

"You have your pistol, yes?" He could dimly see the whites of her eyes, now wide with fear.

"Yes, but if I fire it, that'll attract attention. You be quiet," he said, putting a finger to her lips, "Stay here, I'll handle this." *How will I handle this? What do I do now?*

The man, possibly a fisherman or some such because he wore rubber wellies, a black pork pie hat, and rough work clothes, now left the bicycle and approached but stopped when he saw the body. He shuffled forwards and bent to view it. Straightening, he looked about to assure himself he wasn't being observed, but didn't see them in the dark doorway. The *konoba* side door slammed again and three men emerged, laughing. The fisherman stayed absolutely still, but the three went the other way up the alley and disappeared around the corner. Now he knelt beside the body. Looking at the Italian's face, the staring eyes, he gave a visible shudder, then reached out to close the eyelids. His hands together, he bowed his head and murmured a prayer. When the prayer was finished he crossed himself.

First, he picked up the Carcano and leaned the rifle against the alley's far wall. He began to search through the pockets of the dead man's tunic. Out came a wallet, and from this he pocketed a wad of Italian *lira* notes, then replaced the wallet. Next he found a book of matches and three packs of cigarettes, one of which was open. He pocketed the unopened packs. Reggie stepped down off the threshold. Engrossed in his task, the man didn't notice him. Reggie gave a cough. Startled, the man sprang up, a fist drawn back ready to throw a punch, but relaxed when he saw Reggie was just another Croat, and one that looked vaguely familiar, as they'd seen each other elsewhere in the city. He shook a cigarette from the pack and offered it to Reggie. *What's that word for 'no' again?*

"*Ne*," Reggie said, waving a hand. The man put it to his lips, struck a match and puffed it alight, then exhaled. The man began a conversation in Croatian as he enjoyed his cigarette. He gestured to the body, laughing, and pointed to the sentry box. Reggie put his hands in his pockets and stood relaxed, and chuckled right along with him, nodding in agreement to whatever was being said. Soon the man's sentences had a rising inflection at the end, and Reggie realized he must be asking a question, but he hadn't a clue of how to answer. *Hmm ... I don't know enough Croatian to fool him. I'll just have to try English.*

"Leave the rifle here. You must go home now. You haven't seen any of this," he said, and pointed towards the promenade. The man peered closely at his face, then, pointing back and forth between Reggie and the corpse, he laughed. Putting out his hand he pumped Reggie's hand in congratulations for a job well done. *Blimey, he now knows I'm British, but obviously doesn't care. He's assuming I killed this fellow.*

The man stood silently smoking for many minutes until he finished his cigarette but made no attempt to leave, or indeed, talk to him again. Reggie's mind was not still; it rapidly went over his options. *I can't let him see Pavlina—if he's seen that reward poster, that'll put her in danger. The longer we stand here, the more likely we'll be discovered. He needs to leave, and soon. Somehow, I must make him want to leave of his own accord. There's nothing for it but to order him to leave, but English didn't do the trick. He likely doesn't know any English. I'll need to do it in German. Does he know German? Even if he doesn't, surely he's heard enough of it to recognize it when he hears it. What if he makes a play for the rifle? I should be ready for him if he does. If he doesn't, I also can't shoot down an innocent man in cold blood—that would be despicable! But, in any case, I should be ready for whatever happens.*

The Croat dropped the butt on the ground and stepped on it, then squatted on his heels again to continue his search through the pockets. Now he found a photograph of a smiling young woman who, ankles crossed, leaned against an automobile, her wide hips perched on the boot. After holding this up to the light for a moment it was discarded. The Italian's watch was removed, examined front and back, then the

Croat strapped it on his own wrist. He stood and without warning pivoted to retrieve the rifle from where it leaned. Holding it up to the dim light of the street lamp, he chuckled softly to himself as he examined this prize, caressing the polished wood of the stock.

Now Reggie drew out the pistol from his pocket and used it to wave the man away, towards the promenade, at the same time repeating what he had said before, but in German this time: "Lass das Gewehr hier. Du musst jetzt nach Hause gehen. Sie haben nichts davon gesehen."

The blood drained from the man's face. He raised his hands above his shoulders and began to blubber, the tears rolling down his cheeks as he pleaded for his life. He still held the rifle by its barrel and, realizing this, let it go as if it burnt his hand. When the rifle butt hit the ground it fired, the sound deafening between these close-set buildings. The fiddle music from the *konoba* screeched to a stop. Reggie quickly grabbed the man by the coveralls and propelled him bodily out the mouth of the alley. The man stumbled out, arms flailing, then ran away in a blind panic expecting with every step to be shot in the back.

"Nach Hause gehen!" Reggie shouted after him. From her hiding place he heard Pavlina shout, "*Odlazi! Micati!*" – Go away! Move!

Pavlina burst forth and ran to her bicycle. Reggie pocketed his pistol, then replaced the rifle on the body, not forgetting to replace the thumb in the trigger guard. Snatching up his shaving kit from the doorstep, he ran straight for the ship. She pedalled rapidly past him on her bicycle, the open trench coat flapping behind her like a cape. He paused in the sentry box for a few seconds, to print "Leif Magnuson, Kapitän" at the bottom of the list of names on the clipboard. Behind him, Pavlina took a wide circling path, gaining speed, to align the bicycle with the gangplank. When she hit it, the bicycle's momentum stalled and she dismounted. He chased after her and helped push it up, yelling "L-M! L-M!" to avoid being shot. The guard held his fire, unwilling to shoot a naked woman. They both collapsed on the deck behind the bulwark, out of breath. The guard shaded his eyes against the glare of the flood lamp and looked all about. The promenade was empty. The Swede helped them to their feet. Pavlina propped the bicycle against the bridge house and took down the suitcase from it. She buttoned the trench coat as Reggie made the introductions.

"Captain Leif Magnuson. Pleased to meet you, sir." He produced his fake Swedish passport to show the man.

"Arne Thorsson." They shook hands.

"This is Miss ... Pavlina, of the Yugoslav Government. She'll be leaving again, just as soon as she can dress." *That's innocuous enough. I won't mention 'Buga' because they might have seen that poster.*

Thorsson shook her hand too, then turned and yelled something at an open doorway. A man appeared from inside, to lead them up a long stairway to a door near the top of the bridge, then down a corridor to a stateroom. This turned out to be the captain's quarters. He didn't speak English, and left them alone. After the door was shut behind them, she locked it, then went to the head and rinsed her hands. He put her suitcase on the desk he found there, swept off his Astrakhan and threw it and his kit bag on the bed, then followed her in.

"Buga Pavlina, I was under the impression you were going home!" he admonished in a mock scolding tone, as she dried her hands on a towel.

"Reginald Wallace, the keys to the flat are in your pocket!" He patted his pockets and it was true. They returned to the room.

"How on earth did you kill him with a bicycle pump?" he asked, incredulous. Without a word, she shed her trench coat and turned her back to him. Taking the pump from the coat pocket, she reached behind her and tucked the bicycle pump behind the elastic of her knickers, where it protruded and was held centred between the cheeks of her bum. She turned to face him, holding up her hands as if in surrender to show him they were empty. Reaching behind her then, in the blink of an eye the pump was at his chin. She gave it to him and began to clothe herself, first fastening her brassiere.

"Is not a pump," she explained, "Is silencer from ČZ-27 pistol. I stab Czechoslovakian secret policeman to get this. For many months I use his pistol to kill, but is difficult to conceal." He turned it end for end and examined it: a nine-inch long black cylinder one-and-a-quarter inches in diameter. The aiming sights at each end had been filed off. There was a short pistol barrel at one end held on by a knurled knob, and this barrel also had a shorter knurled knob at its outer end. There was no pistol grip, nor any trigger. It did indeed look similar to a common bicycle pump.

"Then, in window of antique shop I see 1910 'Frommer Stop' pistol from Hungary. Is broken and not working. I take this to machinist — he save only the barrel and bolt and spring, and he throw all the rest away. He makes this barrel short to fit this silencer, then makes the thumb-slide to strike the firing pin." She fluffed her hair out after pulling an emerald green knee-length dress over her head. Sitting on the bed she lay back and raised her legs for him. He obliged by handing her the gun, then tugged off each boot, laying them on the bed. He opened the suitcase and slipped her shoes onto each foot, then helped her stand. Holding the barrel end uppermost she slid the thumb striker back, showing the open underside of the barrel to him.

"See firing pin? See spring?" He nodded. She released the slide, letting it snap the firing pin against the spent cartridge. "Now is hidden in plain sight. No one suspects!"

"This is so very clever. Whitehall should see this!"

"Who is Whitehall?" she asked, puzzled.

"It isn't 'who' — it's 'what'. Whitehall is a shortened name we call the British government."

"Oh. This one time I go to Gestapo building, act like grieving wife to ask for 'husband' to be released. In office behind closed doors I plead, with much tears. The SS Officer tells them 'do not disturb us' – he plan to rape me, you see. I shoot his head. Then I take his boots – *these* boots – and escape from window. It shoots one bullet, very silent. There is no safety – is dangerous!" As she spoke, she gripped the small knurled end of the bolt and pulled it back. The empty shell casing fell out, and he bent to scoop it up. Digging a small canvas drawstring bag from the suitcase, she selected a cartridge and inserted it, pushing the bolt home until it rotated and clicked into place.

"Is loaded. Give me room keys. I will go now." He handed them over, and she pocketed them and her improvised gun. She packed her boots into the suitcase and snapped it shut. They exited the cabin and she followed him down the corridor. He opened the outer door to find a different Swede climbing the stair and nearly at the landing. His hair was blond, not tow-headed like a child but tending on the red side.

"Hello, Captain Magnuson," he said, "My name is Frederik. I'm the—"

"You speak English," he said in surprise.

"Some of us do," the man replied, irritated, "Come with me." Reggie took a step out, but then felt a tug on the hem of his jacket.

"Wait just a moment, please. I think I've forgotten something," he said, looking down and patting his trouser pockets. He shut the door, then turned to her.

"Pavlina, I never thought ... it would be this ... difficult to —" he swallowed the lump in his throat. *In minutes she'll be gone and I'll never see her again.*

"I know, Réži, I know," she purred. "In the past month I think you to be a *good* man, ... an *honourable* man. I wish we —"

"Stop! Stop, you're making it worse!" he choked out. Then they were in each other's arms, kissing passionately as they fell against the wall. Her hand gripped his buttock as she pressed herself against him, her other hand caressing the back of his head. *I've never in my life kissed anybody who has lips as soft as hers. She kisses wonderfully!*

They held each other, making the moment last as long as possible, neither wanting to be the first to let go but finally, it was time. They straightened their clothing. He picked up her suitcase and opened the door for her. The Swede uncrossed his arms and pushed off the rail.

"Mind the stair, Miss, you may find it steep," Frederik said, "and hold tight to the handrail please." Reggie shouldered her suitcase and, bringing up the rear, followed them down the exterior stairway fixed to the after side of the bridge house. A handful of crewmen stood clustered at the foot of the stair and parted to make way for them. Reggie strapped down the suitcase on the bicycle luggage rack while Pavlina inserted the 'bicycle pump' into its holder on the frame. Frederik led her back to the open bulwark gate then stood aside to allow her bicycle to pass. Pavlina shaded her eyes against the glare of the flood lamp to locate the beginning of the gangplank, but suddenly stepped back, bumping into Reggie.

"What – ?"

"Shh!" she shushed him, and pointed. "Look there!" she whispered. An armed Italian stood at the sentry box below. He hadn't looked up. They shrank back out of sight. Across the promenade stood a long, four-door, black Fiat limousine, its boot lid open. Three Bersaglieri officers struggled to fold the body of the dead man into the boot. A small group of civilians holding glasses of beer stood clustered at the open *konoba* entrance and watched from a distance. The music could be heard again, but was now an accordion.

"Bloody hell," Reggie whispered, "They weren't supposed to discover the body until three o'clock. You can't leave now," he said to her. Frederik plucked out his pocket watch and looked at it.

"It's late. Go to your quarters and we'll have a meeting in the morning. I'll arrange a cabin for you, Miss."

"Is no need to do. I sleep with the captain," she responded, without a trace of embarrassment.

"Oh. ... I'll say goodnight, then."

12

"Not So Easy As Described, Eh?"

The meeting was at 0830 hours, after everyone had breakfasted. Reggie finally was able to shave, and this was a good thing because he was uncomfortable having a beard and had found it to be itchy. He dressed in one of the former Swedish captain's uniforms. Söderberg's clothes nearly fit him, just a little tight in places. The man must have been thinner. The man's shoes didn't fit, so he wore his own second-hand shoes. This made him "out of uniform" but he didn't care.

The officer's saloon was cheery, panelled in mahogany and teak, and had an actual fireplace. But that was unlit. Less cheery was the small crew. They were sullen and depressed, having been here a long time, and many had let themselves go. One man sat in the corner and the others avoided him, because he exuded a foul stench of body odour. Reggie stood and addressed himself to a standing Frederik, in English, while the rest of the crew sat and listened.

"This is Miss Pavlina, of the Yugoslav Government. I'm Captain Leif Magnuson, and I've been sent by the British to get this ship out to safety, on behalf of the Swedish Government." Today Frederik had an unlit pipe clamped between his teeth, and now he took it out and pointed the stem toward Reggie.

"Then you had better learn how to say it properly: it isn't 'Leaf', it's pronounced 'Lafe'." He waved his pipe at the people in the room. "These are our laundryman, our cook, and all the stewards and deckhands." He pointed to each man and announced his given name.

"Thank you. I was told your captain was murdered, and that's terrible, but where are all your other officers?"

"You were misinformed. All of them were murdered. Probably by the *Ustaše*, but we don't know for certain." Frederik responded.

"All of them?!" he said, shocked.

"Yes, every one: the captain and mates, the engineers, our radio officer, all dead. All but me; I'm the second engineer."

"Well, that's something."

"Yes, isn't it," he sneered, sarcastically. "We're not allowed off the ship by that guard down there."

"Don't you worry," Reggie announced to the room, "I'll have to teach you how to do the things necessary to get us underway, but we'll do it. I'll have you out of here and on your way to Sweden within a week!" He expected a reaction to this news, if not a cheer, then at least some applause. The crew sat silent, morose. The only woman, a cook with black hair similar to Pavlina's began to cry, and Pavlina went to comfort her. The ill-smelling man in the corner snorted in derision.

Frederik had more to say. "It isn't only that we don't know how to navigate the ship; over many months we've had to run the oil engines daily for a few hours, and do this to heat the living quarters, keep the lights on, heat our water for bathing and laundry, do the cooking and washing-up, and run the refrigeration and freezers for our food. This has depleted our fuel supply so much so, that we now have only enough fuel to reach perhaps the Greek island of Corfu 300 nautical miles away, and that's occupied."

"So, what's the problem? Can you not buy more fuel here?"

"At the time we delivered our cargo of locomotives onto the tracks in the nearby Baldekin neighbourhood, we also delivered a cargo of railway diesel to run them. In hindsight, had we known what would happen, we could have retained it for our own use."

"But you were paid for that fuel, right?"

"Yes, in cash. They do not use credit here during wartime. We then ordered fuel for the ship; Marine Bunker-C."

"And it wasn't delivered?"

"The harbourmaster is refusing to bunker the ship without payment in Croatian Kuna only. Captain Söderberg put the payment for locomotive diesel in the ship's safe before he was killed, and none of us knows the combination. We've all tried many times unsuccessfully. It's very frustrating. Jules had moved the ship here to this quay, and here we sit, since April of last year. Each month that goes by, the port taxes owed just get higher, too."

"Port taxes? Why not anchor out?"

"If we were to leave the seawall of the quay to anchor out, the harbourmaster would refuse us permission to return until we pay the port tax owed. As long as we remain moored to this quay, we are assured our position here. Also, we are visited once a month by the *Svenska Röda Korset*, that's the Swedish Red Cross to you. They provide us with a month's worth of food, via the gangplank, but it often doesn't last a month, and it must be rationed."

"Well, could the Swedish Red Cross bring in enough money to bunker the ship?"

"Alas, they're prohibited from doing that very thing, because the Nazis will confiscate the money, and yes, they are searched thoroughly."

"How much kuna do you need?" Reggie asked. The reply was not encouraging. "That's much more than I have with me now." He sat and thought this information over. A minute passed. A few crewmen got up and wandered out of the room. Frederik asked if the meeting was finished.

"Yes. Give me some time to suss out all these problems, and I'll get back to you. I'll be in Captain Söderberg's office going over his logs." The crewmembers drifted away to various parts of the ship. They each had their own space, to keep from getting on each other's nerves. Pavlina went with the female cook to the galley to help her prepare lunch, as the galley had a difficult to use oil-burning grill and oven. Before Reggie went to the office he put on old Captain Söderberg's white peaked cap, now his, and walked the ship's main deck for awhile, thinking. He started at the forecastle and worked his way to the stern. The ship was held off the quay by a half-dozen worn-out tractor tyres acting as "fenders" hanging by lines cleated to the ship.

There were the three large hatchcovers over each hold, each seventy-five feet long by twenty-five feet wide. Each had its own 100 ton heavy lift crane, and there were smaller five ton derricks in multiple locations. Aft of the third hatch and its crane was the single funnel atop the engine room house along with the two lifeboats. He glanced down into the engine room to see the two massive diesels. He went to the fantail, then started forwards again.

In between hatch numbers one and two there was the five-storey tall bridge, quite narrow, only fifteen feet fore-and-aft. On the aft side of this bridge house there was an exterior stair rising up from starboard to port, and at each level this had a landing, with a door into the interior. He'd never seen a ship like this one, but knew instinctively what he'd find inside. Each level would have a corridor just inside the door, and this would be the width of the house, and the cabin doors would open off the forward side of this corridor. As he climbed the stair he looked inside each level.

At the top, naturally, was the navigation bridge, chart room, and wireless room. Below this were his quarters and those of his missing officers. The next level down were the crew's cabins. Then came the officer's wardroom, or "saloon" as it was known, and opposite the galley in the centre, the plainly furnished crew's mess. Here also was where the gangplank was swivelled at ship side. Finally, at main deck level was the deck equipment storerooms, walk-in refrigerators and freezers, and the large pantry.

He was dismayed to see the filthy condition of the exterior decks and deckhouse. Coils of line and minor pieces of equipment and tools had been left where they were last used, or just dropped. A hardened paintbrush was stuck to the deck, so he pitched it overboard. He could tell which cabin was occupied by whether its porthole had been cleaned. The ship's antenna now lay across hatch covers two and three. He examined it: the antenna had two parallel wires attached to triangular yokes at each end, and these yokes were usually shackled to the masts atop the cranes. The forward yoke or shackle had broken away due to metal fatigue, and no one had had the ability, or the desire, to climb the mast and reattach it. All this pointed to one thing: his main problem was the dispirited crew. He had to get them motivated again, but how?

Someone forward rang a handbell, the signal he'd been told meant come to eat, and so he went. In the officer's saloon he sat with Second Engineer Frederik. The meal sustained him but wasn't appetizing in the least, being a meatless watery soup of parsnips, rutabagas and carrots. There were savoury biscuits for the soup but they were stale. He ate them anyway. For pudding, each had half an orange, this to prevent scurvy. There was tea, the only bright note.

Reggie finished up, and retreated to his cabin below the navigation bridge to go over the logbooks. They were in Swedish and Frederik read certain bits to him. Nothing stood out. It was all rather dry. Frederik did give him a handy warning, though: "The rudder on this ship is undersized, and she steers like a pig." He thanked him and dismissed the man, then rolled out a chart of the Adriatic. Nothing problematic caught his eye. After an hour of such endeavours, he stood and stretched and wandered to the shoreside porthole to look out. There was the guard at the sentry box, a German. There was The Anchor *konoba* across the way. He certainly was thirsty. He sure could use a beer right about now. He went below to the galley where the steward was tidying up. Pavlina was there helping the cook, whose name turned out to be Annika, and introduced her.

"Annika, do you speak Serbo-Croatian?"

"No sir. Swedish and English." Reggie asked them both to come with him to Annika's cabin. He asked to see Annika's passport, and he and Pavlina examined it.

"Do you think," he asked Pavlina, "you could make yourself up sufficiently to pass yourself off as Annika?"

"Maybe I can try this. Annika wears the red lipstick, but this I never do."

"I'll show you how," Annika replied, helpfully.

"Good. Try to make her look as German as you can with whatever clothes you have. Pavlina, meet me at the gangplank in half an hour, and carry this passport. Annika, stay out of sight until we return. We must make them believe there's only one woman aboard who has black hair." She agreed.

Half an hour later on the deck outside the galley, Reggie explained the plan. Pavlina now looked remarkably similar to Annika. The red lipstick was quite becoming. He advised her to say nothing and, since she spoke no German, discussed any non-verbal cues he would give her. He had with him two clean metal buckets of four gallons each procured from a steward, and these he gave to her. In various of his coat pockets he had put identical amounts of Croatian kuna, to be brought out as needed. The two went down the gangplank and approached the sentry, a young lad barely into his eighteenth year. Pavlina set one of the buckets down. Reggie was looking rather impressive wearing

Söderberg's dress-blue captain's uniform with its gold stripes on its sleeves, and brass buttons, and white peaked cap, he hoped impressive enough to intimidate the young man. He saluted the *Soldat* and spoke to him in German.

"Good afternoon. I am Captain Magnuson. This is Annika, my cook. Might I have a word?" The Private checked his clipboard and said yes, I'm listening.

"We Swedes and you Germans are not so different after all, isn't this true?"

Ye-e-es?" the boy answered, warily.

"We both like our beer, isn't this right?"

"You are not allowed off the ship, Captain."

"My sailors are very thirsty. They have not had beer for many months. As a German, I'm certain you can see what a hardship this is for them."

"So?" he smirked, "My orders are clear."

"Absolutely, and I would not want you to disobey your orders, just as I will not allow my men to do the same." He kept his voice sounding official. "I'm not suggesting we be allowed off the ship, Private. I was only thinking you like your beer but you are unfortunately being paid in reichmarks, and these Croats will not sell you a litre unless you give them kuna." The *Soldat* nodded knowingly.

"You can send your reichmarks home to your mother, but that doesn't do you much good out here in this hell-hole of a country, am I right?" Again he nodded, thoughtfully.

"So, I have a proposal to put to you: each day at a certain hour – say, noon – my cook Annika here will cross to the *konoba* for only twenty minutes, to have one bucket filled with beer. She will bring the bucket back here, and pour the beer into the other bucket, so you can see there's nothing hidden in either bucket." He pointed at the *konoba*. At this, Pavlina held up an empty bucket and slapped its bottom. It sounded a hollow metallic thump. She set it down.

"You —" the *Soldat* said. Reggie held up a hand to forestall the interruption, but kept his eyes on the lad.

"Annika?" he prompted. Pavlina produced from the other bucket a handsome and very heavy litre glass, the word "OSLO" etched upon it. "Annika here will give you this glass, a gift for you to keep, and she will fill it with beer every day, and it will taste wonderful with your sandwich." The Private looked thirstily at the glass.

"But —" he began. Reggie held up a hand again.

"I haven't quite finished." He fished a wad of kuna notes from his coat pocket and held it up. "This is enough kuna to buy fifteen beers. We will give this same amount to you every week on Friday. You can treat your comrades at the weekend. In your barracks, think how popular a fellow you will be! This applies to whichever of your comrades happens to be here," said Reggie, "and as a captain in the Royal Swedish Navy I promise you, your superiors will never hear of this." He held the money out. "Agreed?" The *Soldat* looked at a smiling Pavlina and, all on her own, she displayed the glass with both hands and swayed her hips to convey the impression the lad was already at *Oktoberfest* accepting a *Bier* from a pretty *mädchen*. He looked down at the buckets, and finally over at the *konoba*.

"Eleven o'clock. Make it eleven," the lad nodded, "and I keep her passport until she returns." He collected the notes and passport, Pavlina handed him the glass, and she trotted off with one bucket to the *konoba*. Reggie saluted the lad, then climbed the gangplank to the ship. In the galley a half hour later, Pavlina and Annika set out glasses on a table holding the full bucket while Reggie vigorously rang the handbell out in the corridor. Confused crewmen appeared, for hadn't they just eaten? Reggie made the announcement loud and clear.

"Each of you will be getting a litre of beer with your lunch every day, *provided*," he warned, "the decks and portholes are clean, the equipment and lines stowed properly, and we start behaving like sailors again. Lindgren, take a shower. Now, break out the fire hoses and let's get this vessel ship-shape." Pavlina and Annika began to dip each glass in the bucket and hand them out. In coming days, Reggie doled out more kuna, negotiating to allow another crewman to make a weekly trip to the Saturday market, to bring back fresh foods. Reggie used one of the flag halyards to stretch the radio antenna to the foremast again.

"Reggie, do you remember the time you ask me for the radio?" Pavlina asked the Sunday morning following their arrival on board.

"Yes, and you didn't have one. But, I've already looked over this ship's apparatus, and it's not powerful enough to reach Cairo."

"If the radio works, I know the frequency to reach the partisans," she said. They went up to the wireless room on the bridge. Pavlina sat in the chair at the transmitting set. The controls were all in Swedish. Reggie found the operating manual, which fortunately had sections in multiple languages. He switched on the power, and they waited while the set warmed up.

"I think we're in business, fingers crossed." He dragged the other chair over and sat.

"Reggie, here is the Morse key. Is best to send this in a cipher, but we have not the proper cipher to use."

"We'll need to send it out by voice then, and just keep the message short."

"Yes. We send the message to the partisans, and ask them to send it to Cairo in a cipher, yes?"

"Agreed. They'll have the more powerful transmitter."

"What is it you want to say?" She adjusted the microphone.

"Let's write this down." He dragged a small pad of paper over for her to use. "First, we tell them all the officers are dead — no, scratch that." He thought a moment. "First, tell them 'the hedgehog has burrowed' and is safe with Buga."

"You make the joke? Is not funny."

"No, 'the hedgehog' is me. It only means I'm here on the ship now. Don't worry, they'll understand." Pavlina wrote this down. He spoke slowly, choosing his words carefully, until the message was finished, short and concise, and in Croatian. "I think that's it. Must keep the message short. Anything longer than a minute and the Nazis will get a directional fix on us. We don't want to let them know it's us talking to their enemies." After a few minutes the speaker emitted a low hum. Reggie lifted the lid of the transmitter to see all the valves giving off a mellow orange glow. Pavlina tuned the transmitter to the partisan frequency and took hold of the mike. Pressing the button, she spoke in Croatian, and released it.

"*Buga zove, preko vas.*" They waited. Fifteen seconds passed.

"*Buga zove, preko vas.*" They waited. Ten more seconds passed. Then ten more.

"*Veljko, Buga. Preko vas,*" the speaker emitted. She smiled at this and sat forwards.

"*Veljko? To je Buga!*" She spoke a string of Croatian, smiling and laughing. Reggie shook her shoulder.

"The message, keep it short!" She nodded and became serious.

"*Veljko,*" She followed this up in Croatian sentences, within which the only words Reggie could understand were 'Cairo' and 'kuna'.

"*Veljko za Buga. Prenijet ću poruku,*" the speaker emitted and then fell silent. She smiled and sat back.

"Pavlina, you sounded happy. Who was that man?"

"Is Sergeant Veljko Dragićević. He is Chetnik radio operator and my friend."

"Chetnik!" Reggie was stunned. Pavlina was blasé.

"Yes, Veljko Dragićević now is partisan radio operator. He switch sides in war as some do. Now we wait for the response. He will call this time tomorrow, or maybe next day." Reggie could only wonder at the complexity of all these political factions. He could only guess at how they kept track of it all.

* * *

"Featherstone, come with me!" General Stone barked, as he leaned in the anteroom door, "I've a meeting with Stirling in a minute." As they strode down the hallway the general explained: "Stirling tells me the coded message we were expecting five weeks ago from Marko finally came in today, and I think you're going to want to hear this." They entered Stirling's office and sat in a semicircle of chairs around his desk. There was another man there who was introduced as Carruthers, the BHQ(ME) radio officer. Fitzroy Maclean was there as well. His ginger hair reminded Milly of Reggie, though it was not as wavy. The small room was crowded.

"Ah, here you are. We can start," Stirling said. "Gentlemen, ... and lady: 'The hedgehog has burrowed'!"

"What a relief." Stone said.

"It's about time," said Fitzroy Maclean, "If it was me, I'd —"

"Fitz, enough!" Stirling barked. "Carruthers here tells me it came in but a moment ago."

"Yes," said Carruthers, "But there's a problem: it didn't come from Marko. It was sent to us from Sergeant Veljko Dragićević."

"Good lord, that man's a bloody Chetnik!" Fitz erupted, dismayed.

"What is Reggie doing in the Chetnik camp?" asked Stone, "That's extremely dangerous. Is he their prisoner?"

"We honestly don't know." Stirling conceded. "Sergeant Veljko works for Serbian Brigade General Dragoljub 'Draža' Mihailović.

The latest intelligence we have tells us this Draža fellow has been collaborating with the Germans." Milly's head had been swivelling around to follow each speaker. She spoke up.

"I haven't been kept informed all these weeks. Could Mr Carruthers read out the message directly, please?"

"Yes, yes, of course. Carruthers?" Stirling prompted. The man lifted the message from the desk and read aloud.

"Message begins: THE HEDGEHOG HAS BURROWED WITH BUGA. HAVE NOT ENOUGH FUEL. HARBOURMASTER REFUSES TO SELL US MORE. WILL NOT ACCEPT CREDIT OR FOREIGN CURRENCY. KUNA ONLY. PORT TAXES OWED GETTING HIGHER EVERY MONTH. ALL THE LICENSED OFFICERS ASSASSINATED. MARKO A NO-SHOW. Message ends." The group erupted with many questions all at once.

"What is 'kuna'?"

"The officers are dead?"

"Is 'buga' a mistake in transmission?"

"Sounds to me like he's on the ship."

"Where in blazes is Marko?"

"Gentlemen, gentlemen, *please*, one at a time!" Stirling commanded. The room fell silent. "I can fill you in on many of these. We have learnt 'kuna' is the newly established currency they now use up that way. He mentioned the officers are dead and the fuel situation, and this leads us to believe he's on the ship. The word 'burrowed' would seem to confirm this."

"Marko has always gone his own way," Stone remarked, "and we've always overlooked this flaw, but only because he's fluent in the language."

"I'm fluent in the language," Fitz carped.

"We know, as you've reminded us many times," Stirling replied wearily, "As for that word buga, we've no idea. Frankly, we're stumped. It isn't in our Serbo-Croatian dictionary."

"I know!" Sir Fitzroy Maclean stood and stepped to the desk, into the centre of the gathering. The group's attention was on him now. He withdrew a paper folded into quarters from inside his tunic, and smoothed it out on the desk while the others stood to gather around. "This was smuggled out to us." The Nazi poster showed 'Buga' to be a partisan.

Stirling looked down on Fitz from his greater height. "Smuggled out to *you*," he observed. "Had you any intention of giving this to me? If you persist in not being a team player, you'll always be a Lance-corporal, understood?"

"The leader of the partisans," Fitz said, seething, all but gritting his teeth, "is said to be called 'Tito'. My sources tell me little is known of who – or what – this name stands for. It's been rumoured variously it's the *nom de guerre* of a man, or that it's not an individual at all but someone appointed or nominated to a post by a committee that's known as *Tajna Internationalna Teroristička Organizacija*, which means 'Secret International Terrorist Organization'." Fitzroy looked around at the group, relishing the attention directed his way. "Some claim Tito is not a man at all, but a young woman of startling beauty and great force of character. The truth is, we really don't know, and have no way of confirming or disproving any of this." When he finished his monologue there was a moment of silence, broken by the major.

"*Your* sources," Stirling sneered. "Thank you, Lance-corporal Maclean, I'll take this now."

Milly stood on tiptoe. "Sir, take the poster," she whispered in General Stone's ear.

"Thank you, David," Stone objected, "but I'd like to review this document, if I may."

"As you wish, Bob. Meeting adjourned." As the men filed out preceded by Milly, Stirling detained Carruthers. "I'll need you to stay. We've a reply to compose."

In General Stone's office, Milly asked to see the poster again. They unfolded it on his desk.

"What do you see?" she asked. Stone tilted his head this way and that, and shrugged.

"What should I see?" he queried. Milly covered the man's beard and hair with each hand. Stone's jaw dropped.

"Good Lord! He's a woman!"

"And my Reggie has 'burrowed' with her," Milly said, with a pout.

"Miss Featherstone, I can assure you it's only a code-word. Please take this to David and let him know of your discovery."

* * *

The following morning at ten o'clock, a Monday, Pavlina and Reggie sat in the wireless room again, and listened for any reply. It did not come. The next morning at the same time, they sat in the wireless room once again, and listened for any reply. The speaker emitted its steady low hum but still, it did not come. Reggie lifted the lid on the receiver to look. All the valves gave off their cheery orange glow, except one was dark. He searched through the stock of spares in the drawers but there wasn't a replacement for the type. The radio's instruction manual seemed to indicate they could transmit, but not receive. Pavlina sent this sad news out to Sergeant Veljko 'blind' and they shut down the station.

Reggie was disappointed but Pavlina was heartsick, having heard the voice of her good friend Veljko only to have him disappear into the ether, gone. Reggie told her he would do the "beer run" at eleven o'clock in her stead, if the guard allowed. At the top of the gangplank Reggie greeted Jens Ivarsson who was now standing guard duty at the machine gun. At the sentry box he explained to the German guard that "Annika" was feeling ill. The guard, the very same he had made the agreement with, was not only amenable but also thirsty, so Reggie handed over his passport and walked over to The Anchor and entered, bucket in hand. He leaned on the counter and watched as the barman filled it. He laid the usual amount of kuna on the bar and, hoisting the bucket, turned to go.

On his way to the door he spied a familiar face at a booth table. It was Stjepan. Stjepan glanced up at him as he walked by, and did a double take because Reggie was now clean shaven and in uniform; the last time he'd seen him, he'd had a beard and wore peasant gear. Reggie stepped outside and made a beeline for the ship at a fast trot, trying not to spill any. Stjepan stepped outside and shouted, the barman on his heels. Stjepan was grabbed by the shirt and an argument ensued – no doubt about an unpaid bill. Reggie reached the sentry box, set the bucket down, and started up the gangplank. He made it to the deck, panting hard from the effort, and turned to look. The barman still stood at his door yelling after Stjepan, who was already well past the lamp-post and moving fast. He hit the end of the gangplank at full stride and started up. Ivarsson racked the charging handle of his heavy machine-gun and, taking deliberate aim shouted, "Halt!" Stjepan threw his hands in the air and backed down.

"Where is she?" Stjepan barked at Reggie, in German.

"I don't know," he answered, also in German. The young German guard held his rifle at the ready, looking confused at what was happening.

"Liar!" said Stjepan. He lowered his hands.

"She has a flat somewhere in the city, I don't know where."

"She is no longer with you?" Stjepan challenged.

"We had an argument. I left her." *I hope he buys this.* Stjepan smirked and said something to the German guard. Reggie heard her name spoken. The guard re-slung his rifle, checked his clipboard, and shook his head.

"If I see you again," Stjepan warned, pointing a finger at him, "you are a dead man!" He strode back to the *konoba*. Reggie waited ten minutes, then retrieved his bucket of beer and his passport. He explained to the German guard, who had listened to the exchange, that "it was just a lover's quarrel." He went to the galley to deliver the full bucket.

"Pavlina, I just saw Stjepan in the *konoba*," Reggie said, "and he saw me. I barely made it back alive."

"Stjepan! Are you all right? What is he doing here? He is supposed to be in Primošten."

"I'm fine. I've no idea, but now I think about it, he had a stack of your posters on his table. He wanted to know where you were. I told him we'd argued and I'd abandoned you, and didn't know where you lived." He sagged into a chair. "I'll tell you one thing, though: I'm never leaving this ship again without my pistol!"

"Stjepan, *kopile*!" she said vehemently, "I will go tomorrow and have words with him. You will not worry; I will be armed!" Reggie looked up the word in her dictionary later. She had said, "Stjepan, you bastard!"

Reggie went back to the German guard and explained "his cook Annika" was going to be two hours late tomorrow.

Made up and dressed as Annika, at one o'clock the next afternoon Pavlina started down the gangplank with her bucket in hand. Today she wore a bright red woolen skirt and a frilly blouse buttoned up to her chin. She started across to the *konoba*, but then altered course slightly to enter the alley. *That's clever*, Reggie thought, *she's entering through the side door.*

He stood at the rail and awaited her return. Pavlina's bicycle leaned against the after side of the bridge house. He glanced at it briefly and away, then looked again. Her 'bicycle pump' gun was still in its holder!

He began to worry. Ten minutes passed. This became fifteen, and still she hadn't reappeared. Then, out of the corner of his eye, he caught movement on a building to the north. The green shutters of "their room" opened, and it was her pushing them open!

Five minutes later he saw they were shut. It had now been twenty minutes, and the guard was getting impatient. The man checked his wristwatch then scowled up at him, and Reggie shrugged his shoulders. Finally, after twenty-seven minutes she reappeared carrying her bucket. Beer was poured from one bucket to the other, and the guard got his full glass. She waited below until he finished it, then generously dipped out another for him. She ascended the gangplank and went to deliver the bucket of beer to the galley, then followed Reggie up the stairs to their quarters. When they entered, only then did Reggie notice she wore something red tied about her waist, something knitted she hadn't been wearing when she left. She handed it to him. It was Stjepan's jumper.

"Here, this is yours now," she said, tiredly, "My mother knitted it for him; he has no more need of it. Stjepan is not his real name, only the false name he use to pose as a Croat in my country. He had us all fooled." He laid it aside. She seemed exhausted as they sat together on the edge of the bed.

"You look beat," he said, as he rubbed her back.

"Is because killing is very tiring."

"I saw you didn't take your special gun. I was very worried for you." She said nothing, so he asked, "What did you do, strangle him?"

"Strangle? No, I stab him."

"How did you approach him with the kitchen knife? I would have thought he could easily overpower you."

"You are right, he is too strong for me. You are wanting to know *how* I kill him?"

"Well, yes ... I suppose I do."

"I tell you. He is happy to see me. I act happy to see him. First I tell him you abandon me, I am devastated and lonely, without money, and my future is hopeless," she explained. "Next I bring him to the room and beg for him to fuck me, but this also makes him wary because never before do I offer myself to him. I have very little time now, so I must work quickly. He wants to embrace me, but I refuse and complain he is stinking and say we cannot make love until he is clean, so he must have the bath now. I begin to fill the tub."

"So, you went to the kitchen to get the knife while he's in the tub?"

"Do not interrupt," she said, wearily. "He is wary, not really believing me. So, I must convince him! I take off my skirt and panties, and let him see my *stidnica* for the first time ever, and this makes him eager." Reggie had no need to ask what a *stidnica* was; he could guess. "He undresses quickly, and when he is naked I ask him to test the water temperature. When he is bent over the tub, I stab him three times in the side under his ribs and push him in head-first! Before I slit his throat, I force him to confess he is a Nazi Colonel."

"Don't tell me," he said, with a shudder, "I don't want to know how you extracted *that* confession!"

"I cut it off in the tub so there is no mess," she added, not obeying him. "I pay the matron much kuna, and her son will throw his body in the harbour tonight." She stood and removed her skirt. He was alarmed to see her legs above the knees spattered with dried blood. "Now I must have a bath, because I let that fascist beast touch me."

"Wait a bit! You never said *when* you went to get the knife." Instead of answering him, she unfastened her blouse and removed it, and then unbuckled her belt with his knife from around her bare waist. The scabbard had been mounted inverted, nestled between her breasts and held in by her brassiere.

"This you will need to clean. Is no time for me to do," she said. He laughed aloud, and slapped his knee.

"Why you laugh?" she asked, her eyebrows raised. "Is death funny?"

"Yes," he exclaimed, "because the poster is accurate now, and Stjepan is the twenty-eighth!"

She gave the knife to him, and he gingerly carried the bloody thing to the kitchen sink to give it a wash.

13

"Message Retrieved"

Now they all fell back into their daily routine of cleaning and organising the ship, preparing to leave whenever that might be. One of their number was allowed to visit the Saturday market every week, courtesy of the bribed guard. The beer flowed every day, also courtesy of the bribed guard. The flood lamps blazed every night as usual. Reggie plotted a course on the charts to bring them to Alexandria. Pavlina made herself useful wherever she could. Their meals had gotten much better. Morale had improved remarkably, and Reggie was pleased.

He had Pavlina, as "Annika," give the burnt-out valve from their receiver to the barman one day, and she asked the man to find a replacement for it. A few days later the barman gave it back, and reported there were none to be found anywhere. With that event, the only problems remaining were the fuel, and the money to pay for it. He had tried to suss out the combination of the safe, but it was of top-notch Swedish fabrication and he couldn't feel, or even hear, the tumblers.

March had only just turned to April when on the first, a Wednesday, there was an event that changed both their lives forever. It was in the

158

afternoon, about 1415 hours, and as usual the couples and families were strolling on the promenade after lunch. Pavlina and Reggie leaned upon the bulwark rail, wishing they could be down there with them. As usual Reggie wore his Swedish captain's uniform. Pavlina wore her "Bohemian" cream-coloured blouse, the one Reggie liked so much, with an elastic neckline that left her shoulders bare.

A distant rumbling reached their ears and grew louder. It was getting closer, too. He recognised it as the sound of heavy machinery. Tanks, perhaps? He didn't know, but the people on the promenade did. They scattered, screaming in panic, for any exit within reach. The waterfront rapidly emptied. He ran for the supper handbell and rang it vigorously.

"Man the rail! Man the rail! Arm yourselves!" he yelled inside. He ran up to his quarters, pausing at each landing to repeat the call to arms inside. He pocketed his Walther P38—at times like this, every little bit helps. When he returned to the rail it was lined with all his crew crouching behind the bulwark, and some held a pistol or a long rifle. These were the armaments left behind by the officers. He crouched as well. The growling and clanking and squeaking was very loud now.

The German guard stood relaxed. Whoever this was, it could only be his *Wehrmacht* or the Italian army; he wasn't worried. A German motorcycle with a sidecar suddenly emerged from between buildings, coming down the hill on the main road at a high rate of speed. It braked to a stop in front of the sentry box and a machine gun was pointed at the guard. He surrendered at once and was replaced in the box by the soldier in the sidecar. The German guard was handcuffed and gagged, and put in the sidecar. The motorcycle puttered into an alley and turned about, to wait until called.

A Panzer IV tank clattered into view, its bogie wheels squeaking, then rotated and backed into a shadowed space between buildings, its short barrel aimed to cover the northern approach along the promenade.

He knew it was captured because its "Bulgarian shield" identification marking had been crudely overpainted, and there was a five-pointed red star outlined in white. A half-dozen lorries then rounded the corner onto the quay. They could see an insignia on the door of each lorry: a shield of blue, white, and red with a five-pointed red star in its centre.

"Reggie!" Pavlina was ecstatic. "The Tito Escort Battalion! Is partisans!"

"Stand down! Stand down! They're friendly!" he called to his crew, and stood up. This was repeated in Swedish for those non-English speakers.

From one of these lorries a captured Italian Breda Model 35 anti-aircraft gun was manhandled, and this was deployed on its tripod on the mole, in a position to cover the southern approaches along the *Obala hrvatske mornarice* road, and the bay. Troops jumped from the lorries, more than a hundred of them in total. A few carried Simonov anti-tank rifles, most definitely not German issue, but some had *Maschinenpistole* machine guns, which were. Most carried the PPSh-41 sub-machine gun of Russian issue. These troops disappeared into the alleyways to the sound of cheers were quickly silenced. The empty lorries departed the way they'd come. Now two enclosed saloon cars stopped at the ship, green four-door Russian GAZ-61's. From these, four men emerged and strode up the gangplank, one with an enormous grey wolfhound on a lead. All of them were in uniform with the *pilotka* forage cap, most carrying weapons which they now slung upon their shoulders. The cars departed, following the lorries.

When they arrived on deck, the first armed man stood aside at attention and the second man approached Pavlina. She snapped to attention and saluted him with the partisan salute; a clenched fist held to her temple. This man was of medium height and clean-shaven, his face tanned and large. His dark hair tending towards grey at the temples was combed straight back. His eyes were blue. He smiled at her.

"My dear Buga, there is no need to stand on ceremony with me," he said in English. He returned her salute anyway, to put her at ease. Please, introduce your friends."

"Here is Josip Broz," she announced, also in English, "Commander-in-Chief of the National Liberation Army of Yugoslavia."

"Please, use just my name 'Tito', that is all that is required," he said.

"Boško here, and Prlja there, are his bodyguards. The dog is named Tigger," she announced. The last man of the entourage now stepped aboard from the gangplank. "Veljko!" she shouted, and launched herself into his arms. Veljko caught her up and swung her around, then kissed both her cheeks. *So this is her good friend Veljko*, Reggie thought.

"I knew you'd be pleased to see him again," Tito said. They all shook hands. "Now, is there some room where we may talk in private?" he asked, looking about at the Swedish crew who stood listening. Pavlina led the way up to the captain's quarters. Reggie turned to his crew and announced, "Dismissed!" then followed them. Prlja tied the wolfhound's leash to a tank vent pipe and followed.

Reggie wheeled out his desk chair, the only chair, for the Commander to use, but they all chose to remain standing. Tito snapped his fingers and held out his hand. Boško produced and handed over the Nazi 'wanted poster' and Tito gave this to her.

"Buga Pavlina, I have had my eye on you for some time, now. You are one of my very best soldiers. I have seen this, and wondered if it was true, you have killed twenty-eight?"

"Well, 'now' it's twenty-eight, sir." Reggie interjected, and took the poster from her.

"Twenty-eight." He pursed his lips and nodded appreciatively. "How did you kill them?"

"Any way I can, comrade. Some I am shooting with my pistol, some

I choke with a garotte, some I stab. I do what works best at the time," she said.

"This is most impressive. I think, however, you should have a more suitable weapon than a mere pistol. Comrade Boško, your weapon." He motioned between Boško and Buga. Boško stepped forward and offered it held out horizontally with both hands, a Russian PPSh-41 sub-machine gun, its fat barrel ventilated, with a wooden stock and drum magazine.

"I am honoured that it is my weapon to be given the great Buga," Boško stated formally. He clicked his heels and bowed from the neck. Buga accepted this gift, and laid it on the bed. Tito's eyes followed her as she did so, and only then did he seem to notice the rumpled bed had been slept in by two people, and recently so. His gaze travelled between Buga and Reggie, and he smiled.

"Comrade Prlja, let us see the map now." Prlja stepped forward and, taking a large rolled map from his tube, unrolled it on the desk, where the others held it down.

"Comrade Pavlina, on the first of March 1942," Tito began, "I created the Second Proletarian Brigade. They are now in this location, here. My other brigades are here, and we have partisan units here, and here, and here. The Bosniaks are here." He pointed at various locations. "Draža is —" Tito became aware Reggie was listening, so without breaking stride he switched from English to Croatian. Pavlina's attention was focussed on everything Tito was telling her. The group continued discussing various troop positions and movements for some ten minutes. Reggie had a hard time reading the tiny names of villages, so gave up trying. Soon the map was rolled up and put back into the tube, and everyone reverted to speaking in English.

Now Tito snapped his fingers again and held out his hand. Boško produced and opened for him an oblong presentation box of dark blue velvet.

"*Poručnik* Buga Pavlina, *Pažnja!*" Pavlina snapped to attention, hands at her side and shoulders thrown back, her chin up and eyes straight ahead. He looked her square in the eye and intoned, "I, Josip Broz Tito, award you, Lieutenant Buga Pavlina, the Order of the White Eagle, fourth class, Officer with Swords, which award I give and confer for conspicuous bravery by the officer in the field." Tito took a multicoloured ribbon bar showing crossed swords from the box, and opened the hinged pin on its back. Holding it in his right hand, he vacillated, unsure of how to proceed because she was not in partisan uniform. Then, with a shrug of resignation, he plunged his left hand into her cleavage. Pavlina's eyes widened and she caught her breath.

Tito tried multiple times to align the ribbon bar horizontally until finally he was satisfied with its position. The others shifted their feet or rolled their eyes in embarrassment. Now Tito placed a long ribbon of light-blue moire silk over her head, a glittering medal hanging from it. Grasping her shoulders with both hands he kissed her on each cheek, and they exchanged partisan salutes. Boško passed the empty box to Reggie. The group erupted in applause, and everyone came to shake her hand. Veljko hugged her and kissed her cheek. Pavlina looked down and touched the ribbon bar, and the very large glittering eight-pointed star hanging there, of a double-headed white eagle beneath the royal crown. She was trembling and so overcome with emotion, Reggie felt he had to take her arm and slip a hand around her waist for support. He guided her over to the chair, supporting her as she sank into it. Tito noticed this as well.

"I have awarded you this honour," Tito said, "to lend you credibility for a special assignment I have in mind."

"Do you order me to take command of a brigade now?" she asked eagerly, sitting forwards, her eyes bright.

"No, I only inform you of this now so you will know of it," he revealed. "I order you to join the Yugoslav Government-in-exile, in London."

"London!" she exclaimed in amazement.

"Yes. It seems the Croatian and Serbian ministers in our king's cabinet are in serious disagreement: after the extent of Chetnik collaboration with the Axis became evident, they are quarrelling among themselves. I want you to do your utmost to convince King Peter, Mr Churchill, and Mr Roosevelt to switch their support from Draža Mihailović to myself."

"This I will be honoured to do, comrade."

"Our young king – only eighteen years old – is studying at Cambridge, but when he's in London he lives at Claridge's Hotel in Mayfair, where all the other Governments-in-exile are housed. That's where you'll stay. There may also be an opportunity for you to travel to Washington, in America."

"America," she breathed.

"Yes, America, *perhaps.* In London you will liaise with a British SOE agent named Ivar Bryce to keep me informed. He is the flatmate of a man named Ian Fleming. This man Fleming, he has something of a reputation as a 'ladies man' so you should steer clear of him." Tito said, in warning. He turned to his bodyguard and held out his hand. "Boško, the documents now." Tito took them all and handed them over to her one by one as he explained each.

"This is your official appointment. Here is your letter of introduction." She saw these were signed by Tito himself. "This one will allow you to be paid a daily stipend as you travel there, and this next document puts you on the payroll of the Yugoslav Government-in-exile when you arrive. I should mention all of the Governments-in-exile there, the Norwegians, the Free French, the Danes, Dutch and Belgians, most occupied European countries, all of them are financially supported by the British.

"This final document is the most valuable of all. Keep them all very safe, but especially this one. It is your 'letter of transit' – similar to a *laissez-passer* – and will allow you to exit any country while on your way to England. But, naturally, it will be up to each country whether they allow you to enter." At the bottom of this letter were three signatures; King Peter II, Winston Churchill, and Joseph Stalin. The bodyguard Boško gathered up all the documents, refolded each individually, then tucked the stack into the narrow end of a long khaki envelope. He refolded the envelope once, then again, and wrapped a red string around a red cardboard button. He handed it to her, and she saw on its exterior the words "confidential" and "secret" stamped in red ink.

With an arch glance at Reggie, Tito continued, "I may be a half-century old, but I am not blind." He turned and formally addressed himself to her. "Buga Pavlina, you will accompany this Captain Reginald Wallace to London," he ordered, "and for you, I now declare my diktat at an end!"

Diktat? Reggie was confused, for this word meant 'dictation' in various languages, including Croatian, but Pavlina had never been Tito's clerk or secretary, had she? Perhaps he didn't know all there was to know about her.

"Sir," Reggie said, "If I may enlighten you; we haven't enough fuel to reach mainland Greece, let alone London, and the harbourmaster will not sell us any on credit."

"Ah, yes. When we became aware your receiver was broken, Cairo requested we come here in person, to relay to you their reply."

"What did they say?" Reggie's attention was riveted on what he would say next.

"It was very strange, and I don't pretend to understand it but, here it is." He took a slip of paper from a tunic pocket and glanced at it. "Cairo asked if Marko was there, listening. We replied 'no' – then Cairo would say only one word. We asked for clarification, but they would only repeat the one word."

"What was that word?"

"Shlomo." At the utterance of this word, Pavlina bolted from her chair as if galvanised by a jolt of electricity. She raced to the wardrobe and returned with Reggie's knife and his Yugoslavian jacket. Spreading it out upon the desk, she slit open the hem of the lining, and out spilled many dozens of glittering diamonds.

"We can go now!" Reggie beamed, relieved. He scooped up the jewels and poured them into his blazer's pocket. A few minutes later they all stood in a group at the head of the gangplank to bid Tito and his entourage good-bye. Just then the *Kübelwagen* appeared, driving south along the promenade. It must be three o'clock. As usual it stopped in front of the sentry box. A partisan soldier stepped out of the box with his machine gun levelled, and arrested all four occupants. It was all rather neatly accomplished.

"We have another car," Tito said, laughing, "and yet another German officer to interrogate. It seems there's no need to walk back to where the lorries wait." His entourage started down the gangplank.

"Sir, before you go," Reggie called out, "could you give us a ride to the harbourmaster's office? We have some business to transact there."

"Certainly, certainly, get in. Prlja will drive. Our motorcycle will escort us," Tito said.

"Reggie, I stay here until you return," Pavlina said, "I have much to tell to Veljko."

14

Leave-taking

At noon the next day, the Swedish crew lined the port-side rail to watch the long-awaited transfer of fuel. A tanker lay alongside, the warning "*Ne Pušenje*" – No Smoking – painted in large letters on the front of its bridge. Engine-driven pumps thrust fuel through the thick hoses. The noxious fumes of hot Bunker-C oil wafted up and drove them away. The bunkering took most of the afternoon.

"Are you sad about leaving your homeland?" Reggie questioned Pavlina, at lunch. Her face thoughtful, she finished chewing.

"No, not really. I have always wanted to see England again," she mused, "and maybe America. I am happy to go because of the Nazi price on my head—also I am certain Stjepan has revealed my location to others." Even though everyone was excited to finally be going, Reggie decided to delay departure until the following Saturday, as it was bad luck to leave port on a voyage beginning on a Friday.

Reggie made his usual daily inspection tour of the ship at ten-hundred hours on the Friday, a task he had learned to do as a first mate under the tutelage of Captain Roy Mallinson on board the SS *Dominion Empress*. Not for the last time did he think of Roy, and Becky McKenzie. The ship was clean and shipshape. Gear had been stowed properly. They left the booms with their flood lamps swung outboard, for they would need them at night during the passage south. At eleven o'clock Pavlina, dressed as Annika, made the beer run as usual, and the guard got his usual full glass. What was unusual was that she carried both buckets back aboard, "*zum Waschen*," she told the guard, just as Reggie had taught her how to say it. At noon Reggie, with a handful of his crewmen, visited the guard to explain their lines on the bollards "needed adjustment." He ordered the tractor tyre fenders hanging from the ship to be transferred to bollards on the quay, and then ordered the men to "single-up all lines," fairly certain the young guard wouldn't know the significance of what this meant.

They left at daybreak on Saturday. He wondered what the reaction from the townspeople would be, when they discovered the ship gone. At any rate, he was sure they would appreciate having their view back. His first order was to raise the largest Swedish flag they had at the stern staff, and smaller ones at the spreader. These stood out to the west, showing there was an offshore breeze. The deck crew on the foredeck and the fantail retrieved the bow line, stern line and spring lines, and flaked them all down. Another crewman was ordered to stow the gangplank, and used one of the smaller booms to hoist the gangplank off the pavement. The breeze carried the ship slowly away from the quay, and the guard stood panic-stricken, as no one had counselled him on what to do in such a circumstance. The end of the gangplank caught the sentry box. With a screech of splintering wood, it was scraped off the quay and fell into the water. Reggie waved a cheery good-bye from the bridge wing, and the boy waved meekly in return.

To get the HLV *Belfair* out of Šibenik they needed to negotiate Saint Anthony's crooked channel that connected the Bay of Šibenik to the Adriatic sea. A pilot was usually available for this, but all three pilots had been rounded up with others and executed, so there were none.

Reggie had them proceed in channel centre at dead slow, fingers crossed. Once they were clear of Saint Anthony's channel, and Zlarin Island just outside, he set a course of 174 degrees true.

At noon he took a sight with the sextant to fix their position, though this was hardly necessary; he knew exactly where they were because the Island of Vis was abeam to port. Still, he did this out of habit. A new heading of 140 degrees was ordered to bring them down the centre of the Adriatic Sea towards the Mediterranean. Despite the lack of a working receiver, he ordered a wireless transmission be made every hour on the hour, warning all who could hear that they were the H.L.V. *Belfair*, a neutral Swedish ship, and they claimed "diplomatic immunity from attack" as they proceeded. Various members of the crew sent this out in Swedish, English, Croatian, and German. He could only hope the transmission was being heard.

In early afternoon they saw the first results of their efforts, as they were overflown by an Italian reconnaissance 'plane, most likely from Pasquale Liberi Aerodromo at Pescara, Italy. It looked them over and departed. As the sun set, an Italian Motor Torpedo Boat approached, possibly out of Bari, but by then they had switched on the flood lamps, and after giving them the once-over, it too departed.

At two o'clock in the morning on Easter Sunday, Reggie was awakened by an anxious Swede who urged him out of bed. Another Italian MTB, he thought out of Brindisi, was shadowing them and had fired a shell across their bow. He used the megaphone to tell them in his crude schoolboy Latin that the radio receiver was dead, only to see their crew collapse in helpless laughter. After much shouting back and forth in languages no one could understand, it too left. He ordered the helmsman to come to 160 degrees, and to cease the radio transmissions, then went back to bed.

Dawn came, and they were ten miles off the port of Otranto, that port on the very back of the "heel of Italy." Now would come the real test as Reggie held to his course, because he knew, but the crew did not, his destination was in truth Alexandria, Egypt. However, after breakfast one of the English-speaking stewards, a Mr Torstein, casually said he had noticed the direction of the shadows on the ship, and suspected Reggie hadn't turned south-west, and wanted to know their true destination.

"Alexandria, Egypt," He was forced to admit. "But don't you worry. Once there, another crew will take over and bring you all out to Sweden. Those are my orders. Keep it to yourself." Five hours passed, and according to the chart, they had left the occupied Greek Island of Corfu thirty miles abeam to port, although it couldn't be seen. Reggie had just completed a sun sight at noon to fix their position, when a shout went up from the port bridge lookout. A boat was fast approaching from out of the east, and this proved to be a Kriegsmarine *Schnellboote*, a fast torpedo boat, out of Corfu. Mr Torstein appeared on the bridge.

"Oh, great. What do we do now? What if he questions our direction?"

"I've thought of that. I plan to tell them we're on our way to Madagascar to load nickel ore for the German steel factories. But I'll make a dash for Alex when we're close enough."

"God, I hope that works." Torstein muttered. The German captain motored up and matched speed with them, and within hailing distance of his bridge. He spoke to them through a megaphone.

"*Belfair!* Kapitän-Leutnant Kolten. Why have you not answered our transmissions?" Reggie wielded his megaphone once again.

"Kapitän Kolten, Captain Leif Magnuson. We can only transmit. Our receiver is *kaputt*," he called in German. "We are a Swedish ship. Sweden, a neutral nation, and a non-belligerent. By the international principle of freedom of the seas, we claim the right of free passage upon the high seas." The captain of the other ship answered him back.

"We do not dispute this. Your passage is assured. From what port did you depart, Magnuson?"

"Šibenik, Yugoslavia."

"Do you mean Šibenik, the Independent State of Croatia?"

"Yes, I do – my mistake, Herr Kolten."

"What destination?"

"The Vichy-French Colony of Madagascar." *This is critical. I hope this works.*

"Through the Suez canal, then. What cargo?"

"No cargo. We are in ballast as you can see from our boot-stripe. We made a delivery of locomotives one year ago, and have only now been permitted to depart." The man looked over his Plimsoll mark and boot-stripe, then disappeared below. In ten minutes he was back.

"Your destination is Stockholm, Sweden," he announced. "Your route is being reported by every news source and is well known world-wide."

"This is true. We are out of Šibenik for Madagascar, and then from there to Sweden. In Madagascar we will load seven thousand tons of nickel ore for our Swedish furnaces, for the metal we sell to you. "

"We do not make mistakes. Your proper course is for Sweden. Turn about!" the Nazi demanded. Reggie steeled himself for what had to come next.

"I know my orders, and will continue on the course given me by the Swedish Government." He held his breath. Kolten stared at him for a moment, unaccustomed to his orders not being followed.

"We have confirmed your course with your government. It is to Sweden, and you will set a course for Sweden now or we will be forced to sink you. You have been warned."

"A moment if you please, I shall need to consult with my officers." He sauntered into the bridge then raced to the chart room, the steward following, as the helmsman watched them dash by. *Let's see, let's see, course 230 true* – he drew a pencil line on the chart, then set the dividers to nine nautical miles, the length of an hour's motoring.

"Torstein, listen, and tell me if you think this will work." He stepped it off with the dividers as he spoke aloud. "Seven and a half hours till sunset, then fifteen hours after that puts us off Sicily only some thirty miles from Syracuse just at sunrise, *here.* Then it's three and a half hours in daylight until we'll be forced to turn towards Gibraltar just *here*, but instead of turning, what if we maintain our course? Just keep going straight? Then it's a forty-five mile dash to Valletta, Malta, and *hopefully* that'll be under air cover. That is, if we warn them we're coming." *Torstein need not know about the broken receiver but at least we can still transmit.*

"It may be possible, Captain. I mean, it sounds plausible." Torstein shrugged, "But then, I'm only a steward. I'll have to trust your judgement on these matters." Reggie returned to the bridge wing and retrieved the megaphone.

"Kapitän Kolten, we will alter course as you 'suggest', but we will lodge a complaint upon arrival."

"You do that." Kolten sneered.

"In the meanwhile, might I suggest you compose a reply to your Führer, one he may read and dispose of, prior to your execution?"

"Do tell." Kolten laughed.

"Your house-painter boss will not be pleased when your Krupp armament factories output is drastically reduced. We will now go home empty but, as you say, it is *we* that have been warned." Kolten's grin faded. Reggie ordered a change of course to the southwest. The *Schnellboote* matched speed with them and took up station abeam to port. They escorted them for a few hours, until a *Scirocco* wind arose from the south. They then departed for Corfu, not wanting to contend with this nasty weather.

Just before sunrise an aeroplane appeared from out of the west. It was Italian and circled them for five minutes then flew off the way it had come. Reggie, awakened by the drone of engines, rose to see the flood lamps were still on. They were. He checked the chart, and noticed two aerodromes on the Island of Sicily: Magliocco, and the Ponte Olivo. This being late in the season for the *Scirocco* it hadn't lasted long. He greeted Arne at the helm as he stood his four-hour watch. He checked to see they were still on 230 degrees, heading south-west. There were three and a half hours to go before they were to start their dash to Valletta, Malta, and he wanted to prepare. He warmed up the transmitter and checked inside. All the valves but one were glowing. Mr Torstein stood by as he made the transmission.

"Calling all stations, calling all stations, this is the neutral Swedish vessel *Belfair*. Our radio receiver is inoperable. We are now twenty-four miles south-east of Syracuse, Italy, and maintaining a heading of 230 degrees true. I repeat, maintaining a heading of 230 degrees true. That's 230 degrees true." *No need to say 'over' as we can't receive.*

He had written it all down the night before. When he was finished, he told Torstein to send it as written every fifteen minutes, in English, then went down to breakfast, after shutting down the flood lamps.

"Sir, I thought you might want to see this." The radio operator handed over a slip of paper to the group-captain in charge in RAF Luqa, Malta, but announced it anyway. "The MS *Belfair*, a neutral Swedish ship, has been transmitting this every fifteen minutes for the last hour and a half, and it seems they're stressing the ship's course far more than is necessary." The man read it, then laid his glasses aside, stood and turned to a chart of the Mediterranean on the wall. A string hung from a tack at the location of their aerodrome, a compass rose encircling it.

"If they're trying to impart a specific course to listeners," he mused aloud, "it must mean something. Did they give any coordinates?"

"Aye, starting twenty-four miles south-east of Syracuse, Italy." The group-captain took hold of the string.

"Then ... hmmm ... that would put them right about ... here. If they maintain that course, then —" He stood back and smiled. "It puts them smack in the centre of our Grand Harbour. He's a canny one, sergeant. He's on his way here. What he's doing is asking us for air cover, without actually asking us for air cover. He knows he's being listened to."

"Do you want to send it, sir?"

"Yes. Sortie a Spit and a Beaufighter. It's obvious to me this Swede is expecting trouble, if he isn't in it already. He's given us the chance to sink something and I, for one, won't pass up the opportunity!"

15

Stymied Again

They saw it coming from the west at high speed, an Italian Motor Gun Boat, well before it reached them. It was very fast, easily making 50 knots. The MS *Belfair* was off the south-easterly prominence of Sicily, the Portopalo di Capo Passero, and he guessed it was coming from the Italian naval base at Licata. The Italian motored up and matched speed with them, within hailing distance of his starboard bridge wing. On the hull was painted the number MAS 532. The man spoke to him. It was in Italian and he couldn't understand a word. *You would think my scant bit of schoolboy Latin would help, but no*, he thought. Reggie wielded his megaphone once again.

"We are a Swedish ship. Sweden, a neutral nation. *Neutrale. Neutrale*," he shouted over to the man, while pointing at the Swedish flag on the foremast. The captain of the other ship answered him back, again in Italian. It was an impasse. The *Motoscafo Armato Silurante* 532 took up station on their port quarter a hundred yards out and stayed there. Twenty minutes passed and then, all hell broke loose. The MAS 532 roared across their bow going west flat out. At the same time a Spitfire fighter and a Bristol Beaufighter appeared from out of the southwest at wave-top height and, climbing a bit broke left in hot pursuit. The Swedes on deck waved their caps in the air and cheered. The boat dodged left and right and left, all the while firing what sounded like a 20mm anti-aircraft cannon as the aeroplanes dogged them, also firing. They twisted and turned over the wide sea for what seemed like many minutes. The Spitfire was hit and splashed, sinking immediately. The other broke away and headed for Malta. It was soon apparent why, as four Falco fighters came out from Sicily in pursuit.

Reggie maintained course and speed, and scanned the sea with binoculars but there was no yellow raft nor Mae West, nor any sign of the pilot. Soon the MAS 532 returned and took up station again on their port quarter a hundred yards out and stayed there. Half an hour later the MAS accelerated to just off the port bow and turned into their path. It was an obvious attempt to force a turn to starboard.

Reggie held to their course. The Italian fired a shot across the bow, as a warning. Reggie shouted through the megaphone "Sweden! *Neutrale*! *Neutrale*! Neut—" but was cut off as the Italian sent three 20mm cannon shells through the bow of the ship. Their gun swivelled around, and he realized the next rounds might be through the bridge. Resigned, he ordered a change of course to 283 degrees true, on a heading to pass Tunisia on the way to Gibraltar. Five minutes later Pavlina and Annika arrived on the bridge, worried about the shelling and needing reassurance. Reggie went to the chart room, and the others followed.

"Where are we now?" Pavlina asked. He pencilled an X on the chart.

"It looks to me that we're on our way to Sweden." Torstein commented, not unhappily.

"And we're being escorted to the Atlantic, to make sure of it." observed Annika. Frederik arrived and said he'd viewed the damage from the vantage of the foredeck, and it was in the empty forepeak forward of the collision bulkhead, and well above the waterline, so no worries for now.

"Frederik, how much fuel do we have?" Reggie asked. Frederik took his pipe from his mouth.

"We'll need to refuel somewhere. The distance to Stockholm is about 4,500nm from Šibenik—but you're taking us to Britain."

"How do you figure?"

"You wanted to get us to Egypt first, then Malta next, and both are controlled by Britain. You'll likely want to try for Gibraltar next. We're not stupid, captain. There's something you're not telling us."

"Yes, but I'm afraid I cannot divulge it." There was an uncomfortable silence. "Sorry. I've been sworn to secrecy." He looked about at Pavlina, Arne, Torstein, Annika, and Frederik. "Well, what do we do now? Any suggestions?" he prompted. All this was translated for Arne. They all gazed at the chart for a long moment.

"Reggie, I live in area of Mediterranean all my life." Pavlina said.

"How do you mean?"

"We are in the Malta channel. Is between Malta and Sicily."

"Yes, just here," he confirmed, "ten miles south of Pozzallo, Sicily." He pointed at the pencilled mark.

"There is current here, always moving anti-clockwise. Is twenty-five, thirty miles around." With her finger she traced a circle between Sicily and Malta. It touched the X.

"What are you saying?" He asked.

"She is saying," Frederik answered, tapping the stem of his pipe on an island, "That if we were to lose our engines, we couldn't help but be carried to Malta, eventually."

"So we fake a multiple engine breakdown? That's not at all believable. They'd only offer to tow us to the nearest Italian port. Then they'd likely detain us, make the claim we'd 'abandoned ship' and confiscate us under international maritime law as legitimate 'salvage'."

"Certainly true, but what might be believed is a breakdown of our electric steering motor on a hard-over rudder." Frederik announced. "You can't tow that." Reggie grinned at him and slapped him on the back.

"Frederik, what an excellent idea! How long do you reckon it would take you to arrange that?"

"We can do it now," he returned. "Just put the helm hard over and motor in a circle. Reverse engines and do it again. Until they get the point." All of them walked out on the port bridge wing. The Italian was still stationed on their port quarter a hundred yards out. "Just give me time to get to the engine room, to make sure we've enough compressed air. Direct reversing, you know." Reggie didn't know what he meant about needing compressed air, but that wasn't important now. He told them all to keep an eye on the Italian. He waited until the engine room telephone rang, and heard Frederik say "Ready." He walked out on the starboard wing and scanned the sea.

"Helmsman, hard a-starboard and hold it there," he ordered. The man spun the wheel. The *Belfair*, riding high and moving at nine knots, began a turn to starboard. He ordered half ahead all, and let her complete a two full circles, then stopped engines. He ordered half astern all. The *Belfair* backed down to starboard, and the Italian boat scurried to stay out of their way. He ordered port full ahead, starboard stopped, just to emphasize how 'disabled' they were, then ordered all stop. He searched the flag locker for the 'not under command' flag and gave it to Torstein to raise. From the bridge wing he waved the Italian over, and they motored to him. Reggie thought German was worth a try.

"*Sprechen Sie Deutsch?*" – do you speak German? – he asked. A little, the man replied. Reggie pointed to the not-under-command flag and explained the steering problem, miming holding a wheel. Now fully stopped, the pair of them began to drift with the current, he guessed at maybe two, or possibly three knots.

The MGB hung about for a half-hour, maybe using their radio, although he had no way to confirm this. Quite suddenly the Italian roared away in the direction of Licata. Anxiously they scanned the sky for aircraft but there were none. The time was 1030 hours. They drifted all day as the current carried them south. At times during the day they were overflown by Italian aeroplanes, and at other times there was a lone Hurricane. At sunset, nine hours later, they were left alone. The flood lamps were then switched on.

Eleven hours since they'd shut down the engines brought them within sight and due north from the Island of Gozo, Malta's neighbour. With binoculars he could see a few house lights on both islands. The moon had set; what luck! Reggie used his judgement and dead reckoning to place an X where he supposed they were. He stepped off a measurement on the chart: it was twenty-one nautical miles to Valletta, he supposed an hour and forty-five minutes at his top speed of eleven knots. The engines were started and the flood lamps extinguished. In the moonless dark they dashed for Valletta at flank speed, pouring on the power. A RN tug met them well outside with a warning: there were so many mines on the approaches to the harbour that the *Belfair* was to proceed at the slowest possible speed to minimise any vibration and, with the exception of a skeleton crew in the engine room, all other personnel aboard would need to stand on deck wearing life jackets. This would assure a chance of survival if a mine exploded. The tug escorted them though the submarine nets into the Grand Harbour, where they tied up at Valletta's Pinto Wharf before midnight.

After breakfast Reggie dressed in his dress-blue captain's uniform with its brass buttons and white peaked cap. He left the ship and, after asking around, was eventually directed to Malta Command, the island's 'War Rooms' in Fort Lascaris, below the Upper Barrakka Gardens. *That's quite clever*, he thought, *no one would think to waste a bomb on a garden.*

He needed to get a message to BHQ(ME) Cairo, certain they would be relieved to know where they were. The clerk there gave him a time to return, as the radioman wasn't in. He strolled the Upper Barrakka Gardens and admired the view of the Grand Harbour from this overlook. A Royal Navy Lieutenant lighting a cigarette leaned on the parapet and pointed out to him three destroyers, the HMS *Gallant* and the HMS *Kingston*. In the graving dock across the intervening water lay the HMS *Lance*, fallen on her side and partially submerged. All these had been bombed only the Sunday previous, and were undergoing repair. The man proudly pointed out the HMS *Penelope*, known as 'pepperpot' because of all the near misses she'd endured, and explained how important a part her ack–ack guns had played during this siege. Reggie pointed out his own ship for the lieutenant. The man advised him to get his crew off the ship and take rooms in the city. *Hmmm. Not as safe a harbour as I'd supposed, but I'll need some 'dosh' for that.*

At the appointed hour he presented himself and was ushered in to see an RAF Lieutenant. He was shown to the communications centre. He produced his radio's burnt out valve and was gratified when the man was able to supply him a spare. The radioman had him write out his message. He sat, and wrote.

"To Major David Stirling, BHQ(ME) Cairo. Unable to make Alexandria. Forced by Axis to the west. Able to elude and now at Valletta. Send full relief crew Malta. Advise schedule for flight out eighteen personnel. Need pay from January 1942 to this date, and Swedish crew pay from March 1941 to this date. Please authorise Malta paymaster to issue same. Captain Reginald Wallace."

The man reviewed it and then dismissed him. It would be transcribed into a cipher and sent out. Any reply would be decrypted and brought to his ship at Pinto Wharf by courier. Before leaving, he visited the lieutenant to thank the man, who cordially told him his crew was welcome to the "freedom of the city," as such. The man also issued Reggie a cryptic warning.

"Your crew would be well advised to stay away from The Gut." Reggie had no idea what this meant, but the door was now shut and the man hadn't explained himself. He left to return to the ship, but decided to travel by Valletta's city streets instead. It might be easier to find his way there by a grid pattern of streets.

Was he ever wrong! He was astonished at the level of destruction, with entire city streets reduced to rubble, yet within this a single building here and there stood alone, untouched. The Church of St Francis of Assisi was completely demolished. Large sections of the city elsewhere might stand virtually unscathed. The distance from Fort Lascaris to the ship was less than two miles along the route he took, but climbing over and around all this rubble was exhausting. When he reached the *Belfair* he inserted the new valve in the radio receiver. He lay down fully dressed for a bit of a kip. He was just drifting off, but was suddenly awakened by the rising and falling wail of air-raid sirens and the sound of engines overhead. Jumping from bed he raced down to the main deck. His crew had already emerged. He shouted orders to scatter and take cover behind the bulwarks individually, and apart. *If we're hit, hopefully only a few will die*, he thought.

Anxiously he looked for Pavlina but she was nowhere to be seen. A flight of Ju-88 twin engined bombers approached from the north and were engaged by the Spits. He rushed into the galley to find the women cowering next the oil stove, and he joined them. There was the *crump* of explosions, some very nearby, and the deck vibrated under their knees. It seemed to last hours but in reality was but minutes. They emerged when it was all over. Palls of black smoke rose from various locations on the three peninsula cities across the water, Birgu,

Senglea, and Kalkara. There were blocks of stone fallen scattered on the deck, and these seemed to have come from the Pinto Stores on the wharf, which had been reduced to dust and debris. He could hear ambulance sirens in the distance. Reggie rang the handbell, and the crew gathered.

"Anyone hurt? No? Good. It's much too dangerous to be on a ship out here. I've asked for the pay due us all to be issued. When it arrives, I'll find lodgings in the city for us. In the meantime, you should all go to the nearest air-raid shelter. Come back here at 1800 hours to eat supper aboard. I'll stay on the ship for now." He detailed the deckhands to pitch the stone blocks onto the wharf before they left.

Prior to supper a courier on a bicycle arrived at the bulwark gate with a package for him. He opened it in his quarters and counted the cash. It was all there, and there was a sealed note addressed to him personally from a Lieutenant: it seems the crew of destroyer HMS *Penelope* was leaving tomorrow morning and vacating their rooms above some place called the Caffe Cordina. There was an address. No one else knew this now. See them tonight.

Strangely, there was no response to the rest of his message to Stirling. *Sod that man!* Annika rang the handbell for supper. After supper, he selected Pavlina to accompany him, and told her to bring her sub-machine gun, as he carried quite a lot of cash. They made their way along the waterfront on the *Xatt Lascaris* Road, through a tunnel, and then up the *Liess* and through the Victoria Gate. By this route they avoided all the rubble from the ruins of the Opera House further south. Then taking a left on Old Theatre Street they approached Kingsway, and found the Caffe Cordina on their left, a two storey building with the Caffe, a popular restaurant, on the ground floor. Above the door a carved tablet read "Est. 1837".

It was well they'd rushed, for the seamen from HMS *Penelope* were leaving early. Reggie booked ten first floor rooms for a week starting tonight, Annika getting her own room next to theirs, a room with a view of the square. In the square outside they could see, at eye level, the finely carved statue of Queen Victoria seated in a chair on a plinth, protective sandbags stacked up all about her. He paid cash in advance, and they hurried back to the ship to get the others. Reggie had them queue to sign the logbook and issued their pay, and it was joyously received. He assigned Mr Lindgren as watchman this first night, and they all trooped uphill to the hotel along the same route. Pavlina walked with the group, leaving her bicycle on board.

In the morning they all breakfasted together in the Caffe Cordina. Reggie asked for a volunteer to replace Lindgren, and Arne stepped up. He gave the rest the "freedom of the city" and they dispersed, after given instructions to meet for supper together here. Arne and Reggie were halfway to the ship at about 9:30 when again there was the wail of air-raid sirens and Hurricanes from RAF Luqa aerodrome roared overhead. This time it was a squadron of Ju-87 "Stuka" dive bombers that appeared.

A Maltese policeman in a white pith helmet with a spike on top chivvied them along to a nearby cave the local people were using as a shelter. It was an old railway tunnel and the unused tracks were still in place. It was very crowded and noisome here, as it appeared a large number of families had elected to live in this cave permanently. Infants squalled continually. A side gallery had been designated as a latrine. A Maltese fellow next to him said most caves on the island were like this, then added he much preferred being bombed by Germans, rather than Italians. The Germans came in low and knew what military targets they were aiming at, whereas the cowardly Italians stayed high, out of reach of the anti-aircraft batteries. Their bombs fell indiscriminately in the cities killing many civilians. They sat in the dim lighting as they listened to the battle rage overhead, and waited anxiously until it was over. He wondered if they'd find the *Belfair* afloat, or just the tops of the funnel, cranes, and bridge showing above water.

Mr Lindgren was extremely happy to see them. He reported he'd seen a bomb hit the forward part of HMS *Kingston* without exploding. That destroyer was now being manoeuvred to the graving dock for repairs. Arne exchanged places with Lindgren, and they returned to the hotel. There was as yet no further answer to his message. *What could be keeping the response?*

Reggie and Pavlina now left the hotel. They viewed the Queen Victoria statue, then wandered arm-in-arm down Old Theatre Street. In a few more streets they saw the roof of St Paul's Pro-Cathedral had collapsed. Doubling back the way they'd come, they had a peek into the Teatro Manoel, a rather grand theatre. Further along was Old Bakery Street but it was filled with rubble, so they continued on to the next street, the Strada Stretta, which translated as Strait Street in English. This seemed to be clear. They turned left down it. Soon they encountered a bar on their left called the Tico-Tico. It was open and they had a look inside. It was dim and this early in the day there were only a few desultory drinkers. It didn't look inviting, in actuality rather depressing. They continued their stroll. An old man in a blue boiler suit paid them no mind as he swept up broken glass with a push broom. They passed a place called the New Life Music Hall, but it was not open this early. The next place on their right had a large sign, the Malata Bar, in red letters on a white background jutting out from the building's face. It was open. Reggie looked ahead of them. It seemed this street only got narrower further along. They were about to turn about when a "redcap" stepped out of this bar. He wore the khaki shorts and white pipeclayed Sam Browne belt and holster of a British military policeman. His pistol was holstered and secured to a white lanyard about his neck. Reggie hailed the man.

"Excuse me sir! We've only just arrived, the motor ship *Belfair* of Stockholm." The MP glanced at his captain's uniform.

"You're a long way from home, eh?"

"I've been warned to keep my crew away from 'The Gut'. Could you tell me where that is, please?"

"You're standing in it," he smirked. "The Gut is 'Strait Street' going downhill that way, all the way to Saint Elmo Bay." He pointed.

"Huh. Doesn't look like much." Reggie remarked.

"Don't be fooled. It can get fair rough at night," the MP warned.

"Are there restaurants here?" Pavlina asked.

"Yes ma'am," he pointed into the Malata bar, "if you go through here, there's a restaurant on the other side. This is the rear entrance." They thanked the man and entered the Malata, going through the eatery and emerging onto Saint Georges Palace Square.

They spent the afternoon aimlessly wandering the city, choosing their direction by those streets that weren't yet blocked by rubble. In early afternoon they happened upon a restaurant on Boat Street called Cockneys that had a view of Manoel Island. Lunch was *Aljotta* soup, a Maltese fish delicacy. The beer was a lager style brew called 'Cisk' and it was quite tasty. They continued their wandering along the road skirting the shoreline of the peninsula, then strolled back to their hotel, only having to duck into an air-raid shelter or a cave three more times. Entering the square their hotel fronted on, they had to skirt a fresh bomb crater. The glass in all the hotel windows fronting on the square had been blown in. As luck would have it, no one had been in the rooms during the day. He borrowed a broom from the concierge and swept their room. Supper was nourishing if not exactly thrilling, because of the food shortages. Other than seafood, the meat on offer seemed to always be rabbit, either stewed or fried, and always expensive. The other meat offered was a dish called *Bebbux*. Without any idea what this was, he ordered it once, and was surprised to find it was snails in garlic. He ate it anyway, for he was hungry that day. It wasn't until after sundown he remembered he had forgotten to relay the warning from that lieutenant about "the gut" to his crew. He started down the hall and began knocking on doors, but there was no reply. Finally Lindgren answered to his knock.

"Mr Lindgren, I'm so glad to find you in. Where has everybody gone?"

"I think the money must be burning a hole in their pockets, sir. They said they wanted to go drinking and listen to some jazz."

"And you didn't go along?"

"No. I'm not so much for jazz. It's only a lot of noise to my ears."

"Where is this jazz club they went to?"

"It's not one jazz club, sir, it's many jazz clubs. Some place they called the gut. I don't know where it is."

"I do. Thank you, Mr Lindgren. Goodnight."

"Goodnight, sir." Reggie went back to his room. He sat on the bed to unlace his shoes but then paused, and sighed.

"Réži" Pavlina purred, "you are worried of somethings?" She was already partly undressed.

"Everybody has gone out to nightclubs for jazz and drinks. I can't put my finger on it, but it just doesn't feel right to me, you know?"

"Everybody?" she queried, her voice tense.

"Yes." Something was gnawing at his insides.

"Is including Annika?" *That was it!*

"Yes, Lindgren says they've gone to the gut, and I don't like it one bit. I'm going after them." Reggie wasn't worried about the men; they could handle themselves, it was Annika concerned him now.

"Wait! I go with you." Pavlina dressed quickly in her Yugoslav partisan uniform and *pilotka* cap, and they rushed out the door.

16

Maltese Days, and Nights

At this time of night, Strait Street was very different than the street they'd seen only nine hours before. It was heaving. Jazz music erupted from every doorway. Knots of sailors, soldiers, and airmen weaved about unsteadily, beer in hand, shouting to be heard. Reggie and Pavlina went from one club to another, looking briefly inside for the sight of a familiar face, then moving on. At least once on every street they heard the tinkle of a breaking bottle. They reached the first junction and looked into The Splendid Lounge and Bar. They came up empty. They met across the street to stand under the sign for Everybody's Library Booksellers, the door and windows of which were locked and barred tight, only one indication of how hazardous this street could become.

"Pavlina," he shouted, "This isn't getting us anywhere. We should split up. You cover the right side, and I'll take the left? We'll meet at the bottom of this street." She yelled acknowledgement. The next street was even worse than the first. The individual groups had coalesced to become a solid mass of heaving, pushing, humanity. The caps on the heads of the servicemen all around him were the regulation Royal Navy white with a black headband, and each headband had lettering in gold of the ship that man served. He read HMS *Gallant*, HMS *Kingston*, and HMS *Lance.* There were also Maltese civilians in the rabble, and even a number of Yanks. He stepped into the Carmen Bar and looked about the room. Nothing. Out on the street again he forced his way through the mob. At times a brief scuffle might break out, and sometimes develop into a punch-up involving dozens of fighters. The Americans were willing to spend much more, and when a prostitute abandoned a Brit to go with an American, it was rather resented. A bruiser of a man in front of him was bulling his way through the throng. Those that didn't get out of this man's way in time were tossed aside. Reggie fell in step behind him. It made for easier going and he was glad of it. In another fifty yards the big fellow vanished into a doorway on the left. Reggie was still dressed in his captain's uniform with its peaked cap, and noticed the sailors fell silent when they saw him approaching, an officer in their midst. He decided to put this to his advantage, frequently yelling "Gangway," the command to make way for an officer coming through, and it worked. He made better progress. He shouldered his way successively into the Piccadilly Bar, the Black Prince Bar, the Silver Horse, and the White Star, to discover these places were not only bars, but often also bordellos. He should have known, given that there were a few women standing clustered at the entrances to these establishments attempting to entice customers inside. He was about to enter the Egyptian Queen Bar when the door opened and he ran into Second Engineer Frederik just coming out. The man seemed embarrassed. In a moment he understood why. Pavlina appeared from behind Reggie to stand by his side.

"Don't bother going in there," Frederik muttered, "They haven't any beer." Pavlina laughed at his reaction.

"Do not be embarrassed Frederik, we all understand men do what men must do," then, gripping his shoulder, she asked with concern, "but, where is Annika?"

"We left her back at the hotel," he responded, confidently.

"No," Reggie said, "she followed you!"

"*Herre Gud*," Frederik swore, "We must find her!" The three of them started uphill, back the way they'd come, and then encountered Torstein together with Snorri, the ship's laundryman that spoke only Swedish. They brought them along with them. In the next street but one they found another bar, and with alarm Reggie realised he'd missed this one on the way down. He heard a woman scream in anguish from inside. He forced his way in. The room was small but high-ceilinged. By standing on tiptoe he could see over the heads in front of him a bar with two bartenders. To his left was a stage of musicians and they were loud. On the right-hand wall an open staircase rose to the next floor. The same big fellow he'd followed earlier was climbing the stair and dragging Annika behind him by her wrist. She screamed again, inarticulately, as she struggled against his grip. Reggie pulled out his Walther and racked the slide.

"Stop! Let her go!" he shouted. The man turned to face him.

"Or what?" he sneered. Reggie held his arm overhead so the pistol was visible. The sailors around pushed back, away from this armed officer. The jazz music faltered and petered out.

"She is not a prostitute," he yelled. The room fell silent.

"If she's not now, she soon will be," snarled the man. In the silence there came the unnaturally loud click of something being cocked. Reggie turned his head to see the barman waving a side-by-side twelve-bore at them. The men and women in the room squatted, leaving Reggie exposed. Those near the door ran outside.

"Call the police," the bartender spoke over his shoulder without taking his eyes off them. The other barman began dialling. "Turk! You! Both of you, – take it outside!" Reggie backed out the entrance as "Turk" advanced on him, holding Annika before him as a shield. Outside the rabble pushed back to form a clear space. Once outside the

Turk kept advancing on him until he lunged, wrapping his hand over the top of the pistol. Annika was cast aside and fell to the pavement. A sailor bent to help her to her feet. She broke away and ran to Pavlina's arms.

The Turk twisted the gun in Reggie's hand. He was immensely strong and Reggie felt himself losing the struggle, so he squeezed off a round. A pockmark exploded from the nearby wall, and there was the tinkle of broken glass far above. The man let go and put his bleeding hand to his mouth, punching Reggie in the face with his other fist. His cap flew off and he saw stars. When his vision cleared he found he'd been disarmed. He could hear police whistles and they were coming closer.

"It is mine now," Turk said contemptuously. He pocketed it. The throng parted and two Maltese gendarmes entered the clearing. They wore a khaki uniform and a white pith helmet with a chromed spike on top. They were armed only with truncheons. The shorter one spoke to the Turk in the Maltese language. The Turk interrupted him with scorn.

"You are in The Gut. Here everybody is British. Speak English!"

"Turk, you remember how the magistrate warned you?" the MP challenged in a weary tone, as if he'd done this before. He handed his pith helmet to his companion and unlimbered his truncheon.

"Piss on your magistrate!" Reggie noticed only now, under the street lamp, the state of the man. He wore regulation Royal Navy trousers but the tunic was only a threadbare black suit coat with the elbows worn out. The grubby cap on his head was the regulation white with a black headband, but it read HMS *Glasgow*, a ship not here, and some of the letters were missing. *The man's AWOL, out of control*, Reggie thought, *he's gone rogue!*

"He's got my gun in his left trouser pocket," he murmured to the MP, "he's left-handed." The MP acknowledged him with a nod. The MP assumed a fighting stance, left foot forward, his right elbow pointed at the man, holding his truncheon hanging down his back over his right shoulder. The Turk put up his fists and grinned. He took a step forwards.

The MP dropped to one knee, cracking the man across the left shin, and reassumed his position. The Turk winced and stepped back, then advanced again. The MP lifted his forearm over his head and the truncheon swung horizontally, connecting with Turk's right temple. He staggered back, dazed, shook his head to clear it, and advanced again. The MP faked raising his forearm over his head again and the man held up his right arm to block the blow, but the truncheon came straight down on his forehead, and this was followed up with a hard two-handed truncheon jab to the gut.

Each time the MP reassumed his starting position. The MP raised his forearm crossing over the top of his head again, but dropped to one knee, and Turk swung wildly at a face that wasn't there. He was cracked across the right shin. Still he hadn't gone down. He stood breathing heavily. He pulled the pistol from his pocket. In a flash the MP brought the truncheon down on it and the gun went skittering over the pavement. Frederik scooped it up. But Turk had hold of the truncheon now. He jerked the MP towards himself, spinning him about, clutching the smaller man to his gut by the truncheon across his throat, choking him. The MP's legs thrashed and his arms flailed for a grip, his face turning red as he struggled for breath. The second MP drew out his own truncheon. The Turk laughed and laughed, his mouth wide open. Reggie felt Pavlina's hand on his left shoulder and heard her speak from behind him.

"Do not move, Réži," Pavlina whispered in his ear, "His life depends on you." He held his breath. Her silencer braced on his shoulder, she aimed for the Turk's open mouth. *Phut!* sounded in his left ear. The back of the man's neck blew away and the sailors beyond him were showered with blood. The Turk's head dropped unsupported to the rear and he toppled onto his back. Mouth opening and closing like a fish, paralysed from the neck down, his lungs wouldn't respond, and he soon expired. The second MP rushed to the aid of his companion and helped him stand. The two military policemen turned to Reggie. Frederik crossed the clearing and handed Reggie's pistol back to him.

"It wasn't me. Frederik's had it in his pocket all this time." He displayed it to the officers. "You can see for yourself it hasn't a silencer." The MPs looked over the crowd of three or four dozen sailors.

"Thank you anyway, captain," was murmured. They ordered the crowd to disperse. Reggie retrieved his cap and dusted it down. Pavlina stood off to one side and held Annika, ignored by the MPs.

"We go back to the hotel now," she whispered, "You have enough of jazz, yes?" Annika nodded agreement. Back at the hotel the few men of his crew who had returned went to their rooms. He and Pavlina disrobed completely for bed as was their usual practice. Before drifting off to sleep, they heard the sound of Annika sobbing through the wall. Pavlina rose and wrapped a towel around herself. She kissed Reggie.

"I sleep with Annika tonight. She will need the comforting, I think."

Pavlina let herself into the room still wrapped in a towel. Reggie was getting dressed before breakfast.

"Good morning. How is Annika today?" he inquired.

"Annika is doing well." Pavlina laid her towel on the floor and began her usual morning exercise routine, beginning with stretching.

"Did she tell you how she came to be in that predicament last night?"

"Yes. She went from club to club, enjoying music of jazz, having a fun evening while looking for the others. Then, this big man, he pays for her cocktail. She tries to decline but this he will not allow. Then he buys for her another cocktail, and again she tries to decline, but again he does not listen. So she says to him something he did not want to hear. That is when he get so angry!"

"What did she say to him?" Pavlina didn't answer, so he looked over at her, only to see a sly smile on her face. "Pavlina, what was it she said?"

"What is it called when you know a thing about someone, you wish to tell to another someone?" She sat on the towel to begin her sit-ups.

"Gossip?"

"Yes, that. Do you want to hear a gossip?"

"Why not?" Reggie replied, preoccupied with threading his belt through the loops of his trousers.

"Annika, she is – how is said? – a 'Sister of Lesbos'."

"The Greek Island? Really? Annika is Greek? I would have guessed she was Swedish through-and-through." His belt buckled, he reached for his shoes.

"No, Reggie, you do not listen. Annika, she is the lover of women." Reggie dropped his shoes in surprise.

"You mean, Annika is a lesbian?"

"Yes, that." Pavlina rolled this new word around on her tongue. "Less-bee-ann. Lesbian."

"I'd no idea. You couldn't tell just by looking at her. What I mean is, she doesn't wear a necktie nor trousers, only dresses and blouses – just like you!"

"Yes, that." Pavlina nodded in agreement. Reggie knelt and tied his shoelaces, his face thoughtful, then stood. He felt slightly uneasy. He had to know, so he asked.

"So ... did you and Annika ... you know, ... make —"

"No! I am a lover of *you* – of men, not women. I only let her caress me a little amount, and I suppose it maybe was nice," she admitted, and shrugged, "but men are far more a pleasure to me."

"But Pavlina, we've never made love, because of the orders given to you by Tito."

"No we have not," she admitted, and continued, "But, is not all the gossip. Oh, no."

"There's more?"

"Yes. Annika say: if you want to know more, you will be asking Frederik in private. She say, is a thing for the ears of men." *How mysterious*, he thought. He made up his mind to ask Frederik, and sometime soon. Pavlina finished her sit-ups. She started on her star-jump routine.

Reggie sat down for breakfast next to Pavlina and across from Annika. His crew had filled the other seats around the long table. It was tea and a kind of porridge of a grain he couldn't identify, and as usual there was no breakfast meat available. They tucked into it. He interrupted his meal to catch Annika's eye.

"I'm so sorry for last night, Annika. I'd been advised to warn you all to stay away from The Gut, but it just slipped my mind, and I failed you."

"It's no fault of yours, sir." Annika reassured him. "I would have gone anyway. You see, having lived for a year in close quarters with these men, it seems I've become 'just one of the boys'."

"She's a strong one, is our Annika." said Frederik. Agreement was murmured by Torstein and a few others around the table.

"Still, I should've warned you – warned *all* of you." He was interrupted by the appearance of a group of men at their table, a Swede third engineer and three Norwegian deckhands and a second mate from an American merchant ship, eager to sign on. "Sent by Stirling" they told him. They'd gone to the *Belfair* and were redirected here by the man on watch. He told them to leave their details for him at the front desk, and dispatched them back to their lodgings to await further word.

Reggie tucked into his porridge once again. The waiter set down a cup of coffee at his elbow.

"You have coffee?" he asked the man, in surprise.

"No sir," the waiter replied, "it's made of chicory – that is, it's ersatz coffee."

"Not real coffee? Oh, well, I'll drink it anyway. Have you any sugar?"

"No sir, but there is this dish of sweets here," he said, placing a plate of small gelatinous cubes on the table. Annika nicked a cube from the plate and popped it into her mouth.

"Sweets? What kind of sweets?" he asked.

"*Rahat-lokoum*, sir."

"I'm sorry, I don't speak the language. Can you translate it for me, please?"

"In English it's known as 'Turkish Delight'," he responded. Annika coughed, and spit her piece into her hand. She dropped it on the floor under her chair, where a patiently waiting cat gobbled it down.

Once again there was the wail of air-raid sirens and Hurricanes from RAF Luqa roared overhead. He looked at his watch. Half-nine, right on time. They all went down to the cellar, to sit amongst the barrels and crates. The banshee howl of the Stuka dive-bombers came again.

"Sir, what are we doing here?" Frederik asked, as they all sat out the raid under the light from a few bare bulbs. "I mean, you seem to be waiting for something, but we're in a dangerous place, a place we shouldn't be at all and, who is Stirling? Who are these new men?"

"I don't like it any more than you do." He whispered in response. "I'll explain later, but not here." He then asked for a watch-stander to relieve Arne, and Snorri volunteered. Minutes later, the all-clear sirens sounded. This morning's raid over, Snorri was sent off to the ship, and he and Frederik walked to the communication centre at Malta Command. As they walked, they talked.

"You're wondering who Stirling is?" Reggie asked.

"Yes, and why he's sending Scandinavians to you."

"I don't know either. My 'mission' is supposed to be at an end. It's a long story, one I can't divulge yet. I'm an employee of the Ellerman Shipping Lines of London. Stirling is my temporary boss. He doesn't work for Ellerman. That's all I can tell you about Stirling."

"I've a feeling you're involving us in something military. Sweden is neutral, a non-belligerent country. The *Riksdag* isn't going to like this at all."

"Your parliament isn't of concern for our immediate problem. I'm going to get the proper frequency so I can talk directly to Stirling from the ship. We'll soon get our problems sorted."

At Fort Lascaris Reggie reminded the RAF wireless operator he'd still received no reply from BHQ(ME) and demanded he be given the frequency for voice transmission with them. It was written down on a scrap of paper for him. They climbed the stairs to the Upper Barrakka Gardens so Frederik could see the view. As they looked over the Grand Harbour from the parapet, he decided now would be as good a time as any for a chinwag.

"Frederik, Annika had a rough time of it last night. We heard her crying on the other side of the wall from our room."

"Oh, dear. That's not good."

"Yes, and to comfort her, Pavlina went to sleep with her."

"She did? Oh, dear." Frederik wiped a hand over his face. "Is Pavlina angry?"

"No. More amused than anything. We now know Annika is a lesbian."

"And Annika being a lesbian doesn't repulse either of you?" Frederik speculated, surprised.

"Not at all. She told Pavlina the tale of how she came to be attacked by that monster." Reggie relayed this story to Frederik. "We are puzzled by one thing, though. Annika told Pavlina that if I want to know more, I have to ask you."

"She said that?" Frederik asked, then laughed. "Why, that canny bitch, putting me on the spot like this. She didn't tell Pavlina?"

"Apparently not." They both were silent and watched as one of the *dgħajsa*, those narrow taxi boats with the upright stem, left the shoreline far below. It was painted quite colourfully in primary colours, and the eyes of Osiris were painted on its bow to ward off evil. Its pilot stood facing forward and pushing its long sweep oars as he made his way to the far shore. Frederik began his tale.

"Well, I guess Annika is willing to let me reveal it to you, or so it would seem." He cupped his chin in his palm and thought a minute. "Where to begin, where to begin. Hmmm ..." Frederik blew out his cheeks. "I should probably preface this by letting you know Sweden is one of the most progressive societies on earth. Other nations outside Scandinavia know little of the inner workings of our government, and what gets reported in the foreign press usually calls us too permissive.

"We can live with that: we know what we're doing, and we know it's the correct thing to do. So, there is a movement afoot in our society to make same-sex sexual activity legal. As far as I know, the legislation looks to pass by perhaps 1943, but certainly by 1944 at the very latest."

"That must make Annika pleased," he nodded in agreement. Frederik gave him a sidelong look.

"Reggie, or should I call you 'Leif'? – I see by your mild reaction to this news, you might make a good Swede some day. Well, anyway, here's the story Annika has put me on the spot for, unbelievable as it may seem to you: you know already we were stranded in Šibenik since April 1941 until we left in late March 1942. That's eleven long months.

"With our officers murdered, there was no one to give orders. We were leaderless. It was left to me, as the sole remaining officer, to step up and be a captain, of sorts. I am, however, an engineer more comfortable dealing with mute metal machinery. I'm not so good with human beings and their idiosyncrasies."

"Yes, I can understand that," Reggie responded, patting his shoulder, "I'm often at a loss myself when it comes to that." Frederik turned to face Reggie as he warmed to his subject, and leaned an elbow on the parapet.

"In three, maybe four months, we were at each others throats. Everything, and I mean everything, went all to hell. Work stopped completely, we were not speaking to each other. Some of us came to blows. Sometimes the food didn't hold out and we starved for a few days. The ship became our prison."

"It was hard enough for me to get onto it, and you couldn't leave!"

"You saw the state of the ship when you arrived. It had been much, much worse."

"Worse than that? I cannot imagine!"

"We fifteen men were slowly being driven mad. Some of us are married but most of us, like myself, are single. As the only woman in the crew and responsible for feeding us, in normal times we always respected Annika and her cooking abilities. She never shirked her duties, but she had taken to locking herself in her cabin outside of mealtimes. She knew this was no way to live, and it had to change.

"One day she came to me with a germ of an idea, and outlined it for me. Together we sat and hammered out the details. I then called a meeting of the fourteen others, and we all put our names on an old calendar page, one name for every other day of a thirty-day month. This was posted in the galley.

"Annika and I then laid down some firm rules. Annika would, and this is the key point here, without any sex permitted, voluntarily sleep with, and I mean it was indeed actual sleeping, in the bed of each of us once per month. Men knew which day was theirs. They looked forward to it.

"Every other night she would sleep in the bed of a new crewman, and as she held each man, she listened to him, and talked to him, to soothe away his problems and fears. It was sexless, but it worked like a charm. We began speaking to each other again, working together again as a team. She saved us. "

"Frederik, that's remarkable," he complimented, "And Annika came up with this out of whole cloth?"

"Astonishing, isn't it? And her a lesbian. Annika saved our sanity! Oh, there was some little jealousy at the beginning, as certain men suspected she was favouring some but not others. But soon it was realized she was strictly keeping us all to an equal standard – no sex at all, only holding and talking and listening to us."

"When I arrived I remember, uh, ... smelling Mr Lindgren. What's the story there?" Reggie inquired.

"That, my friend," Frederik chortled, "is the proof she was sincere in her efforts. In Lindgren's second time with her, she awoke to find him attempting to enter her."

"NO! – what an arse." He looked about to see if any had heard his outburst. The nearest soldier stood smoking thirty yards distant.

"Oh, yes, I remember it vividly," Frederik crowed, "Annika kept the supper handbell with her, and rang it at three o'clock in the morning to call us all out of bed. She shamed Lindgren in front of us all, and publicly crossed him off the calendar. His time with her was done!"

"Good for her, what a champion woman!"

"As for myself, she has let me hold her all through the night seven times. Annika now knows more about these men than anybody. She and I hold regular confidences about crew problems. Well, that's the story. Does it shock you?" Frederik asked.

"No, not at all." said Reggie, with a twinkle in his eye. "Do you think Annika will agree to add me to her calendar?"

"You dog, you," laughed Frederik.

"I'm only joking. Shall we go?" Frederik returned to the hotel, and Reggie went to the ship to use the transmitter.

Speaking to Carruthers, the radio officer at BHQ(ME), it greatly cheered him to learn a Dakota was scheduled to fly to RAF Luqa aerodrome sometime in the next few days, at an unknown time. Needless to say, the man couldn't mention specifics in a voice transmission. After speaking to Carruthers, he tuned the receiver to the BBC Overseas Service. After only twenty minutes of listening he was gratified to hear mention of the *Belfair*. They repeated Rome Radio was saying the Swedish ship *Belfair* had become disabled and towed to Malta by unknown forces. They also reported they heard the same message from Radio Vaticana, and also heard Herr Goebbels repeating this in a broadcast from the Grossdeutscher Rundfunk, and furthermore, the German propaganda minister made the promise that that neutral ship was to be left strictly alone. He returned to the hotel in time for lunch.

17

A Promise Kept

Late the next afternoon, hours after the third somewhat predictable bombing of the ships in the harbour had ended, a Dakota aeroplane appeared from out of the east, to circle once over the stony fields and bomb-shattered houses of Valletta. Reggie watched as it assumed a shallow glide path for landing at RAF Luqa to the south. *This is it! The new Swedish officers I've been waiting for. At last my mission is at an end!*

There was a knock on his door. He answered it to find a delegation of his crew, there to inform him they'd had enough of the constant bombings and were abandoning the hotel for the nearest air-raid shelter. Having seen at first-hand how noisome these tunnels were he reluctantly agreed, on the condition the men keep to a schedule of showers aboard ship, this to prevent the spread of lice or disease among his crew. He wrote out a list and assigned certain of these crewmen to be on-board watch-standers for the next few days. Frederik was to keep the boilers at the ready during evening hours.

Three hours passed, and he began to be troubled as he awaited the arrival of the new Swedish crew. It was hours past teatime already, but he didn't want to leave the room for fear of missing them. A squeal of brakes outside alerted him, and he rushed to the window. There below was a bus painted in the usual "Malta camouflage", the type disguising the *xarabank* as a small stone building, and on it's side was painted "RAF Luqa". Its door opened and a group of two dozen naval officers and uniformed crew filed out, followed by Lieutenant-General Robert Stone. The man paused to stretch.

"Pavlina, they're here! I was expecting Major Stirling, but it's General Stone, instead. I wish he could see you in your uniform, but there's no time for you to change." Since wearing her uniform during that night in The Gut, she had taken to wearing only her civilian clothing. Pavlina put down the Croatian/English dictionary she'd been reading, and stood. Reggie hoisted her suitcase onto the bed. "You look very nice in that blouse and skirt, but here – find your Order of the White Eagle medal and put that on, ... I want you to look as impressive as possible!"

Pavlina took her sub-machine gun from the case and laid it on the bed. She placed the Order of the White Eagle on its ribbon around her neck and stood at the foot of the bed. Reggie tightened his tie and threw on his captain's blazer, buttoning the double-breasted brass buttons. He quickly combed his hair. Taking a position in the centre of the room and facing the door, he waited. There came a knock.

"Come in," he called. The door opened and General Stone took a few steps into the room. Reggie came to attention, and snapped off a brisk salute. General Stone returned his salute.

"Stand easy, captain," he ordered.

"Am I relieved to see —" Reggie began. Milly stepped out from behind the General and raced across the room to throw her arms about his neck, and with her eyes shut she gave him a long kiss. She released him and opened her eyes, and only then saw Pavlina.

"Oh my! I'm so sorry, I didn't see —"

"Buga!" General Stone interjected in surprise. From behind the general, Sergeant Ellice entered the room. When he saw Reggie his mouth gaped and he dropped the chart tube he'd been carrying. He appeared to shrink two inches in height.

"Perhaps I should make the introductions," Reggie said. He turned to Pavlina to see her standing stiffly erect, eyes half closed and unsmiling as she regarded Milly icily. He coughed into his fist.

"Buga Pavlina, may I present to you Lieutenant-General Robert Stone, general officer commanding British Troops in Egypt. This is Miss Millicent Featherstone, the general's personal clerk, and that is Sergeant Ellice, the general's aide-de-camp." He turned to face the group.

"General Stone, may I present Lieutenant Buga Pavlina, under the direct command of Josip Broz Tito, Commander-in-Chief of the National Liberation Army of Yugoslavia." The general saluted her, and Buga returned his salute in the peculiar way of the partisans.

"Lieutenant Pavlina, I ..."

"Please sir," she interrupted, "we do not address by rank in the partisan forces, only using 'comrade', because we are all equal."

"I see. Very well then, may I call you Buga?"

"Please." He then advanced to her and took her hand in his, patting it with his other hand.

"Buga, I have seen your poster and am most impressed," the general complimented, "Twenty-eight assassinations. Splendid work!" Sergeant Ellice quailed and, looking at the sub-machine gun, gave a whimper. The general looked at Ellice in irritation. "Sergeant Ellice! Where is my briefcase?" Ellice looked about him on the floor.

"I ... I ... I think I left it on the hotel desk?" he stammered. "I'll go get it."

"No, you stay here. *I'll* go get it." He rushed out the door, but paused along the way. "Have I ever told you, sergeant, how useless you are?" he asked, rhetorically. The door shut. Now the four of them stood in the room somewhat uncomfortably. Milly looked at the rumpled bedclothes and the pillows that lay askew, then looked at Pavlina and then to Reggie, where her eyes remained. As little as he wanted to, Reggie felt it was left to him to take hold of the situation. He took both Milly's hands in his. His eyes held Milly eyes, but his remarks were for Pavlina's benefit.

"Pavlina, I met Milly when I was in Egypt, in January of this year. Milly and I, at that time we were lovers." Sergeant Ellice snickered. Without moving his head, over his shoulder Reggie uttered, "Shut up, you," then continued. "I loved Milly then, and I still love her now, but she was not interested in marriage then, and that's still true for you now, – isn't it Milly?" She looked up into Reggie's face, biting her lip, and nodded. She swallowed in an attempt to clear the lump in her throat.

"Reggie, I love you, but you said you would be back in two weeks, and when you didn't come back, we all thought you were dead. Then, three weeks ago I was told you were alive, and when I told the others," – she glanced briefly at Ellice – "I was not believed." Ellice giggled nervously.

"Milly, are you telling me sergeant Ellice did not heed my warning?" She bit her lip, her eyes welling up with tears, and she nodded.

"He even groped me on the flight here. Do you remember that promise you made, at the jeep, just before you boarded that submarine?"

"I do remember my promise. The other clerks, what about them?" She nodded. Sergeant Ellice grimaced. Pavlina picked up her submachine gun and placed it in her suitcase. She snapped the hasps shut. The door opened and General Stone stepped in carrying his briefcase, shutting the door behind him. He paused then, looking from one to the other, as he could sense the tension in the room. Reggie looked at his wristwatch, then at the window. It was dark out. He turned to the general.

"Sir, it's after duty hours. You should possibly release us so we may eat now." Stone looked at his own watch, then at the darkened window.

"Yes, yes, of course, look at the time. My, my! Is the food here good?" he inquired.

"As good as may be expected sir, given the wartime food shortages. I'll show you downstairs." He settled his cap on his head. They all filed out of the room and down the stairs, Reggie and Stone together in front, followed by Milly, then Ellice, and a grim Pavlina brought up the rear, a hand gripping the sergeant's shoulder. The front room of the Caffe Cordina was marble floored, and it had lovely old murals on its plastered barrel vault ceiling. There was a kitchen towards the back, and more table seating in separate rooms off to each side. Reggie pointed into one of these side rooms.

"If you'll just step in there, General, they'll be happy to serve you. I hope you like stewed rabbit. Get us a table, please," he urged. "We're going to step outside for a minute. Be right back." When the general was safely out of sight, at Reggie's direction Pavlina took hold of one of Ellice's arms, and Milly took the other. They all waited while Reggie went to the hotel's front desk. He whispered to the concierge for a moment, and the man picked up a business card to write something down. They all strolled out the entrance together and over to Old Theatre Street, Ellice hanging back in a fruitless attempt to resist, to stand under a street lamp on the corner of the building.

"Sergeant Ellice, are you thirsty?" Reggie inquired. The sergeant nodded, obviously frightened. "They make an excellent lager here, a brand called 'Cisk', isn't that right, Pavlina?" Pavlina agreed. Reggie pulled out his wallet and thumbed through it, bringing out some British pound notes.

"Here's twenty quid. Oh, what the hell, let's make it fifty quid. We wouldn't want you to run short, now would we?" The sergeant was looking a bit confused, as was Milly. Reggie tucked the wad of cash into Ellice's tunic pocket. "Buga, Milly,—turn him loose!" Pavlina and Milly did, and both women stepped over to stand beside Reggie. He held up the hotel card to Ellice's view, and Milly could see the foreign words pencilled on its back, words meaning nothing to her. "This card is the address of the hotel, in case you get lost." He tucked it into the man's other tunic pocket, and placed a comforting hand on his shoulder.

"Now, Sergeant Ellice, if you go one street north from here," – he pointed – "you will find 'Strait Street'. Turn right and follow it. It has jazz clubs, gambling dens, dozens of bars, bordellos and brothels, all sorts really." He patted the sergeant on the shoulder. "You go and have a good time. Play some cards. Gamble. Drink as much as you like. You can even buy a whore, if you feel in the mood!"

"Are you telling me all is forgiven?" Ellice piped up, his voice thin and reedy. "There's no hard feelings?" Reggie smiled broadly at him, and winked.

"You go and you have a *very* good time, and I'll see you in the morning," he answered him solicitously. Sergeant Ellice backed away, then turned and ran away a few yards, while looking back at them, then ran some more, then slowed to a walk. When he reached the junction he stood under a street lamp and looked back at them. Reggie urged both women to wave together with him, and they did. Ellice waved, and then disappeared around the corner. Milly rounded on Reggie and slapped his chest.

"What the hell was that," she yelled. "After all he's done to me," she sobbed, and beat his chest with both fists. Pavlina wrapped her arms around Milly from behind and restrained her by gripping her wrists.

"Stop! Reggie says he will see him in the morning – but he will not be seeing Reggie!"

"I don't understand," Milly pleaded, "what did you have the man at the hotel write on that card?"

"Only instructions, in the Maltese language, to bring him to this address," he answered. He offered an arm to each woman, and together they strolled back inside to join General Stone for supper.

General Stone was hopping mad. Really furious. There'd been no answer his knock. He hadn't seen his aide-de-camp at breakfast. Hadn't seen him until now, that is. The Maltese farmer sat high upon the seat of his donkey cart, lethargically holding the reins of the donkey, while the Maltese policeman braced his clipboard on the donkey's rump for support, so the general could apply his signature where indicated. Milly stood at the rear of the donkey cart with Reggie. Today she wore a "tin hat" and he noticed that, unlike yesterday, she wore her hair loose and hanging straight now, similar to Pavlina's. She gazed down at the face of her recent tormentor. It was repulsive but she found she wasn't bothered in the least. There were bruises and his skull was lopsided as if someone, or maybe a group of some-ones, had stomped on it. Teeth were missing, and there was a torn lip. The nostrils were dark with dried blood. Some kind soul had taken the trouble to close his eyelids. Reggie lifted the sheet, to show her the rest of the body. The tunic was ripped in places, and his wristwatch, belt, shoes, and socks were missing.

"Seen enough?" he asked. Milly turned away.

"Sonofabitch!" General Stone swore, as he completed his signature. "All the paperwork. All the records. I gotta write a letter to his family." The policeman handed a copy of the document to the general, who looked at each of them in turn, then at the corpse, and grit his teeth. "Captain Wallace," the general bellowed, "need I remind you, it's highly inappropriate to show a dead body to a woman!" Reggie draped the sheet over the face. "I need a drink," Stone fumed, and stormed inside the Caffe. The farmer clicked his tongue and gave the reins a flick, and the donkey cart clopped off to the mortuary.

"Know anything about this?" The policeman held up the hotel business card.

"I don't speak *Malti*, and don't read or write it," he answered. "Have you any idea how this happened to him?"

"Witnesses tell me he apparently first visited a bordello. He later began to drink heavily, then joined a card game with some Americans and a few RAF mechanics. When he lost all his money, someone – the wrong someone – advanced him a lot of money against his promise of paying them back out of his future winnings. By all accounts his gambling skills were marginal, at best. There were no witnesses to the beating." The policeman strode away to resume his beat. Reggie turned to Milly.

"Do you feel relieved?" he guessed.

"Strangely, yes."

"Let's go join the general for a drink, ... my treat." They went inside.

Robert Stone sat nursing his second whisky and soda. He'd downed the first one in just a few gulps. Milly sat across the table from him with a gin and tonic in hand, and there was even a rare lime wedge in it. Reggie was just accepting a neat bourbon from the waitress. This was a private booth, and Reggie was glad of that, for he had something important to say to the man. General Stone was the first to speak.

"As much as the man was a pain in my neck and quite useless from the get-go, I had a hard time finding anyone to drive me, and run errands, ... and coordinate travel ..." his voice trailed off. He stared into his Scotch, and sighed.

"General, how long —"

"You might as well call me Bob, captain."

"Fine by me, as long as you agree to call me Reggie."

All right, Reggie, you were saying?"

"Bob, how long was Sergeant Ellice your dogsbody?"

"I beg your pardon, my what?"

"Sorry sir, a dogsbody is an old Royal Navy term for someone who acts as an aide-de-camp. You may already know the Royal Navy has an aversion to using French military terms, so they use their own terminology."

"I wasn't aware – my what? – what was it you said?"

"Dogsbody, sir." The general downed his drink, and held up the empty glass to catch the eye of the passing waitress. She responded promptly, and set down his third whisky and soda.

"Humph." He sat for a time, seeming to struggle with his thoughts. "Dogsbody. Reggie, what was it you were just saying?"

"I was only wondering how long Sergeant Ellice worked for you?"

"Oh, some two years I should imagine."

"And how long has Milly here been your personal clerk?" The general sat back and regarded Milly.

"Perhaps, oh, I don't know … three? Three and a half years?"

"Exactly right. You've a good memory, general." Milly nodded with feeling.

"Bob, do you think it would be advantageous to your career if you could return to Cairo with an aide-de-camp already in place, ready to directly assume the duties, now Ellice is no longer available?"

"Yes, that would be ideal, but —"

"Let me suggest Miss Millicent Featherstone here is the ideal candidate to fill the shoes left vacant, so to speak, by Sergeant Ellice." General Stone's head swivelled in her direction and he looked her over. Milly had reclined on the banquette, drink in hand, and gave him an encouraging nod.

"No. No, that won't be appropriate at all. She's a woman." He shook his head slightly more vigorously than was warranted.

"But sir, … *Bob*, … were you aware many Mechanized Transport

Corps drivers, all of them women, are assigned to be chauffeurs of high-ranking American military officers? Reggie turned to Milly. "You know how to drive, right?" He prompted her directly.

"Yes!"

"Bob, did you know," Reggie informed him, "that General Dwight Eisenhower has a British woman driver?"

"No, I didn't." He looked her over again as she smiled confidently at him. "Eisenhower, eh?"

"I know your schedule, and your files, inside out," Milly bragged, "Who better than me?"

"Bob, she's already more highly qualified than Ellice ever was," he pushed.

"Well, ... if Eisenhower, ... I suppose, ... it might, ... be appropriate ..." he ruminated. Reggie raised his glass, and nudged Milly. She brought her glass up as well. Reggie and Milly clinked their glasses, but froze, holding them outstretched within the general's view.

"Shall we now all agree, Bob, that Milly will be your new aide-de-camp?" General Stone raised his glass and clinked with theirs, and they all drank. The general sighed a weary sigh. He set the glass down and sat back against the cushioned booth. He yawned, a hand over his mouth. His gaze travelled between the pair of them for a moment, then settled on Reggie.

"Yes," he remarked, but then added, "you sneaky bastard." He smiled anyway. The general then turned to Milly.

"Now then, Staff-Sergeant Featherstone, your first task is to —"

"Staff-sergeant!" Milly gasped, a hand to her chest.

"Yes staff-sergeant. I'm giving you a brevet field promotion here. A staff-sergeant is a non-commissioned officer, and the least senior grade of the officer ranks. You don't expect a general to have an *enlisted* aide-de-camp, do you?"

"No, no, of course not," she affirmed. Reggie put his hand out and shook hers in congratulations. She picked up her gin and tonic and clinked glasses with Reggie, then took a sip.

"Staff-Sergeant Featherstone," the general began again, "your first task is to get the key from the front desk and gather up Ellice's things from his room." Milly choked, and coughed, gin dribbling off her chin. The general looked surprised at this. "Oh, were you under the impression your job would be easier?"

"No sir, absolutely not," she replied, blotting her face with a sleeve.

"Sir, ... if I may, I'd like to volunteer to assist Milly," Reggie insisted.

"As you wish, Reggie. Then later, I'll want to discuss with you the disposition of your ship."

"I was just on the verge of suggesting that very thing, sir." General Stone now paused and looked her over, then frowned.

"Sergeant Featherstone, were you in a hurry this morning?"

"Sir?"

"Your hair is not regulation." Milly touched her loose hair, and blushed.

"Yes sir, I'll do something about this immediately!" They finished their drinks, and they all rose to leave. Milly picked up her helmet. Reggie paid the bill. They stopped at the front desk to get the key while accompanying the general to his room, and Reggie and Milly then continued down the corridor passing the rooms of Milly, Annika, Pavlina and Reggie, and the rooms the *Belfair* crewmembers had recently abandoned, rooms now let out to others. When they reached Ellice's room, Reggie stood close behind her with a hand atop her hip as Milly put the skeleton key in the keyhole of the oak door. From back down the corridor they had just walked, the door to Reggie's room opened and Pavlina emerged. When she saw them, her eyes hardened.

"Pavlina," he called out, "Join us!" Pavlina locked their door and strode towards them. As they awaited her arrival, Milly essayed a risqué joke.

"Captain Wallace, you must be aware that, as I'm now a staff-sergeant, that puts me 'under you', hmm?"

"Shush, you, she's here," he said in warning. Milly stuck out her tongue at him, at the same time giving his crotch a pat. He glared at her.

"What is it you do?" Pavlina asked, warily. Reggie explained Milly's field promotion, and their current task. Pavlina congratulated Milly, who turned the key and they all filed into the room. Reggie went to the wardrobe to get the man's kitbag, and gathered up handfuls of clothing and laid them out on the bed. They began folding them to fit the kitbag as he took the hanger from each item. Milly went through each dresser drawer gathering up and transferring its contents to the bed. Suddenly she screamed and backed away, a hand to her mouth. She ran to the bathroom, and Reggie and Pavlina rushed after, entering just as Milly was sick into the wash-basin. Pavlina held her hair back for her, while Reggie massaged her back.

"Milly, are you ill?" Reggie asked, concerned. When she had recovered sufficiently, she rinsed her mouth and washed her face. She blotted her face with a towel.

"The book," she croaked, pointing at a nameless small book on the floor where she'd dropped it. Pavlina picked it up and opened it, fanning the pages under her thumb, as Reggie looked over her shoulder. It appeared to be a listing of one or two names of women on each page. Each had a cryptic series of letters and numbers below the name. There were a handful of photographs pasted in. Quite plain to see, this was a book of the man's 'conquests' or sexual attempts.

"Turn to the fourth from the last entry," Milly instructed. There, a blurry photograph revealed itself of Milly typing at her desk, taken candidly through a slightly open door. "I know about half these women. See this one here, and her? They both told me they'd been raped. I didn't know by who, until just now."

"Milly, I'll take this book," he declared, "and destroy it for you." Pavlina embraced Milly, yet spoke to Reggie.

"No, you will not," she murmured, "Milly will take this."

"Buga's right, Reg. Give it to me. I'll write to them – the ones I know, anyway – to let them know the staff-sergeant is dead, no longer a threat to anyone." She took the book from her and went to her room, returning minutes later to her task.

They had begun a walk to the ship in late afternoon, and were halfway there already. Their small group consisted of Reggie, General Stone, and the volunteer relief watch keeper for that night, a deckhand named Johan Svensson.

"Sir, why did you come here?" Reggie asked, "What I mean is, why you and not Major Stirling?"

"I don't know we should be talking about this, now." the general replied, with a significant nod at Svensson walking up ahead.

"Not to worry, sir – he speaks only Norwegian, no English."

"Oh. Well then, Major Stirling went on an important mission in the desert, and wasn't available when your message came in."

"I suppose that's reasonable."

"Miss Pavlina ... or is it Mrs?"

"It's Miss, sir."

"What is her purpose being here? Here on the ship, I mean?" asked Stone.

"My contact was supposed to be Marko, but he never showed up. Pavlina was ordered to step in and be my contact, and it was a very fortunate thing, too, because she saved my life. If it hadn't been for her, well, I'd be dead now!"

"Ordered? Ordered by whom?"

"Ordered by Tito, Commander-in-Chief of the National Liberation Army of Yugoslavia."

"Ah! The communist faction leader. But if she was your contact in Yugoslavia, what is she doing here? Shouldn't she still be there?"

"It's a long story, but I'll try to condense it for you. I had a difficult time getting aboard, and Pavlina expedited our eventual boarding, but when she tried to leave, she was trapped on board by the Italian guards. By-the-by, Tito's partisans aren't all communist – that's only German propaganda."

"I sense you are not altogether displeased she was forced to stay."

"Well sir, that's true enough. I should probably admit that, at first she was forced to stay, but later she was ordered to stay aboard, by Tito. She's to join the Yugoslav Government-in-exile, and I'm to accompany her on our flight to London."

"Excuse me? Captain Wallace, you are a British merchant navy captain. Since when do you take your orders from a foreigner?"

"Sorry sir, but with my segment of this mission at an end, I just assumed since Pavlina and myself have the same destination, it would be no imposition if we were to go together. If you don't want to fly us home, I suppose we can stay aboard with the new crew, as passengers."

"Ah, ... the new crew?"

"Yes. The officers I saw get off the bus with you last night. I know there's no more room available at the Caffe Cordina, but you've never mentioned where the replacement crew is billeted. I should like the chance to familiarize them with the ship before they depart." The general walked for a bit in silence. He ran his fingers through his hair, then rubbed the back of his neck, replacing his cap. They were at the gangplank of the ship now, and climbed aboard. Mr Ingerman waited at the bulwark gate to be relieved. They'd only begun to disembark when there was the wail of air-raid sirens and Spitfires from RAF Luqa aerodrome roared overhead for the fourth time this day. A squadron of Stuka dive bombers appeared. The nearest shelter was too far to run to, so they all ran into the bridge house for protection from falling shrapnel as the air battle began overhead. It was over in minutes. When they emerged they watched as HMS *Kingston* across the harbour slowly rolled over on her port side and sank in the graving dock.

"This is a very dangerous place." the general said, stating the obvious.

"Yes sir, it certainly is. I cannot wait to get the hell out of here," he said with feeling. The general now resumed the conversation where it had left off before the raid.

"Captain Wallace, I don't know what you were expecting, but those men you saw were not with me. They only boarded when the bus stopped at the port. There is no new crew."

"What!?" he exploded. "Haven't you talked to Major Stirling, or General Auchinleck?"

"Yes, what I mean is, there *was* a Swedish crew waiting for you in Alexandria, but when we heard nothing it was assumed you were dead, so the Swedish government called them home. I'm afraid it's up to you to take it the rest of the way to Britain."

"Well, get them back," he yelled. "This is the limit I signed up for!"

"Captain Wallace, you'll do well to remember to whom you are speaking!"

"Sorry sir," he replied, in a more moderate tone. "What I mean to say is, my part of the mission is at an end. I'm only supposed to be a 'delivery captain'."

"Well, you'll just have to deliver it a further distance than you had expected." Reggie glowered at this news. He turned to the general and came to attention.

"I am British merchant navy, and you are British army. I'm afraid I must insist any new orders to that effect come directly from The Ministry of War Transport, – Sir." General Stone set his mouth in a grim line. He unbuttoned a tunic pocket and produced a folded sheet of paper, the very thing Reggie had only just demanded. It was signed by the head of the ministry, Lord Leathers. Reggie read it with a sinking heart. Mr Svensson looked from Ingerman to Stone to Reggie.

"Isn't this a fine kettle of fish," he said, "and won't Frederik be surprised to hear it!"

"No, I imagine he won't," Reggie said. "I thought you didn't speak English."

"I don't. I'm from Minnesota. I speak American."

18

A Poll is Taken

Reggie called a meeting of the full crew after everyone had breakfasted. It was held in Reggie and Pavlina's hotel room at 0830 hours. People sat anywhere and everywhere, some on the bed, some on the floor. Some had to stand. General Stone and Engineer Frederik commandeered the only two chairs. The only one missing was Pavlina, as she was a foreigner not involved in the mission. Reggie paced the floor as he spoke.

"Men, I have some good news: while at the ship, I heard the BBC Overseas Service announce that both the Italians and Germans are aware we are here, and have made the public promise to not bomb the ship, observing our neutrality." A collective sigh of relief was heard. "That's not to say some overzealous pilot might not bomb us accidentally. Now, as for our current situation, I'm going to give the story to you straight. I've been —"

"Captain Wallace," the general barked, "Remember what you have pledged to keep secret!"

"I haven't forgotten sir. I'll not divulge anything sensitive."

"I'll interrupt if I think otherwise," the general warned. Reggie ran a hand through his hair, then jammed his hands in his pockets.

"I've been on this single mission since January. I was tasked to take your ship out to Alexandria, Egypt, where a full Swedish crew awaited to take it over, and you were all to be flown home to Sweden. The new Swedish crew was to take the ship —"

"Reggie!" Stone warned.

"— to Sweden," he finished.

"To Britain, actually," Frederik announced to the room, "where it's to be used in a military capacity.

"Did Captain Wallace tell you that!?" the general demanded.

"No. It's only rather obvious," Frederik replied. "I made a stab at a guess, but thank you for confirming our suspicions." The general sat back and crossed his arms, glaring at him.

"If I may continue," Reggie said, "the Swedish crew was called home, and we ended up here, not Alexandria. My task has been extended, unwillingly I might add, beyond what was first envisioned. Now then, I am faced with the duty to bring the ship to Britain. However, we have a problem: as Swedish nationals you are all non-belligerents, and none of you are obliged to participate in the delivery of a ship to a belligerent nation, a ship that will soon be involved in war."

"Sir, if I may," said Mr Lindvold, raising a hand, "Mr Torvald, Mr Ingerman, Mr Janssen, Mr Svensson and myself, we all hold dual Norwegian and American citizenship. We all hail from either South Dakota, Iowa, or Minnesota. We have no such qualms at taking up arms."

"And I agree with you, but the five of you are not enough to handle a ship of this size," Reggie revealed. "Mr Lindvold, you are a third engineer, but if I recall correctly, like myself you hold only a steam rating, and know nothing of oil engines." Lindvold had to admit the captain was right.

"Captain," Frederik interrupted, "may I have a moment to translate up to this point?" Reggie agreed and perched on the corner of the dresser, a leg dangling, while this was done. He resumed his narrative, and his pacing.

"So, I put to you the alternatives to consider. Option one: this neutral ship is safe enough staying here. I can fly to Britain and all of you can fly to Sweden, and the ship can be retrieved whenever another crew of whatever nationality can be rounded up. This may delay our plans such that the ship will miss its usefulness to us.

"Option two: we continue our journey all the way to Sweden, and the original plan to involve the ship in a military capacity is forgotten. The danger here is that, as a citizen of Britain, a belligerent nation, I may be incarcerated there for the duration, as Sweden has been known to do with downed aircrew.

"Option three: we continue our journey to Britain as planned, and our original plan to use the ship stands. In this case all of you will be returned to Sweden from Britain and none of you will know of, or have any involvement with, the further disposition of this ship, and in this case you may never see this ship again, as it may not survive our plans for it."

"Good riddance," muttered Lindgren.

"I'll tell you now your *Riksdag* parliament knows of Britain's plans and has concurred with it, clandestinely of course—there is also something else to consider, something of which none of you are now aware. Miss Pavlina has been given an important mission of her own by the Yugoslav forces, and since our ultimate destinations are the same, I have voluntarily chosen to assist her in this, to guarantee her safety."

"Captain Wallace," General Stone interjected, "This mission takes precedence over all other considerations. Remember you are acting under the direct orders of General Claude Auchinleck himself." Reggie turned to face the general.

"Sir, I don't care. Speaking candidly, I will not leave her side, even to the point of abandoning the current mission. I would rather go home in disgrace, my mission incomplete, than leave her side." Milly sat up, beaming broadly, and began to applaud enthusiastically, but since she was the only one, she soon subsided, somewhat embarrassed.

"Yes, captain, we are all well aware you share her bed," said Lindgren, mockingly, "There's no need to rub our faces in your good fortune."

"Mr Lindgren, get your mind out of the gutter," Frederik said in disgust, "Keep your thoughts to yourself and let him continue."

"Thank you, Frederik. I do not think she will mind my telling you she accompanies me as envoy plenipotentiary to prime minister Churchill, representing the Yugoslavian armed forces on the ground in that country. In her efforts, the destiny of post-war Yugoslavia may hang in the balance. Even, perhaps, the continued existence of the country itself. When she reaches Britain, she will act as personal attaché to King Peter the Second of Yugoslavia." A murmur of understanding circulated the room. "I'll appreciate if all of you will accord her the respect she deserves." Reggie paused as Frederik translated this for the non-English speakers. Torstein stood and crossed the room, to whisper in Frederik's ear. Frederik stood, and clapped his hands, once.

"I ask now that all who are not Swedes clear the room. We have much to discuss." General Stone, realizing there was nothing more he could say to affect the outcome, stood and ushered Milly and Reggie into the hallway. They were followed by the new Norwegian-American recruits. They all filed downstairs to the bar, where they were greeted by a waiting Pavlina who sat studying her dictionary. General Stone returned from the front desk with two sheets of hotel stationery to sit at a table alone and write. Reggie ordered drinks all around while they awaited the result of deliberations. Astonishingly, the barman had a partial bottle of aquavit on the shelf. This Reggie commandeered, paid for it, and with some glasses the group occupied a few tables. It was a nervous time, not knowing. A half hour passed. This became forty minutes. While they sat, General Stone approached Reggie and asked for the return of the remaining kuna notes, as it would be more useful to Major Stirling for further use by his agents in Croatia. Reggie handed over all of the Croatian notes. While he thought of it, he counted what he had left of his month's pay. Reggie had begun to despair of the outcome, when Snorri appeared and motioned for them to follow him. They all trooped upstairs to the room. When they had all resumed their places, Frederik made the address.

"General Stone, Captain Wallace, Miss Pavlina, … and you Americans, we have discussed all the options, and others, and have come to a decision. We are to remain aboard as your crew, at least as far as the English shores." General Stone let out his breath, which he had been holding, as did Captain Wallace. "In the end it was Annika who convinced us."

"Yes. May I say now," Annika observed, "Who among us would have denied entry of the Royal Family of Norway to the Kingdom of Sweden during our sister county's hour of need? Are we hard-hearted enough that we would deny the same right of continued existence to the Kingdom of Yugoslavia?" Pavlina crossed the room to hug her, and shake Frederik's hand.

"But there is a caveat," Frederik warned. "Deckhands Jens Ivarsson and Mr Lindgren have declared they cannot, in good conscience, violate Sweden's status as a non-belligerent and so will be leaving the ship." General Stone took two pieces of paper from his pocket, ripped one up and signed the other. He folded it.

"Sergeant Featherstone," the general ordered, "take this message to Malta Command and tell them to transmit it to British Headquarters, Middle East, to the attention of Major Stirling."

"Yes sir, straight away, sir." Milly saluted the general, and pocketed it. As she left the room, Pavlina followed after her.

"May I come with you?" she asked.

"Yes, certainly." They exited the Caffe Cordina and started walking down Saint Lucia's Street. Milly paused to read the message. It told of the Swede's decision, of her promotion to staff-sergeant with its concomitant increase in pay, and that they would be returning to Cairo on a flight leaving sometime that afternoon.

"Milly, may I see the message?" Pavlina inquired.

"What? No, of course not! Why would you even ask a thing like that?" she replied, annoyed.

"Does it mention me?"

"No."

They hadn't walked very far, only approaching *Triq Sant' Orsla* Street, when once again there was the wail of air-raid sirens and a lone Spitfire roared overhead. She looked at her wristwatch. The time was a half-nine. The lone Spit was shot down at once, and there was no opposition to the raid other than the ack-ack batteries. They ran with others to duck into a shelter. The lights failed, and they sat out the raid in the dark. Infants wailed. Out of the darkness Milly heard Pavlina's voice.

"Milly, may I ask a question?"

"If it's about the general's communications, then, no."

"Is about Reggie."

"Oh! ... perhaps after the raid will be better?" Someone had lit a candle. There were explosions nearby and the room shook as dust drifted down from the ceiling. Ten minutes later, the all-clear sirens sounded. The raid over, they continued their walk to the communication centre at Malta Command.

"Milly, you were a lover of Reggie, yes?" Milly stopped in surprise and turned on her.

"Good heavens! What a thing to ask. That's rather personal!"

"But, Friday night when you arrive here, did Reggie not say you are lovers?"

"Well, yes, I guess he did. That is, we were lovers some time ago." They resumed walking. Pavlina was silent for a moment.

"How did Reggie make the love to you?" she asked. Milly hesitated, uncomfortable with the direction the conversation had taken.

"Well, ... you know ..." she said, leaving her answer hanging.

"No, I do not know." Milly stopped again, and gripped Pavlina's arm, stopping her.

"Pavlina, Lindgren says you and Reggie sleep together. Are you telling me you and he have never done anything?"

"For two months now we sleep together, yes, but we have not made the love." Milly staggered over to a section of fallen limestone wall and sank down upon it. Pavlina sat next to her, and they spoke while watching the Maltese civilians clearing rubble away from the street centre.

"That's unbelievable," Milly said, in wonder. "All this time Reggie has stayed faithful to me!"

"Oh, no, he desires me now," Pavlina corrected her, "but Reggie holds himself back. I am partisan soldier, and if I get 'with child,' Reggie thinks Tito will have him executed."

"That's terrible," she said, shocked. "Is it true?"

"This I tell him, when we first meet. Is true then. Now is *not* true."

"Pavlina, in the meeting this morning, Reggie declared he will not leave your side, even to the point of going home in disgrace, rather than leave you."

"Reggie, he say that?" she asked, pleased.

"Yes, he did, and in front of us all, too," Milly affirmed. "What he and I had, it was only to satisfy my ... my, ... er, 'carnal urges', and I have to admit it was exactly what I needed at the time but, that man loves you with all his heart. I'll swear to it! You must tell him he will not be executed!"

"But he knows! He was standing with me listening, when Tito ended his diktat."

"Diktat! He said diktat? Did Tito use that exact word?"

"Yes," she nodded. "He say 'diktat'."

Milly slapped her knees with both hands, and laughed. "Pavlina, do you have that dictionary I saw you reading?"

"No, is in the room."

"Well, when we return, I must show you something that you'll be surprised ... no, wait, ... that Reggie is going to be very surprised to read. Now then, I have a message to send. Let's go." They stood, and continued walking towards Malta Command. Later, shortly after midday, after Milly had packed up her things, they were standing in Pavlina's room with her dictionary when there came a knock on the door. It was General Stone, and in a quite agitated state as he leaned into the room.

"There you are, Sergeant! I have our bags here. Are you ready? Let's go, the 'plane is waiting!"

"Just one minute sir, only a minute. I'll meet you downstairs," she implored.

"Well, hurry, the bus is waiting. We don't want to get caught in an air-raid!"

"Be there in a jiffy sir." The general shut the door. Milly quickly leafed through Pavlina's Serbo-Croatian/English dictionary until she found the entry she wanted. She passed the book over to Pavlina, and pointed. "Read that aloud, please."

"Diktat, noun," she recited, "One: dictation. [from German, 'dictation', 'command'] Two: an order people must obey even if they do not agree with it, especially one which seems unfair. Three: a unilaterally imposed settle—"

"The second one. Read it again." Milly urged.

"An order people must obey even if they do not agree with it, especially one which seems unfair." Pavlina read aloud. "So?" she muttered, "this I know!"

"Yes, but *he* doesn't know it," Milly revealed. "In January when he was preparing for this mission, he was given a very limited dictionary, and I helped drill him on it. It had only the first meaning in it: 'dictation' and nothing else. Don't you see? Reggie thinks Tito was telling you that you're not to be his secretary any longer."

"But secretary of Tito is Olga Humo, and she is — Oh!" A look of sudden understanding dawned on Pavlina's face, and she smiled and nodded. She folded the page corner down and shut the book. Reggie stepped into the room.

"I just saw General Stone. You're leaving? Now?" he asked Milly, concern in his voice.

"Yes. I'm sorry I must go so early." From the glassless window the horn of the bus outside blared twice.

"Reggie," Pavlina purred, "I think you owe Milly a 'thank you kiss'!"

"I think you mean a 'good-bye kiss'," he responded.

"I mean a thank you kiss," Pavlina corrected, "but it can be both." Reggie turned to Milly and she wrapped her arms around him, and he held her too.

"Milly, I've a feeling we won't be seeing each other again," he said, wistfully.

"I know. Being with you has been enormous fun. She won't mind if we kiss like the old days," she said, with a glance at Pavlina, who nodded. They kissed rather passionately. Milly squeezed his hands, then turned to Pavlina to hug her.

"Good luck to you, ... to both of you!" Milly declared, then ran out the door.

In less than an hour Reggie and Pavlina were at the corner of the Caffe Cordina building, at the junction of Kingsway and Old Theatre Street, standing with a few others of the crew. They shaded their eyes and watched towards the south, to see the Dakota transport climb to cruising altitude towards the east, on its way to Cairo. It was accompanied for a short distance by a Spitfire, one which would return to the island shortly.

"There they go," he said, in a manner calculated to raise his spirits.

"Yes, there she goes," Pavlina responded. The group turned and began to walk into the building. Frederik caught up with Reggie, but then slowed to a stroll, forcing Reggie to match speed with him as the others went on ahead.

"Captain, why don't we have a look at the charts Mr Ellice brought."

"Good idea. We'll meet in my room."

"Sir, I wondered if you could tell me when you plan for us to depart Valletta?"

"As soon as possible," Reggie said, and laughed, "quite possibly tonight, I hope."

"When you paid for our hotel rooms last Tuesday night, may I ask for how long a stay that was?"

"Sure. I paid for a week, so we mustn't stay past two more nights. But, we really should leave. We could catch a stray bomb at any moment and then, the jig would be up, as they say." When they ascended the stair, they passed Pavlina and Annika coming down.

"Reggie," she purred, in the special way she always said his name, "I go out now with Annika. We need to find a ... find a place," she said hesitantly.

"You two are going shopping?" he asked.

"Yes, that. Shopping. You have guessed it. That is what we do."

"Very well. You stay safe. Frederik and I will be in our room going over the charts." In the room, Reggie and Frederik rolled the largest chart out on the floor because the table wasn't large enough, and weighted the corners down with books. This chart covered the western Mediterranean from Malta to beyond Gibraltar. They knelt. Reggie traced a path with his finger westward, past Tunisia, all the way to the

Atlantic.

"This is our route. Once in the Atlantic we'll stay well offshore on our way north. Do you recall how much fuel we have remaining?"

"Yes. The morning after we reached Malta I sounded the tanks. If my calculations are correct, we've just short of 74,000 litres."

"Is that enough to reach the closest point of approach to Britain ... say, Falmouth, England? I'd really prefer putting in to London or Portsmouth, but Falmouth will do in a pinch."

"Do you know the distance?"

"Yes, roughly 2,000 nautical miles from here."

"Well, we're burning fuel at the rate of a third of a ton per hour, and that works out to about eight tons a day so, I would have to say, no. We might make Cape Finisterre, but no farther. I have to say I really don't want to let the tanks get very depleted."

"Oh? Why is that?"

"If we suck up debris, such as rust or dirt, from the tank bottoms it might clog the filters or injectors. You do *not* want to lose your engines off a lee shore, believe me!"

"I'm a 'steam man' myself, so I'll need to trust your judgement about oil engine operation."

"We can't get any fuel here?" Frederik asked.

"Oh, no. They have so little, the Maltese and RAF need every drop. It all needs to be brought in by tanker," he explained. "We'll need to stop for fuel at some other place."

"There's a port just beyond Gibraltar, here," – Frederik tapped it with his pipe stem – "Huelva, Spain. Will that do?"

"I'm afraid not. Spain is still recovering from their civil war. Anywhere in Spain will be crawling with German *Abwehr* agents and, from what I hear, Huelva is especially rife with them."

"Portugal, then?"

"Yes. A neutral country," he confirmed. They pushed the chart aside, then unrolled the chart of the Atlantic coast of Portugal. It was immediately apparent that the only port to handle a ship of their size would have to be Lisbon. Well, either there or Peniche, to the north. Reggie slapped his forehead and swore.

"What's the matter now?" Frederik asked.

"I just handed all our remaining kuna to the general," he complained.

"Oh, well, we can't use it anywhere else but in Croatia, so, no great loss there." Frederik shrugged.

"Yes, but we still need to pay for Portuguese fuel, and to do that we'll need to pay in Portuguese *escudo*. Portugal still does business with most every country in this war, and on both sides. We might have exchanged the kuna at a bank there. How could I have been so thoughtless?"

"Don't beat yourself up over it. Say, I've a suggestion for you: why not leave tomorrow, or the day after that?" Frederik speculated. "It would give us a chance to visit The Gut at least one more time."

"Do you have some sort of death wish?" he asked, "Surely you haven't forgotten how dangerous that place was last time?"

"No sir, I haven't – and wasn't that a shock, the manner in which Mr Ellice died," Frederik reflected. "Who could have predicted we would run across an actual murder here?"

"Who, indeed," he replied, without elaboration.

"All I'm suggesting is, our visit to The Gut wouldn't be for pleasure this time, it would be for business," Frederik said, with a conspiratorial wink. Reggie's eyes narrowed.

"What have you got planned?" he asked.

"Let's you and I go and ask around, surreptitious-like, and try to find someone who is *skickliga* – that is, 'talented' with his fingers."

"You want to find a safe-cracker, to retrieve the money from the ship's safe?"

"Exactly," Frederik confirmed. "Where else could we find a useful criminal, if not The Gut?"

"Hmm … what you say has a lot of merit." He stroked his chin in thought. "Let's do it tonight." They shook hands on it.

"Oh, did you have any luck with your shopping?" Reggie was just stepping into the foyer from the stairs, and met Pavlina as she entered the cafe.

"Sadly, no," she replied.

"What was it you were looking for? Perhaps I can help." She pulled him to one side, out of earshot of anyone else.

"I visit a few *ljekarništvo*, here what they call a *farmaćija*. They had not anything."

"A chemist's shop? You aren't ill, are you? Please tell me you aren't ill," he implored.

"Do not worry, I am not ill, – but I am hungry! We will go to eat the supper now, yes? Come!" They looked into the Caffe Cordina, and tonight's menu was the same again, always some preparation of rabbit. "Reggie, I am in mood of seafood. Will we go now to Cockneys restaurant?"

"Certainly, we can have seafood," he said, approvingly. "There'll be a good view, too. It's only three hours until sunset. But, I want to be back here just about nightfall."

"We hire the donkey cart taxi then," she said, decisively. "But why nightfall?"

"Frederik and I are going to The Gut tonight," he stated. Pavlina stiffened, and gripped his shoulder.

"No," she chastised, "You will not put yourself in danger!"

"You don't know why we're going yet," he challenged her.

"Frederik, he will visit the bordello to get the whore, and maybe also you will. This I forbid you!" She pouted.

"What? No!" Reggie laughed and took her in his arms, "I promise you there will be no bordello. He and I are on a special mission tonight, and I'll tell you all about it over supper."

The taxi cart let them out at the restaurant's front door. The waiter informed them that the *Pixxispad Mimli* – grilled swordfish – was out of season, but there was plenty of *Klamari Mimlija*, which the man was kind enough to translate for them: stuffed squid, and there was *Torta tal-Lampuki*; sea bream pie, and *Lampuki il-forn*; lampuki baked with tomatoes, cauliflower and olives, in pastry. Reggie had the man bring *Aljotta* soup as a starter. Supper was delicious, much more satisfying than the rabbit on offer elsewhere, but also much more expensive. She surprised him by asking for a dozen oysters, and was disappointed when told they were out of season. As they ate, Reggie described for her the plan, the "mission" for that night. Pavlina was non-committal but wary all the same. They ordered cocktails to view the sunset by, then hailed a donkey cart to return to the hotel. In the foyer they encountered Annika and Frederik who sat deep in conversation. Frederik stood when they entered.

"Where have you been?" he barked impatiently, "We need to get a move on—oh, hello, Pavlina."

"Hello Frederik." She turned towards Reggie to give his cheek a pat, and brushed a hand down his chest. "Reggie, darling, you will wait for me one minute, yes?" She turned and climbed the stair.

"Bring my gun," he shouted after her.

"What was that?" Frederik gave him a nudge. "She called you 'darling' – I wasn't aware her English was good enough to use a word like that."

"Neither was I, but I like it," he replied. "Say, Frederik, I've been meaning to ask you, why is it you never light that pipe of yours?"

"I don't smoke."

"Then why do you have it?" he asked, in exasperation.

"It was my father's," he said, with a grin. They waited. Pavlina reappeared and handed over his pistol.

"You give me idea," she announced flatly. "Now I have 'mission' in The Gut of my own."

"Oh? What's your plan?"

"I go with you, or I go without you, but I go anyhow." Frederik took a step back and looked over her lethal Russian sub-machine gun, hanging on her back by its strap.

"I like this woman's thinking. Let's go," he said.

19

Criminals Have Their Uses

It was now dark and, other than the occasional lighted bar sign, Strait Street was illuminated only by a single lamp at each junction. It was again heaving. Jazz music came again from every door. It was just as crowded and raucously noisy as before, but this time they were prepared for this. The three of them paused to formulate a plan.

"It occurred to me earlier," Reggie said, "that we shouldn't ask for a safe-cracker at random because that will take all night. Let's focus our questions only on the bartenders."

"Right. They know their own customers the best," agreed Frederik, "and I also think we shouldn't split up. One of us should go in to ask, and the other two wait outside, but always within earshot of each other. Do you agree Pavlina?"

"Yes."

"Then let's go." They started along the street. Reggie entered the first bar and emerged a moment later shaking his head. Frederik tried the next bar with the same result. Reggie tried the third bar. The barman shook his head "no" to Reggie's question. The music from the stage ended. At that moment, an Australian soldier jumped upon the stage and screamed "Oi, mates! Let's 'ave a song!" The drummer obliged with a drum roll and crash of a cymbal. The piano player began a lively syncopated version of the "Colonel Bogey March" and the Aussie began by screaming "Hitler!" to which the room erupted in the well-known song. Reggie had been hearing this popular ditty since 1939, so he joined in.

Hitler has only got one ball,
Göring has two but very small,
Himmler is rather sim'lar,
But poor old Goebbels has no balls at all.

He turned to go, but it seemed there was more to it; refrains he'd not heard before.

Hitler has only got one ball,
The other is in the Albert Hall,
His mother, the dirty bugger,
Chopped it off when Hitler was small.
She threw it into the apple tree,
The wind blew it, into the deep blue sea,
Where the fishes, got out their dishes,
And ate scallops and bollocks for tea.

The British in the room had stopped singing, but now a large contingent of Americans continued with a fourth verse:

Rommel has four or five, I guess,
No one's quite sure 'bout Rudolf Hess,
Max Schmeling's always yelling,
But poor old Goebbels has no balls at all!

Reggie left when the song ended and emerged onto the street laughing, to see Frederik bent double with hands on knees, and also laughing hard.

"*Whoo*," Frederik wheezed, and wiped his eyes on his sleeve. He straightened.

"Hadn't you heard that one before?" Reggie asked.

"Yes, *I* have, but, ... well, I'll let Pavlina explain again," he said. They turned to Pavlina who stood, arms crossed and unsmiling, looking rather haughty. She turned on her heel and stalked into the bar next door.

"Didn't she find it funny?" Reggie asked.

"She told me," – He paused to snort and wheeze again – "She told me this, and I quote: 'Is rude to laugh at men who have such deformities'!" Pavlina reappeared, shaking her head "no", and the three of them started down the street once again. Reggie emerged from another bar, again without a result, and saw Pavlina had disappeared. He stood on tiptoe to look anxiously over the heads all about, until Frederik pointed her out. She was just entering a brothel on the arm of a prostitute. Three minutes later she reappeared to join them. Reggie opened his mouth.

"Do not ask!" she commanded him, sternly. The three of them continued threading their way through the crowd together. Bar after bar yielded not a single lead, until Frederik returned and said he'd been told of a safe-cracker with the given name of "Gregor," but the barman hadn't seen the man for more than a month. Pavlina made them wait for her as she spoke in private with the whores clustered about the entrances of the bordellos and brothels. Rarely, she might hand her machine gun to Frederik or Reggie, select one of these harlots, and take her inside for five minutes while they cooled their heels, leaning against a building. Most of these tarts were quite plain-looking, even, it could be said, quite ugly. Once, when she had been out of sight for nearly fifteen minutes with a stunningly pretty girl, Frederik could remain silent no longer.

"Reggie, are you absolutely certain Pavlina isn't a lesbian? I'm beginning to have my doubts. I mean, it's perfectly fine if she is, I'd just want to know one way or the other." He was silent for a moment. "... for Annika's sake," he added. Reggie set his jaw and didn't answer. He knew, as no one else did, that he and Pavlina had never been sexually intimate beyond only cuddling. Pavlina reappeared and joined them, looking rather satisfied and happy.

"Do not ask!" she snapped again, when she saw the look on their faces. They all continued their search for the needed safe-cracker, but the men became aware she never entered another brothel after that. After checking dozens of bars without any luck, at the bottom of the street they paused for a conference as to what to do next. Just then a uniformed Maltese policeman rounded a corner and began to pass them by, and his sudden appearance gave Reggie inspiration.

"Sir! Sir!" he called out, "Excuse me sir, a moment of your time, please." It was the same policeman the Turk had attacked.

"Yes? May I help?"

"I sure hope so. You see, I'm captain of a ship in port, the *Belfair*, and we have a problem: there's a safe on board and all of us have forgotten the combination. We're in desperate need of the money inside. Do you know of a safe-cracker here?" The policeman warily looked the trio over. He crooked a finger.

"Let's see some identification," he demanded. They all brought out their passports, and the man examined them carefully, comparing them to their faces. He handed them back. "Sure, I know a 'finger-smith' who goes by the name of Gregor Attard. The only one on the island, as it happens."

"Splendid," Reggie said, relieved. "Can you tell us where we can find him? We've canvassed all of Strait Street and had no luck at all."

"He's been remanded to our gaol," the policeman declared. Frederik's shoulders sagged.

"May we hire him?" Pavlina asked.

"You must be joking. He's a convicted criminal," the policeman said, taken aback.

"We know," she replied, blandly, "but we will need him for the one hour only."

"Do you realize what you're saying? This is entirely illegal. No, no, no. *No!*"

"Sir, surely you've seen us," Reggie said, "Do you remember the Turk? Four nights ago? That was some excellent truncheon work on your part, I must say."

"Thank you, kind of you to —" The light of recognition dawned on the man's face, and then froze there. "The Turk. What do you know about the Turk?" he inquired cautiously, his eyes like slits.

"Nothing. We know nothing." Frederik hurriedly interjected. "We just happened to be there and saw the fight." They all nodded, together.

"Well, ...never did like him, —" the policeman mused, staring at the pavement, "— stupid brother-in-law," he muttered. "He was a bully. She's better off without him." The three of them exchanged worried glances, which the policeman fortunately failed to notice.

"Sir, we really do need the money in that safe, to buy fuel when we reach Portugal. Without that fuel, we'll never reach Sweden," he lied. Reggie then made an abrupt change of course in the direction of the conversation. "Tell me, are you a gambling man?" he asked hopefully.

"On occasion, I've had a flutter on a lottery ticket – not every week, you understand," he added hastily.

"We really don't know how much cash is in our safe. How would it be if, when our safe is opened, we voluntarily donate ten per cent of whatever cash is in there to the Maltese Policeman's Benevolent Fund, or whatever it is you call it here?"

"Hmmm." the man scratched his neck in thought.

"You would need to escort Mr Attard to Pinto Wharf and back to gaol yourself. He'd be entirely under your control at all times. You will observe his, and our, every action. I even suggest you bring a Black Maria for extra security."

"Pinto wharf, you say. Could this be done outside of duty hours?" the policeman posited.

"You name the time, and we will accommodate your officers." Frederik said.

"Ah, ... 'officers'?"

"Naturally, you'll want backup security to prevent the prisoner's possibility of escaping, isn't this so?"

"I guess so," he admitted. Another policeman rounded the corner, and this was the first policeman's partner, because they always worked in pairs. He looked the group over.

"Oh, it's you lot," he said. The first policeman was looking some-what sheepish.

"Why not fill your partner in on our proposal?" Reggie urged. "Surely he'll agree?"

"Proposal? What proposal?" the second man asked. The first policeman repeated it, in a condensed version. "Certainly. I think that's possible, don't you?" The two men agreed and a time was set for tomorrow afternoon at three o'clock on Pinto Wharf. On the route back to the hotel they were caught in a sudden brief but heavy downpour and took shelter in a shop doorway. Then they ran for the hotel. Their shoes and trousers were left saturated as they dashed along though miniature rivers in the street. Pavlina told them she had to visit the ship to get her purple leather flats, since her boots were thoroughly soaked. Reggie and Frederik changed their shoes, socks, and soaked trousers, then the captain and the engineer met in the bar to discuss the necessary preparations, for the ship was to depart Valletta as soon as possible the next day. After orderings drinks, Frederik returned from the bar holding a small leather cup filled with dice.

"Want to play a game?" he asked.

"What have you in mind?"

"It's a dice game called Ship, Captain, and Crew. If you don't know it, I'll show you how to play."

"Sure." A woman set down two pints of Cisk lager and left, as Frederik shook the cup and slammed it downside-up on the table. Annika arrived and stood to watch as he counted his points. Reggie rolled. When Pavlina arrived, Annika took her away to the far side of the room. Reggie could see them over Frederik's shoulder. He couldn't hear them, but it looked to be a heated discussion, for Annika was gesticulating while Pavlina stood obstinately, arms crossed and frowning. Then Annika seemed to be enumerating points of her argument because one forefinger was ticking off the fingers of the other hand. Pavlina stood hands on hips, head tilted to one side, listening. In the end, Pavlina nodded and they hugged. It seemed whatever the disagreement had been was now resolved. They returned to the table.

"Who's winning?" Annika asked.

"Reggie, naturally," Frederik admitted, ruefully. "Everything sorted?" he asked.

"Yes," Annika replied. "Well, goodnight! You boys have fun." Pavlina announced she would get out of these damp clothes and go to bed. A "goodnight" was said all around. Annika headed for the stair, and Pavlina began to follow after. Reggie stood to give her a kiss, but she brushed past him coldly and jogged up the stairs. He looked after her, puzzled, as he wondered what had gotten into her.

"Reggie, pay attention. It's your roll. I got six, five, four, and six cargo points. Ha! Beat that!" Frederik crowed. Reggie resumed his seat and gathered up the dice into the cup.

Nearly an hour later, after the engineer had won the last round,

Frederik and Reggie called it a night and went upstairs. Reggie put his key in the lock and entered their room, only to find the room dark and Pavlina already in bed. He didn't want to disturb her, so he brushed his teeth in the bathroom with the door shut. Her damp skirt and blouse hung on hangers from the shower-head. He undressed quietly in the dark. On the way to the bed he stepped on her flats. He used his foot to brush them under the bed.

He had known Pavlina for around two months now and was greatly attracted to her. There was, however, this enforced abstinence between them. Naturally, his libido hadn't gotten the message, so as they prepared for bed each night he was always rigid. Because of the required abstinence this never lasted long, some ten minutes, and then he'd go limp. The same thing happened every night. Pavlina made no secret of how she enjoyed the sight of him like this, and often might compliment him on its length or, more importantly for a woman, the width of it. Once, she teased him over how his tumidity waved about as he walked. He didn't mind this at all, in fact he rather enjoyed hearing her comments. But tonight there was none of this usual playfulness, because she was asleep. He slipped under the bedclothes and lay down behind her on his right side, because she was laying on her right side and facing away from him. He scooted over and snuggled up to her back. He knew then she was awake, because she shifted and adjusted herself on the bed. Since sex was prohibited, they'd had to devise other ways to show each other affection, ways that didn't cross that forbidden line. Oftentimes, she might cradle his balls in the palm of her hand, or else he might cup a hand to her breast, and in this manner they would drift off to sleep. Now he slipped his arm around her and reached for her breast, and for this she raised herself off the bed to allow his hand underneath, then lay down again. Feeling the marvellous heft of her breast as it filled his hand was pleasure enough. He sighed in contentment.

After a minute had passed, he brushed his thumb across her nipple. She seized his wrist and jerked his hand away. *She's never done that before*, he thought. He withdrew his arm and reached down to arrange his shaft to nestle in the cleft between the cheeks of her bum. Her arm dropped between them from atop her hip and she pushed him away. Her arm remained there as a barrier between them, her elbow digging painfully into his chest.

"Are you angry with me?" he asked her.

"No."

"Have I done something wrong?"

"No." *Brilliant. This is going to be our first argument, and I have no clue what it's about. It has to happen sometime, so I might as well give her the opportunity of starting it*, he thought.

"Do you want to talk?" he asked.

"Sure." *Splendid. She's not going to let me know why she's sore*, he thought.

"Go ahead, you start." She didn't answer him, only shifting herself a little further away, her arm still behind her back, between them. He couldn't cuddle to her with her arm blocking his way like this. It suddenly dawned on him how she'd behaved in The Gut earlier that night, and he remembered the question Frederik had asked about her then. Horrified, he had a thought so terrible as to be inconceivable. There was only one way to know for certain: the question had to be asked, whatever the cost may be.

"Are you a lesbian now?" He braced himself for an unwanted answer he did not want to hear. She was silent for a moment, a moment seeming to stretch hours.

"Yes."

Ever since they'd first met, he'd had to hold his desire for her in abeyance, yet always in the recesses of his mind he'd believed one day they would eventually be able to make love. Now, with a single word from her, he knew it was an impossibility. A lump rose in his throat and he fought down the urge to cry. Men don't cry, not in front of women, and he told himself he wouldn't, especially not in front of Pavlina. He sniffed in salty tears and swallowed them. Pavlina sat up in bed and turned to face him. She gently stroked his hair, and when she spoke there was a note in her voice of deep concern for him.

"What's the matter? Let's talk, captain." He threw the bedclothes off in a panic and sat up, snapping on the bedside table lamp, nearly knocking it over.

"Wh-wh-what," He stuttered. "why are you, ... doing in our room?" Annika's eyes drifted downwards.

"*Gode Herre*, Pavlina wasn't kidding," she uttered. He snatched up a pillow to cover himself. Annika remained seated cross-legged, making no attempt to cover herself.

"Why are *you* here?" he demanded.

"Freddy told me you wanted to be added to my calendar so—here I am!"

"I was joking!" he erupted, "Joking! Where's Pavlina?"

"She's in my room."

"Then go back to your room! You need to get her!"

"You don't want to talk about anything that's bothering you?" she probed.

"No!" he replied, strenuously, wiping his eyes on the blanket.

"Well, now I'm insulted, – and after all the arrangements we made, too." She pouted.

"I don't believe this," he groaned, pressing the heels of his palms to his eyes, "What is Pavlina going to think? She must be furious with me!"

"She was hesitant at first, but Freddy and I convinced her."

"And, just like that, she gave you the key to this room?"

"Yes."

"And then you gave your room key to her?"

"No."

"But, if she's in your room, you *must* have given your key to her?" he guessed.

"Don't be ridiculous," she answered, "I gave my key to Freddy."

"Frederik! Why?!"

"We all agreed since you were taking 'his night' on my talking-your-troubles-over calendar, it was only fair he should be allowed to sleep with Pavlina." Four very distinct raps on the wall above the headboard were followed by her muffled voice.

"Will you two hold it down!" Pavlina demanded through the wall. "Some of us try to sleep!"

"Do you understand now?" Annika said, "He treats her exactly as he would treat me. She's fine with it." Reclining upon her back, she stretched her left arm out. "Now, you pillow your head here, and tell me about every little thing that's bothering you." When he had complied, her arm encircled him. "I'm listening," she urged. He heaved a sigh, and began. He brought up his worries of all the possible ways the mission might fail. He described how he and Pavlina had met, and how she had saved his life, and how he was continually consumed by his deep love for her. He admitted his entirely real desire to make love to her, and told her of Tito's threat of execution if he should make her pregnant. Through it all, Annika uttered little phrases to draw him out, and gave him prompts to continue when he faltered. Surprisingly, the tension consuming his existence ever since Croatia melted away. He felt much better. When he was all talked out, Annika allowed him to cuddle to her in a manner only slightly more permissive than she had allowed him at the beginning of the evening, and they fell asleep. This was one episode in his life he was *never* going to forget. Not that he would ever want to.

The next afternoon Frederik was in the engine room tending to his charges, two massive eight-cylinder diesels. All systems were operational. Annika was in the galley going over their food supplies, and there was hot water throughout the ship. The entire crew was due to arrive at the ship at 1600 hours. Reggie had checked them out of the hotel, then arrived at the ship in early afternoon to make his usual ship-wide inspection. He made sure to carry his pistol, because of the large amounts of money to be transferred. Pavlina was with him, and she carried her machine gun. Chuck Janssen, one of the Norwegian-American watch-standers, reported he'd raised the "Blue Peter" flag that morning, as instructed, and when the Royal Navy tug responded he'd relayed to them their planned departure time of six o'clock that very night. These arrangements were never made via wireless because of the danger of waiting submarines listening in.

The police van, an early model Black Maria from the previous decade, motored down the wharf at precisely three o'clock. It came to a stop at the foot of the gangplank, near a work gang of a dozen men engaged in pitching the stone blocks from the destroyed Pinto Stores building onto a lorry. The policeman from the previous evening emerged and went round to the back, to open its doors. A man stepped out and stretched. He was scrawny and wore no hat. He shook hands with the policeman, then sauntered over to the gang of workers. The workers greeted this man enthusiastically, with slaps on the back and hugs and handshakes all around, while the policeman climbed the gangplank to the ship. Reggie and Pavlina greeted the policeman at the deck of the ship when he arrived.

"Welcome aboard," Reggie said. They shook hands.

"Thank you. So this is the steamship *Belfair*, eh? Swedish?" he asked, looking all around.

"Yes, it's Swedish. It's a motor ship, not a steamship. We're just making ready to leave tonight," he answered. "This is Miss Pavlina, my, er, ... bodyguard."

"Pleased to meet you. That's quite the weapon you have there, Miss." She explained how its drum magazine was fully loaded with seventy-one rounds, and informed him its rate of fire was 1,250 rounds per minute, so the entire magazine might possibly be emptied in under four seconds.

"Is why leaving the gun set to semi-automatic mode is wise," she said.

"I'm impressed." the policeman said.

"Did you bring Mr Attard?" Reggie asked.

"I did," he responded. "That's him down there." He pointed at the group below. "Gregor," he shouted, "Come up and I'll introduce you." He waved the man up. Gregor left the group and started over.

"That's Gregor Attard?" Reggie was concerned. "Why is he not in manacles?"

"Funny story, that. I'd forgotten his thirty-day sentence was up today, so he's being released now."

"What was he in for?"

"Oh, all sorts. Every time something different. This latest was for aggravated assault and battery with intent to maim permanently." Gregor began his climb up the gangplank. "He gouged a man's eye out with his thumb, but fortunately the doctor was able to restore it with very little permanent damage."

"And he got thirty days for that?"

"Yes."

"Only thirty days?"

"Yes." the policeman said, a hint of irritation in his voice. Gregor reached the main deck and stood, hands in his pockets. Introductions were made: "This is Gregor Attard, the island's 'fingersmith'. Gregor, this is your new employer, Captain Leif Magnuson of the motor ship *Belfair*." Gregor kept his hands in his pockets. His black coat was threadbare. He had a grin that never left his face, which was unfortunate because a number of his teeth were rotten. He had bad breath and his greasy hair was down to his shoulders. Reggie nodded at the man.

"This —" He turned to introduce Pavlina but had to pause, "— way, gentlemen. It's just up in my quarters," he finished. *Where is she? She was just here a minute ago. Has she gone on ahead?*

"Well, I'll leave you to it. Cheerio!" The policeman said, starting down the gangplank.

"You're not coming with us?" Reggie asked. "What about our agreed ten per cent cash donation to the Maltese Policeman's Benevolent Fund?"

"Oh yes. Police Commissioner Joseph Axisa came down on me rather hard this morning." He grimaced at the thought. "It seems public servants accepting cash donations from foreigners is rather frowned upon, as it creates an appearance of favouritism in the eyes of the public. I'll have to decline."

"That's not to say," Gregor growled, "that I won't mind a ten per cent cash donation. Call it 'payment for services rendered'."

"Suits me," the policeman said, as he strode down the gangplank. He started the Black Maria and they watched it drive away. Reggie directed Gregor up the stairs to his quarters, but was careful to stay behind the man. They entered the room. Reggie went directly to the safe, but Gregor made a detour on his way there, glancing through the open door of the head along the way. Reggie pointed to the safe. It stood five feet tall and was just about two feet wide by close to eighteen inches deep. Something like a gun safe.

"This is it. It's top quality Swedish fabrication," he said. Gregor bent to read aloud a small plaque on the front.

"Rosengrens, Gothenburg, Sweden. Yes, I see it's a Rosengrens model. Top of the line. See these divots here? Some useless git tried to drill it. This is going to be difficult, very difficult, but I'll give it my best, yeah?" There was a three-spoked handle without a rim in the centre of the door, next to a dial. Gregor knelt in front of the safe. "Get me a paper and pencil." Reggie put these on the floor next to him and stepped back. Gregor took a small piece of emery cloth from his coat pocket and rubbed his fingertips rapidly across it a few strokes. He spun the dial several rotations clockwise, then set the knob to rest at zero.

"Now we're 'parked' – I'll need absolute silence. Don't talk," he ordered. He pressed his ear to the safe door. Carefully he rotated the knob slowly in one direction, then the other. He repeated this for many minutes, then stood. His perpetual smile faded. "No luck. My hearing must be going. Can't hear the tumblers, the dog, or the gates." These terms meant nothing to Reggie, but he remained silent. "Do you have a water glass?"

Reggie looked into the head. "No."

"Do you have a screwdriver handy, then?"

Reggie riffled though the desk drawer and came up with a flat-bladed one. Gregor knelt again and put the screwdriver tip on the door near the dial, with its handle on his ear, testing the screwdriver point at various locations until he settled on one. Again he went through the motions but this time he smiled. Every five minutes or so he paused to write down a number. Occasionally he stopped to cross one out. After half an hour he picked up the square of paper, stood up and stretched.

"Bastards put in some false gates. Took me awhile to figure that." He handed the paper to Reggie, who pocketed it. "Try the handle now."

"No, you go ahead, you're the expert here," he replied. He had his snub-nosed Walther P38 in hand. "And no funny stuff, do you hear?" Strangely, Gregor's perpetual grin had returned. He faced the safe and with both hands rotated the centre handle. There was a dull *clunk*, and the heavy door popped loose. He walked backwards as he pulled on it, and it swung outwards though 180 degrees. Now he stood behind the open door of the safe, and this formed a very effective shield. When his hand appeared from behind the open door it held a small automatic, levelled at Reggie's gut.

"I don't believe this," Reggie said, cheesed off. "You were just released from gaol in a police van. How did you manage to get a gun?"

"Them are me mates loading blocks on the wharf, slipped it to me, yeah. That peeler's as dumb as a bag of rocks. Now, toss your 'rod' over here." Reggie put it on the deck and slid it over. Gregor picked it up and tucked it into the waistband of his trousers. "Sit over there, hands on your head," he said, waving the automatic at the alcove bed. Reggie complied. Gregor stepped to the front of the safe and kept him covered while pulling handfuls of paper from it, dropping them on the floor. "Where's the lolly?" he demanded, irritated.

"You're standing on it."

"This?! This foreign shite ain't no money!"

"It is. That's Croatian Kuna. I never said it was in British Sterling."

"Smart Aleck, eh? What's the exchange rate, then?"

"I've really no idea." The wail of air-raid sirens began, and aeroplanes from RAF Luqa aerodrome roared overhead.

"Then I'm taking all of it! All of it, you hear me?" he shouted, frantically. Bombs began exploding over at the Royal Navy docks, but a few also fell nearby, quite loud. A sheen of sweat glistened on his forehead as he looked up, his eyes bulging in fear. Reggie didn't know if the man was a psychopath, but it wouldn't be prudent to push him beyond whatever limits the man had. It was time to bring out the big guns, to re-assume control of the situation.

"You can come out now, Pavlina," he said. There was no response. "Pavlina? Come out!" he repeated. Still no response. Gregor covered him while he backed into the head, to whip the shower curtain aside. There was no one there. As Gregor returned to the centre of the room he looked up, terrified at the banshee shriek of the *Jericho-Trompete* sirens of the Stuka dive-bombers; he should be in a shelter, not out here where he could die at any second. A bomb exploded on Pinto wharf and the ship trembled. The door of the wardrobe rattled.

"Come out of there," Gregor screamed. The door didn't move. Reggie crouched to spring at him, but was too late. Gregor pumped three slugs into the wardrobe cabinet at chest height. Inside the cabinet something heavy fell. Gregor pumped two more slugs into it at its base. Reggie started for it. Gregor waved him back with his automatic.

"Pick up that cash. Put it in a pillowcase. All of it!" Reggie pulled a pillow from its case. He knelt and stuffed bundles of cash into it as fast as he could. The sooner the man was out of here, the sooner he could go help her. Gregor winced with each explosion, looking up as if the ceiling overhead was about to split open, as a bomb travelled straight to his head. Reggie threw the pillowcase at him and it was caught.

"Sit over there on the bed, hands on your head. I'm bugging out now." Gregor backed away to the door, keeping him covered. When he reached it, he pulled the trigger. There was only a click. Reggie sprang for him, but Gregor was too fast, throwing the useless piece at the captain, who ducked too late. It grazed his forehead. Instantly the Walther he'd taken from Reggie earlier was pointed at him, and he froze, hands raised, and backed away again, to sit on the bed.

"Gregor! Gregor, listen," he pleaded, his hands on his head. The man may be a psychopath, but there was a small chance he might be reasoned with. "You may have done a lot of things, but you're no murderer. Listen to me! Murder will get you the death penalty. You don't want that." A bomb exploded on the wharf, making the ship shake. Gregor flinched. Keeping his eyes on Reggie, he pulled on the door handle, but it was locked. Glancing down, there was a skeleton key left in the keyhole. Still holding the Walther trained on

Reggie, he clamped the pillowcase of cash under his arm, turned the key, then seized the bag again. Taking aim at Reggie's chest he pulled the trigger. There was a click. The chamber was empty, because Gregor had forgotten to rack the slide. He couldn't do this with his hands full. There was still a chance he could be tackled! Just as Reggie sprang to his feet, the door burst inward and Pavlina stepped through, her face purposeful and her machine gun levelled. *BRRRT* – the sound in the cabin deafened him. In less than a second, Gregor's chest turned to a spongy pulp. He collapsed to the floor, on his face a look of shock. Reggie dashed across the cabin to snatch up the pillowcase in the nick of time, before the final spirts erupting from Gregor's chest could touch it. He threw it across the room, then turned to hug Pavlina. She hugged him back.

"Reggie," she purred in his ear, in the peculiar way she always said his name, "You will please stop locking doors, yes?"

"I thought you were hiding in the wardrobe cabinet." Reggie sobbed in relief. "I thought he'd killed you. I heard your body fall." They went to the wardrobe and opened the door. Pavlina picked up her knee-high boots and examined the holes piercing them.

"I hang my boots on the bar to dry. Now they are ruined," she fretted.

"I'll buy you another pair, but first we have to get him out of here." Reggie lifted Gregor's body, holding him under his arms, while Pavlina laid her machine gun aside, and took his ankles. They waddled with him out the door and dragged him down the stairs. "This makes twenty-nine," he said, as they dragged him to the side of the ship, leaving a smear of blood on the deck.

"No, he does not count. He is not fascist, only the criminal," she responded. They lifted him to the rail and rolled him over it. The body splashed far below. The all-clear sirens now sounded from the city. Annika appeared from the galley doorway behind them.

"What's going on?" she asked, "I heard shooting close by and …

Herre Gud! Blood!" she wailed, recoiling in horror.

"Do not worry, Annika," Pavlina assured her, "We only dispose of a little rubbish." They leaned on the rail to watch as the current began to take the corpse away. "Is a waste," she commented.

"A waste? So you think Gregor might have had some redeeming qualities?"

"No. My gun is set fully automatic by accident," she said. "I use twenty bullets when only one will do—is waste of bullets." He looked aft to see crewmen moving about on the deck, then turned and followed both women up the stairs and into the cabin. Annika stood, her eyes wide and holding a fist to her mouth, speechless. She looked about her at the machine gun, the blood, the open safe, the two pistols, the money spilling from the pillowcase, and the fractured wardrobe door. The pungent smell of gunpowder hung heavy in the air from a smoky haze in the room.

"Annika, it's four o'clock and I see the crew has arrived," he said. "Would you go below and tell the cabin stewards to bring up buckets and mops, please? Does the ship have a carpenter? Best send him, too."

"Yes sir, right away!" She turned to go, but paused in the doorway long enough to ask Pavlina, "Did you tell him?"

"Tell me what?" Reggie asked her.

"Tomorrow is my birthday. I am thirty-four years old." Pavlina said.

"Oh dear! We're due to leave in less than two hours. Had I known, we could've stayed here another night for a celebration," he groused.

"Do not worry. We will celebrate tomorrow on the ship," she promised.

"I've an idea! Let's you and I take this bag of kuna notes to the bank and exchange it for Pounds Sterling, and Portuguese *escudo*, if they have it. Then I'll buy you a brand new pair of boots. If we hurry we can return before six." He picked up the bag, and Pavlina followed after him with her machine gun. On the way to the gangplank Reggie ordered a fire hose rigged, to wash the blood from the deck before it dried.

In the event, the bank refused to accept the kuna notes, and there were no boots available here. When they returned, the story was all over the ship. The cabin stewards had cleaned up the blood but a steady stream of visitors came to view the cabin, and Reggie was forced to tell the tale until he called a halt, to demand they absolutely must prepare for departure now. When his quarters were clear he shut the safe while it remained empty and tried the combination left by Gregor. It worked, so he locked the cash inside. He left for the engine room where Frederik assured him all was in readiness. While waiting on the bridge for the RN tug, he recorded the safe combination in the ship's log. They cast off at precisely 1800 hours and the tug escorted them past the submarine nets and out the harbour entrance. They had to follow the same procedure as when they'd entered harbour. After motoring north-northwest for an hour he ordered a heading of 287 degrees true, to pass south of the German-occupied island of Pantellaria. He left the crew with instructions to call him for anything suspicious. In twenty-three hours they were to make the turn towards Gibraltar. He'd made up and assigned a roster: the helmsman and all the lookouts knew their schedules, and each would be relieved every four hours. At sunset the flood lamps were switched on to illuminate the painted flags.

Reggie settled into a chair in the officer's saloon to catch a late supper of shepherd's pie which, because of conditions on Malta, Annika had to make using rabbit meat. It was ... adequate. Pavlina came to sit with him, and study her Croatian/English dictionary until he was finished. Another table held off-duty card players. The fireplace was alight and a small cheery fire flickered in the grate. What he was eating was rabbit, not goulash, but still he was reminded of the Primošten safe house and how contented he had felt then. He took his dish to the galley counter, then sat with her and together they regarded the fireplace as the flames leapt and sparked. He reached for her hand and gave it a squeeze before intertwining his fingers with hers. She turned her book face down on the table.

"Do you remember how," he reminisced, "back in the safe house in Primošten, we sat and watched the fire together? The girl was drawing her bears, the grandmother slept, and even though by that time I had known you only a few hours, I was feeling quite contented. It felt to me like I'd be happy to stay that way forever."

"I remember," she nodded. She shut her book. "Réži?" she purred his name.

"Yes?"

"We need to talk," she murmured, keeping her voice low, "but not here."

"Oh? Where should we talk?" he mumbled. *Oh no, oh no no no, it's never a good thing when a woman says she "needs to talk." She's going to tell me she doesn't feel for me the same as I feel for her, and I don't want to hear that.*

"We will go on the deck, yes?" Pavlina stood and pocketed her dictionary. He rose to follow her out on deck. "Where is private place? Front of ship?" she asked.

"There are crew quarters up there, and open portholes. They might hear us. The stern perhaps?" he suggested. He followed her to the fantail, feeling for all the world like a man forced to walk to his own execution. The stars were out, and the moon hung three-quarters full, but just now he wasn't thinking how beautiful it all was. They leaned on the rail here to gaze at the wake, beneath the Swedish flag as it tossed and snapped. Below them he could hear the twin propellers thrashing as the tips broke the surface. From forward there came the distant drone of the diesels through open engine room portholes.

"Reggie, I will tell what I think." Pavlina took a deep breath. "I love my husband. Filip and me, we are perfect together. He is older than me." *And I am not*, he reminded himself.

"Tell me about Filip," he suggested, more as a delaying tactic than anything else. When she spoke he noticed she kept her words deliberately calm and measured, and it occurred to him she did this to keep from triggering emotions she didn't want him to see.

"My Filip, he comes from Gospić, where we lived once. I do not live there now. In village of Gospić, the famous Nikola Tesla lived many decades ago. This inspires Filip so he goes to polytechnic to be the electrician. We marry in 1932 when I was age of twenty-four. Our son was stillborn in 1933. This you know."

"Yes, I remember you told me, at that wedding we attended."

"Then on ninth of October 1934, Our Yugoslav King Alexander is assassinated in Marseilles by the *Ustaše*. My Filip, he becomes politically active. Then in 1936 my Filip is murdered." She gripped the railing, her knuckles white, and was silent. He put his arm about her waist to console her. They stood thus for long moments, the wind from the ship's motion tugging at their hair and clothing. He wanted to know how Filip died, but didn't dare ask. He waited until she continued.

"My Filip, he returns from what he call the 'electrical symposium' in Italy, when the waggon on the train was blown up by the time bomb the *Ustaše* plant. This makes me very depressed. I think of ending my life. I buy the sharp knife, for to slit my wrists." Reggie tightened his hold on her waist, and she felt this. She put her arm around his waist. "On way to flat to do this deed, I am stopped and harassed by Czechoslovakian secret policeman who travels in Yugoslavia. This is too much for me to bear, so I stab him to take his gun. Is first time ever I kill. This makes me feel not depressed. The rest you know."

"You loved Filip very much," he stated, "and you don't think you can ever love any man again as much as you did Filip." *Get it over with. Don't leave me hanging, as I watch my hopes and dreams die here.*

"This I think," she agreed, "for a very long time. I devote all my time to assassinating fascists of any political party, even after I join the partisans I do this thing. Is taking away my pain."

"I understand, Pavlina," he said, "and I promise I'll still stand by my obligation to get you safely to Britain. I'll order the crew to prepare a separate cabin for you," he said with a sigh.

"What do you say? You do not hear me rightly. I say: 'this I think for a very long time', but this now I do not think."

"You … you don't?" he said, stupefied.

"No. Filip, he is the only man I am ever with in my life. Now Filip is gone from this world." She turned to him, and they hugged. "You are the man I love: this I think from the first week we meet, but is only now I truly believe this."

"I love you more than you can ever know," he whispered in her ear.

20

Whores Have Their Uses, Too

"You will follow me, Réži," she purred in that way of hers, "I have something to show you," she said mischievously. She led him by the hand back to the bridge house and up the stair to their quarters. The room was now clean, and the shattered wardrobe door had been removed and taken away by the carpenter to be repaired. Other than the desk chair, there was no other furniture here on which to sit, so she directed him to sit on the bed. She placed her dictionary on the bedside table, then lit three candles there, each in its own holder. She went to snap off the room light, then sat beside him.

"You're being rather mysterious," he observed.

"When we go to The Gut, you remember what I do there?" she prompted.

"Yes, I remember. I was afraid you had become a lesbian, but you weren't – I mean you aren't," he added hastily.

"Yes, I am not." She tapped a finger on her temple. "I think to myself, who will have this thing I seek, if not the whore? I go talk to the harlots because I want to find the condoms, and these I cannot find at the *farmaćija*." A shiver of anticipation ran down Reggie's spine. He was thrilled, bursting with both desire and curiosity.

"And did you find what you were looking for?" Pavlina reached for the bedside table and brought a candleholder over. From the saucer at its base she lifted a small envelope of brown paper some two inches square and handed it to him. He held it up to the light of the candle to read it. The writing on it was in German. On the front was the brand name "*Odilei*" in a curlicue script inside a red oval. Above this oval was printed "3 JAHRE LAGERFÄHIG" – that was "Three Years Storable", and below the oval was printed "DOPPELT GEPRÜFT" – that was "Double Checked". He turned it over, and on the back was printed "Otto Deliner G.m.b.H. Leipzig".

"Is this what I hope it is?" he asked. Her tawny eyes luminous in the candlelight, she nodded, and a smile spread across her face.

"Is costing me much money to buy," she said. "The whore, she tell me the English soldier here from North Africa left it to her, and he tell her, is taken from a dead German." He carefully prised open the little envelope and eased it out. They sat looking at it in the light of a candle. It was brand new.

"Pavlina, even despite the command Tito has given you ... has given us ... to abstain, do you want to make love?" he asked. She laid her head on his shoulder, her eyes shut, before she answered.

"More than anything in my life," she breathed. His heart leapt.

"When?" he asked breathlessly. She raised her head and looked him in the eye.

"We will do this thing on my birthday tomorrow, Réži my love." They stored the precious thing safely away in the desk drawer, and blew out the candles.

On Tuesday Reggie had done his usual round of inspections at 1000 hours, but when he returned to the bridge, found he'd made very few notes and the ones he'd made were nearly illegible.

The noon sight put them abeam of the city of Kelibia on the Cap Bon peninsula of Tunisia, and three nautical miles out as they skirted the peninsula. He'd been warned on Malta the strait between Sicily and the Cape was so heavily mined, he was well advised to keep to with 3nm of the coast. At 1245 hours he got a nagging feeling of doubt and double-checked his calculations, only to discover he'd made an error, so they were complete rubbish. It was hard to concentrate on even the simplest task today.

Lunch was a vegetable soup with a cheese sandwich made with a dense dark bread and good cheese from Gozo. Even with Malta's food shortages you cannot stop a cow from giving milk. Pavlina helped Annika in the galley so he ate alone, and was glad of this, for every time he saw her today he lost his train of thought and found it hard to regain. He caught sight of the two of them looking out at him from the counter pass-through opening, and giggling. Were they gossiping? They better not be. He decided to visit the engine room. Chatting with Frederik might be helpful to take his mind off tonight.

He walked aft, only to find he'd bypassed the engine room door completely and was standing at the fantail rail. Irritated at his inattention, he retraced his steps to the door and descended to the engine room engineering desk. The two engines noisily uttered *broom – broom – broom – broom – broom* as they ran. Frederik welcomed him into his domain.

"So, Frederik, you gave up 'your night' on Annika's calendar for me. How did your night with Pavlina go?" he asked.

"We only slept, if that's what you're asking."

"I know that—what I mean is, was it what you hoped for?"

"What I'd 'hoped for'? No. We talked, that's all." He looked about to make sure his assistant wasn't within earshot. "She's astonishingly lovely, and *very* fit. Let me tell you, you are a lucky man."

Reggie agreed with him wholeheartedly. He then pressed Frederik to fill him in on how these engines operated. Frederik was eager to tell him all about it: the fuel used was "Bunker C" oil and was so thick it wouldn't flow through the lines unless it was heated to between 140 to 170 degrees Fahrenheit. So it had to be heated first. Simple, right? No problem, they had heaters for that.

Naturally, on these two-cycle engines there weren't any spark plugs, nor any glow plugs. Once inside a running engine, the fuel itself would ignite when compressed to a high enough pressure. Simple, right? But when the engine wasn't rotating, there was no compression. That's where compressed air came into the picture.

First, you needed to make certain there was enough pressure in the compressed air bottles, so the air compressor needed to be started, to build thirty "bar" of pressure, and this equated to about 435 pounds per square inch. Nothing could happen, neither starting nor reversing, without air pressure. Simple, right?

These marine diesel engines, unlike a four-cycle engine, were a two-cycle engine and on these the valve timing was the same in either the reverse or forward direction. So to reverse them, all Frederik needed to do was to adjust the fuel injection timing and starting air distributor position (this also was done with compressed air) and this would change the engine's firing order, and they would start in reverse. Simple, right?

On the steam engines Reggie was familiar with, reversing was as simple as closing a valve, throwing a lever, and opening the valve. It could be done in seconds. He gathered it was a much more complicated process with these oil engines all the Scandinavian countries were so fond of using.

Frederik continued, warming to his subject: so you fed compressed air into at least two cylinders that had "overlap" (Frederik didn't explain what this was) to get the crankshaft to be just past "TDC," top dead centre, in the direction you wanted to get the engine rotating, and when it was spinning fast enough you injected the fuel, and it would start. There was an injector pump for this. Simple, right?

Of course, starting an engine that had been sitting unused for more than twenty or thirty minutes was problematic: condensation would form inside the cylinders, and this could create "water hammer" that could break an engine. So compressed air had to be fed in slowly to rotate the engine at no more than five RPM until all the water had been expressed out, before you could do anything else. Nothing could be simpler.

The only part of this massive apparatus even remotely familiar to Reggie was the exhaust gas boiler. He didn't want to hurt Frederik's feelings, or his obvious pride in his machines, so didn't mention how simple steam engines were to operate by comparison. He thanked Frederik for the tour, then left for the bridge.

As the day wore on, and the evening drew closer, Reggie realised he was nervous. He had no reason to be nervous. None. Hadn't they spent over two months comfortably sleeping in the same bed, gradually learning each other's foibles, their likes and dislikes? He wondered if he loved Pavlina for the right reasons. Not "if" he loved her, for he was certain he did, but if it was for the "right" reasons. Saving his life? He was grateful to her for that, but his love for her went deeper than mere gratitude. He found her very beautiful, too, but there was more to it than admiring her physical attributes, though those were quite pleasing – her gorgeous tawny eyes first and foremost, those stunning legs of hers, the way she kept herself physically fit – these were all attractive qualities, but it didn't explain his, ... how could he put it, ... his very deep *passion* for her. He had always been attracted to women who were intelligent, and she was certainly that. Perhaps that explained it.

He then compared Pavlina with prior loves in his life. As the most recent relationship, he considered Milly. She'd been enormous fun, but they'd both entered into that relationship with eyes wide open, expecting and demanding nothing from each other at the time than pure sexual desire. And with Dorothea back in Goudhurst, Kent, it had been the same. There'd been no courtship.

Courtship. Perhaps that was partly it: years ago when he'd been introduced by mutual friends to Laura, he'd begun by asking her vicar father for his permission to court her. Then they'd only been allowed to see each other as part of a larger gathering, such as the horse races at Ascot, or the motor races at Bridgestone, or sometimes church events, although he wasn't really the religious sort. Later, when they'd gone out together to, say, the cinema or a stage play, there'd always been a chaperone present. He'd done everything strictly by the book: the flowers, the candy, never out too late. All of it had been for naught as, when he'd finally gathered the courage to propose marriage, she'd answered she preferred to remain friends. It had taken him some time afterwards before he realized Laura had always held herself reserved from him, even standoffish.

And now Pavlina: he'd woken next to her nude, not even knowing her name. The very next day they'd rented a flat and moved in together! Then there was this enforced abstinence, but also sleeping together in the same bed every night for weeks! All this time he was gradually getting to know her, becoming more comfortable with her in his life. What a crazy, mixed up "courtship" this was, if that was even the proper word for it.

At 1840 hours, Reggie ordered a new heading of 270 degrees true, to put the ship on a preliminary course towards Gibraltar, before going to the saloon for supper. It was Annika who planned the birthday party for Pavlina. It had been initially scheduled for nine o'clock, but she moved the time to be just after supper. By careful use of ingredients she was able to concoct a small birthday cake. This used up the ship's remaining stock of flour from the final Swedish Red Cross food delivery at Šibenik. The cake was brought out as a pudding offering after supper. With generous lashings of sweetened butter, the cake was delicious, and afterwards they all gathered round to sing, "For she's a jolly good fellow." Pavlina thanked them all for their kindnesses to her. She and Reggie then relaxed by the fire in the saloon and watched the snapping flames. Reggie held her hand and his nervousness drained away.

"I'm sorry I've no present to give you," he said, apologetically.

"Do not worry, my love," she whispered low, so the crew playing at cards across the room couldn't hear, "The present you give me, will be the same present I give you." She squeezed his hand. Half an hour passed, and the fire died down. The clatter of dishes being cleaned in the galley ended. Pavlina stood and bent over him, to whisper.

"You will give me fifteen minutes to prepare before coming to room, yes?" she said. He agreed. Those fifteen minutes seemed to him an inordinately long interval, but he kept to his word. Climbing the exterior stair to their quarters had him wondering what the "preparation" was she had planned. The room overhead light wasn't on, but he didn't reach for the switch, because the room was already softly illuminated by more than a dozen candles. She must have scoured the ship for every available one. She was nude and waited for him sitting on the bed, but rose when he entered the room and met him in front of the desk. He removed his captain's blazer and went to lay it on the desk, but hesitated. There was a candle there, and it was placed to illuminate a picture propped up for display against a stack of books: the girl's drawing of a bear family. He laughed, and tossed the jacket on the chair. When they embraced he kissed her neck.

"Is that perfume I smell?"

"You like?"

"You smell like Annika," he said. She laughed, delightedly.

"Nothing wrong with your nose. Who else will it be?" They kissed then, in that way of hers, a hand caressing the back of his head, the other pulling his body to hers. "I will help you," she said, as she began to unfasten his shirt buttons.

"I've got this. You get into bed." He stripped down quickly as she complied. When he sat on the edge of the bed he was already aroused in anticipation. She took the tiny brown envelope from the bedside table and opened it, then extracted the condom. To her surprise he plucked it from her hands.

"Your sharp fingernails, darling," he said. She nodded, understanding it mustn't get damaged. She watched as he carefully rolled it on. He felt it to be very tight, and said so. She giggled at how funny his shaft looked in this brown rubber sheath. She lay back and spread her legs wide for him.

Now they could do what they'd always desired to do, unspoken since the week they'd met. She looked up to his face with eagerness, her pupils large and dark in the light of the candles, and the candlelight gave her skin a warm glow. He knelt between her legs, then hesitated, wondering how she would like him to start. He only needed a clue of where to begin, that was all, just a clue, but she said nothing. He decided the best place to begin was with her breasts. He bent to kiss them, and the condom split.

He stared at the shreds of rubber hanging there. The frustration was too much to bear, especially so after all these months of abstinence. He threw himself down by her side, his hands balled into fists, and an anguished groan of despair escaped his lips. But he was surprised by Pavlina's reaction. Sitting up cross-legged at his side, she calmly and methodically tore away the remnants of the useless thing. She seemed not bothered in the least by this catastrophe. When all the tiny scraps of rubber had been removed to the bedside table, she lay down at his side and cuddled to him.

"You will not worry, my love," she murmured. "We will do again tomorrow."

"Oh, thank goodness, ... what a relief, ... you have another one," he said.

She didn't answer.

21

The Mission Imperilled

Reggie woke well before dawn. Pavlina lay asleep beside him. He gazed at her beautiful face for long minutes while she slept, so calm and composed. He didn't want to disturb her slumber. He carefully got out of bed and dressed silently, then went to the bridge.

When he reached it, he found Second Mate Bruce Torvald on duty, one of the Norwegian-American crewmen. They went to the chart room and chatted for a few minutes about their actual position, since they'd had to revert to using "dead reckoning" because of the captain's bollix up of the previous day's noon sight. Quite suddenly the overhead light flickered and went out, leaving them standing in the dark. A few seconds later it came back on, but dimly. The telephone from the engine room rang. It was Donald Lindvold, the Swedish-American third engineer they'd acquired in Valletta.

"The generator has just packed it in, captain. I've got us on battery power for now, but they're old and there's quite a drain on them. Something's pulling a hell of a lot of juice."

"Could it be the flood lamps, you think?" he asked.

"Sure, that'll do it. Can you manage without them?"

"Stand by." Reggie left the handset dangling and went to the bridge wing to scan the horizon. There was no moon, and the sun wasn't up yet, but it wasn't going to be long now as the sky was already growing light in the east. He returned to the phone. "Yes, shutting them down now." He toggled a series of switches on the panel. The flood lamps went off, and the overhead light brightened marginally.

"How are the engines, Mr Lindvold?"

"Fine, sir. I learned diesels don't need electricity to run. I'll log this, and let the Chief know when he comes on duty."

"Very good. Carry on, Mr Lindvold." He hung up. He and Mr Torvald returned to their discussion over the chart. Some fifteen minutes later, the starboard bridge wing lookout called out. There was a submarine on the surface to the north of them, about six miles distant, and on a reciprocal course. Reggie trained his binoculars. The silhouette told him it was a Kriegsmarine submarine, obviously on the surface to charge its batteries. He tracked its progress. Had they seen him too? Its flag was being lowered. The U-boat submerged to periscope depth. He looked up at their Swedish flags at the yardarms. The breeze was blowing from directly aft, and at the same speed as the ship, so these flags hung limp. Looking aft, it was the same for the large flag at the stern-staff. He continued to track the progress of the periscope as its moved to the east, throwing up a rooster-tail of spray at its base. Soon the spray disappeared, although the periscope itself was still visible. He was puzzled, until it occurred to him the water surface visible in his binoculars field of vision was no longer moving to the left, and this meant the sub was no longer moving to the east. It could mean only one of two things: they'd stopped or, of more concern, were still moving and had turned towards the *Belfair*. They were either setting up for a torpedo shot, or they'd already fired. It was the only possible explanation. The ship's clock showed 0458 hours. Their next hourly wireless transmission wasn't due to be sent out for another two minutes, and a torpedo might be on its way at this very instant!

He jumped for the engine order telegraph and rang for "All Astern Full". The deck underfoot stopped its vibration. In what was certainly less than a minute, but seemed like hours, the deck began to tremble violently as the engines gave it their all. The textbook response for a torpedo attack was to turn either towards or away from them, to narrow the available target. He ordered the helmsman to turn starboard, but the man reported, "Helm not responding sir". *But of course! With both engines fully astern and our speed decreasing the rudder would have little effect. Frederik warned me the rudder on this ship is undersized and she steers like a pig!* As if in a dream, he found himself taking up the microphone of the tannoy. He forced himself to keep his voice calm as he made his announcement.

"D'ye hear there, d'ye hear there! Incoming torpedo! All personnel brace for impact. Repeat, all personnel brace for impact. That is all." There was no one there who could repeat this in Swedish, so he switched off. There was nothing more to be done but hope for the best, so he walked out onto the starboard bridge wing to stand with the lookout, binoculars to their eyes. He watched the placid dawn waters of the Mediterranean, and had a depressing thought: *Splendid! I'm about to become a captain who has lost two ships in the space of only a few months. Brilliant.*

The lookout lowered his binoculars, and his arm shot out to point. Twin tracks below the surface were racing towards them. The *Belfair* had not yet stopped, but still moved slowly forwards. They watched as the tracks approached the bow, and then reappeared on the port side going away. The telephone from the bow lookout rang and Mr Torvald answered. He hung up.

"Missed us by forty feet," he said. Reggie raised his binoculars to find the U-boat was now on the surface and considerably closer to them. As he watched, they raised a white flag. He knew they weren't surrendering but, could it be they wanted to parley? He rang "All Stop" on the telegraph. Picking up the tannoy, he made an announcement.

"D'ye hear there, all clear, all clear. Stand down. That is all." He picked up the telephone to the engine room, and buzzed.

"Chief Engineer," Frederik answered.

"It missed. Was there any damage from the strain?"

"No." The U-boat had approached to within hailing distance of the bridge. It was facing them head-on, so the boat's identifying number on the side of its conning tower wasn't visible to him.

"Stand by for a minute, Frederik." He let the phone dangle.

"Ahoy, *Belfair*." The German Kapitän didn't say who he was, for obvious reasons. Reggie wielded his megaphone.

"Captain Leif Magnuson. What is it you want?" he called in German.

"Captain Magnuson, I would like to apologise for our misunderstanding," he said obsequiously, "We were unaware of your status as a non-belligerent ship. Your transmission came too late, and we did not see your flags in time," he said, as a weak explanation.

"As it happens, there was no harm done," he responded, but he was thinking, *You bloody arse, you took five years off my life, you bell-end.*

"Please proceed on your course, and safe travels to you," the man replied. Reggie saw the plume of blue smoke as they reversed away. Soon they'd submerged while still facing the *Belfair*. Naturally, the German wouldn't want to turn about while surfaced, as that would reveal their true course. He picked up the engine room phone again.

"Still there?"

"Yes. Was that a real torpedo, or were you just testing us?"

"There were two torpedoes, they were real all right, and it took five years off my life. Give us all ahead full, Freddy."

"Mine too, and only Annika gets to call me that. I'll figure out what's wrong with the dynamo, and let you know." He hung up.

Close to lunchtime he took a noon sight, being careful to get it right this time, for there were none aboard who could verify his figures. When plotted, it revealed they were twenty-five nautical miles north of El Marsa, Algeria. He was relieved. His plan had always been to stay that distance offshore, for fear the ship might be bombarded from French Algeria. Not from shore batteries, mind you, as those hadn't the range. What bothered him was that he knew there were Vichy French battleships in North African harbours, he just didn't know which harbours. Though remote, there was a possibility the HLV *Belfair* could be fired on from these. The wireless transmissions they were making announcing their neutrality at the top of the hour didn't include French. Hadn't Pavlina said she spoke French? He called on the tannoy for her to report to the bridge. When she arrived she was wearing one of her more classy ensembles, a white floral print skirt and a sleeveless red cardigan over one of his long-sleeved dress shirts. *Annika's fashion sense is rubbing off on her*, he thought. Acting quite serious she saluted Reggie, British Army style, then threw her arms around his neck and gave him a rather passionate kiss while he lifted her off the deck and swung her around. The helmsman rolled his eyes.

"F'cryin' out loud you two, get a room," he groused.

"We have room," she said, puzzled.

"Ignore him *dušice*, he's American."

"*Dušice*! You know this word?" she exclaimed, pleased.

"You're not the only one who can read a dictionary, 'sweetie'. Now, I have a task for you."

"Anything," she declared.

"We make our neutrality broadcast in German and other languages. Now we're going to be off French North Africa for the next three days. I was thinking we should change it to every other hour in French. Think you can do that *dušice*?"

"Yes, this I will do, darling," she said. Reggie showed her to the wireless room, and gave instructions to start a transmission in French at 1300 hours. Half an hour after her first transmission the port lookout spotted an aeroplane fast approaching from the south, and identified it as a Spitfire. Reggie knew this to be impossible because Algeria was under the control of the Vichy French. He was proved right when it flashed over them at mast-top height at an unheard of 340 mph. It was a Dewoitine D.520 and had a French tricolour on the tail. It pulled up, did a wing-over, then made a few circuits of the ship before departing to the south. Now he felt assured the Vichy government, as well as the Germans and Italians, were aware of their presence and status. Surely this information would be disseminated all along the coast. He felt confident enough in this he rearranged the transmitting schedule to once every four hours during daylight, and at night not at all, for no one in the Mediterranean flew at night if it could be helped. Pavlina appeared on the bridge in mid-afternoon urgently demanding his attention.

"Réži! Réži! Your king! He will speak now on the radio about Malta!"

"I can't leave the bridge at the moment. Can you switch it to be heard all over the ship?"

"This I will try." Before long there came a crackle of static from the overhead. It was the BBC Overseas Service and was not actually King George VI himself speaking, but only a report about what the king had said earlier that day. It cut in suddenly, in the midst of a sentence:

" . . . island's real ordeal began four months ago when Adolf Hitler ordered it should be 'neutralised' in preparation for a German invasion. Since then the Luftwaffe has carried out hundreds of air raids on Malta, at one point averaging seven a day.

"In his message to the island's governor, King George VI said: 'To honour her brave people I award the George Cross to the Island Fortress of Malta, to bear witness to a heroism and a devotion that will long be famous in history.' Malta is the first British Commonwealth country to receive the bravery award – second only in ranking to the Victoria

Cross – which is normally only awarded to individuals.

"The island's governor, Lieutenant-General Sir William Dobbie accepted the award saying: 'By God's help Malta will not weaken but will endure until victory is won.' Reports from Malta say the heavy aerial bombardment is continuing.

"Three raiding Messerschmitts are said to have been shot down and four more damaged in yesterday's raids. Casualty figures for last month suggest 231 civilians were killed and 281 seriously injured. Nearly 300 suffered other lesser injuries. The Germans have concentrated their attacks on the island's harbour and aerodrome and the nearby towns and villages.

"Figures for the period from 24 March to 12 April show 1,869 tons of bombs were dropped on the Grand Harbour and 162 hours were spent under air raid alerts with much of that time underground.

"Shelters have been carved out of the soft limestone rock on which the island is built. At first the Government opened up and enlarged the catacombs used by the early Christians in Malta as burial places. Since then corridors have been dug and families have carved their own rooms to take cover.

"The Times correspondent writing from Malta said: 'The Messerschmitts try to spread terror by machine-gunning over the land; but if their aim is to cow the population, they may as well give up the attempt'.

"That is the latest from the Mediterranean Theatre. Turning now to the Indian Office we bring you our recently inaugurated programme, 'Through Eastern Eyes', presented by Zulfikar Bokhari and George Orwell, our correspondents most familiar with latest developments in the Indian Congres—"

The transmission ended as suddenly as it had begun when the speaker switched off. Pavlina appeared on the bridge, her eyes glowing.

"Do you hear? Such bombing! We lived through it!" she said

excitedly, hugging him.

"Yes we did, and I hope we never experience anything like that ever again!"

The telephone from the engine room rang. It was Frederik asking Reggie to come down, so he could explain their electrical situation. Reggie thanked Pavlina, and excused himself to deal with the problem. He went to the engine room. When he arrived, Frederik seemed to him to be somewhat worried. This was revealed by his very first question.

"How many days until we reach Lisbon?" he asked, without preamble.

"We should arrive there five evenings from now. Why do you ask?" Reggie asked.

"Well, to be blunt about it, I don't think I can repair the damage until we're in port. Can you find us a usable port?"

"You mean, nearby? I'll need to consult the charts but, off the top of my head, no. We're prohibited from putting in to any African port, and Spain is more than a day away."

"Let me show you what's going on here," Frederik said, and blew out his cheeks in vexation. He guided the captain over to a massive dynamo and began to explain. It was waist high, round like a big bass drum, a yard long and connected to a diesel engine through a shaft having a lever-operated clutch, now disconnected. This produced AC, or alternating current, and this was rectified to DC, or direct current, and fed through an external voltage regulator for use all over the ship. It was this rectifier had "given up the ghost." Frederik next showed him over to an electrical panel of circuit breakers. There on the left was a circuit breaker, a Bakelite cube three inches square with a wire bail for a handle, or where one had been, for there was now only a blackened hole in its centre. He could smell the acrid odour of burnt electrical parts, and melted Bakelite.

"So you're telling me we cannot use the flood lamps, and our machine shop?"

"That's it exactly, nor can we use any of the winches on our cranes," he confirmed.

"I see what you mean. But, what about our anchor windlass?" Reggie asked. Frederik's jaw dropped and he did a face-palm.

"That is also DC powered so, I'm afraid not. We will be able to drop anchor by use of the brake and gravity but will be unable to raise it again."

"Don't we have battery banks?" Reggie asked.

"Yes, but without the ability to recharge the batteries our interior lights will get continually more dim until the batteries are exhausted, and then we'll lose our refrigeration and freezers, and worst of all, you may recall our steering is electrically powered."

"Splendid. Just splendid." He thanked Frederik for his work and returned to the bridge, where he made an announcement on the tannoy that use of the interior lights was to be kept to the minimum. He visited Annika and asked her to keep the refrigeration and freezers shut as much as possible until landfall in Lisbon.

After supper, Pavlina and Reggie sat together in the saloon and regarded the flames in the tiny fireplace.

"Do you want fifteen minutes to prepare, like last night?" he asked.

"Five minutes will do, my love." He let her have those five minutes, then climbed the exterior stair up to their quarters. Again, the overhead light was off, the room only illuminated by four candles tonight. She wore nothing but one of his dress shirts, only a single button fastened, and waited for him sitting on the bed. She rose when he entered the room, to meet him at the desk. There was one candle there, and again it illuminated the picture of the bear family. He held her as they regarded it for a moment.

"I will help you," she said, kneeling to pull the laces of his shoes.

She helped him undress. Soon he stood naked, and only then did he unbutton her one button, letting the shirt fall away. He led her to the bed, and tenderly helped her in. Turning to the three candleholders on the bedside table, he found their saucers to be empty. He went back to the desk, but that drawer was empty as well. He opened the other drawers, but the condom wasn't there either. He made his way to her side, to snuggle to her.

"I can't find it. Where did you put it?" he asked.

"Réži," she purred, "You love me, yes?" She tugged on him, and stroked him, doing her utmost to keep him up while looking deep into his eyes.

"You know I do," he said, "I love you to the ends of the earth."

"So, if I am *trudna*, you will be happy or not happy?"

"Trood-nah?" he said, sounding it out phonetically, "What does that mean?" She retrieved her dictionary from the bedside table and looked up the translation.

"Pregnant. If I am pregnant you will be happy or not happy?"

"Happy, always. How could I not be?" he answered. "But Tito —"

"You will forget Tito. He is not important now." She handed her dictionary to him. "Find the page with corner bent." He opened the book and found it. "You read the word 'diktat' now," she said. He did, silently.

"You remember three days ago?" she continued, "Milly, she say to me you do not know true meaning of word 'diktat' – Tito takes his command off from me, and Réži, my love, we are free to do as we please. Only we matter now." She gazed intently into his eyes, and in the light of the candles her tawny eyes glittered with tiny sparkles of gold. "We will make the love now, and what happens is what happens, and we will be happy for whatever comes from it."

"Whatever happens will happen," he repeated, putting the book on the bedside table. He went to the head only to return with a towel, which he folded in half and spread on the bed, and told her to lay on it. She didn't know why he did this, but did as instructed. Kneeling between her upraised legs, he kissed her toes, then the inside of each ankle. Pushing her legs towards her head, he kissed the hollow at the back of each knee, and at this she squirmed and squealed in delight. Gradually he worked his way along the inside of her thighs, getting closer to being able to use his tongue on her. But as he got there, she posed a question he never thought he'd hear coming from a woman's lips.

"What is it you do?" she asked, sounding confused. He looked up into her face from between her thighs.

"I'm going to kiss you."

"Why you kiss me there?"

"It's called foreplay."

"What is this 'foreplay'?"

"You don't know what foreplay is?" He reached for her dictionary from the bedside table to show her the translation. "*Predigra.*" She understood then, and set the book aside.

"My Filip, he never do this thing."

"Well, what did he do? Tell me, and whatever it was, I'll do the same."

"He beat me."

"What!?" he said, outraged, "I've *never* struck a woman!"

"I show you." She knelt and directed him to lay on his back, then straddled his belly. She positioned his palms aside each breast, then braced her arms behind her on his thighs for support, and this made them jut. "Now, you beat me," she insisted.

"I think you mean slap?"

"Yes, that, – you slap me." He gave her a left boob a slap. "Stronger," she said. He tried again. "The other too." He slapped again. "Stronger," she said again. He left a pink handprint this time. A dozen more of these and she let out a moan of pleasure.

He was reminded of the time she danced the *kolo* at the wedding they'd attended, when her breasts had whipped up and down, but now with each slap he made them whip side to side. He couldn't believe she liked it, but she seemed to enjoy it. He pulled lustily at her nipples with the same exuberance as he used with his slaps, until there was felt a wetness on his belly. Now she rolled onto her back, raising her feet up, grasping at his arms, pulling him over her.

"Push in me," she begged him.

"Not yet," he whispered. She caressed his buttocks and sides, pulling on his nipples. He held himself over her on straightened arms, and with his shaft on her nub, he rubbed her with his length. They held each other's gaze, until he saw her mouth open, and with her eyes unfocused, her eyelids fluttered.

"Push in," she pleaded again, urgently. He quickly slid his entire length deep. "Too much," she grunted, and with nails like bear claws gave the skin of his back little white scratches as she gripped him. He pulled away and began to stroke, sometimes long and deep, or shallow where her lips were, and she moaned, and it seemed she liked shallow better. Her heels caught his buttocks and held him in. He took his cue from this, letting her determine how deep she wanted him. That sensation began, the familiar one that always happened to him: it seemed he swelled inside of her, expanding until he filled her body. He knew this to be an illusion – not real – because no man had a cock a yard long and two feet wide, but it meant he was on the edge. But with only the tiniest of movements he held himself back, for he wanted her to be there with him too. Her legs straightened and she cried out, her back arching to lift her bum off the bed. Thrusting once he held himself deep, losing all coordination as his body convulsed. A wave of pleasure spread from his groin, washing outwards throughout his body until every extremity, even the top of his head, thrilled with it.

His toes curled. He held himself deep and they kissed deliriously, and he kissed her neck, and the tears rolling from the corners of her eyes back to her ears, he kissed those away as she laughed and cried all at once.

He began to pull out. "Stay in," she begged, but he was now soft and fell out anyway. He rolled off her and they lay side by side, panting. "Filip, … Filip, … " she gasped, eyes shut, "Filip was *never* like this." They both began to laugh, and couldn't seem to stop laughing.

"My legs are wet and cold," he said, when they'd recovered their senses, "and my balls, too."

"Why?"

"You gushed."

"I did?"

"You did."

"My legs are wet also. That was my first … how you say? … in Croatian is *orgazam*."

"It's the same in English: orgasm. Really? Your first ever?"

"Yes."

"I'm glad." He dried them both with the towel, then blew out the candles, and they cuddled until sleep overcame them.

When he awoke, she lay asleep still. Here was a woman who loved him, and he loved her, and not only that, they seemed to match so well together. This had never happened to him in his entire life, ever. He couldn't believe how happy he felt, how energised, how ebullient. Again, he dressed silently so as to not wake her. When he reached the bridge the mate on duty regarded him with a quizzical look.

"What's the matter with you?" he asked.

"Nothing. Carry on." He retreated to the chart house to review that day's intended course.

The noon sight revealed Algiers to be abeam to port. He wouldn't

portholes. *Phosgene*, was his terrible thought! He dashed for the stairway. He was halfway down, taking the stair treads four at a time, when Pavlina emerged carrying a limp Annika. She dropped her on the deck, then fell to her hands and knees and retched. Both women were coated in white. The cloud was now being blown to leeward. Although banned internationally since the Great War, his father had told him Spain had used chemical weapons in the Moroccan "Rif War" throughout the 1920s. Crewmen raced over to help them, but he waved them back. He began issuing orders.

"Stay away! Don't touch her! Don't touch any of this stuff. It's phosgene – poison! *You*, go to the engine room and get a boiler suit from Freddy, all the protective gear you can muster! *You, and you*, rig a fire hose! Hose them down first, then wash all this residue overboard!" He approached Pavlina who was still on hands and knees, coughing and spitting. "*Dušice*, keep your eyes shut, listen to me. We're going to rinse you off now. I want you to take mouthfuls of water and rinse your mouth out, but don't swallow any of this, understand?" She nodded. A crewman dragged a hose up and pulled back on its handle so a fog spray soaked Pavlina. Frederik appeared, wearing a boiler suit, while struggling into a hood and goggles. Annika began to cough. He put on rubber gloves, then helped Annika sit up. They washed her down as well.

"Frederik, go into the galley and get the bomb, we need to get it off the ship now!" Frederik emerged carrying the cylinder. Its end was rounded, the other end tapered and roughly broken off. Was this where the fins had been attached? As a lad he'd seen a phosgene canister in a French museum clearly labelled "Gaz Phosgéne" and this certainly looked like what he remembered. "Over it goes," Reggie said, pointing to the rail. Frederik carried it to the rail, passing through the spray of water. As the canister was rinsed clean, he suddenly stopped. Whipping off his goggles and hood, he burst out laughing.

"Take this," he said, handing it to the captain, "Don't worry, its safe." Reggie gingerly took it from him and examined it. There was a dark grey label on it in Spanish, that Reggie couldn't read, but at the top of this was a white rectangle enclosing the word "TETRA". Frederik began removing his boiler suit. "It's a fire extinguisher," he explained, "or a part of one anyhow."

"A part of one?" Reggie parroted. Frederik stepped into the galley, soon to return with the broken-off neck. He handed it to the captain. It had a nozzle and a small hand-wheel, and there was a tan coloured paper inspection tag wired to this. He turned the tag over and on the back of it was written a message in bad English. He read it aloud.

"Greetings Beflair. I have folow you voyage from *periódico*. Here I warnings. If you land by España, *Caudillo* will take Beflair ship and keep, or gift to Hitler. Good luck to get Sweden. – Pedro (ruin this message)"

The crewman with the hose was listening, and asked, "Kaw-dee-yo?" sounding it out phonetically.

"Yes, he means Francisco Franco. It's the Spanish equivalent of *Führer* or *Duce*." Looking after the distant bomber he said, "Thank you Pedro, whoever you are." He ordered a change of course to 260 degrees, to bring them through the centre of the strait of Gibraltar the next morning, abandoning his plan to visit Spain. Frederik escorted a soaked Annika to her cabin, while Reggie escorted Pavlina to theirs. He deposited her wet clothing in the tub as she undressed, all the while attempting to cheer her up by making light of the situation. She seemed dispirited still, no matter what he said. He tried again.

"Here I thought I'd lost you forever, but it turned out to be only some harmless powder. Come on, smile! We can laugh about it now," he urged her.

"Yes, that,—harmless," she responded. "The canister, it miss my head by one hand width." Reggie was chilled to his core at how nearly she had met her death. He held her until she had stopped shaking.

That night, as he undressed before bed, as usual he checked all his pockets for bits and bobs. In the right-hand coat pocket of his captain's uniform he felt a small lump. Since Pavlina was already in bed, and he didn't want to disturb her, he went into the head and snapped on the medicine cabinet lamps. He squeezed the pocket lining and it popped loose. It was a diamond, and a big one too. Glittering under the lights he saw it was round with a high table and deep pavilion. It appeared to him to be a flawless Old European cut from the last century, of two-and-a-half or perhaps a full three carats in weight. He then realized it must have been trapped in the pocket seam from when he'd paid the Šibenik harbourmaster for the fuel and port taxes. *Major Stirling purposefully left those diamonds sewn into the disguise jacket for my emergency use, and they had indeed come in handy in just the nick of time, but I've been forced into doing much more than I'd been tasked to do in the first place. Well, I know to what use I can put this windfall.*

He put it safely away in his desk and continued to disrobe.

22

Shore Leave in Lisbon

They passed by Gibraltar without stopping at 0800 hours. Here they began to butt into the Atlantic swells. The waves were thrown upwards and the *Ponente* west wind dashed the spray against the bridge windows. Three hours later when north of Tangier, Morocco, the captain ordered a new heading of 293 degrees. Their pitching changed to an uncomfortable roll.

At 0520 hours they were off the south-west tip of Portugal, the Cape of Saint Vincent. Reggie had the helmsman turn north to a heading of 353 degrees. The seas had moderated. The noon sight put them west of Sines, Portugal. When they approached the mouth of the Tagus River flowing out through Lisbon, late in the afternoon, they encountered a pilot boat drifting while it serviced another ship.

Reggie rang the engine order telegraph for "All Stop" and they wallowed in the swells while they awaited their turn. He had Mr Thorsson raise the square "Yellow Jack" or "Q" flag, and explained its meaning to be "I request free pratique," a plea for a doctor to clear the ship for entry into port. He then ran up the "G" flag, a square with alternating yellow and blue vertical bars, and explained its meaning to be "I require a pilot."

Soon, that other ship went away, but confusingly not into Lisbon, only departing to the south. The pilot boat arrived at their gangplank, hanging deployed from a crane, suspended to just above the water's surface, and a man in a fedora and trench coat jumped for it. He was followed by another man in a flat cap, and then a man in a white coat carrying a black bag. When the trio reached the main deck the captain's eyes widened in surprise and he choked back a guffaw. He could hardly help it. The first man wore a grey wide-brimmed fedora tilted forward, cocked to cover one eye, the other eye glaring at him. He had a "Salvadore Dali" style moustache waxed to short sharp points, and a meticulously manicured fringe of beard at the jawline ending in a vandyke point on his chin—like a Chicago gangster from a bad Italian film.

"I'm sorry," Reggie wheezed, wiping a tear, "it's just I've never seen a ship pilot dressed like you!" The man pushed his trench coat aside to reveal a revolver holstered at his hip. This only made Reggie stifle another laugh all over again. The flat-cap man now stepped on deck, and spoke.

"That's because he isn't the pilot – I am! Now if you do not wish to follow that other ship, I suggest you apologise, and quickly! Do it! Do it now!" he barked. Reggie composed himself. He put out his hand to the first man in greeting.

"Captain Leif Magnuson, of the HLV *Belfair*. Pleased to meet you sir. I am very sorry about my reaction." The pilot relayed this to the first man, who nodded but didn't shake his hand. The pilot shook his hand and continued.

"This is Mr Amorim, of the PVDE or, *Polícia de Vigilância e Defesa do Estado* which I will translate for you as State Surveillance and Defence Police. He does not speak English. Do everything he demands, without complaint, or you will not be allowed into Lisbon. Walk on eggshells here!" The third man was introduced as The Doctor, and Reggie shook his hand. Mr Amorim strutted, one hand on a hip and index finger upraised, and began issuing orders in Portuguese, his mannerisms a carbon copy of newsreels of Mussolini. He seemed unaware of how comical he appeared. The pilot translated his instructions: "Bring out your entire crew and line them up here. Have them bring out all weapons aboard this ship. Do not conceal anything, do you understand?"

Reggie nodded and did as he was told. Soon the crew lined the edge of the hatch, and the doctor went from man to man looking in their throats using a wooden spatula, peeling back their eyelids, and listening to each chest with his stethoscope. He did the same for the women, but apologised first for having to touch them. While this was going on, the pilot arrayed the guns side by side on the hatch and Mr Amorim photographed the grouping, and then the serial number of each weapon, and then each crewmember. The doctor cleared them all for entry, the guns were taken back with a warning to not let them off the ship, and Mr Amorim and the doctor returned to the pilot boat. Reggie and the pilot climbed the stairway to the bridge as the boat left.

"You've no idea how close you came to not being allowed in," the pilot said, as they reached the bridge house.

"I think I do but, can you blame me? I mean, look at him – the little tin-pot Mussolini!" The pilot grabbed his arm and hauled him up short, to make a speech.

"Listen! Prime Minister Salazar was once our finance minister, he knows exactly what he's doing. We have a wonderful nation here. The economy's good, there's no poverty, crime is almost non-existent, wages are good, no one goes hungry, trade between the nations goes on uninterrupted. Salazar has a 'pro-British' bias, and he even surreptitiously aids the Allies. It's so safe living here, even during wartime, important people such as the Duke and Duchess of Windsor, and the Spanish Royal Family, holiday here in Estoril to play our casinos.

"Amorim and all the others of the PVDE aren't just policemen, they're Salazar's 'secret policemen'." He shook Reggie's arm, and hissed, "Listen to me carefully, you didn't hear this from me: they can make anybody,—*anybody*, disappear. Make sure you never criticize our government. You'll have a wonderful time here, if you just don't step out of line." Reggie nodded, chastened and now somewhat fearful. "And another thing: be extremely careful of who you talk to here. German spies will attempt to buy information to help their submarines sink trans-Atlantic shipping. Do not be taken in. They can be very persuasive, understand?"

They anchored in the Tagus basin off Lisbon at 1930 hours, and the pilot was retrieved by the pilot boat. The ships anchored all about had two large flags painted on each side to indicate their neutral nation status. There were a handful of Irish fishing trawlers, and one from Spanish Morocco, but most ships were flagged either Portuguese or Spanish. Most of them, that is, except one small black tanker displaying no flags at all, either on the hull or flying from a yardarm. A crewman from a nearby ship rowed over to warn them to keep a man on watch at the bow, and not allow any lines to dangle overboard; it wasn't unheard of for desperate young men to float downstream at night to climb the anchor chain, wanting to stow away to America, or to anywhere but Europe. Reggie asked him about the unidentified tanker, and the man informed him it was a depot ship for resupplying Kriegsmarine submarines, only briefly here to buy oil, and was not allowed to display their nationality while here, so, no flags.

After breakfast, Reggie assembled the crew on deck, to tell them he was granting them all a shore leave in this neutral port. He did, however, repeat for them the warnings issued to him by the pilot, then advised them to carry their passports at all times and obey the instructions of anybody in authority without question or complaint. He had taken from the safe the entire quantity of kuna notes and pocketed it. Now he gave an advance on their next pay packet to those crew that wanted it. He then dispatched Frederik to find a ship chandler, and detailed two stewards to help Annika bring the provender back from the markets. They all would finally feast well tonight! A skeleton crew was left aboard, and one lifeboat launched. They rowed for the quay adjacent to the Santa Apolonia railway terminal, landing at 0900 hours.

The quay here was wire fenced and guarded by soldiers twenty-four hours a day, to keep the people pressing against the fence away from the ships at the quay, there to be oiled up by a Portuguese tanker rafted outboard of each ship as it arrived. These poor souls stood, suitcases in hand and passports upraised, and their foreign voices pleaded in a murmur, "Amerika." Some of the more observant of them called out "Schweden." He noticed a few still had yellow star cloth badges stitched on their coats. It was a pitiful sight. The soldiers frisked the *Belfair* crew for weapons and, finding nothing, opened the gate. They pushed the crowd back with the butts of their rifles, and allowed the crew through. A straggle of pleading women followed their group for a distance, but soon returned to the fence.

He advised the rest of the crew to be back at the lifeboat by 1800 hours, and he and Pavlina went off to do their errands. He carried her ruined boots, for they had to find a shoemaker or shoe shop. The weather today was mild and warm, the sky blue with only a few puffy clouds. Reggie wore his Swedish captain's uniform, as was usual, and Pavlina her off-the-shoulder blouse paired with a red skirt and her purple flats. Their first stop was the harbourmaster's office where they were told they couldn't fuel up immediately, as there was a queue of ships ahead of them, refuelling at the rate of two or three ships a day. The man scheduled them to refuel on the afternoon of twenty-third April, three days hence. They walked to the nearby railway terminal, to get a map of the city from the information kiosk. The kindly woman marked the locations of the Swedish Embassy at Rua Miguel Lupi 12, and a few of the branches of the Caixa Geral de Depósitos Banco. At his request she also marked the location of the British Embassy at Rua de São Bernardo 33. Reggie asked about any "beauty spots" that may have a nice view, any she considered "romantic" and, because she lived near it, she lavished praise on the park at the top of the Gloria Funicular, in operation since 1885. This connected the Bairro District to the Bairro Alto District. It could be boarded on the west side of Avenida da Liberdade from Restoration Square. They could get to that square by walking through the "Moorish Quarter" just north-west of where they were now, the Alfama District or "Old Quarter." They thanked her and left.

Reggie pocketed his map. They left walking north-west, and enjoyed a leisurely stroll through the picturesque Alfama District. Reggie was impressed by the wonderful architecture here, certainly the equal of any in Paris, and most especially the tree-shaded squares. Lunch had been a fragrant seafood paella with large prawns, and saffron rice, *linguica* sausage sliced into it. Three hours since leaving the rail terminal they found themselves in the Moorish Quarter, standing in a park in front of a statue of a famous doctor, and across from the Faculty of Medical Sciences of Lisbon building. Could it be the architecture here was even more beautiful than the district they had just left? Walking north-west on the Campo dos Mártires da Pátria, in a hundred yards Reggie realized they were lost. He handed Pavlina's ruined boots to her, then brought out his map and unfolded it. A nearby door opened and a man stepped out onto the pavement. As he passed them by he smiled and doffed his hat, then stopped.

"Good afternoon. May I help you find an address?" he asked, politely. He wore a smooth forest green suit, the collar and lapels of black velvet. His matching felted short-brimmed fedora had a small brown feather peeking from the hatband.

"Oh, yes please," Reggie replied, relieved, "We're only attempting to find the Gloria Funicular, sir." The man stepped to his side to view the map with him. His finger traced the route as he spoke.

"Ah! you're too far north. The funicular is on the far side of the Avenida da Liberdade. Look here, if you walk south and turn right at the next corner, at the next junction you will find the Rua do Telhal. Turn left and follow that to the Avenida. Cross it, turn south, and you're there."

"*Obrigado*, sir, *obrigado*. You've been a tremendous help," Reggie said. The man smiled and tipped his hat once again and, turning to Pavlina, he tipped his hat to her as well. His gaze drifted lower for the opportunity to admire her cleavage, but his smile vanished as he saw the bullet-riddled boots she cradled in the crook of her arm.

"Where did you get those?" he demanded, angrily. Only then did Reggie notice on the man's lapel a tiny round cloisonné badge, red with a white circle in its centre, a black swastika on it. It was a Nazi Party member badge. Looking up he saw a Nazi flag hanging on the building above the door. This was the German Embassy. Pavlina opened her mouth to answer but Reggie interrupted her response.

"So kind of you to help, but we really must dash!" He wrapped an arm about her waist and steered her away before she could say a word. The man turned and ran inside the embassy. They ran. In fifty yards a restaurant appeared on their right and they plunged into this, and he ducked behind the desk of the *maître d'hôtel*. Pavlina flattened herself against the inside wall. Outside, two men rushed past going south.

"Table for two, Monsieur?" the *maître d'hôtel* inquired. Reggie glanced about. A number of travel posters on the walls – the Eiffel Tower, the Moulin Rouge, and Tournée du Chat Noir – led him to believe this to be a French restaurant.

"No," he whispered, "we're ... uh, ... only trying to avoid some Nazis.

Do you have a rear entrance by chance?"

"Certainly, I understand completely. Please follow me." He turned and led them through the restaurant and into the kitchen. "There it is," he said, pointing, "Good luck, Monsieur."

It was a terraced courtyard of trees with scattered tables from other eateries under them. They hurried along the inner face of what appeared to be the rear wall of blocks of flats, trying door handles. One was unlocked and they walked down the hallway to its foyer. This turned out to front on the Calçada Moinho de Vento street. He pressed himself against the glass looking up and down the street for a minute, until he realized the car sitting near the next junction was a taxi. They raced for it and piled into the rear seat. The driver put his folded newspaper on the seat and turned his head, awaiting instructions.

"British Embassy, Rua de São Bernardo 33," Reggie said, "and please avoid driving the Rua do Telhal if at all possible." The man turned the taximeter knob and they motored away.

"He saw your boots and recognized them for … what they were," he told her.

"Is too bad we must hurry. I need to describe for him how I get them, and in much detail."

"That's the one thing you mustn't do, sweetie."

"Is no matter – we are safe here." In ten minutes they were approaching the embassy when he caught sight of a branch of the Caixa Geral de Depósitos Banco and ordered the driver to stop and wait. He dashed in. They took all his Croatian kuna notes and provided him with more than enough Pounds Sterling to cover the wages for the crew at the end of the month, and the remainder in Portuguese escudo.

The taxi deposited them in front of the embassy, a handsome building faced with blue-glazed Moorish geometric tiles, the Union Jack proudly displayed from a staff on the balcony. They hurried inside and sank into plush chairs in the reception area. The receptionist noticed his Swedish uniform.

"Sir, the Swedish Embassy is a half mile south of here," she said.

"Yes, I know, but I'm not Swedish, I'm British. May I speak with the ambassador, please?"

"I believe he may be engaged at the moment, but I'll check," she replied, reaching for an intercom. A man in a US Navy uniform poked his head out a nearby doorway and glanced about.

"Swedish? Did you say Swedish? You off that Scandihoovian ship out there? You English?"

"Yes," Reggie answered, slowly, wondering who this stranger was.

"I'll talk with him for a minute, Miss Harriet. Just step this here way, sir." They went in and the door was shut behind them.

"You that Magnuson fella off the *Belfair*, huh? I gotta shake your hand. Mighty impressive what you're doing if I do say so myself." They shook hands. He turned to Pavlina and took her hand, bowing and giving it a kiss as seen in Hollywood films, unaware that his lips weren't actually supposed to touch her hand. "You that assassinating lady, huh? Much too purty a filly to be doing such-like, but you got my respect, miss. The name's Demorest, lieutenant Patrick Demorest, US Navy, of the naval attaché office here. Have a seat." They all sat. Pavlina and Reggie exchanged looks, as she wiped the back of her hand on her dress.

"How may I help you, lieutenant?" he asked.

"Well, now, that's a very interestin' question, 'cos I was fixing to ask for your help, yes sir." He winked. "Seems we got us a fella here that needs a ride – a ride to England kinda 'on the double', and you're just the fella can do it."

"But we're on our way to Sweden, sir. I don't see how we can be of any assistance to you."

"Now, let's not be coy here, Captain Wallace. I'm fully recognizant of just what you're up to." There was a knock and the door opened. A distinguished gentleman in his late fifties stepped into the room.

"Pat, are you stepping on my toes again?" he asked, with a twinkle in his eye.

"Nope. Nothing of the sort. Just trying to smooth things along, if you catch my drift," he answered. "This here's ambassador Sir Ronald Hugh Campbell, and he's got a mess of alphabet soup after his name."

"I'll see you now, captain. Lieutenant, you may remain here."

"Sure enough, I'll just keep the little lady company." Pavlina bolted from her seat before Reggie even had a chance to rise.

"So pleased to meet you. I go now." She was out the door before the man could reply. Reggie followed. As they walked down the hall, Sir Campbell was apologetic. "He can be just a touch enthusiastic." The ambassadors office was lined with books and featured a massive desk. There was a cocktail trolley near the wall, but the ambassador didn't make an offer. The leather of the chairs creaked as they sat. Reggie introduced Pavlina. Sir Campbell registered curiosity at Pavlina's presence.

"May I ask what your connexion is, with this ship and this, ah, ... 'voyage'?" She smiled and didn't answer, only handing over the khaki envelope. The man opened it and spread out the documents, to peruse them silently for a minute. He looked up and his smile crinkled the corners of eyes that twinkled. "Well, I'm satisfied," he said, handing it back. "You may be unaware, but I was once envoy to Yugoslavia some time ago. Say hello to Winston from me, when you see him next."

"This I will do," she promised.

"What did the lieutenant mean by 'a fellow needing a ride'?" Reggie asked, as he tucked all the documents back in and refolded the envelope.

"Let me ask you this: have you ever heard of a man named 'Garbo'?"

"A *man* named Garbo? No."

"Good. That's as it should be. Two months ago Patrick alerted us to a Spaniard working here independently – independently, mind you! – as a double agent. To make a long story short, he's been doing amazing work, simply astonishing really, and we've taken him on. We call him Garbo – not his real name. The Germans call him by a different name I won't reveal. But now, he and his wife must be spirited away to safety in Britain, where they'll continue their work."

"Ah! And you want us to take them aboard when we go, is that it?"

"Yes, that's it exactly. You'll leave tomorrow."

"Well, that's a problem. We don't get fully oiled up until the night of the twenty-third. There's a queue it seems."

"I'm only a 'lowly' ambassador. I'm afraid I don't command the power needed to change your schedule. We'll just have to wait."

"Even with my diplomatic papers?" Pavlina asked.

"Even so. Sorry." He turned to Reggie. "Now, captain Wallace, let me fill you in on the protocol to be followed for our prearranged 'act of piracy'. You're to navigate to these coordinates at this time, and from there proceed on a heading of zero degrees." He pushed a slip of paper at him and Reggie read it silently. "Approximately 15 hours later a Canadian flower class corvette will approach and fire a warning shot across your bow. You will surrender and follow her in, clear?"

"Yes, but this puts us north-west of neutral Ireland."

"It does. We'll be escorting you up The River Clyde in Scotland. We'll be in touch with you later about Garbo. I'll show you out."

Out on the street Reggie consulted his map but, strangely, it didn't show the bus routes, only trams and funiculars. They began to walk, but in only a minute a taxi happened by and he hailed it. He asked the driver for the best shoe shop in Lisbon. In little more than a mile the man dropped them off at the Sapataria do Carmo in the Chiado district. The shoe salesman was shocked at the state of Pavlina's boots, declaring the bullet holes could not be repaired to the state required by one of such 'bespoke' taste. Pavlina smiled and winked at

Reggie, not letting on they'd once been worn by a Gestapo officer. The man then brought out a selection of similar women's calf-high boots in her size, made from the finest top-grade black-dyed Portuguese leather. Reggie sat and waited while she tried on pair after pair. An hour later she settled on a pair she liked, over her calf and with a hidden zip, however she found the block heels to be too high. The cobbler promised he could alter them and they could be picked up tomorrow. The purchase was made. They then left to walk to the "romantic park" that woman had named, only a quarter mile north, along the way passing the upper terminus of the Gloria Funicular.

The city park didn't seem the have an actual name, only a sign proclaiming "Miradouro de São Pedro de Alcântara", – that is, "Viewpoint" of the nearby street name. It was on two levels, the lower having gardens laid out in geometric proportions, the upper level at the street having mature shade trees, a large fountain, beautiful mosaic patterned paths of tiny pavement blocks fit together, and everywhere plenty of benches, and lamp-posts for illumination at night. The railing enclosing the park was of intricate curlicue cast iron. There were plenty of people too; some strolling, some sitting, and there were mothers pushing prams. Schoolboys raced past chasing a *futebol*, and pigeons scurried out of their way. It even had a concession *quiosque* selling drinks and *sanduíches*. He ordered each of them a local favourite, *porto tonico*, a glass of sweet white port and tonic water, and they sat and sipped while they watched elderly men play at *Bocce* in the centre court. Then they strolled the perimeter rail of the upper terrace, admiring the city views. Reggie was keeping an eye out for just the right spot. It had to be ideal. And then he found it. It was at the cast iron railing, directly across from the large pool of the fountain, and in bright sunlight. He leaned on the rail to her right. They could see the Castle of St. George across the valley, and even the *Belfair* anchored in the distance.

"Réži," Pavlina purred, "why you be so quiet? You say nothing for nearly the hour."

"Yes, I guess it's true. It's just, there's something on my mind."

"You are worried of some things?" she asked.

"Worried? No, not really," he said. He turned to her. "How long have we known each other?" he asked. Her brows knitted, she bit her lip and looked up at the trees as she thought. He removed his cap, feeling inside behind the sweatband for the diamond. Because the top of the ornate fence rail was smooth and had no spikes, there was no place to hang his hat, so he dropped it on the ground. She smiled.

"Is almost ten weeks," she said with conviction, then, "your cap, it fall down."

"Pavlina, I love you, and I can't imagine being apart from you for a single day of those ten weeks," he declared. He took her left hand in his and sank to one knee.

"I love you also, Réži." she said, then looked about her. Couples nearby had stopped strolling and were staring at them. "Get your hat. People look at you. Stand up!"

"I want to take those ten weeks and multiply them by a thousand. Will you marry me?" he asked, holding up the diamond pinched between his thumb and forefinger so she could see it. It glittered, giving off brilliant flashes of reflected sunlight. The women standing around them gasped, some with a hand to a mouth or chest. She gasped too, and took the diamond from him, but then frowned.

"Réži, no one lives as long as that."

"You're always being so literal. Pavlina, will you marry me?" he repeated.

"No," she said, decisively.

It seemed to him the buzz of insects from the trees became unnaturally loud, the sun on his back unbearably hot. His heart was pounding now, and he heard his blood roar in his ears. He looked about, and the people there blurred and went out of focus.

"No?" he repeated, dispirited. She helped him to his feet.

"You foolish man. You must have the proper ring for me. Only then will I marry you!" They kissed and hugged while the people all around them applauded.

"We'll go find a jewellery shop, to get your ring size," he said.

"We go now and find one," she said excitedly, and threaded her arm through his. "Do not step on your hat!" she added, as an afterthought. As they left the park they waved their thanks to the people who had applauded. When they approached the stairway down to the funicular, Pavlina began to turn left towards it, but Reggie gripped her arm tightly and forced her to walk straight ahead and past it.

"Reggie —"

"Oh, look, I think I see a museum up ahead!" he exclaimed loudly, then in a whisper to her, "We're being followed. Don't look back." She obeyed him, but he felt her grip tighten as she whispered an answer.

"Please do not let the thief take my diamond!"

They walked the narrow pavement along the Rua de São Pedro de Alcântara for a hundred yards to the end of the museum building, and as they turned left around it, out of the corner of his eye he saw a man in a wide-brimmed fedora and trench coat keeping pace with them some thirty yards behind. He paused for five seconds to read the sign on the building, which was open – "Santa Casa Museu de São Roque" – and then steered her back around the corner of the building to return to the funicular. The man kept his head down as they passed, and the fedora prevented them from seeing his face. Reggie said to her, "It's too bad it's closed. We'll have to come back later."

As they turned to the right to descend the steps to the funicular, he glimpsed the same man twenty yards behind. Now he knew they were definitely being followed. Reggie joined the queue at the ticket window and bought two tickets, then they retreated to stand near the uphill end of the waiting car, a bright yellow electric tram, a pair of pantographs touching wires overhead. The railcar undercarriage matched the slope, but the body of the tramcar was horizontal. The man bought a ticket as well. Reggie unfolded his map and held it before their faces.

"I noticed him watching us in the park," he whispered, "because he was the only one not applauding. I don't know why a PVDE secret policeman is tailing us – we've done nothing wrong. But, we should let him get on first." She nodded assent. People began to board and find their seats. Reggie and Pavlina pretended to read the map until the man had joined the queue, and then were the last to board. It was crowded. An unseen infant squalled continually. The funicular entrance had no door. Standing near the opening they waited. He tucked the map into his pocket, then held onto a pole as she held onto his hand. The man stood gripping a strap two yards away, not looking at them, a few standing passengers between them. He had a toothbrush moustache. A minute later the motor began to hum. A bell jangled. The driver squeezed the handle on the brake lever and eased it over. The car groaned and started moving downslope, slowly gaining speed. Pavlina put her other hand in her pocket.

"No! My wedding ring is gone!" she yelled, and jumped from the car, dragging him off after her. They fetched up against a nearby wall.

"What do you mean it's gone? Is there a hole in your pocket?"

"Is right here," she said, patting her skirt. "We let him go away now."

"He'll only come back, you know. Let's go hail a taxi." They climbed the steps to the street. Minutes passed and there were no cars, let alone any taxis, nor even a bus. The other funicular car, the companion car counterbalancing the one that had left, arrived and people disembarked. But they knew that man might be on the next car, so when they heard the tram's electric motor begin to hum they raced to board this car. The bell jangled and they started down.

"If he's coming up, he'll see us going down," Reggie said.

"We will hide," she declared.

"But if he's *not* coming up, he'll be waiting for us at the bottom. We must make certain he's in the other car now."

"We will stand so he can see us, but we will not look to him, only look sideways, yes?"

"That's perfect. We'll do that, then." They excused themselves to the people around them and manoeuvred over to stand at the window that would face the other car as it ascended the slope. Reggie held his open map low and they pretended to read it. The driver greeted the passing car with a jingle of his bell and was answered in kind as they passed.

"You saw him? Did he see you?"

"Yes, he look forcefully to us, but I did not look to him."

"Good, he's on his way up," he said, relieved, "We're in the clear. Let's find a seat." Most seats were filled, except for a wooden seat near the far end of the car. They apologized to an elderly man and squeezed past him to seat themselves at the side window. His feeling of relief didn't last long, for as they slowed and turned the slight corner approaching the lower station, from fifty yards away he spied another man in a wide-brimmed fedora and trench coat waiting there. *Blimey, there's two of them. I should have expected they'd be working in pairs*, he thought. The conductor was now only yards away punching tickets, his back to them. Reggie whipped off his cap and gave it to Pavlina.

"Quickly! Sit on the floor facing me with your legs crossed and tucked under the seat." She obeyed his instructions immediately as he stood up, legs spread wide and straddling her. He shrugged off his Swedish captain's blazer, pulling the sleeves inside-out as he did so to hide the gold stripes. He sat, then covered her with it, pushing her forehead down against the seat between his legs. The back of the wooden seat in front of them dug into her spine and she murmured

"Ow!" He muttered, "Shh!" He lay the map open on his coat.

"Tickets? Tickets please!" the conductor said. He punched the ticket of the elderly man. The car eased to a stop with a shudder and a groan. Reggie fished a ticket from his white dress-shirt pocket and it was punched and handed back. The conductor noticed the blue coat spread across his lap below the map and raised his eyebrows.

"Ripped my trousers rather badly," Reggie explained, "and I'm wearing nothing underneath." The conductor grimaced in disgust and went back up the aisle, following the old man. When nearly all the riders had exited the single door, the boarding passengers pushed past them and began to take their seats. The PVDE man boarded and stood in the doorway to look over the interior. Reggie sat immobile and looked out the window, keeping an eye on the man by his reflection in it. The secret policeman looked directly at him and then moved on to the next person. People began to push on the man's back, yelling at him, possibly telling him to get a move on, and after a few seconds he disembarked. A harried woman carrying a baby on her hip sat next to him. The baby stood on her lap facing her and squirmed in her grip. The car full, the electric motor began to hum, the bell jangled, and they started upwards. The conductor walked down the aisle to start taking tickets in reverse order, starting at the rear. He punched the woman's ticket.

"Tickets? Tick—." He looked at Reggie in annoyance. "You didn't get out? I'll need to see your ticket, please." Reggie reached into his shirt pocket again but it was empty.

"A moment if you please, sir, I have my ticket here somewhere." He put his hand under the coat as if to check his trouser pocket, stalling for time, knowing all the while it wouldn't be there. He play-acted checking his other trouser pocket where his hand met Pavlina's and she passed him her ticket.

"Ah, here it is!" He brought it out, the conductor punched it and gave it back, then moved on to the next passenger. Reggie knew in a hundred yards the cars would pass each other and, if the first man who *did* know what he looked like was on his way down, then he was seated on the wrong side of the car. There was nowhere for him to hide. He looked about for inspiration but found none. He was up against the window and was knee to knee with the woman holding the thrashing baby on his left. The struggling infant snatched the poor woman's glasses off, waved them up and down, then released them. They hit the window and clattered to the floor. He stretched a hand down but they were too far away. Pavlina picked them up and placed them in his hand.

"Do you speak English?" he asked the woman.

"Yes," she answered. To the baby she said, "*Fique quieto!*" – be still! – It didn't.

"Are these yours?" he asked, holding them up. "I've needed glasses for some time now—tell me, do you happen to recall your prescription?" Reggie put them on and faced towards the front. The driver gave a jingle of his bell, and the two funicular cars rumbled past each other. Not looking through the glasses but off to the side, he saw the PVDE man frantically looking across, and then he was past and gone. "Never mind, these are much too strong for me," he said, handing them to the woman. She scowled at him for his rudeness. Reggie and Pavlina waited until the seats all about had been vacated before standing up themselves. Pavlina was stiff and her back hurt. He helped her off the funicular and they found a bench in the park they'd left so recently. She sat hunched over, elbows on her knees, as he massaged her back.

"I'm so sorry your special day didn't turn out to be so special," he said.

"Why is the secret policeman of Portugal after us? Ow, ow! This I do not understand," she complained. "Ow, ow, ow! We will go to the ship now, yes? I have enough of Lisbon today."

"Yes, lets get away from here in case they return." He escorted her to the street fronting on the park, where they found a tram halt. The signpost indicated a tram was due in a minute and it arrived on time. As they rode it south he kept an eye peeled for jewellery shops, but the ones he saw were shuttered and barred. It was after five o'clock. They changed to an eastbound tram at the Duque da Terceira Square, and when they disembarked in the Alfama district it was but a short walk to the lifeboat where the crew waited.

23

A Failed Proposal and Successful Negotiation

He was already awake in the morning and gazing at her face, so composed in sleep, when she awoke. She gave him a good morning kiss, and snuggled closer. He cradled her in his arm, as she put her head on his chest.

"Réži?"

"Yes, love?"

"You remember, after I assassinate Stjepan, I say I am tired?"

"Yes. You said killing is exhausting."

"I think I give up the assassinating now," she said, decisively.

"Oh? Why is that?"

"You remember what I say, when Filip is murdered, killing takes away my pain?" She looked up into his face. "But, I have no pain now to take away, because I have you!"

"We have each other!" he responded, thrilled. Then they discussed what they had to do today. First thing was to bring "the rock" to a jeweller to have it fit into a right-sized ring. Then they had to collect the altered boots. "How's your back pain?" he asked.

"I am well today."

"Good." He did, however, have another question he had to ask: "Do you want to get married now? I mean, here in Lisbon?"

"But I have not the ring," she reminded him, "and you will need the ring for you also."

"I know, but we'll have it soon enough. Should we be looking for venues, places to do it, so we'll be prepared?"

"The church? Then what church? There are so many you know. Also, you are the atheist. How will you marry in the church? Will it not be you burst in the flames?" He laughed at this old joke.

"They're only buildings to me. They're supposed to have some mystical significance to some people, but I don't see it." She snuggled closer to him.

"I make the joke. This I think also. We will visit some church today."

"For all I care, we could get married on a hilltop, or on a beach," he said.

"Or the gardens? There are so many to choose here," she suggested. They rose and dressed. Reggie gave himself an advance on his next pay packet. Pavlina deposited her precious document envelope in the ship safe, only pocketing her passport, and they went for breakfast, then to the lifeboat. Today she was dressed in a white skirt with a red floral print, one of her favourites, paired with the same blouse as the day before. Frederik remained aboard to install the new electrical parts, and test the systems, before charging the battery bank.

The ship's boat deposited them on the same quay as before. They walked through the Alfama district where they encountered a grandiose Roman Catholic church. When they entered, they were in awe, surrounded as they were by all the gold and statuary, and every wall was covered in gilt framed oil paintings. The further in they got, though, the slower they walked. They stopped to look at some of these pictures. They recognised the usual Madonna with Child but, as for the rest—he shook his head and made an abrupt about-face and exited the building, and she followed after.

"What is wrong?" she asked, concerned.

"Well, the baroque architecture is nice and that, but we were surrounded by oil paintings of various people in the act of being 'martyred' and some were rather gruesome. Did you see the one of the man standing and holding his own severed head in his arms, the blood spurting from his neck?"

"This I see also," she said, shaking her head, "I see names on the picture frames: is reading 'Saint Denis of Paris' – also you are seeing painting of 'Saint Agatha of Sicily'? ... is terrible, I think."

"I just don't want these images associated with our wedding day," he told her.

"We will go on then," she concurred.

The next church they encountered was the Igreja de Santa Luzia, a small 17th-century church. It was quite plain inside, with bare whitewashed walls, but most impressive was its peaceful garden with vistas over the city's old quarter. A handful of parishioners, mostly old women, knelt in prayer up at the front.

"This is more like it," Reggie said, pleased. A man in a robe left off arranging items on the altar and approached them as they wandered about the interior.

"Good morning! he greeted them, "I am Father Nascimento. May I help you?"

"Yes, I hope so. This is my fiancée. We've only just become engaged, and want to get married."

"I can help you with that," the priest replied, smiling. "Did you have a particular day and time in mind?"

"We're leaving Lisbon in two days, so we need to do this quickly, you see. Also, we are . . . not of this denomination. Will that present a problem?" The priest smiled at this.

"Not at all. Many couples who are ... non-believers ... get married in churches. Happens more often than you might think." Pavlina beamed at Reggie, then asked a question of the man.

"Is allowing to marry in gardens of your terrace?" He looked sharply at her.

"Yes, that is allowed, although we prefer performing the ceremony inside," he said, "I assume you have witnesses, and you'll need two, at least."

"Yes, Frederik!" Reggie said to Pavlina.

"And Annika!" she said to Reggie, "See? Is no problem, *dušice*, we marry then, tomorrow!"

"I'm sorry," the priest said, and his shoulders sagged, "may I see your passports, please?" Reggie stiffened at this request.

"I'm British and she's Yugoslavian," he said, slightly defensively.

"Then this will be impossible, I'm afraid," said the priest, sighing and shaking his head sorrowfully.

"We'll go get married at the City Hall, then," Reggie announced to her. The priest held up a hand.

"You misunderstand me. You'll not be able to obtain a marriage licence. There have been far too many 'marriages of convenience' here. Had one of you been Portuguese there would be no problem, *however*, with the number of people attempting to escape Europe our prime minister Salazar has banned all marriages between foreigners," he said. Seeing their reaction, he added, "Of course, you may always have a ceremony performed here in this church, or any other, but in the eyes of the state it will not be a legal marriage. I'm so sorry."

"Can you, at least, recommend a jeweller where we may get some rings?" Reggie asked, defeated.

"Not a specific jeweller, but if you go over to the Chiado district, I believe you'll find many there," he responded. They thanked the man and left.

In the Chiado district, they did indeed find many jewellery shops, but all of the rings on offer were quite expensive, even considering they were supplying their own diamond. But, on the Rua do Alecrim across from an oval park laid to lawn, they spied a tiny hole-in-the-wall shop and went inside. A bell tinkled as they pushed the door open. The place looked as if it had been here for more than a century. In reality so did the proprietor, a bent Jewish man, balding under his *yarmulke*. His eyes were large, swimming behind round glasses, at their earpiece a series of small magnifying monocles. He introduced himself as Mr Mocatel. He measured their fingers for size using a series of chrome rings and a mandrel. Reggie selected a pair of plain gold wedding bands for them, and Mr Mocatel inquired if they wanted any words engraved on the inside, but they declined because of the lack of time. When their diamond was produced, he gleefully identified it as having come from Lodz in Poland, not Russia as they'd thought, and described how he could tell it was over eighty years old by how certain cuts had been made.

Reggie felt comfortable enough with the man to confess how it had come into his possession, and how its "mates" had helped the two of them, and a ship-full of Swedes, to escape the Nazis in Yugoslavia. When Pavlina selected an 18-carat gold ring to complement the stone, Mr Mocatel was so entertained by this tale, he insisted on upgrading her to a similar 22-carat ring for the same cost. This completed her engagement ring. Pavlina hugged the diminutive man, her chin atop his head. Reggie paid for the three rings in advance. They could come back to pick up the finished engagement ring "tomorrow at noon," Mr Mocatel said.

The Sapataria do Carmo shoe shop was a mere five-hundred yard stroll to the north-east. The boots were ready and fit perfectly. Pavlina put them on, and Reggie took her flats from her, tucking one into each pocket of his captain's blazer. Now they settled in for a leisurely lunch at a nearby Brazilian place on the same square, a *churrascaria* restaurant with meats served *rodízio* style: waiters brought various sizzling meats on long skewers, then sliced them onto their plates with a flourish using cavalry sabres. There were also smoky black beans, and fragrant rice, and all sorts of sliced sweet fruits. It was quite filling. So filling, in fact, they retired to the tree-shaded square while nursing *cachaça* cocktails, Brazil's national drink, until they felt ready to resume their stroll. Reggie had ordered a *caipirinha* for himself, and for Pavlina, a *batida* made with coconut milk. They sat and sipped these as they people-watched. A guitarist sat on a stool dozens of feet away and strummed and sang a melancholy *Fado* tune.

"Have you noticed?" he speculated, "I've not seen any men in trench coats at all today. Either we lost them yesterday, or they've lost interest in us." She nodded while sipping her cocktail. "When we're finished with these, where do you want to go to next, ... the botanical gardens?"

"That is maybe nice," she said, "or, the zoo gardens? There will be the animals from Africa, yes?"

"Want to go see some long-necked giraffes?" he wondered aloud. Just then, a long car motored to the kerb in front of the restaurant entrance, the same car they'd glimpsed as it passed them elsewhere in the city. It was a tan 1937 Chrysler Imperial, and a chauffeur got out to hold open the far side rear door. People all about them stood and craned their necks, a murmur arising. An older lady in a wide-brimmed hat emerged. She wore a mink stole low about her bare shoulders and was elegantly gowned and dripping with jewels. The murmur stopped as abruptly as it had started and the people who had stood now resumed their seats. The portly gentleman seated alone at the next table looked up briefly, and then returned his attention to the book he was reading.

"You are speaking only now of the long necks?" Pavlina whispered, pointing, "Look to the woman there."

"Wow! I wonder who she is?" he remarked. He turned to the portly man and interrupted his reading by asking, "Excuse me sir, but, do you know who that woman is?"

"Who knows? Just some woman, not important. People thought it was prime minister Salazar because of the car, that's all," he replied, and then pointedly focused on his book, his mannerism one of, 'don't bother me'. The elegant woman entered the Brazilian restaurant. The chauffeur sat behind the wheel to wait, the limousine ticking over where it parked. Pavlina finished her drink, and sat while he continued sipping his.

"Do you want another?" he asked her. She frowned, and rubbed her belly.

"No. Is delicious, but maybe I think the coconut milk do not agree with me. Now I find toilet for the women." She stood and kissed him, then walked across the street, around the limousine, and into the restaurant. The elegant woman reappeared and the chauffeur emerged to hold the door for her as she entered the vehicle. He left the door open, then sat behind the wheel. Reggie finished his *caipirinha* and listened to the *Fado* guitarist as he waited. A waiter with a tray stopped, to ask him if he wanted another, and he declined. The man cleared the glasses away, taking one from the portly man as well. The door to the restaurant opened and three people emerged, the flanking figures wearing trench coats and fedoras, gripping the arms of the handcuffed centre figure, who had a black bag over their head and wore Pavlina's floral print dress.

"Hey!" shouted Reggie and bolted from his chair. The three piled into the car and it roared off, even before its door had shut completely. He chased after it a few feet until it turned at the next junction, tires squealing in protest, enough to see the number plate contained the letters "UR". *Could be that's not her*, he thought.

He ran into the restaurant, and shouted at the *maitre d'*, "Those three that just left, did that woman come out of the lavatory?"

"She never entered it sir. She was detained the moment she arrived," he said.

"Damn! Damn!" he shouted, looking about helplessly, not knowing what to do.

"Calm yourself sir, or I'll have to ask you to leave."

"Those men, are they secret policemen?" he asked in a lower tone.

"Quite possibly. I don't know. No one questions what they do. They entered through the kitchen minutes ago."

"Where are their headquarters?" he demanded. The man took a blank piece of paper and wrote.

"You didn't get this from me—please leave," he said, passing it across. Reggie went back out to his same chair on the square, and unfolded his map on the table. He couldn't find the street on it. The same gentleman he'd spoken to earlier was still seated nearby.

"Sorry to bother you again, sir. Do you know where this address is?" He asked, showing the paper, "it's the PVDE headquarters." To Reggie's consternation, the man stood and strode rapidly away without looking back. He sat peering closely at his map, wiping his eyes on his sleeve, frantically determined to find it. By inspecting the map closely section by section he eventually found the short street. He folded the map and raced for the nearest tram stop.

In half an hour he stood at a counter in a small foyer just inside the entrance to the building. The clerk took his passport, and instructed him to wait until called. He sat and fidgeted, checking his watch impatiently. A nattily suited man appeared, carrying Reggie's passport, and escorted him down a corridor. They were about to enter a conference room, when another uniformed man passed by, but stopped and turned, to quite obviously look over his Swedish captain's uniform. He took the passport from the first man and dismissed him, then showed Reggie through a door into a different small room, and shut the door. A door that was steel and had no window. He was told to take a seat in a steel chair while the other man occupied the oak chair across the table from it. This table was bolted to the concrete floor, and held only an ashtray and a goose-necked lamp. A bare bulb hung from the ceiling. The room was windowless and smelled strongly of disinfectant.

"You speak English, I presume?" The name tag sewn over the man's pocket read "Agostinho Lourenço" and his military uniform looked much too similar to that of the Gestapo. Disturbingly so.

"Yes."

"You're making an inquiry about a missing person, missing today, correct?" The man held up the pack of cigarettes. Reggie shook his head.

"My fiancée," Reggie said, nodding. "She was snatched by two PVDE men from a restaurant in the Chiado district little more than an hour ago – they wore fedoras and trench coats." He snapped on the goose-necked lamp, picked up Reggie's passport and examined it closely under the light, then held it up and compared it to Reggie's face.

"Nationality?"

"Yugoslavian," Reggie answered. The man smiled tolerantly.

"Not hers.—Yours."

"Oh, uh, Swedish!" Lourenço aimed the lamp at Reggie, who had to squint and drop his gaze away from the glare. Only then did he see the handcuffs attached to the seat of his chair. The floor was wet and there was a grate over a drain in the centre of it. In the light from the bare bulb overhead he could see something white through the slots of this grate. *What is that? It looks like a ... a tooth?*

"But what is your *actual* nationality?" He lit a cigarette, taking his time about it. He exhaled a stream of smoke towards the ceiling. "You needn't worry," he said, "this room is quite soundproof. Take all the time you need." Appearing quite relaxed, Lourenço tapped the ash in the tray and examined the glowing coal on the end of his cigarette.

Reggie sat immobile. He really wanted to squirm uncomfortably in his seat, but forced himself to hold still.

"What makes you think I'm not Swedish?" Reggie asked.

"I asked you if you spoke English, and you didn't hesitate."

"Well, I felt it highly unlikely any Portuguese might know Swedish, – no offence – and English is such a universal language these days."

"No offence taken," Lourenço said. The seconds ticked by while he examined the passport under the lamp again. "Try me. You could begin by telling me your hometown." Reggie felt a bead of sweat trickle down his side from his armpit. It tickled. He squeezed his arm against his side to blot the sweat away, and thought, *My hometown? I never bothered to look.*

He suddenly remembered the litre glass they'd given that German guard back in Šibenik and blurted, "Oslo! It's Oslo."

"Your passport says 'Uppsala'," Lourenço said, tolerantly, "Oslo is in Norway." Reggie groaned inwardly. *Why didn't I say 'Stockholm'? It's on the bloody ship! There's no chance of my explaining this mistake away, now.*

Lourenço closed the passport and it held up. "It's a good effort, don't you think? ... but ...." He reached under the table and pressed a button. "The truth is always the best, no?" *Will they use wooden truncheons on us, or rubber ones? Not that either will make much difference. And to think, I let both of us in for this voluntarily by coming here. If I ask politely, will they take me to her cell and let me see her, before they begin?*

The door opened and the first man appeared. "Mr Mafalda, would you go and fetch me out the —"

"British! I'm British!"

"Ah! You see? That's all we wanted. Just the truth. Now we can begin our procedure. —Mr Mafalda, would you go and fetch me out the admissions ledger, please?" The man returned carrying a thick ledger, then left the room. Lourenço pushed the passport across the table to him. "It's a good effort, but not good enough. I could see the hand of MI6 all over it" he said. Reggie looked down once more at the "tooth" beneath the grate, and quite suddenly it disappeared. *It was only the light reflecting off a bubble in the water.*

"M. I. Six? Who's that?" Reggie asked, relieved. Mr Lourenço looked surprised at this.

"SIS? MI5?" he suggested.

"Sorry, I've no idea. It's all gibberish to me." Lourenço rolled his eyes and shook his head, not answering him, then pulled the ledger towards him and opened it. He extracted a fountain pen from a tunic pocket and uncapped it.

"Your *actual* name, please?"

"Captain Reginald Wallace, British Merchant Navy."

"*Obrigado.*" He wrote this down.

"I would appreciate it, if you don't let that information leave this building."

"*Comandante* Reginaldo, please think for a moment of just who you are asking that?" He smiled patiently.

"Oh, sorry!"

"Was she carrying her passport with her?"

"Yes, always," Reggie answered promptly.

"Nationality on the passport?"

"Yugoslavian."

"Her family name?"

"Pavlina."

"Given name?"

"Buga, ... not her birth name, but it's what she calls herself." Lourenço traced his finger down a page.

"We don't have her."

"You don't?" he said, confused.

"No. It wasn't us."

"Are you sure? She was driven away in a car similar to your prime minister's. Two letters of the number plate were 'U' and 'R'."

"I am certain. We keep very good records." He shut the book. Reggie was given his passport and escorted out of the building. He stood on the pavement and turned first one way, then another, at his wit's end. *If the police hadn't taken her, then who? Had someone who had seen that wanted poster in Croatia tipped off a confederate here? Made a deal to split the reward? Had the Nazis put two-and-two together and somehow connected her with his ship, despite Stjepan's sudden disappearance? Had they followed the voyage of the* Belfair *as reported in the world press, to track her here?*

He truly didn't know what to do. He spent the afternoon riding trams, on the lookout for the Chrysler, his fears quickly solidifying into anger. He returned to the lifeboat before six o'clock. The crew was stunned to hear what had happened but, like Reggie, didn't know what to do. He spent a sleepless night, tossing and turning, mulling over his options.

There was a knock on his cabin door as he dressed, and a crewmember told him he was about to miss his breakfast.

"I'm not hungry. Tell everyone the ship's boat is leaving earlier than usual today," he commanded.

"How much earlier?"

"A.S.A.P! Wait, ... never mind, I'll do it." He went to the bridge to use the tannoy.

When the lifeboat touched the quay, Reggie was the first one off. He turned to the others.

"I don't know how long I'll be. If I'm not here by 1800 hours, go to the ship – I'll find my own way back."

He shouldn't have skipped breakfast. That was a mistake. If he was to spend an entire day and night searching, he needed to eat. He found a café and wolfed down a hearty meal of *bife com ovo a cavalo*: fried eggs atop a pan-fried steak, with rice.

His first stop was the *Ministério dos Transportes*. He gave a description of the car and number plate, but the clerk refused his entreaties, saying that information couldn't be divulged to just anyone. Disappointed, he boarded one of the city's ubiquitous trams, to visit the British Embassy next. If anyone could help him, he was sure it would be Sir Campbell.

The tram ascended the Calçada da Estrela and dropped him at its junction with the Rua de São Bernardo, where he had to walk a quarter mile north to the Consulate entrance. He was escorted in to see the ambassador, who was dismayed to hear about Miss Pavlina. Sir Campbell offered him a noggin of whisky, to calm his nerves. Reggie sipped, and listened.

"The Ministry of Transport declined to help, eh? I'm not surprised. Let me see what I can do." After consulting a 'wheeldex' he lifted his telephone handset and dialled, while Reggie listened. "Hello, Jorge? ... Ambassador Ronald Campbell, British Embassy ... say, I'm wondering if you can help me out here ... I'm trying to trace the owner of a 1937 Chrysler Imperial, the number plate contains the letters 'U, R' ... the colour?" He looked at Reggie and arched an eyebrow.

"Tan," he said.

"Tan in colour, and chauffeur driven ... Thank you." He hung up. "He'll call me back directly. Now then —" He was interrupted by a knock and his receptionist entered carrying a canvas bag marked 'diplomatic pouch', its heavy zip locked with a padlock. "Excuse me." He retrieved a key from his desk and unlocked it. She returned in a moment with its contents transferred to a black dispatch box, and this he opened, lifting out documents one-by-one onto the desk while muttering to himself, "M-mm, ... yes, ... hmm-hm." Suddenly, he exclaimed, "Oh dear!" Reggie sat forwards with a question.

"Something the matter?"

"Dear me, such sad news. One of our top submarines was sunk on fourteenth April and we're only now hearing about it. The *Upholder*, and there were no survivors," he said. Reggie felt like he'd been kicked in the gut, and the ambassador saw this. "Oh, did you know them?"

"Yes. Commander Wanklyn. That was the sub took me to Yugoslavia in February." He downed his drink in one gulp.

"I'm so sorry," Sir Campbell said, in commiseration. The phone rang. He picked it up and listened. "Thank you, Jorge." He hung up and turned to Reggie. "The car belongs to a Mrs Maria Xavier dos Santos de Castelo Branco, an extremely wealthy widow," he relayed, "and also, I might add, a notoriously vocal Nazi sympathiser."

"Where might I find this widow?" he asked.

"In Castelo Branco, about a one-hundred-fifty mile drive north of here."

"Splendid," he groused. "Look, since you saw me last, there's been a change: I've proposed to Pavlina and she's accepted."

"That's wonderful! Congratulations! You won't be able to get a marriage licence here, though."

"Yes, we know."

"So, I gather you're going after her?"

"I don't see how I can, as much as I want to; a three-hundred mile return trip, and no way to get there; Pavlina may not be in Castelo Branco and, in fact, she could be held anywhere; that car may only have been the getaway car. I just don't know."

"I'd loan you the consulate car, but it's at the mechanic's shop with electrical problems. What will you do?"

"I don't know yet. What I do know is I'm due to pick up her ring in less than an hour. I'll do that now, and maybe I'll think of something."

"Good luck," the ambassador said, in parting. Reggie left for the Chiado district.

As he entered the jeweller's shop a few minutes before noon, the little bell tinkled. Mr Mocatel looked up from his workbench, then came hurriedly to the counter. He began talking non-stop, making excuses.

"So good of you to be on time, so prompt, but I'm sorry to say it's not ready yet, you should go away now and come back again, tomorrow, yes tomorrow, or perhaps the day after would be better, and now if you will leave, you can just step this way, and use my back door to the alley, ... yes the alley ... and, and—" The bell tinkled behind Reggie. The blood drained from Mr Mocatel's face and he fell silent. He swallowed. His hands began to shake and he clasped them together to prevent this. Reggie turned. A man with a toothbrush moustache and wearing a fedora had stepped into the shop, his trench coat unbuttoned, and Reggie felt something hard press against his kidney. Looking down, he saw a silencer just like Pavlina's on the man's pistol. He raised his hands, slowly.

"Are you armed?" the man asked.

"No." The man patted him down to make certain, then holstered the gun. The angle of the brown leather strap across the man's chest told him he wore a shoulder holster under his left arm. *He's right-handed*, Reggie thought. He looked beyond him, out the glass of the shop door.

"Where's your partner? Don't you fellows always work in pairs?"

"He's at home, recovering from an illness. Put your hands down."

Reggie then asked the obvious question: "PVDE?"

"No," the man answered.

"Then who the hell are you?"

"Mr Mocatel, you may go." He pulled his trench coat aside to reveal his Nazi party badge with its swastika, pinned to his velvet lapel. Mr Mocatel gave a whimper. "Oh, do shut up will you? You're in Portugal, not Dachau you idiot," the man said in irritation.

Without taking his eyes from the man, Reggie said, "Stay where you are, Mr Mocatel – we're leaving." He went to the door and opened it, bell tinkling, and motioned for the man to precede him. The man shook his head in the negative. Reggie stepped outside onto the pavement, and the man followed after. Reggie continued walking straight ahead, off the pavement, across the street, and into the small oval park on the other side. He found a convenient tree-shaded bench and they sat, Reggie on the man's left. He crossed his legs and rested his right forearm on the bench, his elbow hanging off the back of it.

"How did you manage to get a gun into this country?" he asked.

"Let us just say, there are many things may be carried in a diplomatic pouch, besides mere documents."

"Do you have her?" he asked, casually, while glancing up at a pigeon gliding in for a landing on the head of the nearby statue. The man's gaze followed his.

"Yes, she's–" The words were barely out of his mouth before Reggie punched him in the face. The man went for his gun, but Reggie seized his wrist and crushed the smaller man against the bench with his full body weight. They grappled silently for a few seconds, then froze, locked in a tense balance, neither having an advantage.

"You're not going to shoot me," he grunted through gritted teeth, "If you do, you won't get what you want from me. What *is it* you want from me?"

"That is correct, I won't shoot you. Let me go, and I'll tell you." Slowly, each relaxed their grip on the other, and Reggie slid to the far end of the bench. The man rubbed his jaw. Reggie's hand hurt like the blazes, but he wasn't going to give the man the satisfaction of seeing him massage it.

"Have you harmed her in any way? Injured her? Because if you have …"

"Why would I do that? We're a cultured people, we aren't —"

"Aren't *what*? *Philistines?*" he interrupted, with contempt. The Nazi smirked at this.

"How very droll of you, Herr Magnuson. Need I tell you, the Serbs, the Croats, in fact most all Slavic peoples are a subset of the great Aryan Race."

He called me Magnuson! He hasn't a clue of our real mission, he thought. "You mean a subset of your 'Master Race', but not quite equal."

The man shrugged at this. "Pavlina is quite beautiful. Her Slavic proportions are exquisite. In actuality she embodies the very essence of Aryan motherhood."

"Your racial theory makes me ill."

"Not a theory; it's a fact."

"What is it you want?" he demanded.

"A trade: you give us the *Belfair*, and in return you get Pavlina. We have a crew waiting to take it over. We will depart, and the next moonless night paint over the Swedish flags, give it a new name and new home port. It will then be just another random merchant ship, only one among many."

"I know all about your merchant raider *Kormoran*, because I encountered it on my last voyage. Your plan is to convert the *Belfair* into a merchant raider, isn't it?"

"Perhaps." The man gave a smug smile.

"And my crew, you'll just let them return home to Sweden with me?" he countered.

"Yes, certainly."

"To keep the theft from being discovered, your plan is to murder us all. After all, your fatherland has proven itself so proficient at it."

"I'm afraid you watch too many films, Herr Magnuson," he said, airily.

"If I refuse?"

The man laughed at the suggestion. "There is no chance of that. You've already made the decision." They sat for a moment while the man smirked, and Reggie silently fumed inside.

"I need to see her, to make sure she's not been harmed."

"I've already given you reasons why we would not but, very well." He raised an arm and beckoned towards them. The Chrysler motored up from a side street, and the chauffeur got out and opened the rear door. A few seconds passed, but she didn't emerge. She wasn't there.

"Get in," the Nazi said.

"Get in? Are you mad?" he said, incredulous.

"Not at all."

"I'm not going anywhere with you, certainly not getting in Mrs Maria Xavier's car for you to drive me up to Castelo Branco where you can just make us both 'disappear'."

"How do you —" the man began, but Reggie cut him off.

"Let me tell you how this is going to work: all of our dealings will take place in public, with plenty of people around, and never inside any building or car. You will bring Pavlina to me, *first*, before anything else. Only after I'm assured she's unharmed will we talk."

The man balked at this, opening his mouth to object, but then acquiesced. "Oh, all right, it's but a small matter."

"We'll meet at the viewpoint park where you first saw us. I'm sure you know it. Plenty of people there."

"*Ja, ja*," he looked at his wristwatch, "but it's a long drive to Castelo Branco and return. It will need to be tonight—say, seven o'clock?"

"Seven. I'll be there. She better be unharmed," he warned.

"And you had better come unarmed, otherwise ..." the Nazi warned in return, leaving the threat unsaid, but patting the bulge beneath the coat for emphasis. He boarded the Chrysler and it cruised away. Reggie returned to the jewellery shop and, despite the "SHUT" sign, rapped on the glass. Mr Mocatel provided the engagement ring that had, in fact, been completed. He put the ring in the box with the wedding rings, and gave Mr Mocatel assurances the Nazi would not return; that the German now had business to transact with him alone.

Returning to the Consulate, he sat with Sir Campbell, to fill him in on the morning's events. The ambassador was sympathetic and listened carefully as Reggie wrapped up his narration.

" ... and I didn't think to mention this before but, the Nazis in Croatia have put a price on her head of a half-million reichmarks. The man did call me Herr Magnuson, so I believe the Nazis in Lisbon may not know about the Balkan reward for her capture."

"Let us hope so. Hmmm, ... seven o'clock this evening, you say? He's bringing Pavlina?"

"Yes. He had a silenced pistol in a shoulder holster, and bragged how it came here in a diplomatic pouch. We have guns on board the ship, but he's warned me to come unarmed."

"Wise advice indeed!"

"I actually have available to me an unregistered gun having a silencer. I could —"

"No, no, no, don't even think along those lines! Mere possession will get you twenty years!"

"Well, what am I supposed to do? I feel so helpless!"

"My advice, my boy, is to go back to your ship and wait, yes, wait I said! Remind me, what did you say was the name of that last church you visited yesterday?"

"The, uh ... Church of Santa Luzia, in the Alfama district. We spoke with a Mr Nascimento, I think?"

"Father Nascimento," he said, and wrote it down, "and the park is the one with the viewpoint, at the top of the Gloria Funicular?"

"That's right. It's where I proposed to her, at the railing closest to the fountain."

"I know it well. Now, you go back to your ship. Eat something. Try to get some sleep. You want to be fresh for tonight's negotiations. When you do come, bring your crew – unarmed, mind you! – and I'll meet you there at seven."

"You'll be there? Oh, thank you, sir! It'll be a load off my mind if I have your support to back me up." The receptionist Harriet showed him out. Ambassador Sir Ronald Campbell sat in thought for a time, then buzzed Harriet on the intercom.

"Sir?"

"Would you ring the Igreja de Santa Luzia church in the Alfama district, and ask Father Nascimento to come to the phone?"

"Yes sir." He sat, going over paperwork, until his phone rang, then picked up.

"Father Nascimento? ... this is ambassador Ronald Campbell at the British Consulate here in *Lisboa*. ... Very well, thank you. ... I was wondering if I could prevail upon you to perform a simple wedding ceremony tonight at dusk, at the Miradouro de São Pedro de Alcântara, ... excellent! These are the particulars ..."

Reggie couldn't eat, but forced himself to, swallowing a dry sandwich of tinned beef he fixed himself in the galley. He tried to nap but couldn't sleep. The crew kept out of his way as he paced the length of the deck. As the ship's clock chimed a half-five, he ordered everybody except a minimal skeleton crew into the boat, and they rowed for shore. Landing at the quay, he found a group waiting for the boat, including Annika and Frederik. He explained what was going on, and requested them all to follow him to the park, with no judgement if any one of them declined. No one did. The tram delivered them to the lower terminal of the Gloria Funicular, and they boarded as a group. At the top, he directed them up the stairs and around the corner to the viewpoint. It was dusk, the sky a muted purple, and the pole lamps of the park were lit, bathing the scene in a lovely yellow glow. The lights of Lisbon covered the hillsides across the valley. There were many people out tonight, too. Some couples strolled, and some women pushed baby carriages, their husbands at their side. The husbands were bare-headed and, for the most part, wearing the typical Portuguese open-necked and short-sleeved white shirts. Most were wearing knee-breeches and sandals against the lingering heat of the day.

The crew from the *Belfair* followed Reggie along the ornate iron railing until they encountered the ambassador. Reggie made the introductions. He checked his wristwatch: the time was 6:47. As the ambassador guided their group closer towards the fountain, Reggie was amazed at the tableau arranged before them.

A priest resplendent in alb and chasuble with, behind him, a folding table set up against the railing, covered with a white cloth and laid out with the appropriate silver plate. The full paraphernalia of the Mass was there – candles, chalice, ciborium and paten – leaving no doubt this was the setting for a full Nuptial Mass with all the pomp and ceremony of the Catholic Church. Reggie did, of course, recognise all these things, the memories welling up from his childhood so long ago.

The priest smiled beatifically at them as he clasped a slender volume before him. The flames of the candles guttered in the evening breeze. Facing this table were folding chairs arrayed in two groups, each five abreast and six deep, flanking an aisle centred on the priest at the table.

"What's all this, then?" a bewildered Reggie asked Sir Campbell.

"I've arranged for the two of you to marry. Don't worry, the cost is being covered by the Embassy," he replied. "Would everyone please take their seats, on the *left side* only?" he called out. "Thank you. Ah! Here she is!" The Chrysler Imperial had stopped in the street. The chauffeur got out and opened the rear door. The same Nazi emerged, then helped Pavlina out, her hands enclosed in an expensive ermine fur muff. Reggie waved to them but they didn't wave back. The man kept hold of the crook of her elbow as they walked across the park. The closer the pair approached, the slower they walked, the man appearing confused, then angry, while a broad grin spread on Pavlina's face. Reggie and the ambassador met them at the entrance to the aisle through the grouping of chairs.

"What is this?" the Nazi hissed angrily. Reggie ignored him and went straight to Pavlina to kiss her, while the ambassador answered for him.

"This is their wedding, all prearranged days ago. It shouldn't take long, and then we can all get down to discussing the business about the ship."

"And just who are you?"

"Mr Karlsson, Deputy ambassador to the Swedish legation here in Lisbon. And you are?" he asked, but received no answer. Reggie had been hugging Pavlina, but she wasn't hugging him in return. He put his hands inside her muff, only to discover she was wearing handcuffs.

"Are these handcuffs necessary?" he asked the Nazi, irritated.

"Yes! Get on with it. We have urgent business!" he said, impatiently. Reggie now smoothed her hair away from her forehead, to reveal a purple and yellow bruise above her left eyebrow.

"You're injured! What have they done to you?"

"Is nothing. I do to myself this injury." She grinned at him in triumph.

"She head-butted my partner and broke his nose," the man admitted.

"My dear, will you allow me to escort you up the aisle?" the ambassador asked her.

"Mr Karlsson, when this you do, I will be honoured by you." He took her arm. While the two of them stood there, the Nazi still held tight to her other arm. Sir Campbell cleared his throat and addressed the man.

"The three of us look a bit odd, sir. If you will take a seat in the front row, things will move along much more efficiently," he said, "unless, it is *you* who want to escort her to the altar?" Reluctantly, the man released her arm. "Mr Magnuson, would you please show him where to sit, first row, over there? Thank you."

Reggie did, then went to stand before the priest. "Frederik!" he called out, "Will you stand as my usher? Annika, do you want to be Pavlina's chief bridesmaid? Come on up, then!" The two made their way up, to stand at either side of Reggie, leaving a space for Pavlina.

The priest nodded benevolently and asked in a kindly tone, "Do you have the rings, my son?" Reggie fished a small maroon velvet box from his trouser pocket, handing it to Frederik. The Nazi had sat in the first row, right side, on the aisle, but left his hat on. He kept his right hand inside his trench coat on his weapon, in case they had any plans to whisk her away. Reggie faced the priest and stood waiting somewhat nervously. There was no music, but a courtly Sir Campbell slowly escorted Pavlina up the aisle to "give her away" to Reggie. Reggie and Pavlina turned to face one another. The ambassador now turned to those who walked in the park and clapped his hands, to make an announcement.

"May I have your attention, please!" he called in a stentorian voice, "This is a wedding ceremony, but any and all are welcome to come and observe!" The couples strolling under the trees now approached, to stand at the rear of the chairs. A mother here and there bent over her pram, rocking it to-and-fro while uttering a soothing sound: "Shh-shh-shh."

The ambassador now sat to the man's right, leaving a chair empty between them, but then leaned towards him to say, "Since we're the only ones sitting on the 'bride's side', the distribution appears a bit unequal. I've been told you have crewmen ready to take over the ship. If they're present, perhaps they'll agree to fill these empty seats?" he suggested.

The man stood for a moment to put two fingers in his mouth, and loudly whistled a prearranged signal. More than a dozen short-haired young men, muscular and attired in seamen's togs, promptly appeared. At his direction they all sat.

Now the invocation could begin. The priest opened his "Rite of Marriage" Missal and, raising his hand with two fingers held extended and together, made the sign of the cross before Pavlina and Reggie. He spoke in Latin, beginning to bless them with the words, "*In Nomine Patris, et Filii, et Spiritus Sancti...*"

Now Annika began to weep quietly, and Frederik passed her his handkerchief, behind the backs of the bride and groom. As the priest droned on and on in Latin, Reggie began to smile broadly. He very nearly laughed! Inside the ermine muff he released Pavlina's hand, but she held tight to his.

"Let go!" he urged under his breath through lips held immobile. Her grip only tightened, her brows lowered at him as he struggled. Reggie gazed lovingly into her eyes and, not moving his head a millimetre, flicked his eyes towards the priest then back to hers. She looked at the priest, and without breaking stride in his monologue, the man *winked* at her! Her jaw dropped in surprise, and she released her grip. Now the priest turned for a moment to lay his slender volume on the table. He clasped his hands together and looked over the assemblage to loudly repeat, in English, that time-honoured phrase, "Should anyone present know of any reason that this couple should not be joined in holy matrimony, speak now or forever hold your ... *hands up!*"

There was a flurry of clicking cameras but, strangely, not a single flash was seen. Fifteen Germans turned their heads towards the sound, to see the mothers in the crowd had vanished, and the "husbands" now covered them with handguns. Too late, they realized they hadn't heard the crying of a single infant, for the baby carriages had been empty of all but weapons.

"I said hands up! Police!" shouted the so-called "priest". Many of these plain-clothes "husbands" also shouted out, "Police! Keep your hands high!" Two men bolted and were chased down and tackled.

As the Nazi rose and spun to his left, drawing his pistol, Sir Campbell's foot swept his legs out from under him, and the man fell face first in the dust. Reggie pivoted and put his foot on the hand holding the pistol. The Nazi struggled up to his hands and knees. Pavlina hurried around behind Reggie and Frederik, and planted the toe of her boot in the Nazi's groin. She followed this up with a second kick, for good measure, and the man collapsed with a whimper. She then invited Annika to kick him too, but she declined. A plain-clothes policeman sprinted down the aisle and stuck his pistol barrel in the Nazi's face. The man surrendered. Sir Campbell retrieved the man's pistol and handed it off to a policeman.

"Good aim, sweetie!" Reggie said, "I knew it was a faked ceremony the moment our 'priest' here spoke.—I mean, I know *my* Latin is bad, but *his* was ghastly!" He retrieved the handcuff key from their captive to unlock her, then shackled the wrists of the Nazi. Frederik opened the ring box for him, and Reggie slipped the engagement ring on her finger. They kissed.

"The men here, all are the Nazis, yes?" she asked, "I count many, more than the dozen."

"Yes, you're right. Fifteen I think," he answered, glancing about.

"Thank you, Reggie!"

"I had nothing to do with it. You must thank Sir Campbell, sweetie. He arranged it all without my knowledge."

"Thank you, Sir Campbell. This is the best *faux* wedding day ever!" she enthused.

"You are entirely welcome, my dear," the ambassador replied, "however, let us not call it a 'false' wedding, but rather we shall let it stand in place of your wedding rehearsal."

"If this is our rehearsal, I certainly hope our real wedding is nothing like it," Reggie muttered, with a roll of his eyes. Before he was escorted away, Pavlina collared their captive to retrieve something, and Reggie wanted to know what it was. She opened her hand to reveal she had taken the man's Nazi party member badge.

"I get it! You're wanting a keepsake, a 'souvenir' of our adventures today," he laughed.

Those with weapons were quickly disarmed, and their hands cuffed behind them. A pair of Black Maria vans arrived, and their rear doors were flung open to begin the loading. The manacled chauffeur was prodded towards them by a policeman. One policeman helping the Nazis into the vans paused just long enough to comment to his fellow, "Kidnapping, and having a gun that's *silenced*? I'll lay you odds ten-to-one they won't let him out until at least 1967."

Father Nascimento approached, carrying a box, to blow out the candles and collect all the loaned vestments and silver plate.

24

Wedded Bliss

A motorboat hailed the HLV *Belfair* early on the morning of the 23rd with a message: they were to go to the fuel dock at once, instead of after noon. The reason was the Kriegsmarine submarine tender scheduled to refuel ahead of them couldn't move, as more than half the crew had vanished.

At the quay, Pavlina descended the gangplank alone, telling them all she "needed to get a little shopping done" before departure. She was searched by the soldier at the fence and permitted to enter the city, where she boarded a tramcar.

A bell tinkled as she pushed the door open. Mr Mocatel looked up from his workbench in surprise, having not expected to see her again. He came hurriedly to the counter, worried there might be a problem with his craftsmanship. She displayed the lovely engagement ring on her finger.

"But, if nothing is wrong with the ring, why is it you are coming today?" he asked.

"I have a thing to show you!" She drew him out from behind his counter by the hand, then to the pavement outside. He looked up and down the street, confused at what he was supposed to see. She held out her open hand, and in it lay the Nazi party badge. He shuddered. "You know the man who this is belonging to?" she asked. He nodded, and recited an old Yiddish curse.

"He should have a hundred houses, and in every house a hundred rooms, and in every room twenty beds, and he should have a delirious fever that will drive him from bed to bed to bed!"

"But he has now only one bed, and is in the gaol! Please, I want you to pick a spot on the pavement. Is can be anywhere, but a place maybe is important to you, yes?" Mr Mocatel pointed to the concrete directly in front of the entrance to his shop. She placed the badge there. "Now I think you are wanting to step on this, yes?" Mr Mocatel put his heel atop the badge. There was a crackling sound. He ground his heel upon the cloisonné badge until nothing was left but enamel shards and wire, then stepped away.

"You enjoyed that?" she asked, and he nodded and smiled with satisfaction. She hugged Mr Mocatel, then squatted to sweep the remains into her hand. She crossed the street to the park where she dumped the shards in a rubbish bin, then dusted her hands off and gave a cheerful wave goodbye.

The ship was bunkered with enough fuel to reach Sweden, and this took many hours, until well after lunch. They departed Lisbon shortly after 1400 hours. After the bogus wedding the evening before, the ambassador had informed them the prearranged plans to spirit away "Garbo" out of Lisbon had been cancelled: Garbo and his wife would to go on an aeroplane the following day, for speed.

Out into the Atlantic now, they plunged into the swells, taking a northerly heading of 353 degrees. By nightfall it was tipping it down, and then the rain moderated to a drizzle, continuing for three days with a headwind, and then the weather broke. All day long on the 27th of April the sun shone brightly, and it was a great relief to the captain, and also the helmsmen, the seas had calmed.

His noon sight put them near the coordinates given him by the ambassador, 54°17' 16" North, 12° 22' 36" West, and this was directly west of the Republic of Ireland's Dingle peninsula. Reggie found he was slightly nervous, because he knew they were near the same patch of ocean where the Germans had sunk the SS *Athenia* and the RMS *Lusitania*, both without warning. He ordered a new heading of 0° true, proceeding due north, just as the ambassador had instructed him. As if on cue, a RAF PBY Catalina overflew them, then remained circling for their protection as they proceeded.

At 0300 hours on 28 April, the expected Corvette approached from out of the south-west. HMCS *Battleford* was fresh from Liverpool, Nova Scotia, Canada, where she'd been undergoing a refit since her latest trans-Atlantic HX convoy escort duty. The planned "shot across the bow" was made, flag signals were exchanged, and they were given instructions to proceed to the east-north-east, and north of Ireland as the Corvette followed them in.

By noon on the twenty-ninth it was a relief to be entering the relative safety of the Firth of Forth. The latest PBY Catalina departed. Reggie had the deck crew bring the booms inboard, and stow away all the flood lamps and extension cords. Nine hours later found the *Belfair* adjusting her lines on the bollards of the Titan Shipyard Dock on the river Clyde.

At Reggie's invitation, Pavlina and the Swedes trooped down the gangplank and into Clydebank, to have a celebration party at the nearest pub. They found it a few streets away near the train station, at the venerable Alexander's Bar, on Alexander Street, and Reggie would charge the expense to the Ellerman Company, consequences be hanged!

It was the final day of April and that morning after breakfast, Reggie had the crew pack up their kit bags and queue in the wardroom for him to sign their papers. He issued the pay due them in pounds sterling, then signed off each man's Merchant Navy Seaman's Discharge Book, stamping each in blue ink with the "Very Good" stamp. He then made a final inspection of the ship. Reggie went to his quarters and changed into civilian clothes, leaving old captain Söderberg's uniform hanging in the wardrobe with the other two. Shortly after ten-hundred hours a taxi arrived, and Reggie greeted lieutenant-commander Bruce McPeavey of the Royal Navy, the new captain. The man went down the line of crewmen to congratulate them all on a job well done, and then Reggie dismissed them. He stood at the top of the gangway and shook each man's hand as they departed for the Swedish Consulate in Glasgow. The five Norwegian-Americans remained aboard, sitting on a hatch cover, intending to volunteer for whatever military operation was slated for this ship after Reggie had gone. He spent an hour walking Captain McPeavey about the ship, and gave him much important advice, passing on Frederik's words to him: "The rudder on this ship is undersized, and she steers like a pig," and, "You need to watch yourself in a crosswind, it's easy to lose control." He had to explain once again why the wardrobe door was still missing in the captain's quarters, and McPeavey was amused by the tale, and then he related the story of just why there was a massive dent in the galley bulkhead over the stove, and McPeavey was astonished. The two men exchanged salutes at the gangplank, and Reggie joined Pavlina waiting on the dock with her bicycle and suitcase, and his kitbag. As they walked towards the port gate, an arriving bus braked to a stop and some of the new British crew disembarked. He wished them well as they passed. Reggie couldn't quite grasp their mission was actually at an end. It seemed anticlimactic to him, in a way.

"I feel relieved. Do you feel relieved?" he asked, as they walked to the railway station.

"Yes. Is the new working now for me," she said, patting the khaki envelope of documents in her pocket.

"Yes, we'll need to get settled into Claridge's and meet your King Peter … Oh! And I'll certainly want to show your 'bicycle pump gun' to the Admiralty. It's a handy little device, and there must be a boffin somewhere here who'll want to see it."

"Boffin?" she asked, "You say much strange things I do not understand."

"Sorry, that means 'scientist'," he explained. Suddenly, he smacked a palm against his forehead. "I just remembered, I need to report in at the Ellerman Shipping Line offices. They're probably wondering why they've not heard from me since January. I'll do that in London on Monday." He sent a telegram to alert them of his arrival.

The trip south was uneventful. They boarded at Clydebank Station, changing trains at Glasgow Central Station, and when they reached Edinburgh took a hotel room for the night. Early on Friday morning they boarded the L&NER *Flying Scotsman* steam train. It appeared grimy, and there was no restaurant car but, no matter, as he reminded himself the country had been at war since 1939; some things just had to be endured. He enjoyed pointing out for her the sights in the countryside they raced through, as Pavlina had never before been outside London. At times they napped. Seven hours and twenty minutes later they disembarked at Euston station in the heart of London.

Because of the bomb damage causing so many traffic difficulties they elected to walk to Claridge's Hotel, only one-and-a-half miles. Pavlina presented her papers at the front desk shortly after 2:00pm and was welcomed. The concierge locked her bicycle in the baggage room, and didn't bat an eye when she insisted on retaining possession of its pump – the man had seen many strange behaviours by the residents since the start of the war, and nothing fazed him any more. She was assigned a room on the same floor as the other Yugoslav delegation members. The luggage was deposited in the room and they went out for a late lunch. They boarded the Piccadilly line at Green Park tube station and rode it to Russell Square, then walked to an authentic old place Reggie knew, the Queens Larder Pub on Cosmo Place, but facing Queen's Square. Real English bangers and mash tasted glorious, after all the rabbit they'd had to endure on Malta.

After their lunch, Reggie left Pavlina on her own, and made his way over to the Ellerman Lines Shipping Company offices at 106 Leadenhall Street near Saint Mary Axe, and close to a number of other shipping concerns. The Port Captain, someone Reggie had never seen before, ordered tea be brought. Reggie entertained the man with details of his adventures since the sinking of the *Dominion Empress*. He told of occupied Yugoslavia, the bombing of Malta, the torpedo near-miss, and the fire extinguisher incident off Spain, ending with the capture of fifteen Nazis in Portugal. He didn't mention the Special Operations Executive, nor the planned 'Operation Torch', thinking it wise to hold that information on a 'need to know' basis. A half hour later, the tales exhausted, Reggie stood to depart but the Port Captain had an objection.

"A moment, if you please, Captain Wallace. Have a seat."

"Oh, is there something else?"

"Aye, and I think you may be pleased with it." Reggie sat once again, but nevertheless his radar began to tingle in silent alarm. The man continued, "We've been tasked by the Ministry of Transport to be the managing directors for a new ship, and find a crew for it. We've a qualified captain but as for the rest of the roster, it's wide open. Since you already hold an Extra Master's certificate with qualifications in navigation duties, we thought you'd be an ideal fit to accept the position of First Officer. What do you say?"

"I don't know ... first mate will be a step down for me in my career and —"

"I'm sorry, you must have misheard me. The position is first *officer*, not first *mate*."

"I'm not sure I grasp the difference. Are they not the same?"

"Well, the captain is Royal Navy you see, and so the crew will be Royal Navy as well."

"Sorry, this is a merchant navy ship you're speaking of?"

"Technically, aye – a cargo and supply ship."

"I don't know how long you've held the position of Port Captain, but if you've seen my files I'm sure you will have noted I was rejected by the Royal Navy for medical reasons back in July of nineteen-thirty-one."

"Oh, ... I ... wasn't aware," he said, blushing at this cadet's mistake. Reggie felt uncomfortable for having pointed out the man's error.

"What's the name of this ship, again?" he asked, as a distraction.

"It follows the Ellerman Lines convention of naming our ships after cities. We've decided to name it the *City of Featherstone*." Reggie sat up so abruptly his chair very nearly toppled over backwards. "Ah! I see I've piqued your interest."

"It's just I was startled. – You see, I knew a woman once by the name of Featherstone."

"So, I take it you'll accept the position?"

"I didn't say that. Hmm, ... " He paused to think. "Is this a steamship?"

"I'm afraid not, it's a motor ship"

"Well, that's disappointing. Built in Norway, then?"

"No, built here in Newcastle-on-Tyne by Armstrong & Whitworth. I'm sorry, it's possible I should have clarified some details for you: it's new to us, but it's an older ship. It used to be named the *Belfair*."

"The HLV *Belfair*." Reggie sighed and shook his head, a hand across his eyes.

"Oh, you know it?" the port captain said, astonished.

"It's the ship I've been banging on about for the past half hour. Three shell holes through the forepeak, right? I'm going to have to decline your offer, because I am done with that ship!" he announced definitively. "There is no way in hell I can be convinced to conn that ship into a major invasion of North Africa."

"How is it you know ab—?"

"I've known about Operation Torch far longer than anybody in this company. I'm sorry, but my answer must be no," he said, and went ahead to inform the man of his future plans. "I haven't seen my folks for close on three years. I'll be getting married, very soon I hope, and after that we will be going on our honeymoon, so you see, all my time is already spoken for."

"Well, many people marry and then are parted. It's the nature of war."

"I can always resign."

"Yes, that is an option available to you," the man agreed, pleasantly, "however, you will instantly be called up to the infantry. I can't imagine you accepting that option with good graces. As port captain for the Ellerman Lines, it is in my purview to compel you to take the position."

"How do you reckon that?" Reggie replied, beginning to quietly seethe inside.

"Well, parliament passed the 'Emergency Work (Merchant Navy) Order, Notice No. M198' – you must have heard of it?"

"Yes, certainly, every seaman is aware of its provisions. So?"

"So, I can assign you to a ship," the man replied, airily, "Let us say, for argument's sake, it's a filthy coast-wise collier. If you refuse, I will assign you to a second ship. Again, for the sake of argument, this may be a North Sea search-and-rescue tug which, I'm sure you are aware, are subject to near-constant bombing by the Luftwaffe. If you refuse *that*, then the *third* ship I assign you to, you *must by law* accept the position. Do we understand one another?"

"I see. Unless —" Reggie began.

"There is no 'unless' – this is enshrined in law," the port captain informed him, "also, I understand your rank is 'brevet' captain. I can, depending on how this interview is concluded, recommend to my superiors that that 'brevet' rank be rescinded." Reggie was beginning to hate this truly irritating martinet of a captain.

"Tell me, do you have my dossier available to you now?"

"Yes, it's right here," he said, tapping a folder on his desk.

"When, *exactly*, did I join the merchant navy?" The man opened the folder and leafed through its pages.

"You joined us as a third mate on ... the fifth of August, nineteen-thirty-one."

"How many months is that, since August of nineteen-thirty-one?"

"Erm ... it's, ah ... " The martinet glanced over the dossier.

"I'll tell you: in four days it will be one-hundred-twenty-nine months."

"I'll take your word for that. So?"

"Since then, I've been working my way up the ladder, advancing my career through third mate, then second mate, then first mate, and since Perth, Australia I've been a brevet captain. In all that time it's just been 'shoulder to the wheel' for me, not a single day off for me, correct?" The martinet glanced over the dossier again.

"Ah, ... no. You had three days off in December 1933."

"Huh. Three days in ten years. How much time do you take off?"

"That's no concern of yours!" the man said, heatedly. Reggie stood up and took his jacket from the chair back, folding it over his arm.

"That 'Emergency Work Order' you're quoting to me, it provides for two days paid leave earned per each month served, not counting time off after a sinking. By my reckoning, the Ellerman Lines Shipping Company owes me almost nine months of paid leave. Counting weekends that adds up to just short of eleven months. I'll submit the required paperwork tomorrow."

"But, ... but, ..." the martinet spluttered. There was a knock on the door. "Come!" he barked. The door opened and it was Reggie's old friend Jock standing there.

"Jock!" Reggie said, pleased at seeing his former engineer of many voyages ago, "wait outside, I'll be there in a bit."

"What do *you* want," the martinet bawled in irritation.

"Nowt fer ye, ye pewling maggot," Jock said. "I've a packet here fer me mate." He handed over to Reggie a large and thick envelope. The door shut. He picked up a letter opener and slit the envelope. It was a large amount of pound notes and a telegram. He read it once, silently, then again, aloud. "Welcome home STOP Rank now full captain STOP Enclosed back pay with our thanks for job well done STOP Sir John Ellerman." He tucked the envelope under his arm.

"Thanks for the tea. I'll see you sometime in the last week of March, 1943—that is, if you're still here. Good-bye!" He didn't shake the man's hand. On the way out he asked the clerk for the proper form, and took it with him, then he and Jock went for a pint to catch up on old times.

The next day was a Saturday, so after breakfast Reggie and Pavlina walked to the famous Portobello Road Market. He remarked it was not as large, nor as busy as it had been pre-war. She bought an old Mezzo violin case, cheaply priced for it had no instrument, to carry her Russian machine gun.

"Is getting oil on my clothes, carrying my gun in suitcase," she said, to explain her reasoning for Reggie.

"You'll look like a gangster's moll!" he laughed.

"Moll?" she asked, "You say strange things."

While at supper in Claridge's that evening, the concierge alerted them Mr Ivar Bryce had arrived, and brought the man to their table.

John Felix Charles "Ivar" Bryce was ridiculously handsome with "film-star" good looks, but ineligible for the services because one leg was shorter than the other. He told her she could meet the Yugoslav king's ministers on Monday, but not with the king.

"He's travelling in America on a 'whistle-stop tour' making speeches, drumming up support for their war bond drives. It seems the Americans, not having any royalty of their own, are all at sixes and sevens when they meet an actual king. He's so handsome all the ladies swoon over him," he remarked.

On the Monday, Ivar Bryce introduced Pavlina to the Yugoslavian cabinet ministers. She was not impressed, to say the least. When she returned, Reggie had to listen to her complaints: the Serbian ministers didn't believe Draža was collaborating with the Germans (despite her first-hand knowledge). The Croatian ministers preferred to meet with the king only one-on-one without the Serbs present. The Serbs were convinced by this some trickery was going on behind their backs. Neither side could stand being in the same room as the prime minister Dušan Simović, a Serb army general, considering him to be an inept politician and a coward who had fled Yugoslavia with his family the very day the Italians invaded. Everyone much preferred dealing with the Deputy Prime Minister, Slobodan Jovanović, a university professor and an intellectual, but she had not met with him yet. She had then gone to 10 Downing Street to introduce herself to Prime Minister Winston Churchill, and sat waiting on a hard bench for two hours for nothing, not seeing him, only getting to speak with Foreign Secretary Anthony Eden for a few too-brief minutes. Reggie listened to all this with a sympathetic ear, but there was little he could say, so he waited until she had exhausted her complaints. He then surprised her with the announcement he had submitted the form for his paid time off, so they now had eleven months all to themselves. They had a wedding to plan now, but first he had to introduce her to his family, and to do that they needed to go to Goudhurst, in Kent.

The very next day in the late morning the train deposited them on the Goudhurst station platform, with their luggage and bicycle. It was one mile to the house, walking up Smiths Lane, turning right at the Hammonds Farm Wye, right on Lidwells Lane, and right again on Blind Lane. The house was a two-storey affair, brown weatherboard cladding above and cream-coloured brick below, beneath a steeply-pitched hip roof, and had large many-paned windows. There was a hedge across the front of the property, and another at the back. He pointed out his old bedroom window above, describing for her its excellent views over the High Weald. Pavlina thought the views lovely from where they stood. No one answered to his knock, and he didn't have the key. They left her bicycle with its luggage hidden in the hedge at the rear of the property, and they tramped the public footpath, so familiar to him, across the fields to Goudhurst. When they emerged next to the Great War memorial cross in the centre of the village, she spied the park with its pond across the way and pulled him over to it by the hand. They were quite content to sit for a time, his arm about her, as they watched the ducks dabbling among the reeds. The village hall overlooked this pond from its far side.

"Fancy a spot of lunch?" he asked. She did. "Let's walk up the high street. There's an excellent pub in the Olde Starre and Crowne hotel near Saint Mary's church. We'll eat there." As they walked up the high street towards the church, he waved to Mr Richer across the street sweeping the pavement in front of the Globe and Rainbow, and the man waved in return. Reggie began to be dismayed. Many of the store fronts were different than what he remembered. The Eight Bells was gone, or rather, it had been absorbed into the hotel to lengthen the building. The original half-timbered and brick front of the Olde Starre and Crowne hotel was now a black and white Tudor façade, and it was named the Star and Eagle now.

When they entered the restaurant, a publican he didn't know greeted them, introducing himself as Arthur Holt. At least the interior remained familiar to him, with its horse brasses covering the heavy wood beams and pillars, and the ancient signboard over the fireplace mantelpiece. Mr Holt advised them the new rationing law limited them to three courses, and the cost would be the maximum five shillings if they ordered the beef, or any other meat. They sat and ordered lunch, with a pint of scrumpy each. As they each ate a delicious, though small, Beef Wellington with a dish of the local asparagus, he looked out the window in time to see his mother exit the newsagent's door across the street carrying a grocer's sack and a newspaper, to bustle towards North Road on her way home. *How odd, since when does mum read the newspaper*, he thought. He pointed her out for Pavlina, but didn't want to interrupt the meal to chase after her. The wholemeal bread "national loaf" was not rationed but he found it to be mushy, grey and unappetising. At least there was a good local apple cobbler for pudding. After the meal Reggie walked her up Back Lane to enter the graveyard surrounding the 12th century Saint Mary the Virgin church, and pointed out the headstones there of his grandparents and great-grandparents. They had a peek inside the church, which was empty on a Tuesday afternoon, then retraced their route on the public footpath to his parent's home. Reggie sent Pavlina to retrieve her bicycle from the hedge while he knocked. When the door opened, it was his dad standing there, grey-haired, imperious, and even taller than usual as he was two steps up. After a moment's hesitation, the old man shook his hand, then turned his head over a shoulder.

"The boy's home," he said, laconically. Facing around again he looked over the top of Reggie's head as Pavlina arrived from the drive pushing her bicycle. "Good afternoon. May I help you?"

"Dad, this is Buga, ... Buga Pavlina." Reggie answered for her. The old man looked her up and down, and a slow smile spread upon his face.

"Come in, come in, and welcome," he said, while backing into the interior, "Don't just stand there boy, help her with her things!" He turned and shouted, "Marge!"

"Buga, this is my dad. He's known in the village as 'The Brigadier', but he's long since retired now."

"But, you can call me Percy," the older man corrected. As Reggie leaned her bicycle against the wall, his mother came from the kitchen drying her hands on a tea towel and rushed into his arms, and they hugged.

"Buga, this is my mum, Margaret."

"Pleased to meet you, dear. Any friend of —" Her eyes grew wide as Buga held up her left hand with its diamond ring. She grabbed for dad's hand as her knees went weak. "Oh! Oh, my! Dearie me, ... I'll put the kettle on!" She turned and dashed into the kitchen. Reggie carried her suitcase and violin case up to his old bedroom, and returned to find them just sitting in the lounge.

"Come sit and tell us all about what you've been up to, my boy." They sat, and in a few minutes his mum appeared with a Brown Betty teapot, along with a tray of scones, jams and clotted cream. She served them out as Reggie continued with the tale of his voyages.

" ... and then I was promoted to the rank of captain and took command of the SS *Dominion Empress* at Perth, Australia, after Captain Mallinson retired there. Unfortunately, that command didn't last long because we took a couple of 'Eye-tie' torpedoes as we approached Malta, just after New Year's Day, and had to row for it."

"You were on Malta, dear?"

"Yes, mum. None of my crew were killed, fortunately."

"Well, that *is* fortunate," Percy said. "Captain, eh? Then they must've given you another ship straight away?"

"No. You see, in Egypt I was made a temporary 'secret agent' and sent by submarine to Yugoslavia."

"You were in Yugoslavia, dear?" his mum interrupted.

"Yes, and from there we went back to Malta, and were there during the heaviest bombing, and then we went on to Lisbon, in Portugal."

"You were in Lisbon, dear?" his mum interrupted again. At this, Pavlina had to interrupt.

"Lisbon is where Reggie, he save me from the Nazi men who kidnap me!"

"Kidnapped by Nazis? Goodness me, such adventures!" his mother said. "Well, dear, what sort of a name is 'Boo-gah'?" she asked.

"Is Yugoslav name."

"So, when did you marry – in Yugoslavia?" she asked.

"We meet in Yugoslavia in February, but have the ceremony in Lisbon, but is only the false ceremony we do, to capture the fifteen Nazi men," Buga explained.

"Ah, trickery!" Percy clapped his hands together and rubbed them in glee. "I've always said those Jerries are none too clever – but I think what your mother is trying to pin down is: *where* did you marry; was it in Yugoslavia, or Malta, or Lisbon?"

"Oh, we do not marry," Pavlina replied, blandly, and before Reggie could stop her, added, "We only sleep together since we meet." Reggie took her hand in his and held it up to display the ring.

"This is an *engagement* ring, mum, she's my fiancée. We need to get married, but haven't had the opportunity yet, until now. I was thinking perhaps Saint Mary's church would be —" Margaret stood suddenly, and exploded.

"I should say so! Sleeping together unmarried! Land sakes, what will the neighbours think?" She ran to the kitchen. Reggie rolled his eyes at her outburst. His dad covered his mouth to suppress a laugh, and waved a hand.

"It's all right, never you mind, son. Why, during the Great War there were times we —"

"You'll not be 'sleeping' in this house until after you're wed!" his mother shouted from the kitchen, "and that's final!"

"Well, dad, I guess we can get rooms at the hotel for a few days. Oh, that reminds me, we were eating lunch in the Star and Eagle and saw mum leaving the newsagent. Since when does mum read the newspaper?"

"Oh, she can't get enough of it these days. Every week she buys a copy of *The Daily Telegraph*, but only if they print another episode of that serialized story she's so dotty over. I read it too, and a cracking yarn it is! She's saved every copy, and they're in the library. I'll go have a word with her, son, and get this sorted." He stood and strode to the kitchen. Reggie and Pavlina stepped to the library in the next room, and found the newspapers neatly stacked on the floor next to a wing chair near the inglenook. The issue on top of the stack had a column headlined: "Act Of Piracy" Claims Goebbels (story cont. pg. 5). He turned to page five and found a photo of Captain McPeavey with some crewmen taken aboard the *Belfair*. He took a paper from the bottom of the stack. A grainy photograph credited to some Swedish newspaper showed the *Belfair* in Šibenik, an armed and stern-faced German soldier standing at attention in front of his sentry box, a Swedish Red Cross lorry to one side. He plucked another paper from the centre of the stack and leafed through it, while she looked over his shoulder. There on page five was another story, accompanied by a photograph of Frederik pointing up at three shell holes through the bow of the ship. The shattered buildings in the background had Maltese style balconies. The next issue's story featured an aerial photo of the *Belfair*, snapped over the wing of a Heinkel bomber, its Spanish roundel visible. The issue after this one had a photo of the *Belfair* at anchor off Lisbon, the Swedish flags visible on its side. Pavlina pointed out an apparently unconnected story having a Reuters byline, featuring mugshots of seven recently arrested Germans, along with a Portuguese woman and her chauffeur, all charged with kidnapping and weapons violations. With glee she pointed to one German who had a black eye and sticking plaster across his nose. They'd carefully arranged the stack in order, just as they'd found it, when Percy stepped up behind them.

"She won't budge. I guess it's the hotel for you both," he said, apologetically, "Don't you worry any, son, I'll cover the cost—Ah! I see you've found that story. Your mother was a teacher for many years, and it irks her no end they're always spelling Frederick without the 'C'."

"But Frederik always spell his name without the 'C'," Pavlina replied. The Brigadier's mouth fell open. Margaret stepped into the room.

"Buga," he nearly shouted, "would you like to go out to the garage? See his motorcycle? It's a Triumph, one of the great British marques! Surely he must've mentioned it to you sometime? We'll be right back, Marge." He took Buga's arm and steered her through the kitchen, out the back door and into the garden, Reggie chasing after them. Percy chivvied them past the victory garden of vegetables, and their Anderson shelter covered in flowers. He ushered them inside the garage and snapped on the lights, but had a look outside to make certain his wife wasn't following, before latching the door shut behind them. They were manoeuvred to the far wall around a Jaguar 3½ Litre 4-door Saloon, silver with black wings and sills. It sported large round headlamps.

"Wow, dad! When did you get this?"

"Nineteen-forty. Bought it new. — Here's your motorcycle." The Triumph sat forlornly under a bare bulb, untouched, just as he had left it so many years ago, but now covered in dust and cobwebs and the tyres were flat. The Brigadier lowered his voice. "I didn't bring you out here for this. You saw the story then? It's you, isn't it? You're Leif

Magnuson, right?"

"Yes sir, that's the name I used as an agent to go get that ship. They pronounce it 'Lafe'."

"And this ship of yours, it's to be used in some sort of military operation?"

"Yes sir. The invasion of North Africa later this year. You understand what I'm telling you is on a strictly 'Hush-Hush' basis sir?"

"Understood. I'll be interested in hearing the details later, in private. Don't tell your mother, or it'll be all over Sussex and Kent by morning."

"Yes sir, mum's the word. Buga was my in-country contact. She's a lieutenant in the Yugoslavian partisan army."

"Well, that's ... erm, ... quite unusual, I must say!"

"Dad, I very nearly died on the mission, freezing to death. Buga saved my life."

"Thank you, my dear, we are forever indebted to you." Percy cradled her in his arms, and she laid her cheek against his chest, hugging him back.

"My '*Tatu*' is executed by the Nazi soldiers. He is no more. May I call you '*Tatu*'?" she asked, searching his face for reassurance.

"No, but you may call me 'dad'," he replied, warmly.

The very next day Margaret shooed Reggie and Pavlina off to the village church to speak with the vicar about getting married. The man greeted them pleasantly, but first he had a question for them: had they been resident in the district for longer than seven days? No, only since yesterday. Such a pity – it was a requirement to be here more than a week before even being *allowed* to apply for a licence.

"Seven days? That's not so bad," Reggie responded, "Could you schedule the wedding for 11:00am on the Saturday following? I'll bring the completed paperwork with me, and see you next week, sir." They stood to go.

Hearing this, the vicar had more to tell them: the "banns" must be read out in church once per week for the next three weeks. They sat again. "The 'banns'? What are those?" Only an announcement of intent to marry, and a call for any objection to the union. But, because Pavlina was not a British subject, the vicar let them know there was an alternative to the reading of the banns: for this they would need a "Superintendent Registrar's Marriage Schedule", and to get *that* they'd both need to apply *in person* at the Register Office in Cranbrook. He explained the procedure for them: the Registrar then enters their details in a book open to public inspection, and also displays a notice for 28 days at the Register Office. If no legal reasons to delay or prevent the marriage going ahead are shown within that time, the "SRMS" can be issued, and the marriage may proceed, anytime within a year.

"Unlike in Scotland or Wales," the vicar continued, "the application process in England requires you to swear an oath in person before a legal official, meaning you need to find a judge or sheriff or some such."

Oh dear. Today was the sixth of May. This meant the very soonest they might marry was the middle of June! *Except*, Pavlina's previous husband was dead, so they would also need to produce the death certificate. But they had to inform the vicar *that* document was in Nazi occupied Yugoslavia, and therefore unobtainable. The vicar expressed sympathy about their plight, and stroked his chin, but could come up with no other solution. The vicar went to his office to get the blank SRMS application form for them to take away. While he was out of the room, Reggie muttered aloud to Pavlina they might as well just elope, and "live together in sin." Pavlina responded she didn't want to be held responsible for giving his mother a stroke. They took the document, thanked the vicar, and then walked Back Lane to the Star and Eagle hotel to lunch again.

They strolled back to his parent's home along North Road, the longer scenic route. When they arrived, it was discovered his mother had been very busy herself: she'd spoken to Arthur Holt to ask him to supply a wedding cake – a small one, needs be – and also the victuals and ales for the reception, and the man had agreed. Then she'd gone to the village hall to reserve it for the reception. After doing this she had telephoned the *Kentish Gazette* and placed a wedding announcement in the newspaper, and then sat at the telephone to start a "call cascade" to everybody they knew, to attend if possible on Saturday the sixteenth of May. Reggie was livid at her interference! His mother hadn't known about all these "requirements" but, "What's done is done!" she said, blithely. He left the house, angrily slamming the door. Pavlina caught up with him on the public footpath.

"Just how many weddings does a man have to go through in one lifetime?" Reggie exploded, "On the 16th we're going to have *yet another* fake wedding that will be *illegal*, and when the licence arrives we'll have the *legal* real wedding. Think of the expense!" he groused.

"You are forgetting one more wedding! When this war is over, we will go to Yugoslavia to have the wedding all over again, for my mother," she said.

"Now, that is one thing I'll happily do for you," he said. She hugged him there on the footpath through the fields. Over the next week, Pavlina travelled by train every day to London, meeting in Claridge's hotel with Serbian or Croatian cabinet ministers, always separately, in fruitless discussions and frustrating arguments. She made efforts to meet with prime minister Churchill at number 10 Downing, her documents ready to hand, but again and again she failed, only speaking with various members of his staff.

The only bright spot, she found, was the day mid-week when she was walking past Albany Court Yard just off Piccadilly and, purely by accident, discovered at its entrance the Yugoslav Relief Society. On a whim she stepped inside and volunteered herself for a half day. It made her feel much better having accomplished something.

On the Wednesday prior to the wedding, a bright sunny day, and cloudless, Reggie was seated at the kitchen table after lunch preparing to fill in the application for the Superintendent Registrar's Marriage Schedule. Pavlina's documents and passport were spread out within easy reach. They had now met the requirement of a week's residency in Goudhurst, and he was eager to see it filed at the soonest possible moment. Who knew what other problems mightn't crop up at the last second? Pavlina worked with needle and thread at modifying one of her dresses to use for a wedding dress. His mum was standing at the kitchen sink doing the washing-up, and leaned forwards to look out the window.

"My goodness me, that's a longish car, isn't it?" she said. He went to her side and looked out. It was indeed a long car. An Austin Chalfont limousine, black as jet, now turned up the drive and approached the house. The driver, wearing a military uniform, emerged and strode to their front door. Reggie arrived behind his dad as the knock was answered.

"Yes, may I help you?" the older man asked. The driver consulted a paper in his hand.

"Is this the Pavlina residence?" he asked.

"It's the Wallace residence, but there is a Pavlina here. Please come in. If you'll wait a moment I'll fetch her out. Reggie, will you get her, please?"

"Yes sir." he dashed up the stair and found her in the bedchamber, sewing. "Buga, there's a man here to see you, and he has a rather posh car." She proceeded him down the stairs, where the man stood waiting in the hall. His mum had arrived. It was crowded with all of them here together.

"Miss Pavlina?" the driver asked.

"Yes?"

"You'll pardon me if I get this wrong: Miss Zdravka Pavlina?" Buga flushed scarlet, and seemed flustered.

"Yes."

"I've been sent to get you. Please gather your documents, we must leave directly."

"Just a moment," the Brigadier insisted, "What do you mean, 'get her'? Get her by whom? His Majesty's Immigration Branch of the Home Office?" he said, his chin thrust out disputatiously. His mum gasped, a hand to her chest, and stepped back. The man made no apologies.

"Not at all. Her presence has been requested by the Prime Minister. He's been made aware you've been attempting to see him, and is currently at his home, Chartwell, only twenty-five miles from here. He's an extremely busy man, but he can spare you an hour. Please hurry."

Reggie gathered up all her diplomatic papers and stuffed them into their khaki envelope, while Pavlina raced upstairs. She changed her blouse to the best she had, brushed her hair, and snapped open her violin case just as Reggie arrived.

"What on earth are you doing?" he asked, in irritation.

"I must get my bicycle-pump secret gun. You want him to see this, yes?"

"Yes, of course, but we haven't time for that. Just take the whole case! Wear your Order of the White Eagle award."

"Good idea!" She snapped the case shut and they rushed downstairs and out the front door. The chauffeur stopped Reggie at the car door with a hand on his chest.

"Just a moment! Who are you?"

"Captain Reginald P. Wallace, Merchant Navy; I'm her husband," he lied. The chauffeur referred to the paper in his hand.

"I'm to fetch a *Miss* Pavlina. There's no mention here she's married."

At this, Pavlina put her head out the door, and affecting a most musical lilt to her voice, made a demand.

"Darling, do not make your bride wait on you!" she snapped. Then to the driver said, "Your information is wrong. There has been not any time to change my passport!"

"Very well then, get in." He shut the door after them and climbed behind the wheel. Percy and Margaret Wallace stood on the porch and watched them motor away. She opened the case and put on her medal. They hadn't gone very far before Reggie slid the perspex privacy screen shut, and turned to ask her a one-word question.

"Zdravka?"

"My official name. Is given by my mother." She blushed all over again. "Zdravka is woman form of Zdravko for the man, is comes from South Slavic word 'Zdrav' and is means 'healthy' – is name I not like."

"Zdravka," he repeated, "Zdravka. Zuh-drav-kah.—you're right, Buga fits you better."

Soon the chauffeur was holding the door open for them. Chartwell proved to be a massive pile of a red brick manor house, and they were escorted across the gravel drive and inside. Clementine Churchill met them in the entrance hall.

"Welcome to Chartwell. Would you care for some tea and biscuits?" She nodded to a man standing nearby and he left. "Winnie is out in the garden, painting I believe. I'll show you there." They were ushered through the entrance hall, down a staircase, and out into the garden, where she left them. They crossed the lawn to him, followed by a train of men carrying chairs and a table, and these were positioned at the edge of the terrace for their use. The final man deposited a folded map at the table's edge. Miss Layton, personal secretary to the prime minister, arrived and sat quietly to one side, her stenographer's pad held at the ready. Winston Churchill sat with his back to them, at an easel near the stair to the lower gardens. He wore a straw hat and blue painter's smock, the long sleeves unbuttoned and turned back. His painting was of a pastoral lake scene with cattle. The Prime Minister laid aside his maulstické and brush, then rose to greet them.

"Hullo, you must be Miss Pavlina, the young lady Eden's been rattling on about." He extended his hand and took hers.

"Mr Churchill, I am age of thirty-four, and not a young lady, any more."

"My dear," he responded warmly, looking over his round spectacles at her, with a twinkle in his eye, "when one has reached an age as advanced as I have, every lady younger than myself is a young lady, young lady.

"Mr Churchill, Ambassador Ronald Campbell send to you his greetings from Lisbon."

"Good of him to do so. Ronnie's posted in Lisbon, eh? I hear it's beautiful there." Reggie also shook his hand, and introduced himself. He produced her khaki envelope from an inside pocket and handed it over.

"Here are my documents of the introducing, Mr Churchill," Pavlina said.

"Please, be seated, and call me Winston." They sat. He spread the documents on the table and perused them briefly, while loosely buttoning the cuffs of his sleeves. He began by holding her letter of introduction up to her view, with a question: "I do not recognize the signature. Who is this Tito fellow? I have never heard of him."

"Then I will have the most important news for you," Pavlina replied. "He is only the man who saves my country. My mission is to tell you of his struggles to defeat the Nazis, with successes better than Draža Mihailović!"

"That is a topic I am most eager to hear about, most eager indeed," Winston said, and picked up the next document, but then held it up, in puzzlement. "What's this?" he asked. Reggie leaned over and glanced at it.

"Oh, I'm so sorry, that must've gotten mixed in with those. It's only our marriage licence application. I'll take that," he said, taking it from him. Clementine arrived with a manservant in tow, who set down the tray he carried. She served out the tea for them.

"You're getting married?" she observed, having overheard.

"Yes, this coming Saturday," Reggie replied, "and I was wondering: would it be possible to have your chauffeur stop briefly in Cranbrook on the way back to Goudhurst?"

"I don't see any problem with that." Winston looked up to the manservant. "Mr Sawyers, would you advise the pool driver he's to stop in Cranbrook along the way?"

" – you see," Reggie continued, "the application requires us to swear an oath in person before a legal official, so we need to locate one today, and preferably near the Registrar's Office."

"Winnie!" Clementine interrupted.

"Yes, dear?"

"*You* are a 'legal official', or have you forgotten?"

"Oh, yes, of course I am. I can do that for you." He looked over his round glasses at his wife. "Clemmie, would you excuse us please, there's the little matter of that vile war in Yugoslavia we need to discuss."

"Don't worry," she said to Reggie, sardonically, an eyebrow raised, "I won't let him forget." She returned to the house.

"Now, young lady, I wish to hear all you can tell me about the war in Yugoslavia, and don't leave anything out, however minor you deem it to be. Important matters may turn on the smallest detail." The map was unfolded and Pavlina began her description. Miss Layton began to write. Reggie excused himself, and left them to it. He wandered the perimeter of the upper garden, walking under the trellis to what he was later told they called the Marlborough Pavilion in its corner.

Descending a stair to the lower gardens he peered through the window of a brick cottage there. This revealed itself to be an artist's studio, but he found the door locked. He encountered a new but unfinished brick wall, then strolled the edge of a small lake while he admired the shaggy and red-haired Scottish Highland cattle grazing on the far bank. Mr Sawyers now approached and beckoned him return.

Reggie sat at the table, and the valet refilled his teacup, then stood by attentively. Miss Layton had departed for the house to type up her notes.

"How goes the war?" Reggie asked Churchill, as a conversational gambit.

"You really want to know?" Winston asked, rhetorically, and then continued in that way he had, sometimes muttering but often putting on quick bursts of louder speech. "Well, in the week just past, we were able to land sixty-one Spitfires on Malta, with the aid of the USS *Wasp*. That's the *good* news." Reggie and Pavlina beamed at each other, pleased. The prime minister then continued: "The *bad* news is that the Luftwaffe bombed and sunk three of our destroyers in the Mediterranean, along with a hospital ship. Four more of our merchantmen were torpedoed off the tip of Greenland. Our American friends lost their carrier *Lexington* to the Japanese. The vile Huns have attacked our Russian ally in Kharkov yesterday, and it is suspected that poison gas was employed—it's always something, and usually quite depressing," he mumbled, sounding rather depressed indeed. He was silent for a moment as he examined his cigar, which had gone out, but then his mood seemed to rally. "But, Miss Pavlina, I see you've brought a violin. Will you favour us with a spot of music?"

"Is not a violin." She stood and lifted the case lid to remove her canvas bag of ammunition and bicycle-pump gun. "I make this! Look!" She displayed it to Winston, then aimed it at a nearby large tree trunk and snapped the thumb-slide. *Phut!* A hole was left in its bark. She reloaded it from the canvas bag, then gave the weapon to Winston.

"Is 7.65 millimetre calibre. Careful! Is not any safety. Please, you shoot some things now." The Prime Minister was intrigued at once. He stood and aimed the device at the small lake 180 yards off, and snapped the thumb-slide, just as he had observed her to do. *Phut!* A small geyser erupted in the water.

"My word, this is silent. You invented this?" he asked Pavlina, in astonishment.

"Yes. My Reggie, he say he want you to show to your boffins." He inserted the device down his sleeve, and when he lowered his arm to his side, the gun dropped naturally into his hand.

"I most certainly will! Tell me, may I take this, ... this, ... this 'sleeve gun'?" he asked, inventing a name for it on the fly. "I'd rather like to send it to the boffins over at Welwyn Garden City."

"Yes, this I will allow." He laid it on the table, together with its canvas bag. She gathered up her documents and khaki envelope, fully opening the violin case on the table to deposit them inside. Winston started at the sight of her machine gun.

"What is *that*?" he implored her. She lifted it out and handed it to him.

"Is Russian PPSh-41. In Yugoslavia is used everywhere." She continued explaining the calibre, its drum magazine capacity, and rate of fire while he examined it closely, putting the weapon to his shoulder and gazing down the sights. He lowered it, and turned to address her.

"Miss Pavlina, you may possibly be aware I am something of a gun collector. Might you allow me to *purchase* this fine weapon from you?" he asked, hopefully, "Rest assured I shan't be ungenerous." Her eyes and nostrils flared in alarm. How could she say "no" to the Prime Minister of Great Britain? She touched the Order of the White Eagle hanging by its blue silk ribbon around her neck, and made up her mind.

"I, ... I am thinking *no*. My gun is the gift to me from Josip Broz Tito when he award me this medal. I must say no!" Disappointed, Winston put the weapon to his shoulder, looking down its sights once again at the lake. Knowing this to be quite possibly his only opportunity to handle such a formidable firearm, he squeezed the trigger a three times, and observed each splash in the lake. He flicked it to fully-automatic mode and squeezed the trigger, holding it down. Three dozen geysers stitched a path across the lake until the magazine drum was empty, the sound echoing from the surrounding hills. A Scottish Highland steer on the lake's far slope bolted, ambled a few yards, then went back to his grazing. A tall man burst from the house at a gallop, followed shortly by Clementine and a handful of staff. The man arrived first and snatched the gun from Winston's hands.

"Detective Inspector Walter Thompson," Churchill identified him for those present. "Nothing to worry about Henry, *ahem*, just making a test-firing of this unusual piece. You may return it to Miss Pavlina here." The bodyguard detached the drum magazine, checked to see it was indeed empty, and handed both parts to Pavlina. Winston shed his hat and smock. Clementine bade them all come inside, while the staff remained to clear away everything else. D. I. Thompson disappeared. They gathered in the library, where an oil painting sat displayed on an easel in the corner. A library table dominated the centre of this room. A manservant stepped into the room and made an announcement.

"Lord Beaverbrook has arrived as requested."

"Lord Beaverbrook, Lord Beaverbrook," Churchill muttered, and then shouted, "tell Beaverbrook he will have to wait! Can he not see for himself I am busy!"

"Winnie! Temper!" Clementine remonstrated. She then picked up and held the Churchill family bible for them. The prime minister read out the oath as printed, and with hands raised Pavlina and Reggie swore to it, and then the four of them signed in the provided spaces, as applicants and witnesses.

"Well, that's one more thing finished," Reggie said, with a sigh, "Now all we need do is endure the mandatory twenty-eight day waiting period, and I've still no idea how we're going to obtain that Yugoslavian death certificate. Why does our government continually make every procedure more and more stricter?"

"Stricter?" Winston muttered. "Miss Layton!" he bellowed.

"Sir!" His secretary popped through the doorway immediately, pad and pencil held at the ready.

"Take a memorandum – no, wait, where is your typewriter?"

"In your study."

"The application! Let me have that!" he demanded, snatching it up. "Go, go!" he pushed her out the door ahead of him, pausing long enough to tell them all, "Stay here! Don't move!" before bolting from the room.

"Winston!" Clementine shouted after him, fruitlessly. They listened to their retreating footfalls and the muffled pounding of the typewriter as he dictated. While they waited they viewed the painting on the easel, a pastel desert scene with robed figures holding the traces of recumbent camels. Date palms threw their shadows on a harshly sunlit wall, a Moorish-arched passage through it revealing a tented bazaar just beyond.

In a few minutes he returned. He laid the application on the library table and slapped the memorandum down on top of it. It read that for these named individuals on the attached wedding licence application, the mandatory waiting period was to be eliminated and the licence issued forthwith, no death certificate needed. There at the bottom of the memorandum next to the prime minister's signature was his usual sticker, an adhesive label that read "ACTION THIS DAY." It was red in colour. Before they walked out to the waiting car, the prime minister pressed on them his desert painting as a wedding gift, insisting as he did so that he gave away many of his "daubs" as gifts.

Thursday morning, Reggie asked his dad for the loan of the Jaguar, because he had many errands to attend to. The Brigadier was hesitant. Reggie then whispered conspiratorially in his ear as to what his plans were for the day.

"RAF Northolt? Good lord, that's the far side of London. Why, that's over eighty miles from here!" the old man objected, then agreed, but only reluctantly. He was gone for most of the day, only returning exhausted near supper.

The day before the wedding, a Friday, Margaret and Pavlina finished fitting her wedding dress. It had been made floor length and had a train because his mum had prevailed upon the local constable to let her have the parachute of the German in the cells. In the evening Reggie and Percy dressed the Jaguar with ribbons from hood ornament to boot handle.

Saturday dawned with a sky devoid of clouds, for once. After breakfast Reggie dressed in his dad's old post-war jacket, a Henry Poole & Co three-button formal tailcoat with lapel notches quite out of date. The matching waistcoat also had three buttons. The white bow-tie had to be tied by his dad. They pinned the trouser legs up inside, to shorten them. He sauntered over to the church shortly after ten o'clock. The kerbs of the high street were lined with cars parked nose-to-tail, and at the sight of this, only then did he begin to feel nervous. He stood in the narthex of the church and peeked out as people arrived. Dorothea, or "Dot", arrived and hugged him exuberantly. Laura arrived (her father was the vicar) and hugged him modestly. George and Helen arrived, so he asked if George would stand as his best man. He agreed, and Reggie handed him the ring box. He asked Helen to be Pavlina's matron of honour to round out the group, even though they'd never met, and she agreed to this as well. All the other guests were friends of his mum and dad, or Goudhurst villagers, or both. Soon the Jag motored up to stop in front of the church and he watched as a stunningly beautiful Pavlina emerged. He beat a hasty retreat up the nave to stand at the altar. As he stood looking out over the assembly, an incongruous image forced it's way to the forefront of his mind: including Pavlina, he had slept with five of the women present. He suppressed the thought as wholly inappropriate. The organ in the north transept began to play Mendelssohn's Wedding March for the processional. The Brigadier, wearing his old Regimental uniform, escorted Pavlina up the aisle. The ceremony went by surprisingly quickly. It seemed over in seconds. Soon the bride and groom recessed back down the aisle and outside to be showered with birdseed (rice being rationed) and into the Jag, to be driven to the village hall while the guests walked over.

Mr Holt had come through with a wonderful meal for the guests, even given the restrictions of wartime rationing. The "cake" was a cardboard affair with a small drawer in it holding just enough actual cake for the bride and groom. Most of the men gravitated to the bar to collect pints of bitter. There was a table set with pre-filled stems of shandy or sherry for the women. Reggie was relieved to see the accordionist he had engaged was here, a Pilot Officer from RAF Northolt's No. 308 Polish Fighter Squadron, Jerzy Jakubowski. As promised, the man had collected and brought with him a dozen Croatian ex-pats he knew of from a London church. The chairs were cleared off and the floor prepared for dancing. Reggie was passing behind a knot of women when he overheard his name mentioned. It was Dot, Helen, Laura, his mother, and a handful of others, so he paused to listen in. The gossip was they thought "Pavlina is too exotic." Dot defended her by saying, "But that's what he likes!" He laughed and interrupted their banter.

"Well, as the Yanks say: 'you ain't seen nothing yet'!" He gathered the Croatian guests and guided them to the centre of the floor, then signalled Mr Jakubowski to start playing. It was the Croatian "svadbeno kolo" wedding dance. Pavlina was ecstatic! His mum was confused by it, his dad amused, and Dot was thrilled. This dance would be talked about for weeks afterwards. Reggie even attempted to join Pavlina for a few minutes, with some little success. Mr Jakubowski then began playing old standards for the majority of the guests present. George and Helen wanted to know where the honeymoon was to be. "Our first choice was Scotland," Reggie shouted over the music, "but we settled for four weeks in Brighton." It was all over much too soon. His mum and dad took them home in the Jaguar saloon. Somebody had tied old shoes to drag behind the bumper of the boot.

On the Sunday, after a "wedding breakfast", Pavlina and Reggie with bags packed departed on the train for Brighton. They checked into The Grand, a classic old posh hotel on the waterfront, and from here they had a view of both the West Pier and Palace Pier—not that they were looking at the view much. Both were rather eager to start their family.

They arrived back in Goudhurst by train, four weeks to the day, on Sunday, 14th June. His mum and dad were in quite a pother: that limousine had stopped by only hours before, and Pavlina was to ring *this number* post-haste! It was the number to Chartwell. The phone was answered and passed to the Secretary of State for War, Sir James Grigg. She was told the Prime Minister was leaving for America to attend the Second Washington Conference, and extending an invitation to her to accompany his entourage. It was a tacit assumption this invitation was not to be refused. The limousine would pick her up the next morning. As the trip was by flying-boat, the invitation was for her alone; there was no room for her husband.

While she was away, Reggie kept busy by talking to estate agents.

In ten day's time he viewed a dozen properties on offer, including; a nearly new but expensive chalet bungalow, its walls rendered in pebble-dash, in Wotton-under-Edge (in its "Synwell" development, which name struck him as amusing), and then there was an end-of-terrace Victorian in Weston-super-Mare that had a sea view, but this he had to reject for signs of damp. Also a Georgian flat in Bristol within a terraced crescent that (though elegant) was just a tad old, and a late Regency flat in Bath the cost of which was much too dear. None of these met his requirements. And then, on 26th June he was shown an exquisite cottage in the market town of Chipping Campden that was simply cracking! A thatched "chocolate box" of honey-coloured Cotswold stone tucked away in a hidden lane, it had not only an inglenook fireplace, but also a nursery and a study! It was within walking distance of the market hall, and came furnished. The only thing lacking was a garage, and the garden was much too small. The estate agent advised him, "It's not on the market yet, and the executor is willing to entertain offers. Speaking confidentially you understand, he'll let it go for a song—well, what passes for a song in this neck of the woods, anyhow."

He made an offer and it was accepted, then visited a branch of his bank for the mortgage, put down a deposit to hold it, and telephoned his dad asking for help with the stamp duty. His dad replied he would wire him the funds in the morning, and added Buga had arrived unexpectedly that morning, and a week early. She would arrive at Campden Station on tomorrow's afternoon train.

"Be careful what you say to Buga, son – she's been a little tetchy of late," Percy warned.

Reggie busied himself cleaning up the place for her arrival. The first thing to go was the aspidistra from the front window. He took it outside and binned it. Buga loved the house, especially the little Arts & Crafts touches throughout the interior. Once she'd settled in, Reggie got a crackling fire going and they sat in the inglenook while a summer storm spattered the windows. He asked her how the trip had gone.

"In New York, I never in my life see such big buildings!" she said.

"Yes, I've seen those. They call them sky-scrapers."

"And the food! They ration sugar but no other food! I eat with Churchill's people where the plates are full! I eat from a cooked bird this big," – she held her palms a half yard apart – "and this is delicious!"

"I've had that. It's called a turkey, a traditional dish in America. But what I meant was, how was the conference?" She pulled from her new American purse a sheaf of notes to refresh her memory. She had stopped in London, and Ivar Bryce had transmitted some of these notes to Tito in Yugoslavia. She began her tale: the flying boat had left Scotland late on the evening of 17 June and they arrived in Washington in the early evening of the following day. The two delegations were led by Prime Minister Winston Churchill and American President Franklin Roosevelt.

"On the flying boat everyone call him 'Eff deYarr' and this I think must be his *nom de guerre*, but when we arrive, everyone call him only Franklin. Everyone is relaxed, not formal with everyone. Franklin laughs much. Is much drinking and smoking of cigars. Franklin cannot walk! This I not know before! I meet Canadian Prime Minister Mackenzie King. Also, I meet Crown Princess Märtha from Norway and her children. My King Peter is not there yet; he is late.

"Then the official conference starts. Winston talk with Franklin about a 'mulberry harbour' but I not know where is that. Then they talk of how the Western Allies will best help Russians. The American Generals want to open up a second front in France now, but the British Generals do not think that is the good option yet. Then Winston proposes a joint campaign in the Mediterranean to attack the Italians on the 'soft under-belly' of the Axis. Yes, he say 'under-belly', I write it down here exactly.

"Then they speak of some possible military operations they call 'Bolero', and 'Sledgehammer', and 'Roundup'. These I know nothing about and I have trouble following the talks – is much strange military words. So, then! Everyone agree to start preparing for invading of North African Colonies of Vichy France. This they call 'Operation Torch' but this you know already. For this, Franklin appoints his Brigadier-General Eisenhower as the Commander-in-Chief of American Forces in all Europe. And then he make Yugoslavia eligible for aid that he is naming 'Lend-Lease'.

"Then on 24th June, King Peter arrives. I meet with our Foreign Minister Ninčić and the king in the evening. I am so furious at him! He is the idiot!"

"Who? Ninčić?"

"No, Peter!" she exploded, hands clenched into fists.

"Now, now, you shouldn't speak of your king that way, it's disrespectful, and anyway isn't polite," Reggie said. Buga went on, her temper growing more fiery with each phrase.

"Why not? Is true! He knows *nothing* about what happens in Yugoslavia, and will *not* listen to me! Peter is immature and easily manipulated by his politicians. He change his mind by who speaks to him last! Then he promotes *that Chetnik* Draža Mihailović to full general and make him Chief of Staff of the Royal Yugoslav Army! I am so angry at this! The *only good thing* my king do, is to make Professor Slobodan Jovanović in London the Prime Minister of Yugoslavia. And *then* King Peter agrees that I must go home!"

"Wait a bit!" Reggie interrupted, "He *agrees* you must go home? Agrees with who?"

"Everybody! I eat so much strange foods there my belly makes rumble sounds, so I tell Winston. He tell his Doctor, Mr Charles Wilson: 'look at this woman', and this doctor, he listen to me with his steth–, his steth—"

"Stethoscope."

"Yes, that. Then he tell to *everybody* I am *ill* and must go home! Everybody agrees! All of them! But I am *not* ill, I am only pregnant!"

"Pregnant! That's wonderful! Since when?"

"Mr Wilson tell me I am pregnant two months."

"Two months? That would be since late April. Then you'll be due in … late January, 1943," he reckoned.

"But I am *not* ill. Men are *fools*," she said, pouting.

"Present company excepted, I hope! Never you mind. You're here now, safe and secure, and we have a new home, and everything's just grand!" She stood to put her notes away, and when she turned back around he lifted her blouse and gave the slight bulge of her belly kisses. She smiled and ran her fingers through his hair.

"Oh! Oh yes, I bring a thing from America!" She went to her bicycle where it sat propped on its wheel-stand, and unstrapped a case from its luggage rack. Gripping the top handle tightly with both hands, she grunted as she carried it to the desk, where she dropped it with a *thump*. He followed her into the study.

"It looks heavy. Is it a sewing machine?" he asked. She unclasped the fasteners and removed the cover. It was wide, with rounded edges and was entirely black, but the tab keys and shift keys were red.

"Is electric type-writing machine, for your August birthday! Is called by Americans the IBM Model zero one – is six years old. This I buy used," Buga stated.

"Thank you, sweetie! But, I don't know how to type," he reminded her.

"You will learn, so our child will know how we meet," she told him.

He never did learn how to type properly, but he did work at the project assiduously, pecking at the keys one finger at a time, month after month. He only paused in his efforts to listen to the BBC reports of Operation Torch, but the *City of Featherstone*, the Ex-*Belfair* was not mentioned. At the end of November, Buga would bring him his tea as he typed, and then rest her now-heavy belly on his desk "to let our baby listen to the sound of the machine" (or so she claimed). Sometimes he would hand over a single chapter for her to read, and this often might prompt a suggestion or three. Then, a fortnight before Christmas, he finished the narrative. He proudly handed over the result to her. She hadn't read very far into the first page before she had another suggestion.

"This Swedish man with no name you tell about here: is now obvious you are meaning Frederik, but ..." she hesitated.

"Yes, ... go on, but what?"

"But, no one will know *where* he is, or *when*," she finished.

"You're right! I can easily fix that," he said. He took back the first sheet of the manuscript and wound it into the machine, then centred the carriage and began to type: April 1941, Sibenik, Kingdom of Yugoslavia.

Epilogue

On 28 February 1943 the Allies were finally convinced to switch their allegiance to Tito.

On 12 September 1943, the partisans of the National Liberation Army of Yugoslavia successfully disarmed the Italian garrison in Primošten, capturing four howitzers and 370 rifles.

In December 1943 the City Hall of Šibenik was bombed by the U.S. Army Air Force, because it was used as the headquarters of the occupying German forces. It was the only time Šibenik was bombed during the Second World War.

On 3 November 1944 Tito's partisans liberated Šibenik, one day after Tito became the 23rd Prime Minister of Yugoslavia.

About the Author

I love traveling, having visited Greece, Britain, Japan, Ireland and most recently, Malta and Croatia. Oftentimes, this has given me inspiration to write. HEAVY CARGO is my first novel. THE BELFAIR PINCH is the sequel to it. THE BITTER PIT OF THE CHERRY is the third in this loose trilogy.

Ryan Plut is 67 years old and lives near Seattle, Washington State. He is married to Karen (Keefer) Plut. They are child-free, but have raised many "kids" who meow.

You can connect with me on:

🌐 https://www.ryanplut.com

Subscribe to my newsletter:

✉ https://www.ryanplut.com/contact

Also by Ryan G. Plut

HEAVY CARGO is my first novel. THE BELFAIR PINCH is the sequel to it. THE BITTER PIT OF THE CHERRY is the third in this loose trilogy.

Heavy Cargo

Late autumn 1941.   The Imperial Japanese Army Air Force is terror bombing Chinese cities, sweeping refugees by the untold thousands before their onslaught. The Imperial Japanese Army has invaded French Indochina, and may soon attack Thailand and Burma, perhaps even Singapore!

Captain Roy Mallinson, ageing Royal Navy veteran of the Great War, has been pulled from retirement to aid Britain in this new war. His elderly merchant navy ship, the SS *Dominion Empress* is currently in Singapore having taken on a cargo of surplus US Brewster Buffalo aeroplanes desperately needed in Finland. But Roy has come to a realization; war is for younger men than he.

However, the High Commissioner of British Malaya, and his friend the Dutch banker, have other plans. Roy is forced into altering his route, taking on a disguised cargo so valuable he dare not reveal it, even to his own crew.

On the Island of Java, free-spirited Rebecca McKenzie unexpectedly thrusts herself into the captain's life. She's an Australian nurse stranded here whilst fleeing war-torn China, desperately seeking passage home. How can he say no? But German auxiliary merchant raiders are rumoured to be operating in the area, and although Britain isn't *yet* at war with Japan—Perth is still a further 1,800 nautical miles away, and anything may happen!